been waiting

forever—

biding their
time until
they could
fling off the
mask and
cackle, until
the moment
they could
unleash the
wickedness
inside them.

Is it WRONG to TRY to PICK UP GIRLS in a DUNGEON? ON THE SIDE

Sword Oratoria

FUJINO OMORI

ILLUSTRATION BY
KIYOTAKA HAIMURA

CHARACTER DESIGN BY
SUZUHITO YASUDA

CONTENTS

PROLOGUE ♦ The Final Scene in Her Mind's Eye 001

CHAPTER 1 ♦ The Price of Defeat 005

CHAPTER 2 ♦ An Evil Omen 023

CHAPTER 3 ♦ Rabbit Oracle 045

CHAPTER 4 ♦ Nameless Heroes 057

CHAPTER 5 ♦ Final War 079

CHAPTER 6 ♦ The Divine Providence of Despair 117

CHAPTER 7 ♦ Final War II 197

CHAPTER 8 ♦ A Heroes' Chorus 259

EPILOGUE ♦ Raining Light 351

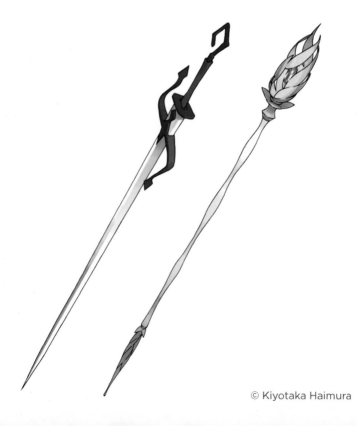

© Kiyotaka Haimura

VOLUME 12

FUJINO OMORI

ILLUSTRATION BY
KIYOTAKA HAIMURA

CHARACTER DESIGN BY
SUZUHITO YASUDA

NEW YORK

IS IT WRONG TO TRY TO PICK UP GIRLS IN A DUNGEON?
ON THE SIDE: SWORD ORATORIA, Volume 12
FUJINO OMORI

Translation by Dale DeLucia
Cover art by Kiyotaka Haimura

This book is a work of fiction. Names, characters, places, and incidents are the product of the author's imagination or are used fictitiously. Any resemblance to actual events, locales, or persons, living or dead, is coincidental.

DUNGEON NI DEAI WO MOTOMERU NO WA MACHIGATTEIRUDAROUKA GAIDEN
SWORD ORATORIA vol. 12
Copyright © 2019 Fujino Omori
Illustration copyright © 2019 Kiyotaka Haimura
Original Character Design © Suzuhito Yasuda
All rights reserved.
Original Japanese edition published in 2019 by SB Creative Corp.
This English edition is published by arrangement with SB Creative Corp., Tokyo, in care of Tuttle-Mori Agency, Inc., Tokyo.

English translation © 2020 by Yen Press, LLC

Yen On
150 West 30th Street, 19th Floor
New York, NY 10001

Visit us at yenpress.com
facebook.com/yenpress
twitter.com/yenpress
yenpress.tumblr.com
instagram.com/yenpress

First Yen On Edition: July 2020

Yen On is an imprint of Yen Press, LLC.
The Yen On name and logo are trademarks of Yen Press, LLC.

The publisher is not responsible for websites (or their content) that are not owned by the publisher.

Library of Congress Cataloging-in-Publication Data
Names: Ōmori, Fujino, author. | Haimura, Kiyotaka, 1973– illustrator. | Yasuda, Suzuhito, designer.
Title: Is it wrong to try to pick up girls in a dungeon? on the side: sword oratoria / story by Fujino Omori ; illustration by Kiyotaka Haimura ; original design by Suzuhito Yasuda.
Other titles: Danjon ni deai wo motomeru no wa machigatteirudarouka gaiden sword oratoria. English.
Description: New York, NY : Yen On, 2016– | Series: Is it wrong to try to pick up girls in a dungeon? on the side: sword oratoria
Identifiers: LCCN 2016023729 | ISBN 9780316315333 (v. 1 : pbk.) | ISBN 9780316318167 (v. 2 : pbk.) | ISBN 9780316318181 (v. 3 : pbk.) | ISBN 9780316318228 (v. 4 : pbk.) | ISBN 9780316442503 (v. 5 : pbk.) | ISBN 9780316442527 (v. 6 : pbk.) | ISBN 9781975302863 (v. 7 : pbk.) | ISBN 9781975327798 (v. 8 : pbk.) | ISBN 9781975327811 (v. 9 : pbk.) | ISBN 9781975331719 (v. 10 : pbk.) | ISBN 9781975331733 (v. 11 : pbk.) | ISBN 9781975313272 (v. 12 : pbk.)
Subjects: CYAC: Fantasy.
Classification: LCC PZ7.1.O54 Isg 2016 | DDC [Fic]—dc23
LC record available at https://lccn.loc.gov/2016023729

ISBNs: 978-1-9753-1327-2 (paperback)
978-1-9753-1328-9 (ebook)

1 3 5 7 9 10 8 6 4 2

LSC-C

Printed in the United States of America

VOLUME 12

FUJINO OMORI

ILLUSTRATION BY **KIYOTAKA HAIMURA**
CHARACTER DESIGN BY **SUZUHITO YASUDA**

THE FINAL SCENE IN HER MIND'S EYE

Гэта казка іншага сям'і.

Погляд дзяўчынкі ў апошні раз бачыў

She could see a crown of light—a ring of bright, scattered motes suspended in the air, woven together to create a white stairway ascending to the heavens.

They had promised to see this together—which meant this had to be an illusion. Her battered consciousness should have already slipped away, but it showed her this fragile, transient, final hallucination reflected in her eyes. Though only a sliver of a dream, it was still so beautiful.

Even if it was a trick of the eye, she had conviction that it was lovelier than anything she had ever seen.

It was the Elf Ring in Lefiya's home forest.

She could hear a miserable voice. A ceaseless lamentation. A plaintive wail of regret and grief that reached the very heavens. A howl coming from that girl's soul.

She was inconsolable, knowing she was the one who'd made this girl cry. It broke her heart to have hurt her.

No matter how much I want to, I can't stop those tears from falling. It would be impossible to soothe that gaping wound that you will shoulder for as long as you continue to live.

There's so much I want to tell you. There is more I wanted you to know. But I know I'll never get the chance.

I won't ever be able to talk to you again. I won't ever be able to use this voice. I won't ever be able to sing another song.

Her body was disappearing, turning to dust. Her thoughts were losing their direction.

Don't cry. Keep moving.

But in all my departing musings, I cannot bring myself to ask you to forget me. And that is my greatest weakness. My lingering attachments. My crazed thoughts.

I know I don't have any right, but I can't help but ask—please begin to smile again...

She could see relentless rain. Unfairly beautiful, a cruel purity, something more precious than anything else in the world. Those unbroken raindrops and tears that caught the light transformed into a tune that made her heart tremble.

Straying from rhyme and reason, the last remnants of her consciousness were fading away.

The scene before her drifted farther into the distance.

She was starting to lose her grasp of the girl's presence.

Even her impure heart and body were shut away in an all-white space. She would forget everything.

Which was why...Which was the only reason why she made one last request to that crown of light.

If miracles exist, then all I ask is this. In exchange for my atonement, let me become fragments of light, pouring down on her shoulders, even after my body and spirit leave no trace in this world. For her, let me always—

For the one like a flower that would wilt at the slightest touch, I want to—

She offered up that final prayer to the heavens, the one place she had sworn never to look for aid again.

THE PRICE OF DEFEAT

Гэта казка іншага сям'і.

Кошт паразы

Why did she have to die? That was all she could think about. That was all she kept asking herself.

But there was no answer in her bleak thoughts, which had become desolate wasteland. There was no response, even when she pleaded with reason, which had frozen over, offering about as many answers as a wall of ice would.

She was not filled with rage, nor was she filled with sadness. There was only white.

Her head and heart were all white—snowy ash covered everything, making all boundaries disappear. Where did her emotions end? Where did her thoughts begin? What was pain? And what wasn't?

She could not understand. She could not move. She could not do anything. In that infinite field of white, memories buried under ash twinkled like jewels.

"Then I will protect you. I won't let you die—even if it's only you."

Her weary heart tried to reject this scene—to stop it from replaying again.

But it would not stop. Unbidden details flashed before her eyes: Her voice. Her gestures. The warmth of her body.

"Once this is all done, we'll go. I promise."

A broken promise. And finally, her smile.

"..."

A tear fell from her sapphire eye. Even though she had already wept until she thought she could weep no more, the tears didn't stop.

Even though she had howled in pain, her reservoir of tears hadn't dried up.

It was as though her body had become a fairy spring, burbling with water. Every time ripples swept across the deep-blue surface of the water, Lefiya was overcome with grief again.

"——, ——."

She could feel someone standing in front of her, trying to say something. But Lefiya could not grasp these unspoken words. Her broken heart could not process anything.

All she did was move her parched lips and whisper a single name.

"Miss Filvis…"

"Lefiya…"

In a voice tinged with sorrow, Aiz called her name one more time. But there was no response. She continued to slouch over, weeping, crumpled on the floor like a doll with broken strings.

They were in Lefiya's room in *Loki Familia*'s home.

The elf girl silently sobbed in a room originally meant for two.

In a word, she looked pitiful. There was nothing resembling an expression on her face, which had become locked in place as it dripped with rivulets of tears.

Her parched lips barely opened, and from time to time, she whispered the name of her friend who was no longer there—like a faulty music box. She was almost an alabaster sculpture with an embedded soul, grief leaking out in immaterial tears.

It had been only five days since Aiz had emerged from her own room after questioning herself in deep isolation. But that was different from what was happening with Lefiya…for Aiz had retreated into herself based on her internal conflicts, while Lefiya had been broken from the outside. Her precious friend Filvis Challia had been taken away from her.

"Lefiya! Lefiyaaa! I'm begging you to look at me…! Smile like you always do…!" tearfully pleaded Lefiya's roommate, Elfie.

Her eyes were puffy and raw from tears, and her voice was already raspy. Over the last few days, she had stuck close to Lefiya.

Nothing Tiona or Tione had said worked. Even Riveria could not get through to her.

Right now, there were only three people in the room. Since they couldn't be by Lefiya's side around the clock, they would drop in during their free moments, but no one could manage to return any spirit to her voice. They just didn't know what to say to her in this situation.

She had watched on as her friend's neck snapped right in front of her eyes—devoured by monsters, slaughtered. For a girl with such a tender heart, it was too cruel a blow.

But behind their concern, they knew she was broken. The first-tier adventurers had all calmly reached the same conclusion: Lefiya Viridis was beyond recovery.

"Stand back up! Get vengeance!" These were words they could never, ever say.

There was no way they could ignite that black fire and add kindling to it. Aiz knew what happened to those burned by that black flame, which was why she could not bring herself to shove the girl into that sea of hellfire.

"Aiiiiz! Lefiya…won't…!"

"…"

Elfie wailed as she clung to Aiz, burying her face in Aiz's shoulder. And Aiz could do nothing but support her. Unwept, all she could do was embrace Elfie as she cried for the both of them.

She averted her gaze, feeling incredibly powerless.

Aiz softly reached out and gripped Lefiya's hand, but the elf remained as empty as a broken doll.

"Y-you guys…"

Raul stood still, lost in thought. There was nothing he could do about the situation unfolding before his eyes.

In the manor cafeteria, the members of *Loki Familia* were all silent, collectively mourning, as though they were attending a funeral. The cafeteria was usually full of cheer, but the hall had gone silent, as if the sound itself had been stolen away. It was uncanny, sending a shiver down Raul's spine.

"...Gh." One of those present was Anakity, the cat person with black hair.

Her expression said she despised the time off they'd been given. She would've much preferred devoting herself to some mindless task, giving her no time to dwell on her thoughts. Noticing the anguish on the face of his beautiful colleague, Raul started to say something, but the right words never came to him.

He already knew what was bothering her: their flight from Knossos the other day. It was not that they had lost to or fallen for their enemy's tricks. It was that the entire chessboard itself had been *flipped on them*.

The path toward victory they had been following completely vanished from underneath them.

It was an event that one of the strongest factions in the city, *Loki Familia*, had never experienced before. Out of desperation to stay alive, they had watched their friends die begging for help with outstretched hands—the poor members of *Dionysus Familia*.

Because they had turned away to save themselves, an entire faction of more than eighty adventurers had been wiped out.

"Y-you guys..."

Raul was disappointed in himself for continuing to whimper the same thing. In the past, he had always been the one who'd made a fool of himself, and his friends in *Loki Familia* were the ones who called out to him, helping him back to his feet.

In a way, Raul's embarrassing behavior maintained the balance and harmony of those around him. This was his unique contribution, the unintentional charisma he brought to the group as a boring human. In every horrible situation, the sight of hapless little Raul Nord carrying on helped the rest of the familia loosen up and smile, knowing that everything would somehow work out for the best.

He was embarrassed by his self-hatred and rage, the unease, the confusion, the fear of it all. But he had managed to overcome it, even though the effort caused his chest to hurt and made him want to tear off his own skin. Since it was just him who had fallen, Raul always managed to stand back up. He knew himself well. That was why he could grit his teeth, bear through it, and keep his head up.

But right now...

Raul didn't have a game plan to address his friends whose heads remained bowed—because he had not been there to witness this himself. He had not been involved in their tragic choice to sacrifice others in order to live on.

To secure a path of escape out of Knossos, Raul had moved to prop open the gates connected to the Dungeon with his team. All that he had done was immediately close the orichalcum door once his fleeing friends had made it out into the Dungeon...to stop the wave of green flesh closing in on them.

He could not share their burden—much less erase it. He couldn't inspire them like Finn and the others. Raul could only look pathetic as he cursed his own incompetence.

"You bastards *still* wallowing?" snapped someone, annoyed, cutting through the funereal hush that hung over the room.

When he snapped his neck around in surprise, Raul saw a single werewolf enter the hall.

"B-Bete..."

He must have come to get food. It was obvious that he didn't expect any to be served, barreling through the cafeteria toward the kitchen where the ingredients were stored. He scoffed as he glanced at the familia members, who trembled in surprise.

Raul hurriedly followed him. "B-Bete, are you okay...?"

Aren't you depressed? Isn't this hard to get over? Raul silently asked Bete, finding himself drawn to the werewolf out of an urge to cling to anything and everything in desperation. Raul might have hoped he would be able to do something with the strength of a first-tier adventurer.

"Spit it out already! If there's something you want to say, then say it to my face!"

"Eep?!"

Bete seemed the same as usual. He was violent and abrasive, as if nothing had changed. But in this moment, this crumb of normalcy was reassuring.

"…If you haven't finished pitying yourselves yet, then just keep wallowing some more."

"…What?"

Which was why that last comment took Raul by surprise. Bete had not snorted or sneered, even though he was one to look down on and verbally assault anyone he deemed a weakling. In a way, he was overlooking their behavior, for now.

"B-Bete, what happened…? Did you eat something weird…?"

The werewolf hadn't unleashed a torrent of scorn—or even an irate shout. This left Raul feeling like he'd run into a monster doing a handstand or something.

As if he was beginning to get annoyed by Raul's slack-jawed look, Bete clicked his tongue in irritation. "It's the same for me. You need time to cool your head."

"What…?"

"Go ahead and sputter gutless complaints until it's time."

That was when Raul realized something: Bete had been a spectator, like him, securing one of the other passages into Knossos. He was frustrated remembering their defeat and escape, but he had still managed to get his emotions under control and move forward.

"'Until it's time'…?" Raul repeated the words without meaning to.

Finally, the werewolf snorted. "While you bastards are wallowing i your own misery, Finn's crew is moving in your stead."

"Give me an update on the situation."

Bete had been right. In the executive office, Finn was poring over information with Riveria and Gareth, living up to the werewolf's expectations, solemnly and resolutely.

"We know *Dionysus Familia*'s members were the only ones to suffer direct casualties. We didn't deal with particularly significant losses, and neither did *Hermes Familia*," said Riveria.

"Aye, but obviously, morale will drop. They've survived this incident by turning their backs on fellow adventurers. This is going to change them," added Gareth.

Finn quietly listened to their reports with neither regret, hatred, nor any visible mental anguish coloring his face. The prum hero was charged with leading *Loki Familia* and their entire alliance of factions, which meant he had to be more stoic than anyone. He had to control himself and present an example to those below him. And Finn was in a state of mind to do it.

I'm surprised that this chance encounter with the Xenos has changed my heart into one of steel, Finn inwardly analyzed. *Is this that growth Loki was talking about?* He almost scoffed out loud.

Of course, he felt a sense of obligation, frustration, and regret. However, after setting those aside, he also felt a desire to meet the coming battle head-on. As the man called Braver, he understood the most important thing he had to achieve right now.

They needed to decided what direction the familia would be taking. The top priority was to work out a plan for the second assault that he had predicted they would need. Additionally, they also had to think of a way to spur on the familia after its morale had been dealt such a devastating blow.

"And the conditions in Knossos?"

"*Ganesha Familia* is leading efforts to remove the green flesh filling the labyrinth. We've sent some of our people with them, too, but..." Gareth trailed off.

"The progress is slower than expected. The flesh attacks as if it has a will of its own," Riveria finished, picking up where the dwarf left off.

Finn slipped back into thought.

The first attack had been necessary to clear Knossos. In the fight with the remnants of the Evils and the creatures, the alliance of familias had been in control from start to finish. Following Finn's blitzkrieg plan, the adventurers and healers from all the factions had overrun the remnants of the Evils and handily crushed the plants that were the source of the vibrantly colored monsters.

But at the final stage, right on the cusp of complete victory, the tables had turned on them. As far as Finn was concerned, that expression didn't even describe the extent of it. It would be more accurate to say the entire table had been sawed in half.

It had started with the invocation of the seemingly sentient flesh. That hideous mass had filled the passages of Knossos in the blink of an eye, preying upon any adventurers it found. Caught up in that onrush of all-consuming green, *Dionysus Familia* had been annihilated. And Lefiya's friend had faced a noble death in front of her. Brimming with green overgrowth even now, Knossos had been transformed from a den of demons into the devil's castle.

"As for those on Ouranos's side…We've had contact with Fels, but…with all these developments, Fels doesn't have a good grasp of the situation, either, except that it might be like a spirit miracle…"

Finn glanced down at the oculus magic item placed atop the desk.

According to Gareth, the patron god of the Evils, Thanatos, had said that Knossos was not a fortress but an altar. An altar for a sacrifice.

The abrupt return of a god had triggered the altar, which was all part of the scheme created by the enemy's ringleader and true mastermind—Enyo.

"If everything went according to Enyo's plan…I can't help but shudder. It means we're not the only ones who are disposable—even the remnants of the Evils are, too. Our enemy is coming at us like a god," Riveria summarized frankly, awe and fear in her voice.

"…Did you notice anything, Finn?" Gareth asked.

Finn was silent before speaking his own mind.

"…I couldn't see a face. Even when I was with Thanatos, I could perceive his expression as he moved his pawns…But with Enyo, I couldn't even grasp their intentions beyond the board. Not even a sliver of them."

"…"

"If Enyo managed to activate the altar by keeping everything a secret—including their true identity—the enemy is a monster beyond our wildest imagination. Riveria is right. From the very beginning, they never intended to have a real fight."

Finn had used his pawns atop the board and his ingenuity to create a perfect advance. However, while Finn played by the rules, the enemy was cheating, *pulling a sword from outside the playing field and stabbing it down into the board.* Enyo had not just tried to kill Finn's pawns—but even tried to kill Finn, the person moving the pawns, too.

"A god, huh…?"

It had afforded a perspective different from mortals, divergent values, leading to a battle of opposing worldviews. Finn had won the match and the battle. But in the end, the god had made it seem as though the battle had never happened to begin with. And he had been overcome by a feeling unlike anything he'd ever experienced before.

Finn laughed—one tinged with humiliation, gained knowledge, and militancy.

"…Anyway, there's nothing we can do except move on. We must create the plan for the second assault, which we have to win at all costs. Cast aside the fear as we go challenge Enyo one more time," Finn said, speaking into existence the promise and courage to raise Riveria's and Gareth's spirits—and his own.

After they nodded in agreement, they started to uncover what Knossos had become. But as the conversation proceeded, they ran into an unavoidable question.

"I get that the enemy used the corrupted spirit to cover all of Knossos. But…then what?"

Riveria was the first to put it into words. Her jade hair quivered as the high elf furrowed her brow at the inexplicable.

"At Thanatos's whim, Enyo was kept from finishing us off. We're certain of that. But do they intend to stay holed up in their castle now?" asked Gareth.

Coated with the green flesh, Knossos was maintaining its silence. There were no signs of monsters or creatures attacking, let alone the demi-spirit.

As the dwarf said, the activation of the altar should have been Enyo's *plan to end this all.* A plan to kill all of *Loki Familia,* those with the potential to become an impediment to the destruction of Orario. Even though it missed its target, Enyo had not reacted in any way. It was ominous, almost.

"Finn, you were worried they might summon the demi-spirit aboveground...but there are no signs of that. Is the enemy pretending to be as slow as a tortoise?"

"..." Gareth's comment had tickled Finn's ears as he slipped deeper into thought.

Though they had gotten a lid on the green flesh, there would eventually come a time when the alliance would attack Knossos again. This silence would lure in the alliance to attempt it.

Or was that the enemy's aim—inviting them into Knossos again? Or was there a totally different objective? But that would mean...

A moment of silence fell in the office as everyone held their tongues.

"...I guess this is the only other lead we have."

Finn pulled a single piece of parchment from the desk's drawer. It depicted a monster that was the very image of an evil dragon and maidens surrounding it in a ring.

It had been sketched from memory and shared by Lefiya before she broke. It was a mural on the wall that she had happened across with Filvis when they bumped into Thanatos during the very first invasion of Knossos. According to Lefiya, Thanatos had said that the mural was *"something that Enyo had brought in from some ruin."*

"If I remember correctly, that's Nidhogg, huh? That was the dragon in the center."

"If we're to believe Thanatos's story."

Gareth and Riveria looked down at the sketch spread across the desk. Nidhogg was said to be a monster that existed in the Ancient Times. When Lefiya had given him the sketch, Finn had investigated it, but all he could find was that it was speculated to be one of the oldest calamities that had been released by the Dungeon, even before Behemoth, Leviathan, or the Black Dragon, the targets of the Three Great Quests.

But this was all speculation, because detailed literature on it could not be found, so it was just Finn's conjecture based on the time frame of the background. According to the minimal accounts of Nidhogg, it had apparently been so overwhelmingly powerful that it had thrust the world into the depths of despair. It had been strong enough that the ancient people had no chance of striking it down themselves.

As for how it was defeated, it was not recorded in any historical documents. All Finn could find was *"when light fell, all was over"* and *"the song of the children's prayer purified the evil dragon"* and other abstractions along those lines.

He had tried to ask Loki if she remembered anything from that time.

"Oh yeah. I dunno much about that. Everyone in the heavens was all like, 'Things are getting bad in the mortal realm,' but that was when I was busy trying to kill gods, so it was all a bit chaotic. If I remember, some god intervened on their own and blew it away, apparently, but…"

That was the extent of her response.

The use of Arcanum in the mortal realm was prohibited. And choosing to intervene was no small thing. If a pillar of light came down from the heavens, it would gouge another hole in the mortal realm besides the Dungeon. That was what Finn had taken away from her story.

"Lefiya was the one who saw this sketch and had the conversation with Thanatos, but she's not in a state of mind to talk. As for her companion, Filvis Challia…" Riveria said, dropping her pitch, lowering her eyes at the fate that had befallen her fellow elves.

Finn stared at the picture again: the evil black dragon Nidhogg in the center. And the maidens surrounding it. The girls had their eyes closed, holding hands. They could have been a sacrifice to the dragon or holy maidens offering up a prayer to suppress Nidhogg. There were six of them.

Six…Six, huh?

Six was an unpleasant number. With narrowed eyes, Finn felt uneasy thinking about its underlying meaning. *Loki Familia* had the pieces to connect that ancient mural to the current situation.

The problem was, if things proceeded as they did in the mural, what would happen in the end?

Finn put those thoughts on hold, keeping the vague answer to himself. He decided that right now, when they were desperately in need of more information, they had no choice but to gather all the clues they could related to the mural of Nidhogg.

"…Is Loki still not back yet?"

When silence had totally fallen over the room, Riveria turned to look to a certain place, as if in search of the jester's advice or hoping to see her. Finn and Gareth looked over in the same direction, too.

But their patron goddess's seat was empty.

"—Are you sober, Loki?"

That was Hermes's first response after hearing her story.

They were in the god's room inside *Hermes Familia*'s home. While Finn was planning, Loki had been let into Hermes's home, facing him as he stared fixedly at her.

"I just told you. I'm serious and sober. Put the other way, I can't think of anyone else who could be Enyo's *identity*."

Loki hadn't stopped talking since she'd stepped foot into the home, elaborating on her hypothesis on the series of events and the true identity of the city destroyer.

Hermes closed his mouth and stared at her, probing her divine will. His orange eyes couldn't conceal his surprise. He was normally an aloof, delicate god, but right now, he seemed to be carefully scrutinizing her declaration inside and out.

"…What basis do you have? Just saying it out loud almost makes me laugh. Do you have any conclusive evidence?" Hermes joked deliberately because they were in this situation.

Loki looked behind her, where the god Soma was standing. She had forced him to accompany her.

Stealing the bottle in his hands, she poured a glass, handing

Hermes a cup of red wine sloshing against the rim, warning him with a sharp gaze not to drink it.

"What is this…? Wait, *this is*…?"

"Yeah, divine wine. I found it in Dionysus's wine cellar when I was looking through it with Soma."

Raising the glass to his face, Hermes took a whiff of the smell. In the next instant, he smashed it on the floor, causing the glass to shatter and a pool of gory red liquid to spread. It wafted a bewitching fragrance. Hermes glared daggers at the shards of glass, not bothering to hide his disdain at the divine wine that had tried to seduce his thoughts.

"With this, even a god could get *wasted*…I guarantee it," Soma said. There was a smidgen of excitement and frustration in his level voice—a reluctance to accept someone who had created a better divine wine than his own and an intense curiosity.

"…There's no proof. And Loki's theory is full of holes. But with this wine…then…" Hermes whispered to himself, having heard Loki's and Soma's speeches.

He let himself drown in a sea of thoughts, pressing his palm over his mouth, and his eyes narrowed as he thought harder. It was as if he was placing a missing puzzle piece and deciphering the final scene.

"…I got it." Finally, Hermes raised his head and responded. "I'll go with your theory, Loki. Or, rather, I'll have to reexamine everything with this missing piece that you found."

This was the path leading to the mastermind. He had the key to unspool the actions of Dionysus, who had kept up his suspicious behaviors. Hermes quickly shifted gears, showing off his mental agility.

"So what do you want me to do? There's no way you came here to share your hypotheses with me, right?"

"A home investigation. If our thoughts are on the mark, we'll need to back it up," Loki replied.

"That's true."

As soon as he heard Loki's response, Hermes shrugged and started to walk.

"I'll make some moves. In search of the answer you seek, Loki."

Leaving the room, he gave orders to his followers who were waiting outside. As they watched him depart, Loki looked down at her hands, left behind in the room with Soma—glancing down at the bottle filled with red wine.

"Search every nook and cranny! I trust we can place the blame on the Guild and Lord Hermes later!" Asfi barked.

From the wild footsteps and the sounds of crashing, you would imagine they were taking part in an emergency break-in operation. They were investigating—which was a better way to say "taking control of" the building.

Hermes Familia had moved quickly. Right after Loki's request, they'd immediately left their home and broken into the indicated familia's home.

"It's no good, Asfi! It's a shell of a home!"

"There's no one here!"

"Gh…!" Asfi bit her lip at the reports from the war tiger Falgar and the chienthrope Lulune.

The manor looked as though it had been torn apart by thieves. The shelves were stripped bare; a sea of parchments and documents was strewn across the floor, littered on top with pieces of broken antiques.

But they could not find anything—as if they were mocked for being a step too late. Hearing the reports from the familia members, Asfi rushed down the stairs to the last area left, underground. She threw open the door to the basement, Falgar's crew in tow.

"Ugh…!"

"Do I…smell blood?"

Asfi stared at the scene as Lulune and Falgar whimpered.

There was nothing particularly special about the underground room, a storage space for fruits and vegetables…other than the distinct smell of blood that Lulune had mentioned—and that thing.

At the back of the dim room, an ominous cluster of red glyphs had been written in blood across the wall—as if jeering at them. As if challenging them. As if cursing them.

PERISH, ORARIO. I SHALL OPEN THE GATES TO THE UNDERWORLD.

With both fists balled up, Asfi was the only one there who could decipher the clump of hieroglyphs—a challenge and a confession.

And then she spat out the name of the familia who owned this home.

"*Demeter Familia…!*"

CHAPTER
2

AN
EVIL
OMEN

Гэта казка іншага сям і.

Прыкметы цемры

© Kiyotaka Haimura

This god had been waiting forever—biding their time until they could fling off the mask and cackle, until the moment they could unleash the wickedness inside them.

Those in the city are nauseatingly blissful in their ignorance. And I wanted to spit on the mortals and gods around me.

Everyone seems to agree that peace is the natural way of the world. But all I carry with me is annoyance and a murderous impulse. To keep those little shits from catching on, I wore the mask of a deity of character and engaged with my surroundings with great care.

Some said I was a righteous deity…What a joke.

Some entreated me, wanting my love…If you knew the real me, would you say the same?

Some wanted a vow to be counted as one of my followers…Fine, then I'll use you until you can give no more.

All this god saw across their plastered smile was a scene of perpetual gray. Reflecting in their eyes was a sight unbearably repulsive—something unlovable, something unfulfilling, something wrong. That was why the god would open the gates of hell.

Throw open the doors to the surface and summon the monsters aboveground.

For the Dungeon desired this, too.

I will become the labyrinth's mouthpiece and go in search of what lies beyond this age of chaos.

That was right. This god had been waiting forever. For the time to be ripe. For the moment when the die would be cast by their own hand. For the instant the bridges would be burned.

There were finally those in search of their identity, attempting to reach out to touch their shadow, but they were already too late.

Even though they had gone to the trouble of leaving hints. Even though they had given the seekers a fair chance to stop this plan. *Even though I enjoyed the game of finding the culprit. Even though I was always watching, deep within the threshold between intoxication and frenzy, jeering at you.*

Enyo laughed out loud at Orario.

"That's impossible!" Fels suddenly shouted.

The four torches were crackling as they burned. The mage's voice echoed in the dim room lit not by magic-stone lamps but by simple fire.

Fels was in the altar beneath Guild Headquarters. The Chamber of Prayers where the old god Ouranos sat.

"To say *Demeter Familia* is…To say the goddess Demeter is… Enyo!" Fels reflexively rebuked this report.

Hermes Familia had investigated *Demeter Familia*'s home. They had just gotten intel that the goddess and every last one of her followers had disappeared—and that there was an ominous message left behind in the basement.

"Demeter is one of the gods who supported Orario, like Zeus and Hera! There's no way she could be Enyo!"

Which was to say, it would be a big disgrace if that was the case, though the mage in the black robe didn't say that out loud.

The primary activity in Demeter's familia was agriculture. From grains to vegetables to fruits, most produce brought into Orario had been harvested by them. *Demeter Familia* had been running all major farms outside the city, single-handedly supplying much of Orario with food. They were even more crucial than *Njǫrðr Familia*, who contributed large amounts of seafood.

In fact, her familia was larger than *Ganesha Familia* if the count included noncombatant workers at the big farm outside the city who had not received a Blessing.

Because they focused on production and business, the familia lacked combat strength, though it was still a C-rank familia.

Many said that if *Demeter Familia* disappeared, people would starve and the city would fall into an eternal winter.

"Just how much do you think she's done to maintain peace and order in Orario?!" Fels yelled, arms swinging wildly in frustration.

"However, there is no changing that Enyo's tracks were left in her home," Ouranos responded, sitting on the altar.

"Gh—"

"And Demeter is the one goddess who can freely go in and out of the city."

Ouranos spoke only of the reality of the situation, leaving Fels at a loss for words.

Leaving the city required a complicated series of formalities due to the regulations set by the Guild. However, Demeter had been exempted from those restrictions, since she ran farms and a base outside the city.

The ability to freely move in and out of the city was crucial to this series of events as nothing less would have allowed the exporting of the Xenos to bankroll Knossos and the trading of man-eating flowers to Meren, among other things. The Evils and their underground allies must have entered and exited Orario often. If she could leave the city without arousing suspicion and keep her true intentions hidden, this entire operation would have been a breeze for Demeter.

The other familias exempted from these formalities were *Ganesha Familia*, who maintained the de facto police force of Orario, and *Hermes Familia*, who dabbled in a little bit of everything. It also went without saying that those two gods had already been taken off the suspect list.

"At the very least, the investigation has raised enough evidence to suspect Demeter."

The greatest blow in this case was how her entire familia had disappeared at a time like this. It would be impossible not to be suspicious of her connection to the incident after that. And more than anything, her relationship with Dionysus seemed suspect.

As the controllers of the food sources for the city, *Demeter Familia* alone—meaning Demeter—could gather the special grapes used to create divine wine and slip it to Dionysus. Demeter could smile like nothing was wrong as she poured him a glass to get him drunk. She could whisper in his ear and turn him into her puppet.

"…What do you think, Ouranos?" Fels managed to ask with no other arguments to offer. The mage struggled with sorrow as the flickering torchlight in the dim room projected an imagined scene.

"……" Ouranos closed his eyes as the mage sought an answer, cloaking himself in silence for a time. The torches crackled, echoing through the room.

"If…" The old god finally began to speak. "If I am right…then we must find where Demeter is now."

"…"

"As soon as possible. Before it is too late," he said, laying down his unyielding divine will. Ouranos declared his intent with regards to the goddess from his homeland.

"…Understood, Ouranos. I will follow your divine will. That is why I am here."

Fels didn't argue against this, promising to carry out the divine will that had been unveiled. To become an attendant to that will, the mage shut off all doubt and agitation—to act as a faithful ghost.

"Ouranos, I'd like to speak to you about another issue," Fels said, shifting to a different topic. "With the extraordinary efforts of *Ganesha Familia*, the general public does not know about the existence of Knossos, but…there is no hiding the pillars reaching for the heavens."

Gods had returned back above during the first assault. The pillars of light had shot up toward the sky with force and deafening explosions, piercing through Knossos and the ground before reaching the heavens.

"Everyone in the city saw the return of Dionysus and Thanatos. Two pillars went up in succession. It's unreasonable to tell them to believe it was nothing."

"Have Royman deal with explaining to the citizens and gods of the city. Fels, continue to assist Ganesha's children and the Xenos and proceed with the investigation of Knossos. Leave the investigation of Demeter to *Hermes Familia*," Ouranos ordered.

"Very well. But, Ouranos..." Fels's black robes trembled, as if announcing the final truth.

"...The people are not stupid...Even if they can't grasp the situation, they will realize something is coming all the same."

Fels was right. News of the omen had spread through the city, slinking around the streets.

"A god returned to the heavens...And two of them at that."

"The Guild said it was just a small dispute, but...they haven't announced which gods were sent back. I feel like they're hiding something."

"And there was that incident in the Pleasure Quarter where Ishtar was sent back, too. Things have been weird lately. Maybe something's happening."

"Also, when the light went off, it was in the southeast side of the city. That was where the monsters appeared on Daedalus Street, too..."

On the street corners, the citizens were trying to handle a ripple of unease gripping the city, though it was far from panic. With the two gods' pillars on their minds, everyone was talking to anyone who would listen. And once people started talking, rumors spread like wildfire.

The people's guesses led to more speculation, which had a hint of the truth as unease spread through the city.

"Apparently, *Ganesha Familia* has set up base on Daedalus Street."

"They've only got gatekeepers out, and I've seen nothing more than the bare minimum number of guards everywhere else."

"I heard *Loki Familia*'s been busy, too."

"Daedalus Street again? Do you think they were lying when they said they had gotten rid of all the monsters on the surface? Maybe there are some monsters that are still lurking around?"

In a bar filled with rough people, adventurers were talking about the current situation, since they were particularly sensitive to the city's undercurrents. The rumors paired well with their beers. A merchant who was socializing got pulled in to the conversation, and the story started to move beyond the city. The more they all talked, the more authentic it began to sound.

"If it comes to that, we can just leave it to Little Rookie—ah, he's supposed to be called Rabbit Foot now, huh? He'll beat that minotaur this time!"

"Ha-ha-ha, that'd be nice!"

Even in moments like these, they didn't forget to throw in the occasional joke, sandwiching the conversation with bouts of laughter. But they undoubtedly possessed the ability to sniff out something fishy. While there were some who went to the Guild the next day, there were others who exchanged information with friendly factions. Most of their patron gods and goddesses smacked their lips, wondering what was coming and what would happen, getting excited by the ache of their divine intuition, waiting for the day that would be arriving soon.

There were many predictions, but most familias did not skimp on preparing for the worst scenario.

"Damn…What is this disgusting wall of meat…?"

Meanwhile, there were some adventurers much closer to the epicenter of events.

The huge dwarf was swinging a battle hammer to break down the oppressive mass, wiping the sweat from his brow. There was no end to the mysterious fleshy matter, even when they dug deep into the earth.

"Keep your hands moving and your lips shut, you asinine dwarf. This is a mission," complained a male elf.

Since he had only one arm, the elf couldn't swing a weapon, so he was whispering a spell and casting magic instead.

"Hmph, quit nagging me, elf! Talk to me again after you've worked a bit yourself!"

"What did you say?!"

"You heard me!"

As if symbolizing relations between the two races, the dwarf and elf were predictably quarrelling. The dwarf's name was Dormul, and the elf was called Luvis.

Though he was a dwarf, Dormul was an adventurer boasting a height of over 170 celches, and Luvis was a handsome but high-strung embodiment of elf-dom. Both were Level 3, making them upper-tier adventurers, and their familia had been rated by the Guild as a mid-level faction with high battle potential.

Along with their comrades, they had been called on to help remove the green flesh. The location was a place connected to the side of the ninth floor of the Dungeon. After passing an orichalcum gate, there was an area covered by the bizarre material—the interior of Knossos.

"Those assholes from the Guild. We just got back from the lower levels of the Dungeon! Working us to the bone…"

"You got that right. Digging holes should be left to dwarves."

Because of a top secret mission handed down by the Guild, there were several other dwarves and elves working around them. The order was to dig a path through the green flesh, so they had carved out a tunnel, with the dwarves taking the lead.

They were shooting the breeze, but Dormul and Luvis were paying close attention. Like a monster, there was no doubt the green flesh was alive, and if they let their guard down, it would try to ensnare them.

"It seems a handful of the prominent guilds have been given this sort of mission. They've sent out other familias with second-tier adventurers like us," Luvis quietly mentioned to Dormul.

Which meant this was a restricted mission given out only to factions that could be trusted.

"Given the timing…do you think it's related to the returns of those gods?"

"You mean what happened while we were in the Dungeon? It would be foolish to tie it all together so simply, but there's certainly enough to think something is up…"

The grotesque wall in front of them continued to undulate. Unable to contain their disgust, the two kept talking quietly to themselves.

"Not just that. We've got folks from *Ganesha Familia*, too…It's almost like they're monitoring us. I don't like it."

Dormul was right. There were upper-tier adventurers from *Ganesha Familia* in their party. With swords at their hips and guards up, the second-tier adventurers were observing Dormul and the others. The atmosphere was tense.

Based on that stance…rather than watching our every move…it's more like they're keeping an eye on this green flesh that couldn't possibly be from the Dungeon…

The sharp elf suspected that the members from *Ganesha Familia* were not there to monitor them at all. They were not observers but protectors who would spring into action in the event of an emergency.

The green flesh had sprouted on the fringes of the Dungeon, which alone cemented its place as an Irregular.

"…Either way, we were given a mission. All we can do is complete it."

They weren't really allowed to question the mission. There was no need for them to know what was going on. Or, more bluntly, they weren't allowed to know. However, these adventurers could see the Guild's discomposure on full display.

While Luvis and Dormul kept clearing the green flesh, they thought about this series of events: the appearance of armed monsters on Daedalus Street and the gods' returns to heaven.

"Lord Dionysus ain't coming…?"

"I'm sure he's busy. He must be if he can't even come to drink some of his beloved wine…"

In a cozy neighborhood of the city, the people's faces were clouded over. A certain god had stopped coming around, even though he had always made a point of dropping by and chatting with them.

Was it a curse that the residents had no way of knowing the events that had transpired? Or was it a blessing? Either way, the god's absence was a noticeable change in their lives and fostered a growing unease.

"Hey, Mom, when is Lord Dionysus coming?"

"Next time, we're gonna get him to let us join his familia."

"You know it."

The innocent laughter of the children echoed toward the cloudless blue sky that should have been so beautiful.

"Ah, Lady Hestia!"

In a different location, the lively voices of more unknowing children called out.

"Hey there, Fina. And you too, Lai and Ruu. I brought Jyaga Maru Kun snacks today, too."

"Thanks, Lady Hestia!"

"Thank you very much…"

Hugging back the chienthrope girl, the goddess smiled at the human and half-elf children.

Because the Labyrinth District was being rebuilt, the residents of the slum had been moved to temporary residences in the northwest. Even though she hadn't told the captain of her familia about it much, Hestia had developed an attachment to the orphanage there, often giving them donations and visiting to regale them with tales of her followers' adventures.

"Has anything strange happened around here lately? Or is anything bothering you?" she asked them nonchalantly.

"Mmmm, we asked Miss Maria and the other adults what was happening with Daedalus Street."

"They told us not to go near there…"

"When will we be able to go back…?"

The children made various faces as they responded, when a human boy suddenly raised his voice.

"Oh yeah! Lady Loki was just here."

"Loki…?"

"Yeah. She was talking with the adults…I think she was looking for someone."

The goddess, who had come to observe the city's situation for herself and to blow off some steam, fell silent at the children's words.

"I've…got a bad feeling about this."

Her soft words disappeared into the unnaturally clear sky. A disturbance was quietly but slowly enveloping the city.

"…Everyone is so agitated. This is different from the usual Orario," Tione murmured as she pulled aside the curtain and peeked out the window.

Beneath the blue sky, the hustle and bustle out in the streets was hard to describe as "peaceful." She turned around and looked back to the room.

"Well, it was worse back when you guys came out aboveground, I guess," Tione said.

"…I am extremely sorry for what happened."

She was talking to someone who was using somewhat clumsy Koine. If a normal person had seen the speaker, they would have passed out from shock or drawn their weapon. For instead of two arms, she had two wings.

"It's so weird to have a monster apologize to me—enough to make even an Amazon like me feel faint and taken aback…Anyway, I'm half-tempted to pinch my cheek and make sure I'm not dreaming."

Rei the siren smiled bitterly as Tione unconsciously made a strange face.

When they had been carrying out the first assault and a trap turned Knossos into a deadly prison, Rei had separated from the other Xenos to rescue the adventurers. Because of that, *Loki Familia* had been saved from a terrible fate by a hairbreadth.

This was why she was alone aboveground in the aftermath. *Loki Familia* had taken her in and brought her to Twilight Manor—under strictest secrecy of course. The lower-level members knew nothing of it. Only a select handful of people knew that Rei was there.

"I should have gone to Fels in the first place, but…"

Rei herself seemed to recognize that her presence in a room of surface dwellers could be compared to a black blotch that had found its way onto a painting. She wrapped her wings around her body and hunched her shoulders, as if apologizing for even being there.

Her actions and posture in the chair were incredibly un-monster-like, which was a weird phrase to Tione, but she could not think of a better way to describe it.

"...It is what it is. Guild Headquarters doesn't have any extra capacity. After all, the flow of people and adventurers going through there is higher than ever, so this is the right place for you to hide."

Tione sighed a little at her own logic and changed direction as she continued the discussion—as if her conversational partner was another person. The speed with which she changed her focus—or rather the level of indifference—was worthy of being called an Amazon.

"And? How long are you planning to keep that up, Alicia?"

"T-Tione..."

"As soon as you lift your head, you go back to staring at the ground."

In this room at the top floor of the northwest spire of Twilight Manor, which was an aggregation of spires, there was one other person besides Tione and Rei—Alicia the elf.

"I know you made a point of bringing this food, but isn't it totally cold by now?"

Tione was right. There was a meal placed on the table. As one of the seniors in the familia, Alicia was one of the people admonishing Aiz, Lefiya, and the other juniors, but at the moment, Tione had taken on that role. If anyone else had seen it, they would have commented on this odd scene.

In other words, that was just how much Rei left Alicia at a loss.

"I tagged along, since you said you were coming. Didn't you have something you wanted to say?"

Alicia was among those who had been saved by Rei. During the battle on Daedalus Street when they had faced off with the Xenos, Rei had protected her from the creature Levis's blade in Knossos.

"I..."

She had not yet been able to put what she wanted to say into words, or perhaps she simply had no idea what she should say. It was difficult enough to even look at Rei. The Xenos woman had an awkward smile on her face, but still, she welcomed it.

Unable to meet her eyes. Unable to exchange words. And yet, Alicia was groping for a way to approach Rei. For a Xenos like Rei, just being allowed to be at Alicia's side was salvation, a step forward—as opposed to rejection and extermination.

"In that case, I'll take care of what I came for first," Tione blurted out.

As if demonstrating the difference between the high-strung elf and the uncomplicated Amazon, Tione walked up to Rei. Without any care if the siren was taken aback by the sudden approach, Tione planted her hands on Rei's shoulders, not shrinking back because they were the shoulders of a monster.

"—Thank you. Thanks to you, the man I love was saved. You have my gratitude."

And she thanked her; as Rei gazed in wonder, Tione looked into the siren's eyes.

Loki Familia had taken on the risk of harboring a monster because she had rescued their captain, Finn. If it had not been for her, they would have lost Braver, and *Loki Familia* would have effectively been unable to stand back up on its two legs. Neither Finn, who owed her his life, nor their patron goddess, Loki, nor the rest would abandon the savior of their familia.

Lowering her head, Tione said, "Thank you so much," one more time.

With visible shock in her eyes, Rei's lips finally parted into a real smile—as if there was nothing more that could move her other than thanks from a human.

"—But if you fall for the captain, I'll crush you."

"What?"

"And if you try to flirt with him, I'll make you wish you were never born."

All of a sudden, there was something pitch-black lurking in Tione's eyes, darker than the abyss itself—as if she was a berserker for

love. Those eyes were more frightening than an adventurer who simply killed monsters. Tione would always be Tione, even when facing an Irregular monster, and this made Alicia drop her tensed shoulders in amicable exasperation.

Despite getting a little flustered, Rei managed to deal with the emotionless eyes focused on her in her own way.

"Your face is really cute for a monster. And you've got a nice rack, too. If you tried to seduce the captain in exchange for saving him…"

"I-I'd never do that! P-plus, I already have someone in mind…! Someone who is totally kind and brave with a cute smile like B-b-beyll-rghllll…!" Rei stammered in a state of panic as she responded to the ominous warnings, muttering the name of the person who instantly came mind, which had come out as an unintelligible "B-b-beyll."

At that, Tione stopped moving and looked puzzled.

"Ohhh? You've got your eye on someone?"

"I'm not sure I'd put it like that…" Looking extremely embarrassed, she softly murmured, "I cannot embrace anyone with these wings…but if there was someone who would hold me…that would make me very happy…"

The siren's fair face reddened, flushing her elven features. She looked like a maiden in love, just like any other girl.

"I see…Monsters can fall in love, too," Tione whispered, letting her go.

"Honestly, I don't really have much of an opinion on Xenos. If you get in our way, I'll slap you down, and if you're willing to help us, I'll gladly accept. About the same as I feel about other adventurers."

"…"

"But yeah…I want to talk a bit more with you." Tione flashed a cheerful smile—though it wasn't because of that.

It was as though she were Tiona. They hadn't reached a mutual understanding yet, but they had found a feeling that was unmistakably shared by a person and a monster. It was not great or noble but just some gossip between young girls.

"In order to do that...we have to crush that stupid labyrinth and clear up the mess in this city."

Tione's expression changed as she looked out the window again. Her eyes locked onto the southeast, to Daedalus Street, where the demonic lair, Knossos, lay in wait. Rei also tensed as she saw the adventurer's focused gaze.

"..."

When Tione glanced at Alicia, she did not look away this time. Her hands clenched in her lap. She had a mountain of things she wanted to say. However, her next words were directed just at Rei.

"...Could you help us?"

The siren smiled in response. "Of course."

As if her response had long been decided.

"To be able to fly in the sky, to be allowed in the light aboveground—and to be able to join hands with you, that is what we dream of."

The howls merged together in layers. It wasn't in any human language.

The monsters' roars overlapped as they worked at destroying the wall blocking their way.

"Ooooh! Ooooooh!"

"Graaaar!"

They were digging a hole—cutting, smashing, carving, breaking, removing the green flesh blocking their way.

An unruly troll swung a giant club. A unicorn struck with its horn like an enraged bull. A giant deadly hornet held lances in both hands. There were other monsters of all shapes and sizes.

Their commonality was that they were all fashioned with equipment, armor, and weapons. They were armed monsters, a pack of Xenos.

"Nooooooooooo! Lido, it's bulging again!" shrieked a lamia, her words tinged with a heavy accent, the cry echoing in the passage encased in the eerie green coating. On the wall, it swelled like a malignant tumor, approaching the Xenos as if trying to swallow them whole. A single lizardman whipped around. He wielded a longsword and scimitar in either hand, but instead of using them, he opened his mouth wide.

"Move!"

After the lamia and everyone else in front scampered out of the way, he unleashed a breath of fire. In an instant, the passage became an inferno. The swelling mass of flesh writhed as if crying out. After bathing in the flames, it turned to ash, and silence returned.

"Whew...Man, to think the Dungeon itself would attack...This place is really something else."

While Lido swung his scimitar and grumbled, the Xenos who couldn't speak human language cried out "Bweh-bweh!" in thanks.

Lido the lizardman was one of the leaders of the Xenos. His strength was comparable to that of a Level-5 adventurer. His scratched-up breastplate and the rest of his armor that covered his red-scaled body were pieces of gear that had originally belonged to adventurers. The lizardman was brawny, which was unusual for his species.

He looked around again, reflexively feeling disgusted by the labyrinth of flesh despite being a monster himself. There was no source of natural light. Were it not for the magic-stone torches in their inventory, the Xenos would have been shrouded in darkness. There was a bulky mass still blocking the way to the front. His orpiment-colored pupils distorted as he looked at the transfigured labyrinth of Knossos.

"Going to the deep levels to help Bellucchi's gang, then immediately coming back to Knossos and digging a hole...Fels is running us ragged."

Facing off against a labyrinth itself was a first, even for Lido.

Once, a segment of the green flesh—too thick to call a tendril, as wide as a giant tree's roots—reached out and grabbed the hand of one of the Xenos and almost sucked them in. If Lido's blade had not been drawn, it would have succeeded. The green flesh was out for prey—whether it was human or monster.

To deal with this strange foe, they bathed it in fire, reducing it to ashes and injuring the parts that recoiled. Rinse and repeat. Despite knowing that fire was its weak point, and despite being stronger than the average upper-tier adventurers, it had been rough going for the Xenos to reach this point.

"Are you okay, Lido?"

"Oh, Wiene. I'm fine. It's dangerous here, so make sure you hang back."

Wiene the vouivre had called out to him from behind. Lido tapped his breastplate to reassure his friend who was totally covered in a black robe, but she did not leave.

"…Do you think Rei is all right?"

The name of the siren who had been separated from them crossed her lips. She was still worried about Rei. Her amber eyes were quivering like ripples running across the surface of water. The lizardman warrior stopped moving for a second and smiled a toothy grin.

"She's fine, Wiene. According to Fels, Rei is under *Loki Familia*'s protection."

"Pro-tec-tion?"

"Yeah, like how Bellucchi's crew took care of you. I'm willing to guess she's getting along with those scary adventurers."

At the reference to a certain group of adventurers, Wiene broke into a smile and seemed to finally be at ease.

Lido himself was curious how Rei was doing, but he had heard from Fels that she was safe through the oculus, a magic item in his possession. The captain of *Loki Familia* had reported as much.

People protecting a monster. That concept would have felt unbelievable just a few days ago. Something was changing—ever since that battle in the Labyrinth District. Or, put another way, a certain boy had thrust Lido, Rei, and the adventurers into motion.

——*If that's true, then there's nothing more gratifying.*

At the end of that fight, Rei's sacrifice might have touched the hearts of the adventurers. Lido wanted to believe that, prayed it was the case.

"Let's cut the chatter there. There's no end to this repulsive flesh. We don't have time to waste our breath," a gargoyle cut in.

"I got it, Gros." Lido shrugged like a human at his old friend, who did not allow him to indulge in sentimentality, as he returned to the hole digging.

"Telling us to make a route to the enemy's boss…That's really gonna take a lot of work," Lido complained as he alternated breathing fire and slashing his sword.

"It's not like this is the first time Fels has come to us with an absurd request," Gros responded as his claws flashed.

The Xenos were currently at a depth equivalent to the Dungeon's ninth floor. Unlike *Ganesha Familia*, who were excavating from the surface, they were clearing the green flesh from inside the Dungeon.

For the Xenos, any activity above the tenth floor was risky. Generally, they did not venture onto the upper floors where there were many lower-tier adventurers. Unlike the middle floors and below, the highest floors were smaller, so there was the concern of accidentally running into an adventurer. This time, they had Ouranos's help, though, so they had been able to get to the ninth floor without anyone noticing.

That said, it would take time to reach their target, the enemy's inner citadel.

"But still…it feels like this thing's resistance is weaker than when we started."

"Yes, there's no mistaking it. It was more intense the first time. We almost lost some people then."

When they had been investigating at first, the green flesh was incredibly active, attacking from all directions—floor, walls, and ceiling. It was almost like the labyrinth itself was a living organism lashing out.

Compared to that, its movements now were much more localized, attacking just as though it remembered that was what it was supposed to do. Clearing away what remained was hard work, but it wasn't dangerous, per se.

That was how it felt to Lido.

"!"

As they were carving through the green flesh, they heard a soggy *plop*, followed by several corpses falling out of the flesh in front of them. The bodies were covered in armor that just barely maintained its original shape.

Adventurers.

The members of *Dionysus Familia* who had been swallowed up by the green flesh on that nightmarish day.

"...They were pushed all the way to here, huh?"

The corpses were hideous. Some were desiccated; others were decomposing, barely recognizable. Their common denominator was the pulpy faces and skin. There was no identifying them from their facial features or even from analyzing the Blessings engraved on their backs. To borrow a phrase of the surface dwellers', the flesh seemed to consume everything in its path without any table manners, leaving only a ruin in its wake.

Lido and Gros immediately tried to cover the sight with their backs, but Wiene managed to catch a glimpse, reflexively covering her mouth as she gagged.

"Fels was right. The flesh seems to be using the adventurers for sustenance," Gros speculated as he leaned in, inspecting the remnants.

Animosity seeped onto Lido's face, but there was a sense of doubt swirling in his chest.

The problem is...what is this thing trying to achieve after getting these nutrients?

Fels had a theory that the green flesh covering the labyrinth was the work of the corrupted spirit. However, the enemy's objective was not immediately clear. Was it to wipe out the adventurers who had been drawn in to Knossos? Or something else altogether?

Is the weakening resistance from the flesh related to how it is using the nutrients...?

Lido had a hunch—based on his intuition as a monster, born of the Dungeon. One that he could not put into human words. As if reverting to his wild instincts, he bellowed and shook his head intensely.

"——" Lido stopped moving.

"Lido...?"

The dragon girl behind him tilted her head, her bluish-silver hair swaying. The lizardman did not respond as he reached out to the scorched, slashed, mercilessly silenced green flesh and put his hand flat against it.

"Lido! What are you doing?!" Gros shouted wildly.

Lido responded quietly.

"It's vibrating." Ignoring his frozen comrades, he murmured, "*Something* is...echoing."

Rabbit Oracle

Гэта казка іншага сям'і.

Трус Oracle

"I can't find it!"

In the center of a spacious library, Tiona cried out in frustration, surrounded by a mountain of books that had been removed from the shelves.

"Are you stupid, Tiona? Don't make a scene! This isn't our home library!"

"You too, Tione. Please keep your voice down..." Aiz whispered, begging Tione, who had snapped loudly at her sister.

Her efforts were in vain as daggers of annoyed glances were shot toward them.

The Great Library of the Gnomes.

An institution in the east of the Labyrinth City run by gnomes living in Orario, like the Gnome Vaults.

Of all the spirits, gnomes had the most dexterous fingers, which allowed them to easily integrate into human society. Among them were particularly skilled gnomes who managed various establishments, including the safe points where valuables could be deposited. These gnomes were called landlords. Using jewels they mined themselves as starting capital, they created services that put even the gods and greatest merchants to shame. The Great Library and the Gnome Vaults were examples of their skill at business. Incidentally, the Great Library had an entry fee with a not-insignificant price—as gnomes considered knowledge a treasure—meaning the average city resident and lower-level factions tended not to visit very often.

There were many people from familias in the spacious open-access area with high ceilings, researching things. When Tiona and Tione raised their voices in the center of the building, they drew glares of annoyance. "Loki Familia *again*...?" they seemed to want to say.

Unable to endure the glares, Aiz shrank back, trying to avoid their eyes.

"A dragon called Nidhogg isn't showing up in aaany of the books!" Tiona lay flat on the desk, not noticing how people were reacting around them.

They had come to research the mural of the evil dragon and the six maidens. As Finn had the familia members prepare for the battle, some received instructions to gather information about Nidhogg. Since the library in the manor had already been searched to no avail, their search brought them to the Great Library of the Gnomes, which claimed to have the most books in the city.

They had heard that Finn had already attempted to find it in ancient literature, so Aiz and the sisters were investigating Tiona's beloved heroic epics, but…they had not stumbled across any clues at all.

"Hey, Mr. Librarian. Do you recognize this mural?"

Raising her head from the desk, Tiona caught a librarian trotting by. She must have forgotten that it was supposed to be secret, because she showed him the sketch of the mural without hesitation. Shorter than a prum and wearing an expensive-looking uniform like a banker, the elderly gnome quietly shook his head, his beard swaying back and forth.

Tiona's face smashed back down to the tabletop again.

"Did any of you find anything, Narfi?"

"Sorry, Miss Aiz. We couldn't find anything, either…"

"I mean, the Great Library is huge, but our study has a bunch of books, too. If we couldn't find anything in either of these places… Plus, we've checked a ton, too," she responded. Narfi was looking exhausted as she tried to balance a tower of books.

Tione tore at her bangs, trying to contain a headache. She was not used to dealing with books.

Currently, other than Bete and Anakity and those who had been explicitly given other jobs, every member of *Loki Familia* was at the Great Library seeking leads.

"Nidhogg is probably some really old fairy tale. Back when monsters were coming out of the big hole, back in the earliest days."

Tiona slowly raised her head, throwing herself into the search again as she cracked open one of the books carelessly sprawled across the table and glared at it.

"That's why the information is so fuzzy...Like in this book, it's not a dragon; it's a snake. And its name is 'the world devourer' or 'the one who dwells in burning rage.'"

"'The world devourer'..."

"When I first heard the name Nidhogg, I didn't recognize it at all," Tiona added.

From when Tiona was young, she had always loved reading the epics. If she did not know anything about it at all, Nidhogg must have really been a faceless monster. Aiz started to think back on the faceless mastermind, subconsciously superimposing Enyo over the evil dragon.

"What hero defeated your version of Nidhogg, Tiona?" Aiz asked.

"Ummm, there wasn't a hero in the story about the world devourer."

"Then who defeated it?" Tione responded with another question.

"I dunno."

"Huh?"

"Everything is vague, like 'it was erased by a great god' or 'it was purified by the heavens,'" Tiona responded with a sullen look. "Plus, I don't know anything about the six maidens..."

As Tiona compared the sketch of the mural to the book, Aiz and Tione glanced at each other. They wanted to know more, but even if they tried to research it, there just wasn't enough information to go on. They weren't making any progress.

"At this rate, we should just try going to the Guild! We can get them to let us check out the books in their archive!" Tiona's brow was furrowed as she stood up all of a sudden.

"Investigate the books that the Guild keeps...?" Aiz tilted her head.

"The captain must have already asked the Guild to gather information. And their material is mostly about the Dungeon and Orario..." Tione looked at her sister, frowning.

"But Nidhogg was born in the Dungeon, wasn't it? Then they

might know something about it! If the Guild is no good, we can try asking some other gods or goddesses about it!"

It was not particularly promising, but she had a point. Tiona's argument that they should do everything in their power had Narfi and the others nodding along, especially while the enemy was maintaining its unsettling silence.

"...Let's split up into different squads: some people stay at this library, others go to the Guild, and in the meanwhile, a group will ask around. As my idiot sister said, we'll go through the whole city with a fine-tooth comb." Tione made a decision.

She had been left in charge of the group there by Finn and her sister had set her into motion once again. With this, *Loki Familia* scattered throughout the city.

"Hurry up, Aiz! Tione!"

"Don't rush me. Sheesh..."

Beneath a wide blue sky, the streets of Orario were filled with a morass of demi-humans. Tione grew exasperated as Tiona weaved through the crowds in the middle of the packed street like a monkey and kept impatiently waving at them to follow. Aiz and the sisters were in the northwest section of the city, proceeding toward Guild Headquarters.

...But the odds of finding what we are looking for are...quite low.

Like Tione had said, Finn must have already asked the Guild for information, and there had not been any response from them, meaning that the Guild had not found anything notable.

Contrary to Tiona's expectations, Aiz secretly believed it would be better to not anticipate too much from their efforts here.

Their current mission was the equivalent of trying to find a specific flake of gold that may or may not even exist in a giant desert. That was what Aiz thought, at least.

...Lefiya...

As she found her list of problems growing longer, Aiz started wondering about the elf girl. Of course, she wanted to ask her about everything she had learned about Nidhogg from Thanatos, but more importantly, she was concerned about the girl herself. Tiona and Tione were probably thinking the same thing, too. They didn't say anything aloud, but the way their faces suddenly clouded over told the tale. The obviously missing member of their four-person party left a feeling of loneliness hanging over them.

Would she be able to stand back up? Would that smile ever bloom across her face again? Aiz silently looked up at the sky. It was a beautiful, clear azure blue and totally oblivious to what was happening.

"Come on—Miss Amid told you not to exert yourself. You can't go out walking all the time! I understand how you feel but you have to keep it under control!"

"Ah-ha-ha…Sorry, Lilly."

At that time, they heard a pair of voices amid the clamor of the street.

——*That's…*

Looking back down at the street, she saw his silhouette. White hair and rubellite red eyes. Aiz was shocked to see the boy approaching them from the crowd.

"Oh?! It's Argonaut!" Tiona cried out.

The pair noticed Aiz and the two sisters.

"Miss Tiona, Miss Tione? And Miss Aiz…"

Bell Cranell was as surprised as they were that he had run into them on the street corner, and it showed on his face.

"What a coincidence! What are you up to, Argonaut?"

"Ummm…I was finally able to walk again after coming back from the Dungeon, so I was taking a little stroll…"

Bell seemed a bit dazed as he responded to Tiona. She considered herself a fan of Argonaut, who was as close to a character out of one of the old epics as she could get.

The boy was dressed the same as usual except for an odd piece of armor on his left arm. The elbow, arm, and finger joints were all covered with metal plating. The collection of parts looked almost like a gauntlet missing a piece of armor or an incomplete artificial hand.

The surface was silver with a mysterious blue tint. It was enough for them to infer it was a magic item. It must have been a support for his injured arm. Based on the polished construction, it had almost certainly been made by Amid. Next to Bell was a prum girl escorting him. She was watching them dubiously after Tiona had called out, obviously not enjoying this situation.

"..."

"..."

Suddenly, Bell glanced at Aiz after responding to Tiona. They looked at each other.

"...Back from your expedition?"

It had been the talk of the town that *Hestia Familia* had gone out on their first expedition after receiving a mission from the Guild, even getting picked up in one of the news publications. The Little Rookie—or rather, the newly minted Level-4 Rabbit Foot—was the center of the town's attention because of it. The fact that he was standing there in front of Aiz meant that he had overcome another adventure.

"...Yes." Bell nodded quietly in response.

Slowly, a small smile spread across her lips. The last time they had met had been almost four weeks ago. She felt like she barely recognized him.

——*Miss Aiz.*

——*I want to become stronger.*

Just like he had said that morning on the city walls, he was moving forward. And Aiz started to smile when she recognized that fact.

There was something she had wanted to say, but for the moment, she was overcome with jealousy and happiness.

"Oh yeah! Argonaut! Do you know anything about this picture?!" Tiona spoke up all of a sudden. As Bell tilted his head in confusion, she thrust the sketch of the mural in front of his face.

"Hey, idiot!" Tione shouted at her sister, but her younger sister showed no hesitation asking questions involving confidential information.

"We want to know about this picture! You know a ton about the heroic epics, right? This is Nidhogg. Do you know anything about it?" Tiona paid no heed to her older sister as she approached Bell.

Bell started to sweat as the Amazon pounced on him like a large dog, but he scrutinized the sketch of the mural, the evil black dragon and the surrounding six maidens.

"This picture…"

"Tiona, I told you to quit randomly showing that to people! There's no way Rabbit Foot knows—"

"Oh yes, I recognize this." The boy nodded.

"—What?" Tione fell silent, and Aiz froze. Tiona was also wide-eyed. Even she had not expected that answer.

"I read about it in one of the old stories my grandpa showed me. Wow, that brings back memories."

The boy acted as if it was nothing at all. There was no way he could guess how they were feeling. His eyes slowly closed, and he sank into his memories.

Then, with a smile, he said, "This is the spirits' six-ring that destroyed the evil dragon Nidhogg, right?"

As the sun went down, twilight darkness began to crawl across a sky on the cusp of sunset and the coming night. A weighty comment from Finn stirred the air in the office in *Loki Familia*'s home.

"So that's what it is…"

A large gathering filled the room: the leaders Finn, Riveria, and Gareth; Aiz and the other first-tier adventurers of the main fighting force; Raul and Anakity and those who were the bridge to the lower-level familia members; and Loki, who had just returned to the manor. Urgency hung over them.

A giant sketch of the floor plan of Knossos was spread across the multiple desks pushed together in the center of the room. While Bete and the rest crowded around the map, Finn glanced at Aiz.

"The spirits' six-ring…Are you sure that's what Bell Cranell said?"

"Yes…Nidhogg was defeated using the power of those spirits."

Aiz nodded as he gazed at her. They had asked Bell for everything he knew regarding Nidhogg.

"*There isn't a hero in the story of Nidhogg.*"

"*Instead, six great spirits appear at the behest of a deity.*"

"*And they sacrificed their lives to defeat Nidhogg.*"

What were the looks on their faces when he had first explained it to them? What clamor had resounded in their chests?

"*They sealed the dragon in a powerful barrier and sang a song... Chanting a spell if I had to guess.*"

"*Finally, they activated their ultimate attack and defeated the fiendish dragon.*"

"*That's what was written in the tale I read.*"

After listening to his story, Aiz's voice had trembled as she asked her next question.

"*So the maidens in this picture aren't sacrifices or saints—?*"

And the boy had answered without any hesitation.

"*No. I believe those are the six great spirits of the Ancient Times who created the spell rings and vanquished Nidhogg.*"

Six spirits from Ancient Times. The encircling spell. In other words—

"—The ancient ultimate spell that destroyed Nidhogg will be resurrected in Orario?" Finn concluded, his cold, sharp voice resounding around the room.

Riveria pursed her lips and leaned forward, drawing six circles on the map of Knossos in red ink. One in the north, one in the northeast, one in the southeast, one in the south, one in the southwest, and one in the northwest. They were centered on the large halls on Knossos's tenth floor where they expected the demi-spirits were being concealed. When she connected the six points, it created a perfect circle, completing the ring.

"...These six chambers—this ring...Just how much of Orario does it cover?" Gareth asked.

"The center of Orario—no, the central area surrounding the Dungeon's entrance. That would make it a little bigger than Central Park," Finn responded.

Anakity placed a map of Orario with a similar scale atop the blueprint of Knossos. Just like Finn had said, it overlapped with the area at the center of the city. No one needed further elaboration to understand what the enemy wanted—what Enyo, the city destroyer, was trying to do.

"Blowing away Orario...Using crazy magic that destroyed a crazy-strong monster in Ancient Times...?" Raul looked pale as his voice filled the room.

The enemy had incomparably powerful demi-spirits at their command. But Enyo was not planning to simply set them loose, instead attempting to turn them into a magic reactor core to wreak mass destruction...

"...I saw seven flasks when I was inside Knossos."

When they had invaded Knossos the very first time, Aiz had encountered Levis in a chamber equipped with several flasks for nurturing crystal orb fetuses. Gareth picked up on Aiz's apprehension as she remembered the scene.

"If you discount the bull-type demi-spirit we defeated...then the numbers match."

Given what they knew, they could anticipate six demi-spirits. The number of flasks tied it all together.

"So then...what? You're saying the enemy isn't holing up to weather a siege but that they're biding their time to set off a giant bomb...?!" Tione said, vocalizing the current situation.

As silence filled the room, Loki finally opened her mouth.

"I already checked with Ouranos about whether the demi-spirits would be able to perform the ritual and activate the spell if the corrupted spirit's main body had *consumed* any of the ancient great spirits—"

Loki borrowed the blood feather from Riveria as she spoke and drew more crimson lines on the map. Inside the ring created by connecting the six circles, she drew simplified figures. It was a giant magic circle formed using the six cores as origin points, maintaining the circle shape.

"—The answer is almost certainly yes."

The ultimate spell. The spirits' six rings. The extermination ritual that once destroyed the evil dragon.

It had to be the greatest destructive miracle in the mortal realm, one that approached the power of Arcanum.

"This ceremony is known as *Heaven's Gate*. Placing the spirits around the massive magic circle and using the spirits themselves as mediums, it summons the power of the heavens, creating a pillar that approaches the power of the gods. A spell that brings death but one that could only be performed once multiple great spirits had already gathered together and joined their power…It's almost too powerful."

Raul was not the only one at a loss for words. Everyone was silent in shock.

A power close to that of the gods. A special loophole that had been allowed to occur when the mortal realm was being overrun by monsters.

The brain could not comprehend its scale.

"And its destructive power?" Bete followed up.

"Powerful enough to *blow away all of Orario and the surrounding area*."

Everyone but Finn froze at her response. That was why Tiona's team had not been able to find anything about Nidhogg in the books. It was not that the ancient people had not left behind any records of it. It was that all the people who had observed the ceremony had disappeared in a sea of light.

"This isn't just something like bringing the city into ruin…The enemy is trying to literally erase Orario," Finn concluded solemnly.

At that time, the provocative words of a certain man echoed in Bete's head. It was what Vendetta—the creature Olivas Act—had said when they crossed paths at the pantry on the twenty-fourth floor.

"I will destroy Orario."

That had not been an exaggeration, a threat, or a joke. They actually intended to have the six spirits resonate, amplify, and annihilate everything aboveground in a massive ritual. Once Babel and Orario, the lid on the Dungeon, were removed, the giant hole that gave birth to monsters would be exposed again, spewing forth renewed horrors. That was the scenario that Enyo and the underground forces had in mind.

Outside the window, night had fallen, and darkness had settled in the city. With night as his backdrop, Finn announced, "This is an emergency. There's no time left to spare."

That day, certain people in the city felt something.

"...Do I hear a song?"

Reverberating from belowground, singing in unison, six voices were overlapping, serene and repulsive.

The curtain of night drew on Orario. As the moon looked down on the city, the prelude to destruction began quietly.

CHAPTER 4

NAMELESS HEROES

Гэта казка іншага сям'і.

Героі без імя

A small bird was whistling, chirping in song. The morning sun streamed through the window again, marking the coming of yet another day.

But even as the bright rays lit up the room, Lefiya did not respond in any way. She was lost in darkness. She could not tell what was ahead or behind, which way led left or right, up or down. She did not know where she should go. There was no beam of light to show her the way. She was taut like the skin under a fresh scab, blood ready to pump out of the wound again at a moment's notice. The knife of despair gouged Lefiya's heart over and over and over again.

Are you really okay like this?

Are you really okay letting it end without doing anything?

The dawn poured down on her as she sat there, crumpled on the ground, her eyes empty and fixed on the floor, her heart withered.

"Lefiya, I'm coming in," someone called out from behind the door. The one entering the room was Loki. The patron goddess walked straight to Lefiya and stopped there.

"Lefiya…I've got something to tell you."

Taking a knee so that she could talk eye to eye with Lefiya, Loki began to speak.

"I understand what you are feeling right now. And I'm going to say something that is going to be hard for you to hear. But we…we need you to get back up," she explained to the elf, who had become incapacitated, unable to look up with her eyes that reflected nothing. Loki concealed her guilt as a parental figure, acting the part of a goddess. There was no water of mercy to douse a withered soul. Instead, Loki offered a blaze to set Lefiya's parched soul afire.

"It's about that masked creature…the one who killed Dionysus's follower."

There was a twitch. Though listless as a rag doll, the young girl's hand trembled—forming a fist.

"Will Loki be okay...?" Tiona managed to whisper.

Aiz, Tiona, Tione, and Elfie were outside Lefiya's room. It had already been half an hour since Loki had gone inside.

"Lefiya is essential to take on that hellhole," Loki had told them.

Some had protested that it was heartless. But they all recognized their patron goddess was right. Everyone wished for the recovery of Lefiya, of the Thousand Elf.

There was nothing they could do save wait in front of the door. They were irritated by the sense of helplessness, but there was nothing left for them to do but pray to their goddess.

"!"

At that time, a voice rang out inside the room—a true scream. As if someone was desperately working a throat that had forgotten how to move. As if a battered pipe had a raging stream of water rushing through it.

As they stood frozen, the screams repeated over and over. They could not make out the words, but Aiz could detect the rage. It was undoubtedly a response to what the goddess must have said. Finally, the voice petered out. Those assembled outside forgot to breathe as they stared at the door.

"——!!"

"Lefiya!"

As the door creaked open, they saw first Loki and then Lefiya appear. Tiona and the others gathered in front of the girl who walked out with eyes glued to the floor, her long hair down instead of tied up as usual.

"Lefiya! Lefiyaaaa!" cried a teary Elfie.

"Calm down, Elfie," Tione said, gently stopping her.

"Lefiya...are you okay?" Tiona asked, looking concerned.

Lefiya responded without glancing up. "...Yes...I'm sorry...for worrying you."

She responded clearly—though she was extremely hoarse, nothing at all like her usual voice. It must have been because she had been grieving for so long. Peeking out from behind her hair, her eyes were red. Her face was pale and haggard.

But there was determination in her eyes—a resolve strong enough to bring her back to her feet when she had been beyond recovery, a tragically heroic conviction.

Everyone closed their mouths and opened a path for her.

"Lefiya…"

Aiz's eyes were filled with heartache. She could guess how Loki had gotten Lefiya to stand back up. Their encouragement and appeals had not reached her, which meant the only thing left was revenge: to talk about the being that had stolen away Filvis and set Lefiya's withered soul ablaze.

A dark unease crossed Aiz's mind as she glanced over at her patron goddess, who remained silent.

Will she become trapped by the idea of revenge?

Will she become like me?

Will she get burned by that black inferno?

There was no sign of the sweet girl in the elf standing before Aiz's eyes. Aiz started to reach out to Lefiya, who passed right in front of her.

"___"

But just then, Lefiya looked up, and Aiz saw her eyes. She was captivated by the azure eyes looking back at her. Every last word in Aiz's thoughts immediately evaporated. The elven girl walked past her.

"…Is it really okay to let her go?" Tiona asked, unable to hide the concern in her voice.

Aiz did not respond. She just watched the elf from behind as she grew distant—observing her as she kept moving forward.

"To think it would be the great spirits' ultimate spell…" muttered the mage, bitter, in the chamber lit by magic-stone torches. The location was in the center of the city. The thirtieth floor of the white tower, Babel.

Ouranos had arranged for the space with the giant round table where the Denatus was normally held to be opened for use. In the room were Finn, Fels, Shakti, Tsubaki, and others, the representatives of each organization. The so-called factions of justice had gathered to plan their strategy. The goal was nothing less than protecting Orario from the plot threatening to destroy the city.

"The encircling spell…They intend to create a resonance among the six demi-spirits, circulate the magic energy, and destroy everything when it is unleashed…?" Shakti trailed off after hearing Finn's explanation.

"Sheesh, that's damn serious," Tsubaki murmured to herself.

Just as the Xenos excavating Knossos had guessed, a giant-scale spell activated by a superlong chant had started to take shape underground. If the spell was to be completed, Orario would be destroyed.

While all their patron gods and goddesses were busy running around taking care of other things in preparation, their followers were sharing information and discussing their next course of action.

"You're trying to say the activation of the altar…and the reason for the transformation of Knossos into a spirit realm…wasn't just to wipe us out but to procure enough magic to sustain the demi-spirits?" Fels asked.

They were hinting at the tragedy that had occurred, the total annihilation of *Dionysus Familia*. There was a shudder and a hint of admiration in Fels's weighty voice.

"Just how long has this plan been going under our noses…?" Shakti wondered.

"Enyo, huh? It's true this is beyond the limits of mortal comprehension. But…it may be that all gods and goddesses inherently have this side to them," Tsubaki said.

They were candid about their reaction to Enyo, but it was tinged with a more general awe at the works of the deusdea, who existed on a higher plane. As everyone stood there around the table, a moment of silence settled over the room.

"But right now, we have to defeat one of those deities." Finn's voice dispelled the quiet. "If we don't, our people and places will all be stolen from us, and the world will face unprecedented despair. Whoever the enemy may be, there is no way out for us—save victory. Who's with me?" he asked, the lone hero undaunted and calm, encouraging them. There was no longer any path of retreat. There was no future left for those who would not fight.

Hardening their resolve, the adventurers nodded.

"As mentioned before, the enemy has six cores—the starting points from which they are carrying out the city's destruction. We have to crush all six of them."

"Finn, you're making it sound like you're planning to attack all six of the chambers on the tenth floor at once," Tsubaki said.

"Yes, that's right."

"That's bold. But aren't those demi-spirits stronger than even floor bosses?"

"The time for half measures has passed. If we don't do everything in our power to win this, we won't."

Tsubaki's lips twisted into a grin as Finn confirmed her suspicion.

"Wait a minute. Wouldn't the spell become inactive if we manage to cut off one of the six spirits performing the chant?" Shakti asked.

"No, even if we get one, another can continue the chant where it was left off. It would buy us some time, but the spell will still go off unless we defeat every last one. Ouranos and others confirmed that much," Fels responded.

Shakti and the others grimaced at the explanation.

"Shakti, what about the route through Knossos?"

"Right now, Ilta's crew is operating at full speed to dig the hole. Ironically, the closer that spell gets to completion, the weaker the attacks by the green flesh become and the better our progress. I imagine it's siphoning more of its power to power the ritual."

"Then?" Finn prompted.

"Yeah, we'll have the path to the tenth floor open in time for the second assault," Shakti responded.

"The Xenos are making progress in the Dungeon. And several other strong familias have been given missions, too," Fels chipped in.

The Guild was not holding back in the lead-up to the final clash. This imbued a sense of impending crisis and desperate exaltation to the buildup. Orario was uniting to face a powerful enemy—an adventure the likes of which few had seen before.

Finn nodded in satisfaction and then proceeded with the full-scale discussion of the plan.

"First of all, the operation will begin with *Ganesha*, *Hephaistos*, and *Loki Familias* invading Knossos from aboveground and inside the Dungeon. We'll be splitting into five different squads."

A map was spread out across the table. Chess pieces were placed atop the map.

"I'll command the main force and the first squad. From there, Riveria and Aiz will take the second squad, Gareth the third, Tiona and Tione the fourth, and Bete the fifth..."

As he rattled off the names of first-tier adventurers, he split up the pieces. He placed them at each chamber on the tenth floor of Knossos, where a demi-spirit lay waiting, starting in the north and moving clockwise—the first in the north, second in the northeast, and so on until all five pieces had been placed.

"The second-tier adventurers and below will be spread among the squads. And we'll have the other factions split up among these squads, too."

"I see. Splitting *Loki Familia*'s forces into five even parts to make a set of elite corps and then have us fill in the gaps?" Tsubaki asked, a look of understanding in her eyes.

"Yes. Tsubaki, you'll be with Gareth in the third squad. Shakti, you'll be with me in the first. *Ganesha Familia*'s other first-tier adventurers and all other notable forces will be split around among the other squads."

Finn continued. "Paluza—Ilta Faana will be in the second; Amid from *Dian Cecht Familia* will be in the fourth. Aki and Lefiya from our familia will be in the fifth..."

Finn listed off the names of adventurers and healers to maintain a balance among the various squads.

"Wait, Finn." Shakti stopped him there. "There are six demi-spirits to defeat. There aren't enough squads in your strategy...What are you planning?"

She was right. Finn was pulling together only five squads. The sixth squad was elusive.

Are you saying we don't have enough fighters? No way. Are you planning to leave one of the demi-spirits? But you wanted it to be a simultaneous attack. Are you scheming to concentrate forces into one squad that will bear the load of taking out two different spirits?

Shakti probed him with a sharp gaze.

Do you intend to form a suicide squad with no hope of returning alive?

"—The Xenos will do it."

The one who answered was not Finn but Fels.

"I've asked them to gather the most skilled of their comrades in the Dungeon to take on this battle. There are no individuals as adept as Braver and the other elites of *Loki Familia*, but they all hold a potential beyond Level Three, meaning they should not fall behind the other squads."

Everyone in the room already knew of the existence of the Xenos, and Fels's argument was persuasive and reasonable. The mage detailed the utility of the monsters well.

"...If you can bear this poison, then I'd ask you to trust them."

I'd like you to allow the Xenos to bear the responsibility for one of the fronts in this crucial battle to determine the fate of the city.

The mage was asking them to join hands with the lizardman and other monsters who dreamed of living alongside humans in the world aboveground—not just from a cold calculation of military gain but with compassion and understanding.

The silence lasted only a moment.

"This is exactly the time we'd want to borrow the strength of the monsters. I've no objection."

It was Tsubaki. "I've heard about them from Welfy...a former colleague. And from my patron goddess, too. That there were oddities of monsters who trusted humans. Like they were house cats. If those two believe in them, what do I got to lose?"

"Cyclops..."

"Besides, beggars can't be choosers. If someone's willing to lend a hand, I'll take it. Isn't that right?" Tsubaki's lips curled as her uncovered eye narrowed.

"…Yes. That's Ganesha's will as well," Shakti responded.

"I wasn't against it to begin with." Finn chimed in, too.

Tsubaki was the one who'd had the least interaction with the Xenos among all of them. Shakti and Finn smiled at the craftswoman who moved not based on reason but on faith—or her own belief system. Fels's hood trembled. As the mage looked downward, a quiet "Thank you" slipped out.

"Let's continue. Fels, there's been a change of plans. You won't be joining any particular squad. I'll have you moving on your own."

"More dirty tricks, huh? Fine with me."

"In addition, there will be several other noncombat squads led by Raul and a few others. They will maintain supply lines and serve as a reserve force. In an emergency, I'll have them join the main squads as support if necessary, but don't expect too much of them. At the end of the day, these six main squads will have to do what needs to be done. To that end, each squad will have an oculus for maintaining open lines of communication."

"Finn, what's your plan for dealing with that strange creature with red hair? My understanding is that the one who killed Hashana is the only one among the remnants of the enemy's forces who needs special attention."

"The enemy's plan is in its final stages. There's no more reason for her to take the role of the spirits' guardian. That creature will almost certainly focus on Aiz."

The battle planning proceeded apace with Finn leading the discussion. Despite all being from different factions, there was no wasted time and they were quickly able to reach an understanding on strategy and tactics.

All of a sudden, Tsubaki spoke up.

"Finn, what of *Hermes Familia*?"

"…They're working on something else. They need to take care of something…to *confirm* it."

After Finn answered, no one else brought it up again. They all knew that the true identity of the mastermind still needed to be uncovered. Finally, Fels touched on the time limit.

"We've researched the enemy's ritual. There will be some inherent differences from the original ceremony—for starters, they've become monsters, but..."

Fels had calculated their time limit based on the chanting that was even now resounding underground, quiet enough that most people had not noticed it yet.

"The time limit is—tonight."

Distress crossed the faces of the people in the room.

"...We won't be able to evacuate the city in time. In fact, trying to move everyone out of the city will just invite needless chaos," Shakti said.

"Yeah, we just had two gods sent back; the whole city's already in an uproar," Tsubaki responded.

"We don't have the leeway to split our forces further in order to maintain the peace and oversee an evacuation. If it's just going to cause a panic, then we should act as if nothing's happening," Shakti concluded.

Finn and Fels watched as Shakti and Tsubaki spoke. The half-dwarf's eye narrowed.

"So we're to put an end to this without anyone ever knowing about it?"

"Yes."

"If we mess up, innocent people will lose their lives. Is that okay with you, follower of Ganesha?"

"Finn already has the right of it. If we fail, the Dungeon will be revived. That would be a crisis for the mortal realm. All those saved lives would just be lost later if we don't win," Shakti responded to Tsubaki's point.

There was determination in every word, prioritizing the second assault above all, even if it meant she had to abandon her primary duty. It was the resolve of one who had made her decision and already overcome any lingering inner conflicts.

It all depended on victory. If they did not win, they would lose everything. In that case, they had to devote themselves to whatever it took to stack the odds in their favor.

"If Shakti has made that judgment, then I'll respect her opinion," Finn said after watching their exchange silently. "She is exactly right. Right now, we have to remove as many elements of uncertainty as possible, even if they seem trivial. We need to gather all our forces and then eradicate the enemy hiding away in that underground den of evil. If we yield here, it's not just Orario. The entire world will meet the worst possible fate…The fate that Enyo must be hoping to achieve," Finn said.

Shakti, Tsubaki, and Fels took Finn's words and locked them in their hearts. As he met their gazes, Finn grinned playfully.

"Let's save the city without anyone knowing. That's just the job for adventurers like us."

A hint of a smile crossed all their lips. No one disagreed with him.

"…Shakti, I'll leave the rest of this to you. I need to attend to something."

"Finn? Where are you going?"

Finn turned his back on them and started to head for the door. When her voice reached him, the prum hero looked up—at the room's high ceiling, supported by countless pillars. And beyond that, to the heavens that the tower's heights reached for.

"I have an important job to do that will determine how this plan will go."

"It seems Braver has settled on a plan with the others."

Hermes was moving through the backstreets of Orario with Asfi at his side.

"Tonight, they're going to attack with everything they've got, right?" he asked.

"That's right."

"Yeah, there's not much else to do. If they can't strike down the spirits before time runs out, then it's all over."

There was no one else around in the dim alleyway. As he listened to Asfi's answer, Hermes smiled. Glancing at the face of her patron god, who was grinning even though they were hours from the decisive battle, Asfi added to the report.

"Also…we've found *Demeter Familia*'s hideout."

This caused Hermes's eyes to narrow.

"It's in the Beor Mountain Range due north of Orario. A building tucked away in the mountainside. I've heard Demeter had a storehouse for keeping food in preparation for a famine. That must be it."

Demeter Familia had disappeared—with all their familia members and Demeter herself. With a giant warehouse, she would be able to hide her familia members and hole up.

"Asfi."

"What?"

"That Goddess of Abundance can get quite scary when you make her mad. Do you think she is waiting deep in the labyrinth close to the entrance to hell? Or do you think she's aboveground, counting down the seconds until the end?"

"…I don't know. But either way, we've no choice but to break in and investigate."

Was there a hidden meaning to his question? Or was he just asking for her opinion? Either way, Asfi responded in a grave voice.

"That's true, I guess." The god chuckled softly from beneath the hat pulled low over his eyes. "I'll be going along with you to their hideout. Tell Laurier and the others not to move out until I give the word."

"…Understood."

Asfi noticed that Hermes's voice had dropped an octave lower. But as one of his followers, she pointedly did not comment on it.

"Is that all for reports? In that case, I've got a task for you to do. Can you take care of an errand for me?"

"…Okay, but I'm sure that I'll die from overwork if you give me any more to do."

"If we lose this battle, you'll die sooner or later anyway. Please just endure it for now."

Asfi let out a long sigh, hiding the bags under her eyes behind her silver glasses. Hermes lightly dismissed the familia leader's complaints about all the jobs that had fallen on her shoulders. Instead, he stopped moving and rested his hand on her head. A rare smile crossed his face. After a few seconds of silence, Asfi knocked away his hand, still in a bad mood.

"Please deliver this letter to the specified place."

"What is this for…?"

"Preparation. To increase the odds of victory even just a little."

Asfi looked dubious when he handed her the scrolls of parchment— not just one but several. However, she kept her doubts to herself and did not even check the contents of the letter as she resigned herself to accepting her patron god's order.

"Also, make sure that the city gates are opened."

"The city gates…? For what? *Ganesha Familia* has judged that an evacuation would not get the citizens out in time. And the very act of evacuating the city would—"

"It will be necessary later. If you can get those letters delivered."

Asfi heaved another sigh as Hermes aloofly insisted on not explaining himself. She pulled out a pitch-black helmet from her gear and tugged it on. Thanks to the Hades Head magic item, she became invisible.

"Good luck."

Those were his parting words. However, that was sufficient. Hermes smiled as he headed down countless back alleys. Taking a shortcut, he arrived at the building he was looking for.

"All right, then, time for me to do my part for the sake of hope, too."

Before his eyes was a palatial mansion adorned with an emblem bearing a ball of light and medicinal herbs.

"Hey, Amid."

The god had appeared before Amid right as her entire familia was rushing around.

"How might I help you, Lord Hermes? As you can see, we have our hands full at the moment."

"Are you joining in the attack on Knossos, too?"

"But of course. In continuance with the last assault, I've no intention of shirking my duty. This time, our entire familia will support *Loki Familia* and everyone else with our healing."

The location was not *Dian Cecht Familia*'s clinic but the large mansion that was their home.

Many of the familia members were running past Amid. All of them were focused on preparing items, staffs, and other supplies for support from the back lines.

This time, *Dian Cecht Familia* intended to dispatch all their healers. They would take care of each squad's healing and resupplies, allowing them to focus their attentions on defeating the spirits. Behind her, their patron god, Dian Cecht, was shouting, "Just leave the difficult stuff to Loki and the others! Focus on getting ready to run away!" But they were all ignoring him.

They understood it was just because he was worried about them, but they also knew that if they did not finish things with the second assault, there would be no future for Orario or the rest of the world.

"I shall spare no efforts if there is anything I might be able to contribute."

The total annihilation of *Dionysus Familia* had left a deep scar on Amid, too. But she intended to face this battle, upholding her duty as a healer to prevent any further sacrifices. Because of that, she had no reason not to cooperate with Finn and the rest of them.

"So how might I help you? If at all possible, keep it brief," she responded curtly, seeing how they were busy preparing.

Hermes shrugged and broached the subject directly, as she requested.

"It's about the matter I asked about before. Were you able to take care of it?"

"…? Thanks to your ingredients, I was able to prepare a sufficient magic item, but…"

Suspicion was the first thing to cross Amid's face. He was asking about his request that she had just finished up the other day.

"Since you asked whether I was able to take care of it, all I can answer is that I did the best I could do."

"If Dea Saint is willing to say that much, then I can rest at ease."

Hermes nodded magnanimously. Then the mood suddenly changed. "And—*the progress?*"

Amid froze for a moment. "…It has been excellent. But what of it?"

"Is that so? Good."

"Lord Hermes, what are you talking about?"

"What do you mean? I just inquired about the progress of my request."

"Are you trying to get him *involved*?" While her face was delicate and dollish, there was fierce reproach in her eyes. "I must be clear that as a healer, I'm absolutely against this. In fact, I should stop—"

"Amid," Hermes interrupted her, a smile on his face. "I can't be choosy with my methods anymore."

"…"

"You said it yourself. *'I shall spare no efforts if there is anything I might be able to contribute.'*"

"…"

"The truth is, I'd have liked to be able to keep this in reserve, but—"

As if thinking back to the past to bring success to now, Hermes's eyes flared with determination.

"I'm going to play the ace up my sleeve."

A single drop of blood dripped down, rippling out.

Thousands of years ago, it had apparently been a ceremonial rite. When a human received a spilled drop of blood from a deity, they climbed the stairs of sublimation, becoming something greater. It was said to be the key to seize the future, the power to crush evil to overcome hardships.

Remembering that story, Lefiya's thoughts moved to the divine blood dancing across her back.

If this power is the key to possessing the future, to squashing evil, then what am I going to do with it? What do I intend to achieve with it?

I—

To Lefiya, it was a ritual—and it always would be one. A mechanism for confirming her final decision. An act of resolve to cut off all routes of escape and face the battle head-on. It was questionable whether this ritual could be called "holy." But she suspected calling it "tragically heroic" was not right, either.

I'm going…to put an end to everything.

If she did not go through with this, she would not be able to move forward or backward. She knew that much.

"…It's done, Lefiya." The god finished redrawing the map on her back.

After a new page was added to her story, Lefiya's eyes opened. Reflected in her eyes was a messy room, bottles of alcohol and antiques strewn across the floor. It was a disorganized room of a goddess that was rarely cleaned, but to Lefiya, it was like a reflection of her own heart and left her somehow at ease. Or it would be more accurate to say she was filled with a strange feeling.

"Your Status has been updated. You've leveled up, too," Loki said as she removed her finger that had been tracing on Lefiya's back.

Lefiya stood, her upper body naked as the day she was born, and she took the update sheet from Loki's hands.

Lefiya Viridis

LEVEL 4

Strength: Io Defense: Io

Dexterity: Io Agility: Io Magic: Io

Conjure: H Abnormal Resistance: I Magic Resistance: I

MAGIC

Arcs Ray
- Single-target magic.
- Homes in on its designated target.

Fusillade Fallarica
- Wide-range attack magic.
- Contains fire element.

Elf Ring
- Summon Burst.
- Only able to be cast by an elf.
- Must know chant and effects beforehand as a prerequisite.
- Expends Mind for this spell and the summoned magic.

SKILLS
Fairy Cannon
- Increases magic power.
- Doubles power for attack magic only.

Double Cannon
- Active trigger.
- Preserves magic circle of preceding spell.
- The activation key is "Cannon."

"You've gone up the level that we held back on last time. What you've stored up in your abilities are now reflected in your extra points."

During the expedition to the unreached territory of the fifty-ninth floor, Lefiya had already met the requirements to reach a new level. However, at Loki's instruction, she had waited to let her abilities grow to their full potential for that level. That restriction had been removed. She was now Level 4, and a new Skill had manifested itself.

This was a ritual to escape from the past version of herself, who was weak.

"What was the final reading in magic?"

"S960."

She was asking about the final number on her Level-3 Status. Magic was the only thing on her mind, since Lefiya Viridis had only ever been a mage—one who used magic to save her friends and break out of predicaments. Or to put it another way, without magic, she was nothing more than a helpless fairy, someone who could do nothing but watch on as her precious friend was brutally murdered before her eyes. As she had done in the past.

"…"

Lefiya held the update sheet above the burning torch. She watched as the paper turned black and burned, quietly clenching her fist.

Loki studied her, not saying anything as the girl put on her clothes and pinned up her bright blond hair with her silver barrette.

Taking the magic staff Forest Teardrop, she looked out the window. Past the townscape visible from the window, the evening sun was threatening to fall below the city walls.

As the light disappeared, it welcomed a long night.

The night sky was a dark blue—a deep indigo like the sea, like a blue flame burning quietly. The sky was lit by stars that sparkled like gems and the shine of the bright moon. There was not a single cloud in the sky.

Aiz stared up at the sky—beautiful, filled with the brilliant pin-pricks of stars, and tranquil. It was hard to believe that the city was on the verge of destruction.

"Now is the time! This is it, sister! We'll protect the peace of the city and get revenge for Hashana!"

"Calm down, Ilta."

Looking back down on earth, there were an uncountable number of adventurers milling around. *Ganesha Familia*'s second-in-command, Ilta the Amazon, was shouting passionately as their captain, Shakti, chided her. But Ilta was not the only one from their familia in high spirits.

And it was not just *Ganesha Familia*. *Hephaistos Familia*. *Dian Cecht Familia*. And *Loki Familia*. The notable adventurers, smiths, and healers had gathered in that plaza—in the center of Daedalus Street.

"…"

Aiz could hear all sorts of different voices around her: impatient sighs, nervous breaths, commotion from those who could not hide their unease.

Amid all that, Aiz turned around. The girl was not there—the elf girl who would get flustered with tears in her eyes, who would often ask for help. She was nowhere to be seen.

The first, second, and third squads were using the aboveground route to invade Knossos, while the fourth, fifth, and sixth would enter from the Dungeon's ninth floor to avoid the confusion of trying to advance with a single large group. Everyone was to take the shortest possible route to their target area where a demi-spirit was lying in wait.

Aiz was with Riveria in the second squad. Lefiya was in the fifth squad. While Aiz was standing by aboveground, she had already headed into the Dungeon, waiting with the others down there. This had never happened before, not even on the expedition to uncharted depths, which was why Aiz had ended up subconsciously looking around for Lefiya.

Lefiya has changed, *too…*

When they had left the home where she had last seen Lefiya, the elf was quiet. There was no trace of eagerness, bloodlust, or hatred. Just a quiet militancy as she had taken her staff and focused on what she needed to do.

That's right. The girl who's ashamed of her weakness is nowhere to be found. She's moved far away. Like the boy with white hair, she's gone past the point of no return. Aiz felt a sense of déjà vu.

Me too—I have something that I have to do, too.

Closing her eyes, she gently touched the hilt of her beloved sword in its scabbard. The image that appeared in her mind was one of crimson hair like blood belonging to that person—no, to that creature. The one who she swore to settle up with today.

Aiz renewed the quiet combativeness burning away in her heart.

"—Listen up."

Ten minutes before the operation began.

Of course, it was Finn who caused the wave of commotion to ebb and drew all the adventurers' attention.

"We're about to begin the operation. As you've been told, each squad will charge into Knossos as we planned. Each one is setting out for the tenth floor. Our goal is to destroy the six demi-spirits."

The high elf mage and great warrior dwarf stood to either side of him. His voice was quiet, but it did not waver in the slightest.

There was a flickering oculus in his hand that transmitted his voice deep belowground. In the Labyrinth District and in the Dungeon, all those listening hung on his every word.

"I should be clear: There will be no wealth to be won from this battle. No fame. We will be facing almost certain death, and no one will know it. We will be thrusting ourselves into a mortal combat with no reward. Those who die here will have their names engraved into tombstones without anyone ever learning of their bravery—just like *Dionysus Familia*."

The name of that familia was transmitted through the oculus. Aboveground and in the Dungeon, more than a few people looked down at the ground, masking their troubled thoughts. Among those were Amid and the healers of *Dian Cecht Familia*, the members of *Loki Familia*'s reserve like Cruz and Narfi and even Anakity, who would normally be seen keeping the others in line. Raul, who happened to be beside her and notice her reaction, started to say something, but he bit his lip instead, unable to put his thoughts into words.

The wounds were still fresh, patched with only limitless regret—and the fear and worry of facing the same end. The seeds of those inescapable feelings left those adventurers unable to put up a front, stealing away their ability to roar.

"—However, we must not let these deaths be without meaning. And the same goes for the lives that will inevitably be lost in this battle, too. I will not let their sacrifices be in vain!" he added, resolute in his decision, causing Raul, Anakity, and the members of *Loki Familia* to snap their heads up to look at him.

"If we must fall to save others, it is a fight worth continuing! In exchange for their sacrifice, we must become even more relentless warriors! Our lives must be used to prove their deaths were not wasted!"

Along with everyone else in their familia, Anakity recognized in an instant that his words were aimed at them specifically, as well as at the army as a whole. He was speaking for the dead, explaining the duty expected of those who had survived by turning their backs on *Dionysus Familia*.

"There is no way to atone! Or to condemn! There are no adventurers who wish for these things! They would want one thing and one thing only—*'Make that god of shit howl!'*"

"!!!"

"Take the names and voices of those who have joined the funeral procession in the heavens and engrave them into your hearts. Then go win this fight!"

Anakity clenched her fist. Raul's chest thumped. The members of *Loki Familia* were filled with a raging resolve, the healers of *Dian Cecht Familia* were overcome with pure prayers, the smiths of *Hephaistos Familia* were moved by a burning blaze, and the warriors of *Ganesha Familia* were determined in their will to fight.

Tiona and Tione thought about their comrades who had returned to heaven and clenched their fists. The tears and blood spilled by Leene became wounds in Bete's heart, fueling his strength as he bared his fangs. Aiz swore a vow, her golden eyes flickering. Their fiery resolve spread beyond the first-tier adventurers.

"Right now, history is repeating itself—with us at center stage! Like the heroes of the past who protected humanity and struggled against destruction that threatened the world!"

Dungeon Oratoria. That was the title of the story. The history that occurred around Orario. The true story of those heroes who continued to fight in order to protect their land, their races, their pride, and their loved ones, even at the cost of their own lives. The path lined by their great works and accomplishments.

"Yes, this is a story that will never be told! This battle will not bring riches! Nor will it bring glory! But we will become the nameless heroes and save this world!!"

"!!"

The hero declared the beginning of another legend. The second coming of those ancient heroes' determination, of the heroic epic from long ago.

"A thousand years later, we will become the cornerstone of the mortal realm's peace, just like they were before!"

And he finished the proclamation with the name of that story.

"We'll write the opening chapter to a new *Oratoria*!"

"RAAAAAAAAAAAAAAAAAAAAAAAAAAAAAAAAAAAAAA AAAAAAAH!"

The sky trembled. The ground quaked. Bete howled, Tiona and Tione roared, and the battle cries of adventurers thundered toward the skies. The gods standing away from the crowd burned the images of their followers into their eyes. Their war cries passed through the ground and the message even reached those lying in wait below.

"——*Try me.*"

The labyrinth that had been transformed into a devil's castle cackled, carried by the melody of the spirits.

"——*I'll crush you.*"

The adventurers roared with heroic spirits.

"Gh!"

A flash of silver, a sword's voice as it was unleashed from its scabbard. Aiz led the way, raising her sword above her head, and more and more weapons pierced the sky in her wake.

The fairy girl closed her eyes, starting a prayer, clutching her chest as the torrent of shouts roared.

"Begin the operation! All members attack! Our target is—Knossos!"

The curtain raised on the battle to decide the fate of the world, a story that would never be told.

The adventurers' cries coalesced into a great bellow as they charged into the darkness of the repulsive labyrinth.

CHAPTER
5

Final War

Гэта казка іншага сям'і.

Заключная вайна

In contrast to the adventurers' cries and the intense thundering of their advance, the start of the battle was silent. The adventurers descended directly to the ninth floor of Knossos using the shaft that *Ganesha Familia* had tirelessly excavated.

Some used the prepared ladders, some leaped through the air, but all descended straight down. The adventurers landed in a chamber, a giant space packed with a forest of pillars. There was a clump of green flesh, gnarled like the outline of a person's body, where Thanatos had turned his blade on himself and returned, creating the giant shaft. The location where a certain God of Death had come to the aid of Loki and her familia.

Because Thanatos had shot through to Daedalus Street to return to the heavens, his shaft was the shortest route from aboveground to their target on the tenth floor, allowing them to pass through directly to the ninth floor.

Looking around, Finn glanced at the *Thanatos Familia* flag that had been deformed almost beyond recognition. Suppressing his welling emotions, he dashed forward.

"The flesh has ceased all activity! There are no monsters, either!" Shakti said as she joined Finn.

Her voice encouraged the others, creating an avalanche of adventurers pressing in behind them. Immediately afterward, they entered the labyrinth master's room. It was the large chamber that Thanatos and the Evils' Remnants had used as their base, but it had now lost all meaning. The enemy's true core had moved below it to the tenth floor.

"The first squad to the north! The second to the northeast! The third to the southeast! Advance to the chambers where each demi-spirit is hiding!"

Faced with the diverging paths forking off from the labyrinth master's room, Finn quickly fired off orders.

Three squads had broken into the ninth floor from the pit that connected to the surface. In addition to Finn's first squad, there was the second led by Riveria and Aiz and the third, led by Gareth.

Over a hundred and fifty adventurers, supporters, and healers were moving in coordination with each squad, advancing down the passages that *Ganesha Familia* had already cleared.

"Gareth, Riveria! I'm counting on you! Don't screw up!"

"Worry about yourself, Finn!"

"Let's toast with some of Loki's secret stash when we get back!"

The three comrades taunted one another as they went their separate ways, sharing one smile before they left.

"Finn, Gareth! Don't lose!" Aiz called out as she left with Riveria, setting off the other adventurers laughing, taunting, and wishing one another luck.

Each squad had their own path to follow, avoiding and passing by the green flesh without difficulty. The sounds of boots and greaves scraping against one another filled the passage.

The grotesque mass was still clinging to the ceilings and walls as the elite squads proceeded. Finn resumed his commander's attitude again and roared into the crystal he took out of his pocket as he ran along with Shakti and the rest of the first squad.

"Every squad needs to follow their predetermined routes and head for the tenth floor! We're going to press in from all six directions!"

"There are six demi-spirits on the tenth floor! We have to take care of all of them! Pay attention and follow the shortest routes as we discussed!"

Listening to the captain's voice from the oculus, the fifth squad charged into the remade Knossos with Lefiya.

The location was the entrance connecting to Knossos on the Dungeon's ninth floor.

Using a Daedalus Orb, they opened the orichalcum gate and

rushed inside. This route had not been dug by *Ganesha Familia* but by *Magni* and *Modi Familias* as part of the Guild's mission. The other two routes on the ninth floor had also been dug by other familias under the utmost secrecy.

There was no connection between Knossos and the Dungeon between the ninth and twelfth floors. There were field notes about gates on the tenth and eleventh floors in Daedalus's Notebook, the labyrinth's blueprints, but those entrances had been removed, as if Enyo had already foreseen this future. Because of that, the fastest possible route to Knossos's tenth floor was through the ninth floor of the Dungeon or through the shaft created by Thanatos's return.

"Hey, don't hold back on me!" Bete warned.

"How could I?! Not after the captain set the stage!"

At the head of the fifth squad, Bete's comment warranted an angry shout from Anakity without even a second glance. "I came here to win!"

As the squad's second-in-command and de facto commander, she was the one who had received the oculus from Finn. With her eyes flaring at the scene before her, she blew off the werewolf's needless concern. Anakity's improved mood naturally strengthened the familia's resolve.

A wide passage spread out beyond the opened gate. It was the location of their heartbreak, the place where they had turned their backs on *Dionysus Familia*. It was also the place where an elven girl had lost her arm before being mercilessly torn apart by monsters.

"…"

Everyone's gazes turned to Lefiya. Ignoring the concerned looks from the rest of *Loki Familia*, she stopped for only a second. Filvis's arm was nowhere to be seen. It must have been swallowed up by the green flesh. Instead—

"This is…"

"A sword…and a wand?"

The ownerless weapons were lying limp on the floor. Filvis Challia had wielded sword and staff in either hand when she flew into a rage and suicidally rushed toward the masked creature. The magic swordsman had dropped the weapons when her neck had been cruelly snapped.

"Gh..."

Lefiya picked up the sword and wand, pressing them to her cheek. She closed her eyes tightly, as if the feelings she had sealed away were starting to seep back through.

The other familia members, even Anakity, could not find the words to say to her in that moment.

"—Quit slacking, slowpoke! We've gotta hurry up and kill that damn spirit! If you're gonna hold us back, I'll leave you behind!"

It must have been expected that Bete would take the initiative, hurling his bile at her. His words were rough but intent. He kicked any weakling's ass, just like always.

Anakity glared at him, but Lefiya herself was grateful for his unchanging demeanor and words.

"Sorry! I'm coming!"

Looking up, she started running. She stashed away the sword and wand. At the head of the group, Bete snorted, Anakity smiled, and the rest of the adventurers continued their advance.

"Nine Hell! That's the gate!"

"Got it. Leave it to me."

In the northeast of the ninth floor, Riveria's second squad advanced. From *Ganesha Familia*, Ilta the Amazon called out. At the edge of their vision was a mass of crimson tentacles that seemed to be overlapping like a multilayered spiderweb. This was the one gate that *Ganesha Familia* had not been able to break through when they were excavating. According to the blueprints of Knossos, it was also the point where the stairs leading down to the tenth floor were located.

"Harbinger of the end, white snow. Gust before the twilight—"

As Riveria stopped and readied Magna Alfs, that highest-tier magic staff, the crimson tentacles peeled away from the gate. The speared tendrils rushed toward the high elf, drawn to her powerful magic.

"Ha!"

As they flew toward her, Aiz suddenly twisted and severed them all—three slashes in the span of time that it took a single tendril to approach. It was a high-speed series of attacks, and her unbreakable sword, Desperate, became a blur to those watching. As if a knight protecting her queen, she created a barrier with her sword. While Ilta and the others from different factions were in awe at the tremendous display of swordsmanship, Riveria finished her spell.

"*Wynn Fimbulvetr!*"

Three arctic gusts blasted out. When the bunch of tendrils were hit with the blast that froze everything in its path, they held on for a moment, but by the next instant, they burst open, as if crying out in agony. They froze and then shattered into countless fragments of ice, revealing the staircase leading to the next floor.

Aiz, who immediately dashed through like a whirlwind, was at the head of the squad, and the others poured in behind her with a roar. And then—

"—!!"

The tenth floor of Knossos—the castle of demons.

As Aiz stepped onto the stage of the decisive battle where their target lay waiting, before anything else could happen, her eyes opened wide.

As expected, the tenth floor was covered in the green flesh, but unlike the other floor where it was flabby, almost like a lesion, here it had been formed into a proper passage.

It was as if a thin layer of green carpet had been laid over the original stone passage. The surface looked smooth. There were no visible gaps. It perfectly covered the floor, the walls, and the ceiling, as if a master stonemason had constructed it. Ironically, its outrageous beauty proved that it had not been crafted by people.

The color was not the poisonous dark green of the other floors but sea-foam. The green passage gave off a dim light that seemed almost mystical, evoking the image of a holy altar.

"...It's almost like the Dungeon."

That was how much the scene had changed. It was reminiscent

of the Dungeon that left adventurers in wonder at the scenes of the unknown. While Aiz murmured to herself, the others from *Loki Familia* and *Ganesha Familia* were dumbfounded.

"...?" When Aiz glanced around her, she noticed something.

There were several veins of light running through the pale-green flesh on the ground beneath their feet.

"...A light strip?"

It looked almost like the circuits in magic-stone items. There were many straight lines and some curves, combined like a coded pattern. Some adventurers shuffled their feet and looked down as they tilted their heads in confusion.

"—No. This is a magic circle," Riveria declared as she came up from behind them, cutting through their doubt.

"A magic circle...?"

"It must be the ritual that Loki spoke of...The great ring that the six spirits are creating."

Everyone understood at once. This was the bypass that each spirit was creating. A giant ring for the magic to circulate. It was the foundation of the enormous ritual that would erase the Labyrinth City from the map.

"Then if we just break up this magic circle...!" Ilta leaned forward.

"No, attacking it and trying to cut off the flow of magic won't work. What we see running through the floor is nothing more than the outer layer." Riveria shook her head. "It's not just the floor. The entire spirit composition covering the whole labyrinth is a giant magic circle."

Riveria jabbed the bottom of her staff into the floor, removing a chunk of it, but in an instant, the light-green flesh covered that wound as if nothing had happened. As if it had an abundance of magic to spare, as if it was using the nutrients it had absorbed from *Dionysus Familia*.

"The structure of the flesh on this floor is clearly different. The magic particles filling the air are terrible...As soon as I stepped onto this floor, it made me a little dizzy," Riveria spat as her thin eyebrows warped in disgust.

It was bad enough that it felt like it might get her magic drunk.

Looking around, she could confirm it wasn't just her. The other mages were all looking a little pale.

"...This must be a container of magic powerful enough to destroy Orario," said the high elf, which caused Aiz and the others to forget the situation for a second and pause. They did not know what to say.

It was a powder keg about to explode, strong enough to blow away Orario above them. A dastardly minefield. The subtext of what Riveria had said caused them to gulp.

"...A song..."

And when she realized it, Aiz had been the one to break the silence. From deep in the passage, she could hear a high-pitched singing voice, like that of an innocent young girl.

"The spirits' chanting, huh...?!"

At the same time, the Xenos had reached the tenth floor of Knossos from the Dungeon's ninth floor, and they could hear the chanting, too.

"Even though I can't use any magic, I know this feeling! Something reaaally bad is about to happen!"

"That voice is...scary and disgusting..."

As the monsters were perturbed, Lido and Wiene both trembled. That uninterrupted spell—one far surpassing the longest-cast magics—was proof enough of the boundless supply of magic.

It was bewitching and beautiful, repulsive yet pure, a devilish and corrupted spirit that would bring about the destruction of humanity. Something neither human nor monster, that disgusting voice sounded heretical to the Xenos.

"If it reaches the end of this spell, we lose! Hurry! Get to the source of the chanting!"

The rest of the Xenos shouted in response to Lido's roar. The group of monsters rushed in the direction of the song of destruction.

"—Huh?"

When, all of a sudden, Wiene looked up, her dragon's ears trembling. Just as she did that, there was a sparkle in the depths of the passage ahead of them: from the walls, the ceiling, and the floor.

Magic circles of all sizes filled their field of view. Magic that had already been loaded, just about to fire.

"____"

The other Xenos noticed, but too late. The magic circles activated all at once.

"Dooooooooooodge!"

When the lizardman's warning boomed out, the explosion flared.

"Gaaaaaaaaaaaaaaaaaaaaaaaaaaaaaaaaaaaaaaaaaaaah?!"

In the fourth squad, led by Tiona and Tione, a number of adventurers screamed out. A sudden blaze had started.

"The walls are blowing fire?!"

"You guys!"

A complete and utter surprise attack. Right after they thought they heard a high-pitched whining, magic circles appeared on the pale-green wall of flesh, unleashing flame magic.

"A surprise attack?! Were they aiming for this?! Where's the enemy?!"

It was an entirely different magic circle from the giant ring running along the floor that the demi-spirits were creating. Tione was rightfully confused by the sudden activation of these spells. There were no suspicious mages around. It was as if *the passage itself had used magic—*

"—Tione, up ahead."

She was shaken for a second but, drawn by her sister's stunned voice, her head snapped up, and she was at a loss for words.

Red, blue, and gold. Dozens of magic circles in every color imaginable. A magic cannon was set up at the end of the passage. They took aim for Tione's squad as they called forth sparks of flame, freezing tremors, and crackles of electricity.

It was an enormous deployment that not even a squad full of mages would be able to pull off.

Tione had finally come to the answer.

"Are you telling me the Dungeon itself is using magic?!" she shrieked.

As if to say she was right, the magic circles sparkled and fired off a fusillade that seemed to scoff at their resistance.

"——————————————————————Ghhh?!"

A whirlpool of light poured down on the adventurers. It was a wide passage, but it was an intricate barrage of spells in a limited space. The animal-people adventurers were blown away by the bombing while the human healers were frozen and the dwarf tanks were bathed in lightning.

Fire, ice, and lightning. It was a flood of magic with no commonalities. The force behind each spell was equivalent to that of an upper-tier mage performing a long chant.

"Is the spirit doing all this?!" Tione's scream was tinted with anger as she barely managed to dodge blasts. The tenth floor had become a container charged with magic, a terrain that the spirits had absolute control over.

Circulating an exorbitant amount of magic, the beings at the cores could cast spells remotely. Tione realized that was why they had not seen any trace of monsters and why there had not been any efforts to slow them down before now.

With such an absurd trick up their sleeve, who would need gatekeepers or fodder soldiers? The entire floor itself served both as a counterattack installation and the field on which intruders would be executed.

"I didn't think they'd just let us pass, but this is crazy!"

Hail poured down from above, a spear of lightning bolted from the side, and a pillar of flame burst up from where she landed. The adventurers fell into a panic in the blink of an eye.

The Dungeon itself is using magic.

For adventurers who explored the Dungeon, the deadly implication of that phrase needed no explanation. It would be fair to call it "absurd."

"This is way worse than a swarm of monsters!"

Even a first-tier adventurer like Tiona could not help but scream at it. A barrage of magic. A never-ending attack. The menacing assault from every direction caused one adventurer after the other to fall. In a short amount of time, the squad was on the verge of losing half its fighting force. Faced with an inexhaustible supply of spells, defending and dodging were both impossible.

"At this rate…?!"

We'll get killed.

And it wasn't just Tione and Tiona's fourth squad, either. That thought crossed the minds of everyone who had charged into Knossos.

"Use the spirit cloth!"

Finn's shout roared through the oculus that each squad was carrying.

""""!!"""""

"The spirits cloths should resist the spirits' magic! Each squad needs to deal with the barrage using the spirit flags prepared by the smiths!"

Finn shouted his orders into the oculus in his hand as he avoided the blasts from all directions with divine precision.

The members of the first squad he was leading, particularly the members of *Loki Familia*, responded to his orders almost reflexively. The supporters tore the poles from their backpacks and passed them to those in the middle guard. Taking the poles, the middle guard moved in front of the struggling vanguard, gritted their teeth, and mowed down the incoming fire magic with them.

"Raaaaah!"

The poles had a flag stuck to them made of spirit cloth—in this case, salamander wool. The flames entwined with the flag and then burned out with a sizzling sound.

"It…it worked!"

"We can cancel out the magic with these flags!"

In an instant, the adventurers started to cheer. The flags were one of the pieces of equipment that Finn had prepared and passed out to every squad in the lead-up to the second assault.

Spirit cloths. Fabric infused with the protection of spirits, they had high defensive capabilities against certain elemental attacks. For example, the salamander wool was imbued with fire resistance, undine cloth with water resistance, and so on. On top of that, when used against a spirit's magic, it created a massive repulsion, negating the magic.

Since it was clear that the remaining enemies were the demi-spirits, it was the optimal answer. Knowing from experience just how powerful spirit magic was from the encounter on the fifty-ninth floor, Finn had gathered up countless spirit cloths to raise the squads' survival rates as much as possible. He had used the Guild's cooperation to its utmost, incurring a bill for the battle preparations high enough to almost cause the Guild head, Royman, to collapse as he clutched his stomach.

The battle clothes that the adventurers were wearing beneath their armor were made using a blend of all the different types of spirit cloths.

"Gather the squads into a tight formation! Don't spread out! Vanguards, take the spirit flags and defend against the enemy's attack!"

The spirit flags were a custom defensive gear created by *Hephaistos Familia*. They were not shields but flags. Salamander wool was crimson, undine cloth was blue, and so on. By using the matching cloth, they wielded a tremendous defensive ability against spirit magic. But the one difficulty was that unlike a shield, they could not just be held up to receive the attack. Instead, they had to be swung into the oncoming magic. But the effects were just what the adventurers had demonstrated.

They were matching the storm of counterattack spells filling the passage.

"Observe the color of the magic circles! Be decisive and defend with the appropriate spirit flag! Don't let me down!" Finn fired off.

The orders were extraordinarily difficult, but the adventurers could not help but smile as they tried to meet his expectations.

The people were all warriors with plentiful experience. Top-tier adventurers chosen from each faction who were all confident in their abilities. They had both the dynamic vision to determine the magic circle's element in an instant and the strength to swing the flag before the magic landed. The combination of those two made it possible to shoot down the incoming spells with ease.

"Don't fall behind *Loki Familia*! Show them you can do this much without breaking a sweat!"

""Yes, ma'am!""

The members of *Ganesha Familia* roared at Shakti's words. Everyone was a fearless veteran of the deep levels in the Dungeon, so they readily put their all into fulfilling Braver's orders.

"Advance! Advance to the hall where the spirit is waiting!"

Even in the extremely dangerous area where a violent storm of magic was swirling, even in the midst of a deadly scene, the indomitable adventurers wielded a frightening level of adaptability and escaped the rain of counterattack magic.

"To think the armor Finn ordered would be useful here!"

In the southeast of the tenth floor, Gareth was laughing ferociously in the midst of the third squad. He had a gnome toga spirit flag in his right hand and a Tonitrus mohair spirit flag in his left hand. Wielding the both of them to deftly cancel out earth- and lightning-element spells, the dwarven leader's daring charge raised the squad's morale.

"Ugh, Finn! You forced me to make this boring-ass item, but at least it's not totally wasted!"

In response to Gareth, Tsubaki had only venom for the tiny hero. Because the spirit cloths themselves were the main source of the defensive ability, they were basically unmodified. As a smith at heart, it pained her craftsman's soul that the cloths were basically untouched, only blended together, yet they still had produced this powerful item. The effectiveness of the equipment wounded the pride of the craftsmen of *Hephaistos Familia* even as it let them breathe easily. It created a complex feeling.

"As if that impertinent little prum would ever make you put together something that useless!"

"That's true enough! Argh, this is awful! I'm going to have to vent all this frustration with Finn by making him into my body pillow when we're done!"

Between the dwarf and half-dwarf's hard-charging advance and their fortresslike defense, the third squad was closing in on the source of the chanting faster than any other squad.

"It's trying to cast magic, but it's not any different from the Dungeon! Anywhere works, but just hit it!"

"Follow Bete's orders! The attack is weakening!"

"Y-yes!"

And there were some adventurers who were using methods other than what Finn had said in order to get out from between a rock and a hard place.

The fifth squad centered around Bete and Anakity. The werewolf used the spaces between attacks to move in and smash the green flesh on the walls where magic circles were forming. The wounds immediately started healing, but until they were fully healed, no new magic circles could form.

When the Dungeon took damage, the structure prioritized repairing itself to creating new monsters, which was the same system in this demon's den. Until the wounds were fully healed, it would not form new magic circles. The sharp-eyed werewolf did not overlook that similarity. With the labyrinth prioritizing healing to attacking, the fifth squad set out to attack back.

"Lefiya!"

Ignoring Bete, who was leading the vanguard destroying the labyrinth's walls, Anakity was giving out instructions—in charge of orders back in the middle guard. The ace up their sleeve—the one who had just reached Level 4—was Concurrent Casting to keep up with Bete's counterattack. Lefiya was moving and dodging, in no need of anyone to protect her. She ground to a halt, stopping her attack on the structure of the floor while simultaneously summoning a bright-yellow magic circle.

"Fusillade Fallarica!"

She unleashed a scattershot of fireballs. A ferocious hail of fire that went far beyond mere intimidation. The thunderous boom resembled a giant cascade as she unleashed a tremendous attack that even her comrades struggled to endure. It was a raging bombardment.

As the arrows of fire arced, they brought destruction wherever they landed. Beneath that unending onslaught, the demon's lair cried out in anguish.

"That's crazy..."

As the sparks and smoke cleared, the flesh walls covering the passage were strewn all around, and the original stone labyrinth was laid bare. There were gleams of adamantite shining from behind the battered and collapsing stone from obsidian soldiers—the stone slabs that diminished the effect of magic.

To repair the significant damage dealt there, the labyrinth diverted its resources to recovery.

"Keep moving!" Bete shouted.

The fifth squad picked up the pace, dashing through the passage that had fallen silent.

Bete did not concern himself with Lefiya, who had unleashed her magic with impeccable timing. He had finally acknowledged her growth—recognized that she was not just a weakling anymore. Oddly enough, Aiz had felt the same way before the operation had begun.

——*I'm fired up, but my head is still clear.*

There was resolve hidden behind her eyes. Her focus was keener than anyone else's as she followed after Bete.

"...!!"

And so, the first to reach their destination was Gareth's squad. Before them was an absurdly large space. The ceiling towered over fifty meders above, and the width was easily more than twice that. Just like everywhere else, it was covered with a layer of pale-green flesh.

And *it* was there, waiting at the back of the chamber, an enormous trunk like a pillar. A shining, poisonous deep-purple magic circle seeped on the floor as the upper body of a woman continued to chant sonorously.

"The demi-spirit!"

The adventurers' final target.

The demi-spirit that was trying to destroy the city.

"What even *is* that thing…?!" There was an audible tremor in Tsubaki's voice.

In the simplest terms, what they saw was an impossibly large pillar of green flesh. Glued to the wall, it extended all the way to the ceiling, its imposing form easily surpassing the sizes of Goliath and the other floor bosses. The entire body was undulating as venomous red, purple, and black rings bloomed from it, like parasitic flowers. On top of that, it had several tentacles the size of full-grown tree trunks wriggling ominously.

The thing that caught everyone's eye was not far from the floor—the bottom half of the pillar, for simplicity's sake. There were three different faces. The faces were oriented to the left, right, and straight ahead, the very image of a hideous monster. They did not have eyes, housing a vaguely inorganic feel, almost as if they were only masks.

One had a smile, another a frown, and the last one was crying. Its fleshy lips were a deep red, creating an eerie contrast with the pearly teeth. The mouths were large enough to swallow a large-scale monster in a single gulp.

The three repulsive, gigantic sets of features filled the adventurers with an instinctive hatred and dread.

"How could something be so hideous…?!" Even Gareth couldn't conceal his disgust, even though he had seen more than his fair share of variant species.

The faces and tentacles made it look like a three-faced creature with a bunch of arms. A three-faced monster that used its giant tentacles to mow down any enemies who approached.

That was the entirety of the bottom half of the spirit pillar.

"The crystal orb fetus is parasitizing a Grand Treant…! Not just that…From the looks of it, it's drawn in three different bodies!"

It was a monster from the deepest regions of the Dungeon, an extremely large tree monster with a face, similar to titan alms, which had been host to the demi-spirit they had encountered on the fifty-ninth floor. It was a trap monster that had no way of moving itself, so it must have been offered up as a sacrifice to become the spirit's stout, gigantic body.

"It's certainly repulsive, but…the real target must be up there!"

In the fourth squad, Tione looked up with narrowed eyes as they reached their target. In the middle of the pillar was a female body.

"Distant destruction, the promised land, the salvation of heaven, summoned by the words of God—" sang out a beautiful voice, conducting a lovely melody of destruction from a three-meder-tall upper body.

Its skin was pale green, its eyes a stagnant golden color. Its long pale-green hair billowed. It was a transformed spirit.

"The demi-spirit's actual body…! As the captain predicted, it's preparing for its ultimate spell!"

The giant female body protruding from the pillar's flesh had its eyes glued to the ground as it continued to sing its song. Its gaze seemed almost innocent, as if it were anxious to finally be able to see the sky again. Like an innocent child who breaks its toys, it was trying to reach the sky even if it destroyed everything in the process.

"We have to destroy that as soon as possible! I'm going, Tione!"

Tiona bravely dashed off.

Several other adventurers roared and followed after the Amazon wielding her enormous Urga. Even though they had lost a not-insignificant number of people on the way there, they valiantly charged forward to take down the enemy's pillar, supported by the healers.

"Pierce, spear of lightning. Your envoy beseeches thee, Tonitrus. Incarnate of thunder! Queen of lightning——"

"Gh?!"

While the spirit's real body continued the ritual, a spell resounded from one of the three faces.

Tiona recognized the rhythm, but it was already too late by then. It was a high-speed cast conducted at the approaching squad. The gigantic lips blasted out a different spell from what the spirit's upper body was chanting.

"*Thunder Ray.*"

A golden magic circle appeared in response to the hair-raising voice, unleashing a lance of thunder. Right before it was about to activate, the hair on Tiona's body stood on end, and she barely managed to evade it safely with an animalistic leap, but it landed squarely in the ranks of the squad, who were seconds too late to avoid it. The victims were scorched and thrown back against the wall before helplessly crumpling to the floor.

"Are there two different chants...?!"

With the rest of the sixth squad, Lido was taken aback when one of the faces on the bottom part of the pillar unleashed a spell instead of from the demi-spirit's main body. The Xenos were blown away that the pillar's upper and lower parts continued to double cast.

"The main body of the spirit is continuing to chant the spell to destroy the city..."

"And if anyone tries to stop it, those repulsive faces will eliminate them!"

Fia the harpy and Lett the red-cap spoke in fluent Koine, comments tinged with fear. Their lizardman leader, Lido, saw through the enemy's structure with his orpiment eyes.

"One monster filling two different roles, huh?!"

With dozens of requests under their belt from Ouranos regarding Irregulars in the Dungeon, the Xenos had developed very discerning eyes, and they were correct.

The spirit's upper body was gathering magic for the ritual to destroy the city while the three faces at the bottom counterattacked to deal with any enemies. It was a massive fortress, exterminating the enemies even as it prepared the enormous spell worthy of being called an "ultimate attack."

"*Freeze over as though the eternal permafrost, untold blades. Your envoy beseeches thee, Undine. Incarnate of water. Queen of aqua—*"

"Flash, rays of light. Tear through the darkness. Your envoy beseeches thee, Lux. Incarnate of light. Queen of luminosity—"

"Run wild, darkness. Devour the light in night's peace. Your envoy beseeches thee, Shade. Incarnate of darkness. Queen of shadows—"

"What?! All three at once?!"

Three different high-speed chants had been sung without a moment's hesitation. While Lido and the Xenos turned pale as they realized the three big faces were all casting spells, the spirit pillar mercilessly let loose its magic.

"Icicle Edge."

"Light Burst."

"Dark Roar."

A blade of ice. A flash of light. Oncoming darkness. The wave of blasts swallowed up the monsters.

"AAAAAAAAH!"

As the group of Xenos desperately evaded with perfect coordination, the dragon girl shrieked in the arms of the lizardman who carried her.

"Disperse!"

The first squad was enduring the enemy's bombardment, but Finn's orders were even more precise than his opponent's barrage. He immediately started firing off orders to the adventurers who had just barely managed to drop to the ground to avoid the blasts.

"Every squad needs to split into parties of five and move separately to attack! Don't give the enemy an easy target by bunching together!"

His orders were transmitted through the oculus to all the other adventurers. He was able to come up with guidance fast enough that the squads who had almost been blown away by the enemies' absurd triple cannon were still able to keep up and stem the losses.

Against a powerful enemy and a preposterous situation, the most effective weapon was the commander's loud voice. A brave command was as reassuring as any weapon or magic to subordinates dealing with adversity. Braver's immediate orders nipped the loss in morale and avoided the worst result.

Finn himself was enduring the enemies' fusillade using the spirit flags while simultaneously taking command and raising his soldiers' spirits.

"Shakti! The enemy's magic resembles the elemental counter spells we dealt with on the way here! The patterns for the elements are the same!"

"But its strength is incomparable…! Even a single one of these spells has immense firepower!" Shakti snapped back, as if to say that the two spells were on entirely different levels.

Interwoven with the spirit protective cloths, their battle uniforms were already scorched as they used the spirit flags to protect the mages in the back lines who had been ordered to fire a broadside attack. It was all on target, blowing away hunks of flesh. But then there was a burble, and almost immediately, the giant green pillar healed itself, filling the gaps with fresh meat, frustrating Ankusha.

"It's controlling the flow of magic. I bet those masks can control the labyrinth's magic—"

Finn did not finish his thought. What he saw in the corner of his eye caused even him to stop moving.

"Shakti…I've got some more bad news."

"What—?" Shakti had a sinking feeling about this as she spun around, but she was at a loss for words at the sight.

It wasn't the pillar this time—but *the rest of the entire space.* There was a great number of magic circles appearing throughout the cavern covered in green flesh.

"It isn't just the pillar itself…The enemy can fire off blasts from anywhere, it seems."

From all four walls and the ceiling far above.

The adventurers froze as they realized the impending disaster, as they saw the dozens of magic circles blooming from thin air.

"This is…"

"I wish my guess had been off the mark, but it seems our investigation was correct. The enemy's lower part acts as a defense mechanism to protect the demi-spirit's real body. It can use powerful magic itself and summon counterattack magic *anywhere on the tenth floor.*"

The three looming faces on the bottom part of the pillar were gimmicks that linked with the labyrinth itself.

Six pillars were equipped with three masks each—for a total of eighteen fixtures for suppressing intruders. They were the ones controlling the counter magic on the tenth floor. Until they were destroyed, anyone who set foot on the tenth floor could be attacked at any point and kept from advancing. And even if they made it to the chambers, they would be surrounded by a whole barrage of artillery blasts, just like what was happening to them now.

If the body in the upper part was the demi-spirit, then the three faces were the spirit altar, a defense mechanism for the purposes of completing the ritual to destroy Orario.

"Can we win this, Finn…?!" Shakti growled as she swiped off the dried blood from the wound on her cheek.

As the demi-spirit looked down on the adventurers, its eyes narrowed. The smile never left its face as it kept singing. It was the song of destruction, without a doubt. Despair gnawed away at the adventurers' spirits, and the fiendish requiem that would destroy the city moved slowly but surely toward completion.

As the will to fight wavered under the gazes of the demi-spirit and the spirit altar, Finn quietly licked the back of his thumb. The light of hope had not disappeared from that hero's blue eyes. Instead, he raised a rallying cry to push back against the anguish.

"All squads! Target the lower part of the pillar first! Neutralize the labyrinth so it can't attack us anymore!"

While he shouted his forceful order, the enemy opened fire from all directions. A colonnade of ice poured down from above. A stream of lightning cut through the air itself. Intending to kill, magic circles spread a carpet of flames like a minefield across the floor.

Slipping through the rain of magic coming from every which way, the front of the adventurers' armor was scorched in an instant as they dashed forward to attack the spirit altar.

The vanguard led a gallant charge. Under their protection, the back lines sniped the monster in front of them.

Faced with a thunderous artillery barrage trying to obliterate them, the adventurers shut out their fear and raised a battle cry.

It was a battle far beyond anything mere mortals could inflict on each other. The opening of a battle the likes of which the world had never seen.

They could feel the tremors. Far away, the sounds of battle reached them through the rumbling ground.

"Hurry it up, you slowpokes! Finn's group has already started!"

Lefiya was sprinting. As Bete raced ahead at the front of the pack and peppered them with abuse, she listened and picked up the pace, just like everyone else.

The fifth squad was made up of members of *Loki Familia* and *Ganesha Familia*. They were closing in on the chamber where the demi-spirit lay waiting.

——*My heart is calm.*

The passage seemed to quake with every step. Her heart pounded against her chest every time her feet hit the floor. But Lefiya was calm on the inside. Considering it was a battle with the fate of the city at stake, it was shocking to her that she was unemotional. The old Lefiya Viridis would have been desperately trying to squash her unease, holding back the tears as she fought to keep her heart from beating out of her chest.

But now, her lips smoothly conducted her chants, and there was no sign of her messing up. She had long forgotten the number of adventurers she had helped by scorching the labyrinth. Right now, she was confident she would be able to maintain her Concurrent Casting even if she was facing off against a floor boss by herself.

She was in a state of mind that had no remaining ties to her past self. Her spirit was a clear white, like the sea-foam from waves crashing silently on a moonlit beach. She almost felt like she was in a different world from the adventurers around her who were getting worked up.

There was no nervousness, no bluffing, and no wrath. Just resolve—and a determination not to run, to face whatever lay before her and fight as best she could.

That was why. That was why she had a premonition, a feeling that there was no way they would make it to the demi-spirit that simply. She was sure something was going to happen.

"E-enemy attack!!!"

And just as she expected, it came. The counter magic in the passage stopped for an instant. In that small window of opportunity, a single enemy appeared from a side path. As warnings flew from the rest of her team, the figure in a hooded dark-purple robe approached quickly.

——*The masked creature!*

That sinister mask. Those metal gloves. The mysterious creature that left no bit of skin exposed. I'll never forget it. I could never forget it. This is what I came here for—!

Lefiya's eyes filled with emotion. She clenched her fists. Her calm heart suddenly transformed into a raging sea, as if she had been waiting for this very moment.

"Lefiya! Fall back!" Anakity called out to her.

The masked creature was attacking perfectly into the middle of their squad. It would take a few moments before Bete at the front would be able to deal with it. To help fill those few seconds, she ordered a counterattack from her position at the tail end of the formation. However, the masked creature paid no heed to Anakity, holding out an orb in its right hand.

A Daedalus Orb?! What good is that going to do now—?

Knossos was already covered with green flesh. Like soil that had a matured tree's roots growing through it, even if someone tried to lower the orichalcum doors, the doors would not be able to move. And there were not even any doors near them. As Lefiya wondered what the creature was trying to do with the key—

"Out of the way." A ghastly voice spoke from behind the mask.

The layer of green flesh covering the floor withdrew like a wave slipping back into the sea.

"_____"

The stone floor appeared, and there was a bright-red jewel inset into the floor right beneath the center of the squad. When the hidden trap appeared, Anakity realized what the enemy was trying to do. She realized it—and that she was already too late.

"Fall."

The jewel on the floor shone, resonating with the masked creature's key. The next moment, the floor violently split open.

"Wha—?!"

The familia members were horrified, and even Bete could only watch in wonder. It was a function that remained from Knossos, a trap activated by the Daedalus Orb. By removing the parasitic flesh, the creature had been able to trigger the pitfall.

"Damn it!"

Its area of effect extended from the front of the squad all the way to the middle. As Bete's curse echoed, the adventurers were yanked down by gravity. The masked creature then jumped in itself and followed after them.

"Lefiya! Bete!"

They disappeared into the darkness below, beyond the reach of Anakity's outstretched hand. She immediately started to take out the key that they had brought along, but the film of green flesh suddenly covered up the ground again with a burble. At a loss for words at the sudden surprise attack, Anakity stood there with the remnants of the squad, her brow furrowed as she held the crystal up to her mouth.

"Captain! We were caught by an enemy trap! Bete, Lefiya, and several others fell through a shaft to somewhere below the tenth floor!"

She reported back to the oculus as artillery blasts thundered from the other end. She knew that they were even then in a fight for their lives, but she still could not help shouting. Finally, after a chain of four hair-raising explosions, Finn's voice responded.

"Can you join back up with them?!"

"...No! We cannot figure out where they fell, and we cannot use the same pitfall because it has already been covered up again by the altar's structure!"

After a brief consideration of the possibility, she forced herself to respond in a way that tore her apart. The commander whose face she could not see gave her an order quickly.

"Take whoever's left and continue the advance. I'll send some of the reserve forces over to you. Move immediately to attack the demi-spirit!"

"...Understood!"

His coolheaded voice resounded in her ears. There was no change in their priorities. It was clearly the correct answer. Even if they lost half their comrades, the demi-spirits had to be defeated. They had joined this battle with that in mind.

Anakity was consumed with regret as she rushed through the passage with the remnants of the squad.

While Lefiya's squad was split up...

"—!!" Aiz sensed an intense presence.

"Riveria! It's coming!" Aiz shouted.

"!"

She was sprinting in the middle of the squad when she noticed it. Riveria's shoulders twitched in response.

The location was still in the long passage where they had been exposed to the counter magic. In the distance, the entrance to the chamber with the demi-spirit was just barely visible. All of a sudden, the flesh wall to the side of the squad opened like a maw, revealing a large passage.

"...!"

The passage was completely dark. Not a single light shone in its depths. From the darkness emerged hair the color of blood. It was the strongest creature, wielding a single pitch-black cursed sword. It was Levis.

"You came, Aria."

When she appeared, the magic circles in the passage fell silent, as if respectfully deferring to her. The queen of slaughter sauntered out as the fragments of magic circles dissipated and dissolved to magic particles.

"This will be the end."

"…"

"You and me. Our final battle."

She did not say much. The entire second squad had frozen, facing off against her. The adventurers' terrified gazes focused on Levis, but she had eyes only for Aiz. There was a moment of silence as the adventurers forgot they were amid a decisive battle. In that passage, where the adventurers' battle cries and the labyrinth's magic had fallen quiet, two pairs of eyes, golden and crimson, stared each other down.

"Riveria." It did not take long for her to reach a decision. "Let me go."

Desperate trembled in her hand as she gripped it. It was hard to tell where the hilt ended and the curled fingers began, as Aiz started to transform herself into a sword. The reflection of her face on the silver blade was filled with militancy.

"…"

As the girl pleaded with her, never taking her eyes off Levis, Riveria closed her eyes. There was a brief moment's pause, but then she immediately fluttered her lids open and nodded in response. She did not say anything. Turning her back on the two of them, the high elf led the rest of the squad to continue the advance.

Her silhouette told the entire picture:

——Don't lose. Win this.

——Win and come back.

As Riveria left, Aiz did not say anything in response. She just nodded.

Levis let them pass, as if she had no interest in the fate that would be decided by the adventurers' battle.

"You don't need to make a speech or anything, I'm sure."

"No."

"And no last words?"

"Not necessary."

Their exchange was succinct and dispassionate. It was not very fitting for a final battle. Despite being mortal enemies, the two were cold and clinical. They were not rivals, nor would they ever be.

From the moment they'd met, they had been bound together by an odd combination of blood and ice. Neither had any sort of burning belief in the other.

"I am going to defeat you."

On the surface, at least.

"I will defeat you and put an end to all this."

"I've heard enough of these boasts."

But even though they did not share any common belief, even if they did not have any motive beyond clearing away the flying sparks, both of them were fighters.

"That was on the twenty-fourth floor. After losing to me once, you stopped your doll act. Your eyes were flaring, and you were acting awfully high and mighty."

Levis was satisfied. She had not noticed it herself, but the task that she carried out with something akin to inertia had become her one reason to keep living—once it involved the fights with Aria. She had not noticed that her emotions—*which had rotted away during those numb days a long time ago*—had gradually returned as the girl kept standing back up and kicking up a roaring wind, even though Levis had tried to destroy her many times. If her emotions had not been returning, then there would have been no reason for her to let Aiz escape when last they'd faced each other. If they were not coming back, then there would have been no reason for her to want a battle between just the two of them on this day.

"Then I'll say the same thing I said before, too," Aiz added.

She had pulled together an overpowering hostility—an unyielding spirit that loathed to lose. She had overcome the powerlessness in her heart that had crushed her spirit. And most importantly, she had filled herself with a resolve to protect the people and places most important to her. She was not good at expressing herself verbally, so she did not have the means to put those thoughts into words. But under her skin, in the depths of her heart, the boiling emotions in her soul pumped through her body with each heartbeat.

"I will not lose to you."

A glint of light flashed from the silver sword. The black cursed sword raised into the air as it whined. The passage was watching and waiting—and spectating. Levis must have willed it to not intervene using magic.

They stared each other down.

"—Let's do this."

Levis quietly announced the beginning. With her arm holding the sword hanging loose by her side, the true monster shifted into battle mode. Aiz had not taken a real stance with her sword, either, when the trigger went off in her heart. Everything except the enemy before her quickly slipped away from her vision.

"That said, this is going to be one-sided."

Levis had no doubt of the fact that she was overwhelmingly superior, but she still wanted a fitting finale for their last battle. At those words, Aiz closed her eyes for an instant.

Levis was right. It would have been a one-sided battle had they fought not that long ago. There would have been no way for Aiz to overcome the creature. But it was different this time. This time, Aiz was different.

"—Here I come."

When Aiz opened her eyes, there was something different about what she saw.

The creature standing before her, the hybrid between a person and a monster, the enhanced species that had eaten magic stones to grow stronger, the being whose battle potential was far beyond that of Aiz or the other first-tier adventurers in *Loki Familia*—it was a true monster.

Yes, that's right.

Aiz perceived the contours of a human woman, which morphed and changed with *an audible squash*, melting like hard candy under heat. Levis darkened, becoming a pitch-black color. The humanoid form warped into a more grotesque form. There was a sound of a switch being flipped on her back. In the dark depths of her heart, a fragment of power rose.

"…What?"

Her vision was clouded. Lines formed, evoking images of a storm. The being standing before Aiz noticed her change, but even so, it was too late. It did not matter anymore whether she noticed or not. Aiz's golden eyes were filled with a dark light. A pitch-black circle filled the outer edges of her irises.

Alter. Adjust. Change.

The being before her was transforming—changing from a human to something more disgusting, and from that nauseating form into a full-fledged monster. Levis had become a monster covered by a mixture of pitch-black and bloodred.

"—!"

Aiz's back was burning. The raging fire crackled, distorted, and howled as it gave off black sparks. Aiz was embracing the torrent of power—but she was controlling it, like Warlord had taught her. She did not become a puppet to the black inferno ravaging her body. She integrated it into herself—not allowing the black blaze to burn her body but weaponizing it to defeat her enemy.

Aiz readied the sword in her right hand.

"Tempest——Avenger."

And then she cast it—the spell to summon the wind. The forbidden chant to *combine* the strongest Skill and the spirits' Airiel.

In the next instant, the world around her changed dramatically. She could no longer hear the violent tornado roaring. The wind whipping about her took on a darker color. It gave birth to a spiral of wind. The wind's flow created gashes in the nearby green flesh.

Because of the wind running wild in the passage, the boundaries between them became blurred.

It was not the melody of a beautiful wind.

The spirit wind that the creature had seen so many times before turned into an inky storm swirling around Aiz.

"——————————————————————————————*Gh?!*"

In that same moment, in places far from their fight, in the six chambers, the six spirits all simultaneously screamed.

"Wh…?!"

Finn, Gareth, Tiona, Tione, the Xenos, and all the other adventurers engaging with the demi-spirits saw it happen. Even the demi-spirits' bodies stopped singing as they held their heads and cried out in anguish. All the intricate counterattack spells cut off, as if they were recoiling in fear from the sinister black storm that had been summoned inside them.

"_____"

While Knossos was consumed in a chaotic quake, time stopped for Levis. Her green eyes snapped open wide. It was the first time that genuine monster had set eyes upon a true beast besides herself.

"_____*!!*"

Though it had ground to a halt for a moment, the green flesh started creating magic circles again. The attack spells that had stopped because of Levis's thoughts all of a sudden began again as one. They had received the spirits' command and created a cage of more than a hundred magic circles, with every last one aimed at Aiz.

All the elements and all the magic. If it could manage to fire, this simultaneous barrage would completely destroy the girl and her black storm.

However, none of that meant a thing to Aiz now.

"*Nizelle.*"

She launched herself off the floor with just her right foot. That alone was enough to make the flesh burst apart. The black gust of air whipped

© Kiyotaka Haimura

into a gale that almost looked like a raging fire, blasting away the film of green flesh on the floor and even the stone paving beneath it.

She broke free from the magic cannons' encirclement, leaving it behind in the blink of an eye. As the accelerating shock wave from impact spread outward and the hundred magic circles were being shredded to pieces, Aiz appeared directly in front of Levis.

"——Gh?!"

From a close range, the black storm brought Levis back to her senses. The girl was expressionless as she prepared to attack. She held her sword raised high above her head. And then she swung it down with a single vertical slash. It was a stance for striking down an enemy who had left themselves open to attack, and she was using it despite the fact that she was assaulting Levis head-on. But even that meant nothing to Aiz now.

In truth, Levis was not able to fully respond to it in her current state. Using the wind pressure that was brutally blowing right in front of her, the creature used all her strength to retreat as the blade swung down.

And it *broke*.

"What?!"

Aiz's sword broke the adamantite floor—and the structure of Knossos was supposed to be indestructible.

Green flesh splattered. Fragments of stone and metal blasted through the air. The floor shattered, making a giant crater like a meteorite had fallen there. And a hole opened.

Levis was struck by a sense of weightlessness. And then she was swallowed up by the darkness leading to the next floor, still shuddering as she fell.

"I will beat you."

"—Ghhh, Ariaaaaaaaaaaaaaaaaaaaaa!"

Levis screamed as the girl leaped into the hole to pursue her. Using her black storm, Aiz accelerated in midair, closing in on the creature who had no foothold, mercilessly hitting her with a slash.

The *splattering of flesh and shattering of bones* were melodic.

Losing an arm to a single blow, Levis crossed blades with Aiz at a disadvantage. But if she had not done so, she would have died.

As the creature took the brunt of that charge, the top half of the cursed sword broke off, but she still desperately swung it. She was able to avoid lethal blows; however, there was a lot of blood pumping from her stomach. Her lips were red with fresh blood. With one exchange, Levis fell, and Aiz used her wind to kick off the wall and immediately chase the creature. Levis would not be allowed to escape. The black wind billowed, lashing out.

Overpowered by the wind, her sword broken, tossed about by the gale, she was pierced through while in the air.

One, two, three, four. As Aiz's sword transformed into wind and roared, she broke through four adamantite walls and then through the floor again.

Despite being in an underground labyrinth, Levis was experiencing the weightlessness of free-falling through the air. As rage and fear filled Levis's eyes, fragments of metal and thousands of bits of green flesh filled her vision, making it hard to see. She fell and fell and fell some more. She fell to a far deeper floor as pieces of her body were carved away.

And then…

"Gaaaah?!" Levis slammed into the floor of a big chamber with a resounding boom. It was a wide area blanketed in green flesh. Levis could immediately guess it was the twelfth floor due to the distance from the demi-spirits.

"This will do."

After knocking Levis down through two whole floors, Aiz landed gently using her wind as a rain of adamantite and flesh crashed down around her. This would be the true location of their final battle.

"Aria, you bitch…"

Levis no longer had her right arm; her gnarled left foot had lost all shape and form. Anyone who did not know better would surely believe she was down for the count. She had been stretched to her limit by the sword's wind, and her whole body was covered in lacerations. There was nowhere on her without some open wound.

With a face warped in rage, Levis got up, wounds giving off a hot steam as the creature's regeneration kicked in. The severed right arm was quickly mended. She slammed the last bit of her sword's hilt that remained into the ground.

"Where were you keeping that monster?! Why haven't you used it before?!"

"*I couldn't use it.* Because I was always imagining you were human. Even though you have extreme power, somewhere in my heart, I thought you weren't a monster, since we could communicate with each other."

Avenger. According to Loki, it was an incomparably powerful rare Skill—the most potent one, even among all her followers. The effect was a strong increase in power based on the strength of her desire for revenge. Its target was hideous monsters.

Until now, Aiz had not been able to view Levis as a monster. Or, rather, Levis did not fall into the neat box that the girl had created to define them. But she had overcome this obstacle by training with a certain strongest.

"But after fighting him...after fighting Warlord, he taught me: I need to use everything I have to beat you."

And more importantly...

"...There are monsters who can speak human words. There was a dragon with a human heart."

A troubled look appeared on Aiz's otherwise expressionless face as she put her heartbreaking thoughts into words. The image of a single vouivre crossed her mind. Under that moonlit night, there was the dragon girl who had been protected by that boy, who then had protected him—the dragon girl who had cried as she pleaded with Aiz.

"The exact opposite of you. You have a monster's heart."

Aiz did not know the answer to this question: If a monster could reason and cry, could it really be a monster? Or was someone in a human shell committing atrocities the true monster?

She had been at a loss after meeting the Xenos. Were monsters an absolute evil that needed to be destroyed or not?

"I'll be the one to decide who is a person and who is a monster."

And now, she finally spoke the answer she had been avoiding.

"I'll decide with my own eyes who to use this power on!"

That was the answer Aiz had reached after the chance encounter with the Xenos. She would not burn everything down indiscriminately with that black blaze. She would not become a puppet to the raging howls of her Skill. Instead, she would use her golden eyes to direct her sword. Even as she was eaten away by the black flames, her eyes were lit with the light of that resolve like a sword.

Levis stood dumbfounded as the girl's glare pierced her.

"…Bh." Finally, air passed through the creature's lips. "Ha-ha-ha-ha-ha-ha-ha-ha-ha-ha-ha!"

Levis laughed. It was the first time Aiz had ever heard her chuckle.

"You've changed, Aria…Yes…you've changed."

"…"

"Compared to our first encounter…Your eyes never looked like that before. When your eyes were black all the way to the bottom, it was similar to ours."

While the creature's body was recovering, giving off a hot steam, Levis compared a scene from her memory with what stood before her now.

"What changed you? How did you become that strong? For the first time, I'm a bit curious about you."

True to her words, her eyes were filled with interest as she ran her fingers over her wounded stomach that had fixed itself, up across her own voluptuous bosom, her neck, and then her cheek.

"Aria, until today, you were my everything. Stealing you away was my job."

"…"

"Everything in this world is worthless. I'm not even sure what meaning there is in doing this. Even though I have something that I must protect at all costs, it's really just inertia pushing me forward."

The pessimistic creature finally unveiled her own thoughts for the first time. Stowed away in her gradually strengthening tone was a fighting spirit that did pale in comparison to Aiz's.

"But when I'm chasing you! When I'm facing off against you! When that happened, surprisingly, that might have been the only time I was happy! When I was crossing blades with you, it might have been the only time I could forget myself!" Levis howled, as if her withered emotions were returning with their full force.

"That must be why I'm so happy to face off against you now that you've changed into this!"

"That's not how I feel."

And on the other end, Aiz stared down the monster before her, her eyes giving off a sort of black glint.

—*Don't be consumed by it. Control it. And remember.*

——*The enemy facing you now is…*

Aiz had an enemy she needed to defeat, a being that could not be forgiven. She had an irreplaceable wish. However, her target was not Levis.

"You are my enemy. And a stepping-stone. I will defeat you and then go fulfill my wish."

Levis cackled even more maniacally.

"That's in your nature, Aria! A dollish face and a childish determination not to lose! How horribly impertinent! But that's fine. You are fine just the way you are!"

In the next instant, her eyes flared as she stuck her arm into the green flesh on the floor.

"Come, you useless fragments!"

"‼"

Shock flashed through Aiz's eyes. Starting where she stuck her hand into the floor, the green flesh began to gradually rise, eating into Levis. It was a flesh brimming with magic, an armor created by the corrupted spirit that granted power beyond human understanding.

Crawling from Levis's right hand, arm, and shoulder, the green flesh violated Levis's right side, synchronizing with her and turning a crimson color. It became an armor of flesh bonded to her body.

The red surface was gnarled with vessels like leafy veins adhering to her skin. The enormous, eyelike organ embedded in her right shoulder stared at Aiz.

"If you've changed, then…I have to change, too."

As Levis stood up from her kneeling position, she withdrew something as she pulled out the arm she had thrust into the floor.

She drew a crimson longsword from the floor with a ghastly burbling sound. The sword was steeped in magic, the spirits' corrupted sword.

"Let's begin. This really will be our final battle."

There was a popping sound as the vessel running along Levis's cheek burst, letting out an explosion of magic that her body could not contain. The wound was immediately healed by her regeneration, but there was just another pop in a different location as boiling blood splattered across the floor.

The creature's body was gradually self-destructing. However, Aiz was in the same position. The black wind blasting all around her was steadily eating away at her slender body. Levis was not the only one summoning a power beyond what her body could withstand.

"   "
 . . .
"   "
 . . .

They both quietly readied their blades. The violent waves from the black wind whipped their hair through the air, and the unsightly flesh armor trembled in the face of its prey.

This was the fourth time. The fourth time that they had crossed blades. When one lost, they would train to win the next time, causing the other to go off in search of strength.

To stamp the last ticket in that unending relationship, they both rampaged wildly.

"*Haaaaaaaaaaaaaaaaaaaaaaaaaaaaaaaaaaaaaaaah!*"

With a howl, the creature sprinted, tearing up the floor where she'd launched off. Aiz responded by lowering her body and disappearing. The black wind shattered the ground in a single blow as she accelerated even faster than the monstrous woman, closing the distance between them.

The monster howled against the roar of the black wind as they clashed.

CHAPTER 6

THE DIVINE PROVIDENCE OF DESPAIR

Гэта казка іншага сям'і.

Цёмны Бог

The night was swarming with silence. The vast expanse of darkness could be an ocean of black ink. Of course, there was no sound of waves crashing. There wasn't even wind as the sky remained cloudless. There was only the moon frozen high in the sky, calmly looking down on the land.

A stream of cold moonlight poured into a building tucked away in the side of a certain mountain. Nestled amid the trees, it was almost glued onto the mountainside. There was not even a single light. The building was quiet and dark. There weren't even animal sounds to break the silence.

"..."

A rustling approached the building.

Hermes climbed the stairs that creaked with each step. When he came to a sudden halt, he put a hand on the handrail and turned around. Visible in the distance, a white tower, Babel, rose into the night sky. He narrowed his eyes as his thoughts shifted to the adventurers fighting below it who the people would never know about. It lasted only a moment before he turned forward again and finished his climb.

Hermes was alone. There was no trace of anyone in the building. It was almost disappointing that it was this empty. Climbing the large spiral staircase outside, he left the building and headed to the balcony.

It was a broad space to be called a balcony. Made of wooden planks, there were plants kept on either end of the space—flowers, of course, and cultivars of agricultural products. All the plants made it feel like a big greenhouse.

At the other end of the balcony, there was a magnificent night sky that came into view. It was the ideal observation deck, with a view of the Labyrinth City overflowing with the light of magic-stone lamps in the distance.

And in the middle of that nightscape, in the midst of that superb view, there was a deity staring toward the city, back to Hermes.

"Hey, I found you."

He took off his hat and stepped closer. It was a certain goddess's hideaway. A giant storehouse for saving up food. The second home for a certain familia.

"..."

Maintaining her silence, the goddess turned around slowly, a blank, passive mask on her face.

"Don't you think it's about time we ended this, Demeter?"

Her honey-colored hair fluttered as she looked back at Hermes, though her face was as still as a mask.

"I see. You actually came, Hermes."

"Ow! That hurts! Your claws are digging into my shoulder!"

"I-I'm sorry..."

Loki reflexively recoiled, swinging her arms and legs like a child. As they slowly *descended*, Rei the siren struggled to not grip too hard with her talons as she spread her wings.

They were in Knossos, descending through the middle of the shaft created by Thanatos, down the hundreds of meders that it extended. They had secretly dodged the adventurers on watch and snuck in from the Labyrinth District.

Finally, they reached the ground on the ninth floor of Knossos, and Loki looked up.

"Man, this is reaaaaally far down," she said. "Sorry for forcing you to bring me here, Rei-Rei."

"R-Rei-Rei..."

"But parachuting with a monster was a neat experience."

Paying no heed to Rei, who was shocked by the nickname, Loki kept talking to herself in her usual laid-back manner. Lighting the magic-stone lamp at her waist, she started moving down the path that Finn and the others had taken.

"It sure has changed…"

It didn't take long for them to reach the labyrinth master's room, the long passage, and the routes the three squads had gone down after splitting up. As they proceeded through the transformed labyrinth, Loki stopped at a place she remembered.

It was the main area nearest the Evils' base, the one closest to the labyrinth master's room. It was the location of the fateful crossroads from the day of the first attack. It was the place where Gareth and Loki had discussed their strategy for the endgame after cornering Thanatos. And as they were leaving, it was the place where Dionysus had gone off on his own.

"*Ganesha Familia* did a damn fine job clearing a path all the way to here."

"Yes…the surrounding flesh is completely dead."

Almost all of the green flesh had been scorched, and even the bare stones showing in the gaps of flesh were charred. Loki approached one part of the passage. It was dark, a shadow that even the magic-stone lamp could not pierce. There was a passage that blended perfectly into the darkness that the adventurers—and even Loki—had overlooked before. She held the lamp up above her head to light the long passage that was cloaked in shadow.

"…Rei-Rei, you don't need to guard me anymore."

"What?"

"I mean, I was just dragging you along on my whim. You should go help out where the big fights are happening. That's what Finn planned."

"B-but to leave a goddess alone…" Rei tried to persuade her, uneasy.

"I'll be fine." Loki smiled slightly. "There aren't any more monsters around here."

Her voice was full of confidence that left the siren at a loss for words. There was no way Rei could stand up to a goddess in a war of words.

"…Very well. If a goddess is saying that, then…"

"Sorry for dragging you along on impulse."

"It's fine. I'll be on my way, then."

The siren flew off quickly, curious about how things were going elsewhere in the labyrinth. She spread her blue-tipped, golden wings and headed toward the tenth floor.

"...All right, then."

Loki started walking. The light from the magic-stone lamp dangling below her outstretched hand cut through the darkness as she proceeded down the passage. She was following in the footsteps Dionysus had taken before.

The passage was filled with half-rotten flesh. That area had probably been almost entirely used up to power the tenth floor already. The flesh sagged to the ground like a deflated balloon that clung around Loki's calves, evoking the sensation of trudging through a swamp. All around her smelled like a dense jungle, though wafting toward her from the distance was the sickly smell of honey. It was as if the whole place had been doused in it, and it left her grimacing in disgust.

Along the path, corpses of vibrantly colored monsters that had been drained of their magic stones were piled high. When she ran her hand through them, they turned to ash that trickled between her fingers. And like the monsters, there was an arm sticking out of the swamp of flesh, the corpse of an adventurer that had been pushed all the way there. Loki was silent, faced with images that spoke to the ghastliness of what had happened that night. Before long, she reached the end of the passage.

There was an open space. The giant shaft created by the god's return was still filled with green mass all the way to the surface, but in the rest of the space, the flesh on the walls and floor was rotting away.

Loki opened her crimson eyes a bit. She had come there for a reason: to find decisive proof of the identity of Enyo.

"...This is..."

There was an ancient-looking chair, a cord, and a mirror. And traces of liquid spilled on the floor.

"This smell...There's no mistaking it. It's the same smell as the one in Dionysus's wine cellar."

A faint, sweet, bewitching fragrance. The remnant smell of the wine of the gods. That was enough to tempt Loki's senses all by itself.

"I've come to check my answers, Demeter," Hermes announced.

He put his hat back on and traced his finger along its brim as he looked at the deity before him.

"Ah…you found me. You found me."

Demeter responded in a melodical way that almost sounded grief-stricken, but she was entirely at ease. In fact, it even caused the rear guard of *Hermes Familia* members hiding away on the stairs or in shadows at the front of the balcony to shudder. Her gown billowed and whipped around slightly as she gradually turned to face Hermes.

Her public face—the image of a warm goddess—was nowhere to be seen. She did not have any expression at all. There was a terrifying emptiness to her face, showing the depths of the goddess, her hidden true self.

"Just you and your children, Hermes? A miscalculation…or, rather, a misfortune. Even if we didn't draw Loki and her followers, it would have been nice if some of Ouranos's mercenaries had come to me, too," Demeter said.

The goddess saw through the existence of those hiding their presence. The gaze focused on Hermes was colder than he had ever seen from her, even though they had known each other for a long time.

"…To split our forces?" he asked.

"Yes. After all, the preparations are complete. The die has already been cast. Whatever you might try to do now—arrest me, send me back to the heavens—none of it matters. The door to the underworld will still be opened."

There were no signs of any of her familia members in the surroundings. They were nowhere to be found in *Demeter Familia*'s storehouse. There was a chilling calmness to her. An ominous silence filled the air.

"…And your followers?" he ventured.

"They aren't here. Or, rather, they aren't anywhere."

"…Why?"

"Who's to say? Perhaps I sent them to the den of demons or they became fertilizer to allow flowers to bloom…Now, which do you suppose it is?"

In her current state, Demeter was so repulsive that the members of *Hermes Familia* who heard her trembled, their armor grating audibly. Cold sweat trickled down their cheeks as they struggled to keep breathing steadily. There was a tone, an intonation, to her voice that they had never heard before. She was not even unleashing her divine will, yet they were still shaking. Was that the inherent hideousness of the deusdea—the true nature of deities?

The mortals' hearts were jumbled, filled with a fear far from what they'd experienced against monsters.

"Hermes…Didn't I tell you before?"

Her bangs swayed. Her empty eyes looked like pure quartz that had not been stained by anything.

"As I've said before, I am not satisfied. I am the goddess whose very name means 'the mother of the earth.' The mortal realm is not as it should be. And I cannot tolerate it."

Her voice grew in intensity. Her eyes opened wide as she shouted.

"I cannot tolerate its unreasonableness! Its discrimination! Its distinctions!"

She vented her raging emotions.

Hermes's followers felt as if something were gripping their hearts, but they could not understand what she was saying. It did not make any sense to them. It was beyond human understanding. But if nothing else, they were still determined to throw away their lives to protect their patron god, should it come to that.

"…Yes, I've heard that. I've heard it from your lips before: the paradox that you, the very incarnation of love, cannot love everything about this mortal realm. And the conflict that it's caused."

"Then don't you get it?"

The two deities stared each other down as they stood on the balcony. The air almost seemed to crackle, electrified by the tension between them. Her arms drooping listlessly, Demeter looked down.

"You understand why I…did this—?"

"Let's *quit this farce*, Demeter. The jig is already up." Hermes cut her off, shaking his head.

Her eyes focusing sharply as the smell wafted up from the floor, Loki started looking around the area…as if she was sure of something.

"…There it is."

Hooking her finger into a small gap in the stone flooring, she pushed it down, and one part of the stone made a noise and slid to the side. It was a hidden passage.

—*"I'd expect them to have a secret path out for when their stronghold was about to fall!"*

—*"Don't miss any hidden passages!"*

What Gareth had said during the end stages of the first assault found its proof there.

The mastermind, Enyo, had lured the deity here, set off the return pillar, and then managed to escape from the rampaging green flesh using the hidden passage. Stairs continued downward into the floor. Before the door could close again, she slipped in the hidden passage.

Loki held out her torch with one hand as she descended the stairs. The narrow stone steps continued into the darkness, creating an overwhelming sense of claustrophobia, but Loki's vermilion eyes did not waver in the slightest as she kept looking straight ahead.

"…"

At the end of the stairs, she reached a wall blocking her way. She found a switch for a hidden door in the area, triggering it to open. At the end of the hidden passage was a space filled with pillars. There was a spiderweb of interlocking passages, each surely the end of another hidden passage.

The surrounding walls were covered in ancient murals: People fleeing in terror from monsters. A sea of flames. Lives being greedily devoured. Destruction and slaughter. Violation and chaos. A gruesome feast of death. A vision of hell.

"_____"

And standing in the center of the chamber was a being in a

dark-purple robe that covered its whole body and a jet-black cape. The cape was decorated with different masks. It was an eerie appearance, seemingly symbolizing the different faces of a deity.

Loki glared at it.

"So you're Enyo."

"Wh-what did you say...?"

Demeter's face snapped back up as she managed to respond, but her voice was trembling.

"I'm saying this will make you more pitiful. And I don't want to see you like that. The sight of you lowering yourself to the role of a jester is not something I ever wanted to see."

Hermes's voice was coated in sadness as he fixed her with a melancholy gaze.

"Demeter, the Goddess of Fertility. As I said before, an incarnation of an all-encompassing love. Terrifying if you ever make her mad. Able to lay waste to the entire world...but this kind of *direct method* isn't your style."

Demeter's face paled. He did not know what she was feeling: the regret, the resentment, the despair. Even a fellow deity like Hermes could not understand that. But Hermes believed it was necessary to release her from that painful role.

"You're not Enyo," he proclaimed.

After pitching through the air for some time, Lefiya and the other adventurers landed on a stone floor. They were in a large open chamber. Nearly half of the fifth squad had been separated from Anakity's group, but there was still plenty of room for all of them in the stone chamber. Calculating back the length of their fall, the location had to be the eleventh or twelfth floor of Knossos.

Lefiya quickly looked around as those thoughts crossed her mind. And while she was thinking, she caught sight of the masked creature who had landed right in front of them.

"Tch! That was a stupid trap to fall for…!"

Bete's frustration was as directed at himself as the pitfall above their heads that had been covered up entirely by the green flesh on the ceiling.

They would not be able to return to the tenth floor from this place. At the very least, they wouldn't be able to without taking a round-about path. The chamber was connected to several passages. There were entrances visible in the walls even above their heads. It felt like they were in a chamber that served as a relay point connecting all parts of the labyrinth.

It might have been intentional or because the energy was being directed to the tenth floor, but more than half of the surface area of the chamber had the view of the original Knossos. Chunks of yel-lowed flesh were rotting off the walls and ceiling, creating an almost sluglike appearance.

The adventurers grimaced about getting split up easily and imme-diately prepared their weapons.

"…"

However, the masked figure did nothing. It just stood there, unmoving. There was not even the sound of breathing from behind that eerie mask. Its purple robe trembled from the shock waves caused by the heavy battle occurring on the floor above.

…Why isn't the figure doing anything?

At that moment, that was what every adventurer was thinking. They had reached an odd stalemate. After triggering the pitfall trap, the masked creature did not do anything. Even though the adventurers had an obvious advantage in numbers, the creature was being too passive. It was unnatural. Even Bete furrowed his brow in suspicion.

"…"

Lefiya was the only one who did not feel that way. With her yellow hair streaming behind her, she stepped out from the line of adven-turers by herself.

"Lefiya…!"

The members from *Loki Familia* had a bad feeling as she stood square across from the enemy. The masked creature was the one who had murdered Filvis. A desire for vengeance could have threatened to set her heart afire. They had the feeling that the current silence might just be the calm before the storm. The members of *Loki Familia* immediately tried to stop Lefiya, a mage, who was facing the enemy from the closest possible range.

"I always..." Lefiya was quiet, deviating from their collective anxiety.

Her dark-blue eyes were fixed on the masked creature.

"...I always thought it was strange. This question in the back of my mind, wondering who you were."

"..."

"You were constantly in Enyo's shadow, but I thought you were always odd, too."

"..."

"I always felt something off about you."

Her voice resounded in the chamber. The masked figure was silent, unresponsive. The adventurers did not know what Lefiya was talking about. Bete raised an eyebrow—*"What the hell are you trying to say?"* he seemed to ask—as he watched her.

Everyone was still, unable to do anything but watch in silence as Lefiya eloquently pressed the masked figure.

"You *appeared before me*—every single time, all the time."

"No intention of introducing yourself, eh? Then let's start with checking answers."

Loki violently tossed the magic-stone lamp to the ground in front of Enyo in black clothes. There were several torches set around the chamber with flames flickering. Loki raised her chin and glared defiantly at the deity before her while Enyo simply watched her, as if ready to laugh if her answer was off its mark.

"First of all, you kept your identity hidden to the very end so that the plan to destroy the city would not be leaked...*Except it had nothing to do with that at all.*"

"..."

"And it had nothing to do with prudence or cowardice, either. Because you had already shown yourselves to us straight-up. You kept this side of yourself hidden and acted like you'd never even harm a flea."

Loki was acknowledging that Enyo had been somewhere close to them. That was effectively an admission of defeat. Enyo had blended into their daily life with skill, without apology, and with an innocent face that neither the heavens' trickster, Loki, nor Hermes had been able to see through.

"Second, you started this plan six years ago. Maybe you had the evil idea to crush Orario long before that, but...the six-year mark is undoubtedly when the actual plan itself started to take shape."

"..."

"And the catalyst was the Twenty-Seventh-Floor Nightmare." Loki kept showering Enyo with words as her opponent maintained a tight-lipped silence. "On that awful day, the corrupted spirit hiding in the deep levels—or, more precisely, a fragment of it—had been drawn to the lower floors by *something*. That was where you first learned of its existence—the final piece you needed to complete your plan."

The day when the mastermind of that incident, Olivas Act, had become a creature. The fragment of the corrupted spirit had been in the lower floors that day. Loki was declaring that Enyo had been the lone deity who realized that.

"And then, related to that, the third point. After contacting the corrupted spirit and successfully negotiating with it, you brought together the remnants of the Evils and the spirit's underground forces. Never showing yourself, you just used Levis and the masked creature to pass on orders."

"..."

"While it seemed like you were skillfully manipulating the Evils and the underground forces, you were actually between a rock and a hard place. And that was because you had to accept the creature's irrational desire to search for Aria."

Loki stepped closer, speaking as if she saw through Enyo's black clothes completely, but Enyo did not interrupt her. Quite the opposite. Enyo seemed to be pleased, silently egging her on to continue her revelations.

"Our first encounter with those man-eating flowers...that incident during Monsterphilia. That happened because the creature was pestering you. You did it to search for Aria. You did not actually want to go through with it—or maybe you didn't really care either way."

"..."

"When I found out that the Guild...that Ouranos was hiding something, you tried a bunch of schemes to sever any trust I had in him, didn't you? So that it would be easier for you to move around in secret. And those drunken warnings about Ouranos were in service of that goal."

Loki spoke with supreme confidence as she touched on the fact that Dionysus had constantly prevented them from cooperating with the Guild. Enyo's only miscalculation had been that a certain Goddess of Beauty had also caused an incident at the same time to test a certain boy's strength.

Because of the size of the disturbance at Monsterphilia, several adventurers would have been called in. But because the charmed monsters started rampaging first, *Ganesha Familia* and *Loki Familia* had been the fastest to react. And because of the speed of their initial reaction, Enyo had missed the timing to unleash all the man-eating flowers waiting in the sewer system.

The violas that Loki and Bete had encountered in the water tank and that Finn and the others had wiped out all throughout the sewer system were the ones that Enyo had not been able to recover.

"I should tell you now—I know who Aria is. If the corrupted spirit that has consumed many spirits is looking for it, then Aria can only be a being descended from a spirit. Which means either an actual spirit or someone who has the blood of a spirit in their veins."

Basically, they had found Aria. This was a coincidence that Enyo had not anticipated, the miscalculation that the creatures would discover Aria themselves. In other words, Aiz.

"The corrupted spirit at the Twenty-Seventh-Floor Nightmare, it had been drawn there by *something*—by Aiz. The corrupted spirit first noticed her existence when she used Airiel in the Dungeon after joining my familia."

That was right. The true genesis of it all had been nine years ago. When the girl named Aiz Wallenstein had first started walking down her current path. Perhaps it was fate. On that day when she unleashed her magic for the first time, it had been to defeat the black wyvern that Thanatos had summoned into the Dungeon.

Even though they were deep belowground, the corrupted spirit had recognized the traces of a fellow spirit. It had taken years, but it had moved out toward the lower floors. And the real reason that it had started moving from its position hidden away in the depths of the Dungeon since Ancient Times was because of the existence of Aiz.

"To gain the cooperation of the underground forces, you had no choice but to go after Aiz like you meant it."

"…"

"That was why you had no choice but to *get us wrapped up in this.*"

That had been the worst possible result that Enyo could imagine happening. It left them with no choice but to drag *Loki Familia*, the strongest faction in the city, right into the middle of everything.

"…Here's my answer." Loki glared sharply as she spoke, while Enyo still had not said a word.

"The true identity of Enyo is—"

"The first time I felt there was something out of place was when I headed for the pantry on the twenty-fourth floor chasing Miss Aiz." Lefiya addressed the mask directly. "Back then, when I was talking to Mr. Bete, I felt magic. I was the only one who felt it."

"Huh?" Bete cocked his eyebrow when she mentioned his name.

—*"As long as your Magic is the only useful thing you got, you'll never be anything more than baggage,"* Bete had said when he had berated her so harshly.

—*Magic…?*

Lefiya had definitely sensed magic then. She—and it had been only her—had noticed the presence of the masked figure tailing after them from the shadows. And that disconcerting magic would become one of the clues that helped her hypothesis get a better grip on reality.

"The next strange thing was the very first time I entered Knossos."

That was the day when Finn had been badly battered by Levis and their squad had been scattered. While Aiz and Gareth's group had been separated by Barca Perdix's traps, the two elves had been left behind on the upper floors.

"You *intentionally appeared in front of us there*. You pretended not to notice us while *purposely letting us follow you*. All so that you could lead us all the way to the entrance to the labyrinth."

At the time, Lefiya had been lost in the labyrinth with Filvis. And then all of a sudden, the masked creature had suddenly appeared all by itself. They had followed it and discovered a gate leading out of Knossos to the outside. Thinking back on it after the fact, that coincidence was just too good to be true. The masked creature's appearance was too convenient, and it was all the more suspicious that a creature would not notice the likes of them following it.

"After we were separated from the captain and lost inside Knossos, you were trying to let us…No, you were trying to let *me flee outside*."

A murmur spread through the adventurers. They were confused by what she was saying, and more than a few of them were starting to doubt her sanity. Even Bete was looking at her suspiciously. But Lefiya did not stop there.

"And the last oddity was when…my precious friend was slaughtered before my eyes."

The masked creature's purple robe twitched at that.

It hurt just to remember what had happened at the time, and she struggled to even say the girl's name, and yet Lefiya continued, pushing through the pain to get to the truth.

"It doesn't make any sense. Why did you bother to help me?"

There was doubt that she had no longer been able to ignore.

"We were in the same *middle section* of the ninth floor as Mr. Gareth's group. How did we end up all the way at the entrance to the Dungeon?"

Her voice was getting rougher, more emotional.

"How did we manage to escape all the way until we were right in front of the exit?!"

The dam burst on all the emotions she had been holding back.

"Even then, you were pretending to attack us, but you were really just chasing me to the entrance to the labyrinth!" she screamed, which echoed in the chamber. It sounded as though her heart was being ripped out of her chest.

"You were trying to keep me away from Knossos, even if it meant breaking my heart..."

Lefiya's blue eyes were teary, and her lip quivered.

"You were always...*protecting me.*"

Time stopped. The adventurers were at a loss for words. Bete was standing still, struck with awe. The mask remained silent, as if trying to ride it out. Everyone's eyes were focused on her as Lefiya spoke the name of the figure standing in front of her.

"Isn't that right, Miss Filvis?"

She heard an auditory hallucination. Like the sound of glass shattering. Like the sound of stopped time being forced into motion again. The masked creature's arms hung limply, like a broken doll. Its neck bent like it was staring at the ground, and its clenched metal gloves relaxed, losing all their strength. It looked like a criminal who'd had all its crimes exposed in broad daylight. Slowly, it raised one hand and placed it on the mask.

"...When did you figure it out?"

The mask came off, letting the hood fall back to reveal red eyes and jet-black hair—the elf who had been murdered before Lefiya's eyes, Filvis Challia.

"Gh...!"

Lefiya was on the verge of tears. She had exposed it herself, and yet she had still clung to the hope that she had been wrong.

"That's not possible…How…?!"

One of the adventurers who had been reporting to Anakity on that day was startled. Those who had witnessed Filvis's last moments with Lefiya stared at the masked figure's face in disbelief. They were as close to seeing a ghost as they could get. Left without the ability to process the events in front of them, they lost themselves when they saw her face and gasped, clasping their hands to their mouths. While everyone else was speechless, Lefiya wrenched her lips open again.

"I didn't figure it out…Until Loki talked to me with the others, I never even considered the inconsistencies…" Lefiya responded with her clenched fist quivering, her heart beating out of her chest.

"The masked creature is someone you know well, Lefiya."

Before the start of the operation, when Loki had come to her room, her patron goddess had told her as she sat in a trance. She had said there was a high likelihood that Ein's true identity was Filvis Challia. When Lefiya had first heard the hypothesis, it was like she saw fireworks. In the depths of her misery, she became enraged at the insult to her friend and screamed at her patron goddess.

"But the more I listened to Loki's story, I became less certain! Did you really die?! I started thinking you really might be still alive!"

The goddess's words had connected all the inconsistencies scattered throughout Lefiya's memories.

What had caused Lefiya to stand back up was not revenge. She had risen to disprove Loki's theory and learn the truth.

"After I talked to the captain's team, there was nowhere left to run! I couldn't sit still!"

After Aiz and the others had watched her leave the room, Lefiya had gone with Loki to the office where Finn, Riveria, and Gareth were waiting.

"Lefiya, we'll tell you everything we know about the masked creature, as well as our theory. We'd like you to consider it from the

perspective of someone who knows Filvis Challia. Once we are done, we'd like to hear your thoughts."

Finn's voice was so cool, it had almost made her shudder. While her red-hot emotions had melted together, they calmly shared their knowledge to reach a conclusion about the identity of the masked creature.

"During the last expedition, when we were setting up to advance into the new depths, when we were split up by the Dragon's Urn, the masked creature attacked, leading a swarm of vibrantly colored monsters."

"We're talking about the time when we advanced to the fifty-third floor to meet up with your group."

Riveria's and Finn's first point was something that had happened four months ago. While Lefiya and Bete and their group had fallen down the shaft created by the valgang dragon, Finn's group had taken the standard route heading for the fifty-eighth floor. That was their meetup spot.

"During that time, the masked creature was searching for some-thing *while threatening us."*

While Aiz's group was uneasy and under attack, Finn had noticed something about the enemy's movements.

"——The question is, what is that thing looking for? Aiz?"

At the time, Finn had chalked up this search for *something* as a quest to locate Aiz, whom Levis had been after. But what if that was not the case?

"What if the masked creature was searching for you?"

What if it was trying to guarantee Lefiya was still alive? What if it was trying to make sure that Lefiya alone did not die? When he'd said that, Lefiya's throat clamped shut.

"Our biggest suspicion was when you first entered Knossos together with Maenad and somehow made it out safe."

Gareth picked up on this clue. Finn, Gareth, and Aiz had all been in dire situations after they got split up by Knossos's traps. And while all that was going on, Lefiya had been the only one who had not ended up in any kind of jeopardy. It was unnatural. She had even run into Thanatos and escaped unscathed.

That itself was suspicious.

Lefiya and Filvis had not had a Daedalus Orb. And yet they had somehow survived without triggering any of Knossos's traps. As more time passed after the event, it became more apparent just how crucial having a key was to move around Knossos. The opposite had become just as clear: just how hopeless it was to be stuck in Knossos without a key. It would be fair to say that Lefiya moving around Knossos to find Aiz's group was nothing short of a miracle. And in truth, were it not for what Lefiya and Filvis had done, Aiz's group would have died, locked away in Knossos.

But what if that had not been a miracle? What if it had been inevitable? If it had all gone as intended by the person standing beside Lefiya. If it had been a bitter choice taken to save her.

"If the person beside you had been a double agent working with the enemy...it would be possible for you to avoid Knossos's traps and escape to a safe area."

Filvis had taken the lead to protect Lefiya. She had been able to escape Barca's traps, avoid all the eyes set around the Dungeon, and nudge Lefiya's thoughts in the right direction. When Finn had pointed that out, Lefiya immediately tried to deny it, but the words would not come. The growing suspicion had robbed her of her ability to deny their theory.

"There is something we still can't figure out. You had reached an opened gate once already."

The masked creature they had followed had gone outside to meet Ishtar, leaving the orichalcum gate open. Even if it was designed to close on its own, leaving the entrance to a secret hideout open was just too careless. Riveria had even been waiting outside Knossos on standby still.

In other words, the masked creature—Filvis—had feigned going out to meet Ishtar...all so that Lefiya would have a way to get out.

She thought back to what Filvis had said at the time.

"——Lefiya...I think it would be best to search for the exit."

"—While I understand your desire to pursue your fallen comrades—"

"—Finding a way out and soliciting help seems the wisest path."

Filvis had kept saying it—that Lefiya should escape the labyrinth by herself!

"—*You...you think I can just leave a selfish, stubborn...wreck like you...?*"

"—*Do you even care at all how I feel?*"

"—*I can't let you die!*"

When they were at the exit, Filvis had expressed a bitterness that overflowed into words when Lefiya said she was going back into the labyrinth.

"*Lefiya...What do you think?*" Finn had prompted.

Upon hearing Loki's conjecture, Finn's group had quickly come across a suspect for the identity of the masked creature after a rapid investigation. When they said the name of their suspect, Lefiya could not help but nod as all the mysterious circumstances flashed through her mind.

"When we first entered Knossos...When the creature cut down the captain and Mr. Raul and the people with him fled to the lower floors, when we were separated from Mr. Bete...When it was just Miss Filvis and me by ourselves."

Coming back to her senses, Lefiya let her shoulders tremble as she forced herself to face the reality before her. And then she screamed at Filvis Challia, who was standing there, gloomily looking down.

"That was the final piece!"

Lefiya looked up, tears spilling from the corners of her eyes. Her azure eyes still replayed the scene as her voice poured down like rain.

"The creature with red hair let me go even though I had been left behind! But what if she wasn't letting me go at all?! What if she had just decided that she didn't have to bother herself, since one of her comrades was standing right beside me?!"

It was not that she had been overlooked. It was that Levis had already assumed that Lefiya's fate was sealed. That was why the creature had ignored Lefiya.

"—*Can you not even do a single job correctly?*"

"—*Why is it still alive?*"

There were the words that Lefiya had not been around to hear, dialogue exchanged between the creature with red hair and the masked creature in the depths of Knossos.

"..."

Even though Lefiya screamed, Filvis did not respond, simply continuing to look down, as if acknowledging that it was all true. Filvis still did not deny Lefiya's accusations. Tears streamed down Lefiya's face as she shook her head like a whining child.

"I wanted to scream that it was all a lie. I wanted you to be alive. I wanted to be happy that you lived. But...but...! I...!"

Delight and despair. Lefiya felt those two clashing emotions about the girl standing before her.

Lefiya was screaming inside her disheveled heart herself even as she desperately tried to endure the shock racing through her body.

"Wait! What are you talking about?!" Bete shouted.

While all the other adventurers were left behind by the situation, Bete gave voice to their thoughts.

"What the hell do you think you're saying?! That sinister elf and the masked bastard have been in the same place at the same time before!"

During the incident in the pantry on the twenty-fourth floor, both Filvis and the masked creature had been seen together in the same location. And the first time they had entered Knossos, the two of them had been in two different places at the exact same time.

"And didn't you watch a monster eat her right in front of you?!"

And above all, it was the masked creature's hand that had snapped Filvis's neck, murdering her. The fact that she was even standing there before them was a paradox in itself. Bete glared suspiciously at the ghost in front of him.

"That's why I told you to cast aside your emotions."

A single shadow leaped down from a passage above their heads. It was wearing the same mask and same gloves as Filvis. A second masked creature that looked identical to the first.

"Wh—?!"

"—This is all because of your shameful behavior."

Ignoring the adventurer's shock, it flung off its mask, revealing Filvis's face. Once she had removed the mask, the layered voices turned into the voice of Maenad, with which *Loki Familia* had become so familiar.

It wasn't something as simple as similar features. They were exact replicas, like a reflection in a mirror. The one and only difference was that the second one had red eyes that appeared clouded, as if reflecting the abyss.

"What the hell is going on…?!"

The first Filvis kept her eyes cast down, and the second Filvis viciously berated her. While Bete and the others were struggling to come to any meaningful terms with this situation, Lefiya wiped away her tears and looked up.

"Up until now, Miss Filvis only ever used two spells in front of us. The first was for an extremely short-cast lightning. And the second was for a barrier…But what if she had actually developed a third type of magic—one that she had *kept hidden* from us?"

The adventurers gasped. Bete's eyes widened. And the Filvis standing across from Lefiya closed her eyes.

"A third spell that she never revealed. It would have to be—"

The second Filvis. The two fairies. Lefiya was sure of her answer as tears welled in her eyes.

"Cloning magic."

"You're wrong…You've got it all wrong, Hermes! I'm Enyo! It's me!"

Beneath the moonlit sky, standing on a mountainside balcony, Demeter's hair lashed out violently as she shouted. Hermes was not moved at all as he took her in and mercilessly denied her claim.

"There's no way you were forced to drink the divine wine, too. I don't believe that."

"You have it wrong! I'm the mastermind! I'm the one who did everything…!"

"Demeter." Hermes interrupted her quietly but firmly. "I'm asking you here. Please stop this already. I don't want to see you embarrass yourself any more than this."

That caused all the strength to drain out of Demeter's body. There were tears in her eyes as she sank to her knees.

"…You debased yourself by becoming the scapegoat, but that had nothing to do with protecting Enyo, right?"

"…"

"Was there some kind of deal?…Or was it blackmail?" Hermes stepped forward and knelt on one knee to talk to her.

She must have realized there was no more turning things around, because the goddess resigned herself and started to talk.

"I got in too deep…"

"…"

"A certain god was behaving oddly, so I went looking for him. And because I was careless, he…kidnapped Persephone and my other followers." Demeter hugged her knees, remembering what had happened at the time, and her face turned deathly pale.

"He said if I didn't do what he said, he would kill my children. I rejected it at first. But when I did, he *killed one of them*, like it was nothing. I was shaken. And then he killed *another one*. I screamed, begging him to stop. And then *another one*. I started weeping. And then *another one*…"

Her memories were stained with fresh blood. It began to sound like she was holding back her sobs. For deities who were nigh eternal, it was not so long in the grand scheme of things to wait for humans to be reborn. But this optimistic perspective that they would eventually meet again would still never allow them to accept their followers being murdered.

And that went doubly so for the loving goddess Demeter, who in her kindness could not bear their suffering.

"After deciding I was sufficiently broken, that monster said, '*You don't have to do anything. You don't have to kill anything. Just keep your mouth shut.'"*

"…"

"He has his sly side, but when he makes a deal, he keeps his word. I behaved myself and he didn't kill anyone. And if I tried anything, he would immediately slaughter my children, which robbed me of any will to resist…"

There was the Falna engraved into her followers' backs. The patron goddess could sense them from the connection created by the Ichor she had shared with her children.

As long as she behaved herself, the number of Blessings would not go down. But if she did anything out of the ordinary, made notes, used secret signals, tried to contact people, she could sense the number of Blessings shrinking.

It was an incredibly simple and brutal calculation that went on for days, wearing away at Demeter's heart.

"…I think it was around the time when Ares's kingdom decided to come attack. I talked to Takemikazuchi. He said that something about you was off but that he couldn't understand a woman's heart… He asked me to help you," Hermes murmured.

Demeter smiled slightly as she nodded. "That sounds like Takemikazuchi…

"But, Hermes, if you had believed him at face value and tried to contact me, I would definitely have run away. I would have hidden here by myself to avoid suspicion and not let anyone get close to me."

"…"

"That was why…by the time he noticed, it was already too late."

Finally, tears started falling from Demeter's eyes. She must have figured out what the true mastermind was trying to accomplish. She had effectively weighed the fate of all of Orario on the scales against her followers' lives. But even that was already too late.

"…So you were set up as the mastermind?"

"Yes. I never could see through him. I never knew just how twisted he really was…Even back in the heavens, I never understood him."

Demeter's damp eyes looked up to the sky as she spoke.
"Enyo's true identity is—"

"*—Dionysus.*"

Loki declared as she glared at the personification of darkness in front of her.

"The farce ends here."

The sound of laughter seeped from the robe. In the next instant, a hand grasped the robe and yanked it away. The purple-and-black cloth fluttered as the mask fell to the ground. Blond hair revealed itself, accompanied by the sweet facade he always wore.

His identity revealed, Enyo—Dionysus—unveiled himself.

"Well done, Loki."

His smile was no different from what he always had around Loki—as if it were just a snapshot from an everyday scene.

It was so excessively repulsive, it made Loki want to throw up.

"So you figured me out? No, I suppose I should say you saw through me. As expected, I could not pull off my fool's performance in front of you."

He started to clap. The dry sound grated on Loki's ears: A whole-hearted praise. A compliment from the bottom of his heart. An earnest celebration for the person who had discovered Enyo's true identity.

His eyes were clear. They were not *clouded by alcohol*. His smile and his way of speaking and carrying himself were the god Dionysus's true self.

Loki's vermilion eyes flashed, flaring with rage.

"You *intentionally kept yourself drunk* in front of us...!"

Dionysus just smiled faintly, as if to confirm her accusation. It had not been some other deity who had gotten him drunk and manipulated him. He had done it to himself. He would sit in the

© Kiyotaka Haimura

underground wine cellar at his home, drink divine wine, and whisper to the reflection of his eyes in the glass. Telling himself that he was an ally of justice and that he was going to strike down evil together with Loki and Hermes.

While he was drunk, Dionysus genuinely believed he was a righteous god. It was almost like a split personality. That was why Loki and Hermes had not been able to doubt him entirely.

And of course not. How could they suspect a fool who honestly believed himself to be just? Dionysus had blended in with them perfectly. They had been unsure whether he was an enemy or a friend or a spectator.

He had been watching them from the closest location possible, hiding his true self in his intoxication.

Loki's body seethed with humiliation. Dionysus seemed to be enjoying himself as he probed further.

"When did you figure out that I was Enyo?"

"...Right after 'you' blasted off, I really thought it was Demeter. I was following the clues you left while drunk."

"And then?"

"First of all, I was suspicious about whether Demeter could even make a crazy-potent wine. Demeter's purview is the harvest. Even if she could gather the ingredients for the wine, did she really have a handle on how to make it?"

"She might have just been hiding it. Those sorts of parlor tricks and white lies are standard for gods, right?"

"Exactly. It wasn't conclusive, just enough to raise the question. The next thing that didn't quite fit was that the number of deities sent back to the heavens and the number of deities left didn't match."

"Oh?"

"There was the one who was supposed to be you and then there was Thanatos, who went flying right in front of me...But I noticed that one other deity had gone missing. Someone else besides Demeter, who had gone into hiding."

Dionysus's eyes narrowed, pupils contracting.

"There's no more point to it, but...since we're already here, let's check your work all the way to the end." He prodded Loki for her answer.

His tone was that of someone enjoying a game. It was a god's amusement.

"If it wasn't me, who was sent back in that pillar?"

"*Penia.*" Loki responded immediately with the name of the goddess who lived on Daedalus Street and ruled over poverty. "Before we busted in this time, I stopped by to visit the location where the residents of Daedalus Street are evacuating. When I asked around, the children of the slums were saying, '*I haven't seen Lady Penia around lately.*'"

"Heh-heh…"

"In addition to getting yourself drunk to give yourself suggestions, you got Penia drunk to make her your puppet."

He must have approached her with a bit of friendliness as kindred deities from the same homeland, or all it had taken were gifts of food and drinks to that greedy Goddess of Destitution. The specifics of how he had gotten Penia to drink the divine wine did not matter much to Loki. But one thing was for certain: The one other deity had abruptly disappeared from Orario. Demeter had not been the only scapegoat.

"There was another reason to get Penia drunk. It was so that I could convert all my children to be followers of Penia."

As for *Dionysus Familia*'s simultaneous Status seal, this was the explanation for what had happened.

"You even got *your own followers* drunk."

That included all the adventurers who had participated in the first assault on Knossos, from the familia's second-in-command, Aura Moriel, down. They had not actually been *Dionysus Familia*. They had been *Penia Familia*. Dionysus had even made *his former followers* drink the divine wine.

There was no need to keep them constantly drunk—just before their Status update. He could pour them a glass of red wine—"*the one for special occasions*"—as a reward for their work. Once they had drunk the divine liquid, they would have been completely drunk and easily manipulated by his words, mistaking Penia for their patron god, Dionysus, after he swapped places with her. All that remained was to have them receive the conversion from Penia.

It was an absurd puppet show. He tugged at the wet red strings, and people and deities alike danced along to his show. Just imagining it was ludicrous and ghastly.

It was sad. Aura and the others who had sworn adoration and loyalty to Dionysus had not even been his followers in reality. Their bodies and their hearts had been manipulated by the god standing there before Loki.

"…At the start of all this, you said some shit about revenge for your children who were killed. But after the drunken stupor wore off, those were just ones who had started to realize they weren't followers of Dionysus anymore…which is why you disposed of them. Right?"

Dionysus could not hold back his laughter anymore.

"Heh-ha-ha-ha-ha-ha-ha-ha! Amazing, Loki! You got it in one!"

——*"One month ago, several of my children were slain."*

——*"The killer's method was simple: approach from the front, grab the neck, then break it."*

——*"As far as I'm concerned, every god and goddess in Orario is a suspect."*

After she had investigated the sewers with Bete, Dionysus had declared that to her face, determined. And it had all been a lie.

As Loki guessed, the three followers who had been sacrificed were ones who had sobered up while they were still getting their Status from Penia. Perhaps they had not been drunk enough. Regardless, they had panicked and fled the home, running into the deserted streets—where they were murdered by a creature. Dionysus had the masked creature take care of them. And the rest had been just like he told Loki. The bodies were discovered in a way that it would not matter if the Guild investigated it, and he pretended to be the victim, making a show of his pretend grief and anger.

And then all he had to do was show Loki the vibrantly colored magic stones and link it back to Monsterphilia.

At the time, Dionysus was drunk, of course. And because his emotions seemed real, at least in his moment of intoxication, Loki did not see through the lie.

But there had never been any revenge. No battle for their honor. It was all just a charade set up by Dionysus. There was no revenge to be had for anyone. Every last one of his followers had been dancing to his tune the whole time.

"You piece of garbage..."

Loki unleashed her rage in his children's stead. The god before her laughed and laughed, the cruel cackle unbefitting his elegant young aristocratic image.

It had all been possible because of the divine wine. It was a farce sparked by the creation of a liquor that far surpassed Soma's. But it was not just a farce. It was also a tragedy of immeasurable proportions.

"Penia was really a magnificent cover for me. As soon as my plan became feasible, I immediately thought of using her. As backup when it came to looking for the culprit. Of course, she's a deity herself, so she had a foible or two, but..."

Because Penia ruled over poverty, she was an odd goddess who had absolutely no followers. So even if Dionysus secretly converted his children to her, as long as she was drunk and there was plausible deniability, there would not be anyone suspicious of the situation—because *she did not have any followers to point out that something weird was going on.*

There was no better choice for Dionysus's deceptive ploy than her, so she became his scapegoat.

"Yeah, that old coot did a good job leaving behind a hint for me."

"What's that?"

"I recognized that wine from somewhere else...besides in your wine cellar."

"!"

"Penia had it. When I first ran into her on Daedalus Street, that old hag was holding a wine bottle with the same label as the one in your cellar. I remembered that."

It had been the first time they had gone to Daedalus Street to investigate. Penia had been holding a piece of meat on the bone and a bottle of wine. It appeared to be the same as the one in the wine cellar, and the label had the overflowing goblet, too.

"Ah...sheesh. I forgot that she could be a real glutton. And I had wasted effort in warning her not to drink more than was necessary. She was drinking extra on the side and hiding it from me, huh?"

Taking the wine and making a mess of things, acting under no one's orders. Dionysus sighed. His reaction made Loki want to throw up again.

Without realizing she was getting drunk, Penia must have been sipping the divine wine like it was any old drink.

"...And then you killed Penia here."

Dionysus's lips curled into a smile at that.

Loki imagined the scene at the time, the events during that first assault. Following the suggestions that he had given himself from the start, Dionysus had separated from Loki and the adventurers. He had followed the illusion of Enyo that he had seen, drunk from the divine wine, and without anyone knowing—no, without letting anyone notice—he had gone off on his own.

And everything after that was exactly as he had set it into motion: his little act with Loki on the oculus and waking up from his drunken stupor. That had triggered the throbbing headache, splitting his personality apart, shattering the mask of a righteous god that he had been hiding behind.

And afterward, he had become drunk on darkness, awakening his true character, an abyss of evil. He used the mirror that had been prepared to immediately convey everything to himself. The reflection in the mirror sneered, smirking as the progress report came in after he had awakened as Enyo. And tied up on the chair was the pitiful scapegoat who had been brought there beforehand.

Bound and gagged, Penia could not even scream as Dionysus slowly gouged her chest with the dagger in his hand—

That was the whole story of that day.

Once Penia was sent back, Aura and the rest whose abilities had been sealed were wiped out. And Enyo, who had set that atrocity into motion, fled to this hidden passage, living on, happy as a clam.

He had faked his own death with a bonus on top. Thinking back on it, killing all his supposed followers served another purpose besides providing sustenance for the altar. It also prevented any fear of someone discovering his deception by checking the Status on any of the corpses.

"And you were correct, Loki. You were the one deity I never wanted to have as an enemy."

Belying his words, Dionysus's face looked reinvigorated—like a mastermind enjoying the sparring with the detective who was hunting for the culprit. As Loki's rage grew, he had another question for her.

"Allow me this one last question. How did you become convinced that I was Enyo?"

"..."

"With Demeter still hiding herself, she should have been a prime suspect, even if you had your doubts. And Penia's wine bottle supports your theory, but it isn't a decisive clue, either. You could just as easily use it to argue the reverse, that I really had been the one who was sent back and Penia had been making herself drunk to avoid suspicion…So what convinced you it was me?"

It was a genuine question. He wanted to know how she had become sure that the villain was Dionysus.

"…The truth is that I couldn't be sure up until the very end. As you said, there were multiple possibilities." Loki acknowledged his argument as she reached back into her memory. "But that was when I remembered what that shrimp had said."

Hestia. Dionysus's eyes widened at the unexpected mention of the deity.

"While we were watching you, I talked with her about a couple of things. About how you acted back up in the heavens. About your sickness and the way you tried to pick fights with other gods, just like I did…"

Loki remembered the childish goddess's eyes as she watched Dionysus playing with the children in that neighborhood. Recalling that look, Loki delivered the conclusive blow.

"You know, Dionysus, that shrimp didn't call you *'strange'* or *'weird.'* She said you were *'scary.'*"

Not "odd" but "scary." It had nothing to do with him being drunk or not. There was a fundamental part of his nature that struck fear into others. Hestia had unconsciously noticed Dionysus's darkness. None of the other gods or goddesses must have noticed his pitch-black divine will, not even Demeter, who was closest to him. But the Goddess who embodied the Ever-Burning, Sacred Hearth had picked up on that.

"As much as I hate to admit it…and I really do hate it…I believed her. That's all."

She had believed Hestia's word over Dionysus's. That had been the decisive difference. That was how she had chosen the true villain from among all the gods.

Dionysus froze up at her declaration and suddenly looked down.

"Ah…Hestia again, huh…?"

There was a stifled laugh, inaudible to anyone not listening closely. His eyes were covered by his bangs; his mouth broke into a smile that seemed almost to split open his cheeks.

"Sheesh. She's been ruining my plans ever since our time in the heavens…*That troublesome goddess,*" he growled.

His tone changed in an instant. His divine will was on full display. Watching him like a hawk, Loki finally asked a question of her own.

"Let me ask you. That masked creature…is your follower, right?"

His one and only follower. Dionysus, or rather Enyo, had cast aside all his other familia members, even Aura, leaving himself one piece to play.

The god looked up, smiling as his eyes narrowed.

"Yes, that's exactly right. My cute little Ein—my two dolls."

"Correct," Filvis casually responded when Lefiya mentioned cloning magic, as if she had totally given up.

"…On the fifty-third floor, when the captain's crew was fighting, I heard that the masked creature had evaded Lady Riveria's magic.

That it had used the split second to flee from the attack when the blizzard lowered everyone's visibility."

Lefiya tried to contain her turbulent emotions as she stood across from Filvis, putting Finn's and Riveria's thoughts into words.

That had been a barrage with a wide range that the city's strongest mage, Riveria, had unleashed with perfect timing. Was it really possible that someone could not only evade it but use it to escape without anyone noticing?

The answer was obviously no.

"But what if that wasn't to escape? What if it was undoing a spell?"

That was what Riveria and Finn had theorized. They had lost sight of the enemy as if it had just disappeared. That was another of the hints that had nudged them in the direction of a preposterous answer: cloning magic.

In terms of proof, they had the fact that the enemy's equipment, mask, hooded robe, and metal gloves had been left behind, encased in ice. It was possible that Filvis had immediately released her magic, and the body that had been created by a spell turned back into magic particles. And after that, the wave of ice scattered the remnants of magic. Nothing remained of the masked creature's figure. That was the trick that had rendered Riveria's blast seemingly ineffective.

"If there were two of you, Miss Filvis, then...then that would resolve all the inconsistencies."

The other Filvis with darkened eyes—henceforth referred to as Ein to avoid any confusion—was standing behind Filvis, glancing over at Lefiya.

It was not a mirage that would disappear into mist if someone touched it. It was a real body that could attack and defend, and it even had its own thoughts and will, functioning entirely autonomously. It was undoubtedly a rare magic—no, it had to be a magic that Filvis Challia alone could use.

"To guess all of that from little information...Hmm. *Loki Familia* members aren't to be trifled with...I was a fool to leave you any clues..."

There was wonder and self-deprecation in Filvis's warped voice.

"You are undoubtedly a fool. Your ego hindered Lord Dionysus's plan. You should be ashamed of yourself, Filvis."

Ein's voice was cold, filled with scorn and anger.

The uncanniness of their performance forced the other adventurers to accept Lefiya's theory. Cloning magic. The implication of its existence changed everything about their understanding of the incidents that had occurred leading up to this.

They had reconsidered the identity of the masked creature—all because Loki had guessed that Enyo was Dionysus.

"—Who gives a shit about some stupid spell," Bete spat. The tattoo engraved on his cheek distorted as he made no effort to hide his annoyance. "Are you a monster like that redhead or not?"

The masked figure could control the vibrantly colored monsters just like the creature Levis. The surrounding adventurers were startled by the werewolf's dangerous, bloodthirsty glare.

"I am," Filvis responded without any hesitation.

There was no emotion on her face, just an empty expression. Lefiya desperately tried not to stagger back. She had prepared herself, but she still felt like she was about to faint. Her voice welled with a feeling that was neither fear nor agitation as she probed further.

"Did it have to do...with the Twenty-Seventh-Floor Nightmare, Miss Filvis?"

"..."

This time, Filvis did not immediately respond. But her silence was an acknowledgment of a kind. Seeing that, Ein sneered, showing emotion for the first time.

"What? You've come this far. Just tell her."

"Shut up..."

"You want to explain yourself to your beloved Lefiya, right? Just tell her so she'll sympathize and comfort you."

"Stop..."

"Or should I tell her?"

"—Quit it!"

Lefiya could not help but gasp at the bizarre scene. It was a conversation between two different Filvises. An argument with the same voice on both sides. If she closed her eyes, it would have sounded like a one-woman skit. An internal conflict was playing out due to cloning magic.

Right now, Filvis's conflict and true feelings were being laid bare. To Lefiya—and to all the adventurers there—she looked extremely unstable and insecure.

"...Lefiya, you're right. On the day of that nightmare, I was sullied."

Before the darker clone could reveal it, Filvis bared her own past for Lefiya.

"Or, rather, I was *corrupted*."

The Twenty-Seventh-Floor Nightmare.

A sacrificial pass parade that the Evils had started in the middle of the floor. The awful incident had caused significant losses for both the Evils and the adventurers gathered under the Guild's banner.

A young Filvis had been there that day, along with the rest of *Dionysus Familia*.

"Back then, I was still filled with pride that was very fragile. I considered myself some envoy of order...I headed to the twenty-seventh floor with the rest of the familia, and I lost myself escaping from that hell..."

At the time, Dionysus was effectively a hidden third faction. He was pretending to ally himself with the Guild's goals while probing the Evils' movements, always on the lookout for an opportunity to overthrow Orario. But that was just his divine will that he kept hidden, so Filvis and his other followers were involved in the Twenty-Seventh-Floor Nightmare as members of one of the righteous factions.

"And that was where...we encountered it."

"It...?"

"The corrupted spirit's avatar."

"*Ts*—"

She was talking about the corrupted spirit's feeler that had been drawn out by Aria. Lefiya's heart skipped a beat as she listened to Filvis's dark confession.

"The others were wiped out, leaving me behind. There was no time to fight back. It was overwhelming. A tragedy. It broke my spirit."

The undulating green flesh, the mysterious shrill voice, her comrades trampled with no means of fighting back. This was the spectacle that had unfolded itself in Filvis's sorrowful eyes for an instant.

But Lefiya was confused.

"...Wait. Didn't you abandon your party?! If you turned tail and ran like a coward, when'd you become a monster?!" Bete snapped.

He must have noticed the same inconsistency as Lefiya, for he hounded her with a scorn-riddled accusation.

That was right. Filvis had abandoned her friends and sprinted for her life from the twenty-seventh floor. She was one of the few who had survived that nightmare. Bors had even seen her wandering around Rivira on the eighteenth floor, seemingly dead on the inside, wallowing in the depths of her despair. That had been the origin of the name Banshee—a nickname that she was called with such contempt even to this day.

Banshee, the party-killing elf.

Filvis paused at their suspicion.

"She *didn't run away*," Ein answered in her stead.

"Wha—?"

Filvis had not run away. Lefiya's eyes went wide at the implication.

"I heard them crying for help, so I turned to face it, and it killed me. It was an utterly meaningless, wasted death."

"Gh...?!"

"You can guess the rest, right?"

Her fallen body must have had a magic stone embedded in it. She had been reborn as a creature. Lefiya's throat went dry. Bete's brows furrowed, rage visible. He clearly did not like what he was hearing.

Filvis Challia had not abandoned her friends to survive. She had come back to protect them, sacrificing herself with the pride of an elf. After dying, she had been transformed into a monster.

As Ein spoke, Filvis fell silent, the wails and lamentations of that day ringing in her ears.

—*"Run, Filvis!"*

—*"Hurry! Go now!"*

—*"Aaarghhh..."*

—*"Go, Filvis...Get away."*

—*"Run, Filvis!"*

—*"Fil...vis..."*

Her brave and gallant comrades had fallen, one after the other. Even the second-in-command, who was like an older sister to all the younger members in the familia, had been eaten. Even the strongest of them, their leader, was on the verge of being pulled into the spirit's body as he desperately tried to let Filvis escape. The elf who was the most inexperienced of them all had turned her back as tears streamed down her face.

——*"Help me."*

But then she'd heard that final murmur. The captain had whispered something that he had tried to hold back so she would not hear. His words gripped her heart. With tears running down her cheeks, she gritted her teeth and turned around to face that repulsive enemy.

It was the most hideous irony of all. She had proven herself noble and virtuous and pure. However, for that very reason, she had ended up corrupted.

"Th-that's..."

That was the truth of what had happened to Filvis Challia's body on the day of the Twenty-Seventh-Floor Nightmare. As a fellow elf, Lefiya felt her heart ache, as though she had been pitched into the pits of hell.

"It was not a coincidence that the spirit's avatar was on the twenty-seventh floor that day. It was drawn by the smell of blood... It was looking for new feelers from the large number of adventurers gathered there," Filvis said, her voice full of hatred for the sin that the mastermind of the incident, Olivas Act, had committed.

The dead bodies of the rest of *Dionysus Familia* had all been implanted with magic stones, but every last one had just turned into lumps of flesh that could do little more than moan incoherently.

Only Filvis had the compatibility, the strong character to be reborn as a creature.

"So then...When Mr. Bors and the others saw your despair in Rivira...that wasn't because you had abandoned your familia..."

"Yes. It was *the anguish in myself* for being degraded into a monster."

She'd had tattered clothes and hair matted with blood, features that seemed devoid of all life, and she had slowly dragged herself around, trying not to approach anyone. It had all been Filvis's distress as she wandered around the town like a ghost barely clinging to life, searching for the illusion of her lost comrades, begging to wake up from a nightmare.

"After that...I tried to kill myself."

"...!"

"Too many times to count. I tried everything I could think of. But..."

Filvis had not died. She had torn off her arms. She had opened gaping holes in her body. She had hacked at herself. She had burned her body over and over with magic. She had bled herself dry. She had snapped her own neck. She had even tried letting monsters eat her. But she had not been able to end her own life.

The unbelievable regenerative abilities of a creature forced her to survive the most lethal wounds.

So then she had tried to scrape out the magic stone and reach the same ashy fate as a hideous monster—but she could not do that, either.

——*Why?! Why?! Why??!!*

The vibrantly colored magic stone in her chest seemed to have control of her body. It would not allow her to deal any fatal wounds. Even when she came to death, her corrupted body would not allow her to cross that final line.

Filvis had become a feeler, a servant of the corrupted spirit. Her ability to control her own fate had been stolen away from her.

Finally, the whispers started to echo in her head, the offensive voice of the spirit—the mother who had created this form of her.

——*"Why don't we get along?"*
——*"What is your name?"*
——*"I want to see the sky."*
——*"Fulfill my wish."*

Filvis had screamed. She was a proud elf, but she had been degraded into an unsightly monster. This living hell had completely broken her.

"…!"

What if I had been in her position? Lefiya thought, but even that threatened to break her heart. But that pain didn't begin to come close to the pain that Filvis had endured. No one could comprehend her suffering.

"I developed the cloning magic after I had become this…"

—I can't accept what I have become, but I can't die.

It could have been a form of escapism or because of her strong desire to be an uncorrupted version of herself. But even that could do nothing to distract her. Filvis became a puppet who did nothing but cry. Her eyes became hollow, and she was filled with darkness as the whispers in her head tormented her—just like Lefiya had been in the aftermath of Filvis's final moments.

"You grieve and suffer, but you try to hang on to your pride. You are beautiful."

And then.

"I love you. I am in love with your beautiful self."

Someone loved Filvis as she was.

"That's right. I love you no matter what. If you can't forgive yourself, then—" whispered either a god or a devil.

"Let's make all the other children the same as you."

The destruction of Orario. The corrupted spirit dominating the surface. If that happened, then the mortal realm would overflow with monsters, and a small handful of chosen people would be turned into creatures by the corrupted spirit, following in the steps of Filvis. After the world had been turned on its head, it would be able to accept the existence of that broken, beautiful, hideous girl. Dionysus had used his sweet words to douse her cracked heart in a poison disguised as the sweetest noble rot wine, wafting like honey.

"But that's...?!" Lefiya shouted, unable to endure this confession any longer.

If the corrupted spirit took control of the world aboveground, people would lose their lives. It was a sinful path that could never be allowed to pass.

And as she cried out, rage welled up inside her. For the first time, Lefiya felt white-hot anger for a deity—fury at Dionysus for sneaking into Filvis's helpless soul and whispering sweet, fake words to manipulate her.

"But to me at that time...his words were salvation."

"Gh?!"

"Lord Dionysus said that he loved me even though I was so unclean. To be able to be with him while achieving his dream...That was the only path I had left."

"Miss...Filvis..."

"Because he was the only one...No one would accept me as I was other than him..."

However, on the verge of breaking down and with no one else to turn to, Filvis had accepted those sweet words, drunk that forbidden honey. She had joined hands with the devil.

"You're a real piece of shit..."

At the end of a hidden passage, in the chamber filled with columns, Loki cursed Dionysus again, after she'd heard Filvis's story in his own words.

"You hurt me, Loki. And after all I did to save my beloved child who was broken in body and spirit," Dionysus responded, not bothered in the slightest.

The torches set on the wall surrounding them flickered, casting a shadow on his handsome face. With the characteristic perfect features of the deusdea, he almost looked like an inhuman sculpture.

"And above all, I praised her. I honored Filvis for sacrificing her familia comrades, living on, and proving the existence of the corrupted spirit with her own body!"

His voice swelled with passion. He had learned of the existence of the corrupted spirit thanks to Filvis, who had been turned into a creature. And because of that, he had been able to quickly contact the corrupted spirit and bring it over to his side.

"I was delighted! There was nothing more gratifying! I knew right away it would become the key to my plan—especially since we cannot use Arcanum here!"

After that, it was just as Loki had deduced. Using Filvis, Dionysus had made contact with the corrupted spirit's underground forces, with Levis. He had kept moving behind the scenes up until that fateful day to bring his plan to fruition.

"…Why are you trying to destroy Orario?" Loki asked as Dionysus displayed an exaggerated delight, like an actor performing on a stage.

Even though you had to kill all your followers. Even though you had to make a puppet of your beloved one. You planned the destruction of Orario while sacrificing everything. What was it for?

Dionysus was silent for a second. His smile slipped off his lips as he regained his composure.

"To correct the mortal realm," he responded. His face resumed a deity's divine mask. "The mortal realm is impure as it is now. Gods and goddesses are just doing as they please. It is necessary to change things, to return the realm to how it was supposed to be."

"How it was supposed to be…?"

"I'm sure you know, Loki. Unlike the adventurers of today, the heroes of the past did not have any Blessing from the gods when they faced the monsters emerging aboveground."

During the Ancient Times, before any deities had descended to the mortal realm, the swarms of monsters flowing out of the big hole invaded the territory of every race, overrunning them.

It was the darkest hour of humanity, when the most blood flowed. That was what Enyo was looking to achieve by destroying Orario. It was supposed to be a cruel world where monsters rampaged aboveground.

"Those valiant heroes did not have the protection of any deity, overwhelmed by monsters at first. However, as time passed, they started to resist, and eventually they became able to push back the grotesque hordes!" Dionysus's calm voice became heated. "They grew! Those children! Those residents of the mortal realm! I won't deny there were miracles wrought by the spirits sent from the heavens! But those heroes overcame mortal limits with nothing but their own strength!"

"…"

"And without borrowing the power of Falna to draw out their potential! With their noble blood and tears and an unyielding will, they cut through that age of darkness!"

It was true. Even though there were interventions by spirits, the residents of the mortal world had broken free from the monsters' domination by their own hands, stealing back the land that had been taken from them. In the end, they had pushed the monsters all the way back to the big hole that was the start of it all. And then they had constructed a fortress—the predecessor to Orario—to stop the flow of monsters.

"…Yeah, that's right. The children of that time were really monstrous. Just giant clumps of the unknown."

These were the great works of the people called "heroes"—an achievement great enough that even the gods watching from the heavens had to acknowledge it. Those chosen people had grown, made great strides, and evolved. It was like a familia leveling up now. They had continued to break out of their shells, growing to accomplish their dearest wishes.

From the perspective of the modern era, they were some of the most unbelievable Irregulars of the mortal realm. That was the age of heroes, before the arrival of the age of gods.

"That was *Oratoria*—pure and unadulterated! The path taken by children! One to which deities should pay the ultimate respect! That was the reason! That was why this mortal realm has no need for deities!"

He was talking about the start of the *Dungeon Oratoria*, the true heroes whose names had been added to those epics. To praise that, Dionysus was talking bombastically about destroying Orario, about destroying Babel—the symbol of the gods' descent to the mortal realm.

"I don't care if you call me cruel or self-righteous or evil! I will use any means necessary to open the gates of hell! To manifest that realm of death, for life to shine again, I will return the world to that wonderful era!"

To reset it all.

"I will bring this age of gods to an end!"

This was a perspective that he could hold only as a god. To the mortals enjoying peace around the world, it was incomprehensible, a cruel verdict that they would curse.

However, that was a divine perspective, too. Because he was a supernatural existence, he loved the children of the mortal realm. It was a form of agape, the ultimate love of a god for man that respected their pure brilliance. There had to be many deities who would express an understanding of that love. And Dionysus announced it with a lofty look, with the clearest of eyes.

Loki opened her mouth, surer than ever.

"Liar."

As the room fell silent, her voice sliced through the air.

"You just want to *see children screaming and crying.*"

With her vermilion eyes open, she sent daggers to the frozen god with her chilled gaze.

"You went to the trouble of decorating this place with these murals—proof enough of your rotten core!"

On all sides, the walls were adorned with ancient murals: People fleeing from monsters. A sea of fire. Lives consumed whole. Destruction and slaughter. Ravishment and chaos. A gruesome feast of death. Scenes of hell, of the underworld.

They were all rooted in a wild mania.

It was almost audible if she listened closely: the cries of the people fleeing without any hope, the despair, and the broken laughter of someone who was already beyond fear. In one part of the murals, there were people dancing in wild revelry, praying to the heavens, while beside them, others were gouged open by monsters' claws and fangs, spewing a fountain of blood.

It was a vision of hell as the people lost themselves in an unending repetition of screams and laughter. At times, it resembled a violent, intoxicated ceremony from the way they indulged in meat and wine.

Loki shouted, pointing out that all the tragedies displayed around them were a window into the obsession of the one who had assembled them.

"You just want to see children running for their lives, crying and shouting, broken. You want to witness an *orgia*!"

She could tell because she was a goddess, too. Looking back on Dionysus's words and actions, on his constructed character, she could easily discount his speech waxing love for the mortal realm.

Dionysus quietly looked down as Loki rejected his answer.

"Hee-hee-hee-hee-hee-hee!"

And then a complete change came over him.

"Oh gosh…Guess you've figured it all out, huh?"

When he looked up, there was no trace of the aristocratic god anywhere to be seen. Brushing his hair back with his hand, he twisted his eyes like an animal's. The gruesome smile adorning his face transfigured his handsome features, making them utterly repulsive.

Even the devil could not begin to compare with the being standing before Loki. He hacked out a ghastly laugh as his true nature revealed itself. His disguise finally came off completely.

"Come on, Loki! If you get that far, that's boring! You don't know anything about me. We have no past together, yet you still saw through everything!"

"…!"

"But you're right! You were spot-on! There is only one thing I want!"

Loki was assaulted by a hatred unlike any she had ever felt when she saw the transformed Dionysus. But he paid her no heed as he spread his arms and shouted to the heavens.

"Ah, *orgia*! The sweetest feast of madness!"

His unsightly face seemed intoxicated, warped. His body trembled in excitement, imagining the exaltation and pleasure that he so desired.

"Those days before the heroes flourished—when the mortal world was overrun by monsters! That was the best! Their screams could burst eardrums, filling the air as everyone ran in terror from ghastly monsters! My heart always raced as I watched them from the skies above!"

His cheeks were flushed like a maiden in love. His eyes were full of ecstasy. There was an aberrant lustfulness in his words as he continued his praise.

"Did you know, Loki? Right after weak and frail children shook off the bonds of reason, they *laughed*!"

"!!"

"A devastating amount of fear turns into a magnificent climax, and their mind and soul are released! They can consume as much meat or wine as they want, but nothing can compare to that ultimate moment of euphoria! It can only occur amid the blood and entrails brought by monster fangs and claws! Those charming young maenads offered their own bodies in sacrifice, giving themselves as an offering to me!"

Dionysus was a deviant god—a god who delighted in bringing about resentment and derangement, in causing chaos in the virtuous world, in creating an explosion of mystical ecstasy. He was aloof and misunderstood, one who occupied a position that had little to do with the social order.

Upon finally uncovering his true nature that had stayed hidden until the very end, Loki opened her own eyes in shock.

"The crazed cries of children are even better than the finest wine!"

Those who he had arbitrarily declared his maenads were really just young mortal women. It was as if he was saying that the mad chaos spun by those beautiful, innocent people was the ultimate truth of reality. Clenching his right hand that covered half his face, Dionysus cackled. His facial bones creaked under the pressure. It was too sinister a sight.

"But that paradise came to an end with the arrival of the age of gods!" In a fit of passion, he expressed his discontent. "It's all Ouranos's fault! Because that old god made a secret deal and sealed the hole, the monsters' rampage, that hellish landscape ended! My *orgia* disappeared!"

"...That's why you saw Ouranos as an enemy, huh?"

"Damn right! That senile old shit is still offering up prayers...! Thanks to him, I could never be satisfied! Even back in the heavens! He always got in my way!"

His fingers tore through his hair as he spat scornfully. He was the very image of a foolish, egotistical god interested only in his own pleasure. His words housed this single-minded frenzy. The image of the righteous god that he showed to the children of that tranquil neighborhood was nowhere to be seen.

But at the same time, Loki understood that those were Dionysus's true feelings. His repeated warnings about Ouranos and general hostility to the old god when he had been drunk were based in his truth, the darkness deep in his heart. In fact, *hostility* did not begin to do it justice. The truth was that Dionysus loathed Ouranos with a homicidal rage.

"Ah, speaking of the heavens. Hestia got in my way, too. That stupid goddess...After I worked so hard to draw the other gods into a murderous fight and create an *orgia* in the heavens..."

"Gh...!"

"But...that might have been for the best. If she hadn't stopped me, I would have been consumed by murder and unable to control myself."

He was quiet, as if remembering the distant past, but it lasted only a second. His eyes flared, taking on a new fury.

"A game?! What game?! No matter how much I tried to kill them, they just keep laughing right up until the end! Deities are deviant beings who can't feel fear or despair! You bastards could never experience a true *orgia*!"

In his eyes, Dionysus's world was always gray. It always seemed to be blocked off by an enormous obstacle.

He found it something unlovable, something unfulfilling, something wrong. And because of that, he would bring hell to the mortal realm and create a new *orgia*.

"...So basically, you couldn't start a feast of madness in the heavens, so you tried to re-create it in the mortal realm instead?"

Monsters flowing out aboveground and the hand of the corrupted spirit were what lay beyond the destruction of Orario. That was Dionysus's true goal. He was warping the mortal realm for the sake of his own desires. It was to be expected of the works of an evil god.

"That's why you took this roundabout path?"

"Roundabout path? Do you take me for a fool, Loki? If I *messed up even a little* and used my Arcanum, then it would just end up as if it had never happened, between the other deities and the world's ability to fix itself—even if the land here was obliterated."

"..."

"If I wanted to achieve my goal using only the power available to me, then by extension, I would have to get rid of every other god besides myself."

Making it impossible. Dionysus's mind was twisted, but he was entirely calm and rational in his reasoning. He could not directly intervene as a god. That was why he had to use only elements that existed in the mortal realm and manipulate things from behind the scenes. He had to bring about the destruction while following all the worldly rules.

"Let me ask one last question."

Loki had been silent for a minute before finally asking something to clear up the remaining fragment of doubt tucked in a corner of her heart.

"It's about what you said when we were at the grave where your children were buried. Was that apology...a lie, too?"

——*"From time to time, I come here so I don't forget this feeling."*

——*"An apology. Nothing more."*

She was talking about when she had visited the Adventurers Graveyard with Lefiya, Filvis, and Dionysus. Dionysus had laid flowers at his followers' headstones and offered up an apology. Loki had not doubted his promise. His words and underlying divine will had been the real deal. Even if he was drunk. Even knowing his true nature now. She still could not see that scene as the untruth, which left Loki with a plain and simple doubt.

"...Don't misunderstand me. At that time, I was apologizing from the depths of my heart to my children who had died early."

A pure smile crossed Dionysus's face.

"Yes, those were my *sincere* feelings for losing their lives carelessly before the promised time. *'I'm sorry I couldn't offer you up along with Aura and everyone else! Oh, you'll be so lonely when you're sacrificed! I'm sorry you weren't awarded a beautiful death, fulfilling our agreement when you became part of my familia!'* Something along those lines!"

But then his face twisted grotesquely, appearing almost monstrous.

Loki clenched her fist audibly.

"Don't misunderstand, Loki. I love my children. Just like you do. But I just love them in my own way. Ha-ha-ha-ha-ha-ha-ha-ha-ha-ha-ha-ha!"

Loki reached her boiling point and passed her limit. She maintained a quiet expression, but inside, she swore an oath in wrath. With her divine will, she promised that she would bring down this god who was an insult to the mortal realm.

"Filvis is an extension of that."

After laughing for a while, Dionysus touched on his one remaining follower.

"I love *it*. Maybe more than I love anyone else. Oh, how it despaired at its own existence. Its lamentation was close to destruction…Ah, it does not even pale in comparison to the *orgia*."

"Lord Dionysus did not tell me that Olivas Act had lived on as a creature…"

A smile appeared on Filvis's face. It was a self-deprecating smile at her own inability to become a useful puppet.

"It must have been because he thought I might rebel against him or because he thought it would get in the way of his plan…Either way, I was nothing more than a single cog in the machine to him, to put it nicely."

The battle at the pantry on the twenty-fourth floor. Filvis's shock upon seeing Vendetta Olivas Act had been real.

On the same day Filvis had become a creature, Olivas had become a hybrid between human and monster. What fate! But Filvis had spent her time mutilating and trying to destroy herself. She had not noticed that the mastermind of the incident had survived. Well, it was better to say that Dionysus had not let her discover it. To carry out his plan to destroy Orario, he could not afford to have conflict among the underground forces.

"And of all things, that was the day I met you, Lefiya."

"!"

The day that she had set eyes upon the creature Olivas, Filvis's shock was immeasurable. And a small fissure had formed at that time. She had doubted Dionysus once, and her heart inched away from him. At that very same moment, someone had appeared: the girl named Lefiya Viridis, the one who had called Filvis *"beautiful"* even though she had been corrupted. Lefiya had no way of knowing just how precious that had been to Filvis on that day.

"You are not unclean!"

Without knowing anything, she had enveloped Filvis's hand in hers. Filvis had been avoided by everyone because she was the Banshee. But *Lefiya had grabbed her hand.*

The hideous beauty had gone as far as to brandish a blade to reject contact with others. Filvis was the girl whose corrupted body only Dionysus would touch.

But Lefiya had accepted her.

That changed Filvis's heart. It was a light in her darkness.

"At the very least, I wanted you…not to die. That's what I thought as I carried out Lord Dionysus's orders."

During the destruction of the twenty-fourth floor, she had protected Lefiya even at the cost of her own body. Right before the expedition, she had gone along with Lefiya's training and shared her magic with her. Without going against Dionysus's orders, she had continued to protect Lefiya while participating in the assault on Knossos. And then, she had been slaughtered by her clone, in hopes of keeping Lefiya far from the coming battle…

All her actions behind the scenes as Ein, all her inconsistent behaviors, all of it had been for Lefiya's sake.

"Miss Filvis…!"

When they had been separated from everyone else during the first invasion of Knossos and before the first assault, Filvis had kept trying. She had kept pleading with Lefiya, though she would not explain herself, only begging her "*to not die.*" She could have forced the matter. She could have knocked Lefiya out and locked her away. There were any number of solutions to this problem. But she had not done any of them.

"When you told me that the magic I shared with you had saved your friends...I desperately regretted sharing it. But at the same time...I was happy."

"!"

"Because you proved that my magic was something for protecting precious people. I was saved by you, Lefiya. You're a noble elf, achieving something I could never again do myself."

It was because Lefiya had always been Filvis's hope. For Filvis, for the corrupted, *sullying* Lefiya's virtue was the one thing she could not do. The last fragment of Filvis's elven heart had dulled her judgment to the very end. Her red eyes filled with tears, trembling like the surface of a moonlit lake.

"...!"

Faced with Filvis's fragile and teary smile, Lefiya was hit by yet another torrent of emotions. She was somehow able to squeeze out a response as she braced herself against its impact.

"Let's fight together, Miss Filvis! There is still time! One more time! Like we did before...!"

Her voice was loud as she pleaded with Filvis to abandon Dionysus—to fight together again, if she wanted. This mad wish burned itself into the back of Lefiya's mind: a dream where they were walking together in the sunlight, exchanging smiles.

But Filvis responded quietly, as if she had already anticipated that.

"That's impossible, Lefiya..."

"Why...?!"

"Because I'm Lord Dionysus's follower..."

"...But he's just using you as a pawn! He doesn't think of you as a follower! Didn't you just say so yourself?!"

"…"

"You're being deceived!"

"…I suppose so…I suppose I am."

"If you know that, then why are you still…?!"

Ein's dark, clouded eyes watched silently as the corrupted girl looked down at the floor. Pressured by Lefiya's sustained pleas, Filvis was at a loss for words, but she still managed to listlessly shake her head.

"I can't…"

"Why not?!"

"It's already too late…"

"No, it isn't!"

At some point, they started to repeat themselves, but this time, Filvis looked up with a decidedly different kind of sorrow.

"Because you already know my true nature!"

"!!"

"You know about my sullied body. My corrupted soul!"

In the next instant, Filvis's hand thrust into her chest. Lefiya was at a loss for words as she *tore into her skin and peeled it up.* As the clothes, skin, and flesh were stripped off her body, blood pumped out, spraying far. The adventurers paled at the sight, and Lefiya saw something as she was frozen in place. In the girl's chest cavity was a vibrantly colored magic stone, one that was sickening.

"Lord Dionysus said I was beautiful! He was the only one! He's the only one who would hold me! Even though my body is like this!"

Filvis was crying. Her eyes were opened wide. A broken smile crossed her face as tears streamed down her cheeks.

"Well, Lefiya? You said I was beautiful before, too. How about now? Can you still say that after seeing me like this?!"

Lefiya saw Filvis's repulsive inner body, the magic stone and the undulating green flesh. She saw the reality of the defiled girl. Lefiya desperately tried to say something, to express her thoughts about Filvis, but nothing came.

"—There's your answer." The former elf hung her head like a puppet with undone strings.

"This farce is over, huh," said Ein, the twin who had quietly watched on from the side. "You don't have any more regrets. Now there will be no more disruptions to Lord Dionysus's plan...Oh, Filvis, you fool. Our path was set long ago."

Ein soberly handed down Filvis's fate.

"Even if he is using you, he loves you. Even if it is twisted, his love is real. He's the only one who will accept us as we are. Isn't that right?"

"..."

"And what are you even blabbing on about? Rage, despair, hatred... You foisted all of that on me. Quit acting like some tragic heroine. You pushed all the dirty work onto me. You were never as pure as you pretended to be for Lefiya."

Ein approached Filvis from behind with wild eyes as she ridiculed the girl, as if claiming her pound of flesh and reopening the wounds. It must have been the effect of the cloning magic—or of her personality. Ein, the second Filvis, had a blackened heart. As if Filvis Challia had separated from her darkness. As if that body had absorbed all her negative emotions.

"Miss Filvis, please wait! I...!" Lefiya pleaded, trying to stop it.

"It's useless, Lefiya."

But for the first time, a smile seeped onto Ein's face. Her lips curled into a sneer as she continued.

"From the start, we have already killed too many people."

"___"

Banshee. That nickname wasn't for nothing. She had killed innocent adventurers who wandered too close to the trail of the corrupted spirit out of curiosity and those who happened to get too close to Enyo's plan by chance. They had been eliminated in a way to make it seem like an accident.

All told, it had happened four times. More if she counted the ones who had never been discovered. Her role as a party killer was not some tragic fate. It was something that she had brought on herself.

"Can you cover for the monster that watched on as Aura's group died, Lefiya?"

Ein had even killed members of her familia—the people who had realized that they'd been converted to Penia's followers.

"There is no turning back for me," Ein said, delivering the conclusion in Filvis's stead.

There was a small distance between Lefiya and Filvis. If she stepped forward, it would have been closed, but there was something there—an unbridgeable gulf between them. It had become too vast. For their positions were—

"Let's begin the fight to the death. I'll bury you along with all my lingering attachments to this world," Ein said without any trace of compassion.

Filvis remained silent, entrusting herself to her copy's words. Tension ran through the crowd of adventurers, and Lefiya's heart broke when it was time for the unavoidable battle.

"Ah, Lefiya—"

It was Ein who spoke—not Filvis. With a sneer still curling her lips, a tear ran down one of her cheeks.

"If only I had met you before Lord Dionysus…"

"___"

Time stopped as Lefiya felt the weight of complete powerlessness. The two Filvises did not look back at their fellow elf again as they chanted.

""*At the end of illusion, the spirit returns—forming an unbreakable bond.*""

They chanted the spell to *undo their magic*. Both Filvises spoke the name of the spell.

""*Einsel.*""

There was a flash of light. A gleam that melted black and white together. Lefiya immediately covered her eyes with her arm, but she saw it. Ein transformed into particles of light, absorbed into Filvis's true body.

The two silhouettes became one.

In an instant, a wild rush of magic wind swirled around the

chamber. On impact, the blue circlet that bound Filvis's hair shot off her head. But that wasn't all. As the two returned the magic power that had been split into the clone, the creature's flesh—Filvis's body—became active. Her raven-black hair extended to the ground. The exposed magic stone blinked violently. The overflowing power that she could not keep inside her generated a pale-crimson organ at the center of her chest like roots. It violated her white skin, creating a vessel that covered her body.

Her eyes became sunken, and her beautiful red irises became a clouded green jasper. Her white skin became sickly pale. And finally, as the tremendous magic howl settled, the particles of light dispersed with the smoke. Everyone was at a loss for words as she slowly lifted her head.

"Is that...the real Miss Filvis...?" Lefiya murmured.

Joined with her clone, Filvis was far removed from the girl Lefiya knew. She was the elf eaten away at by despair, the epitome of corruption, the personification of a fallen fairy who had become a monster.

"...Let's bring this to an end."

There was now a dark tremor in her voice, as if the void were speaking. That was all she said as she stood across from them, her gaze entirely dark.

"...Get ready, dumbass!"

"M-Mr. Bete...!"

With his gray hair swaying, Bete stood in front of Lefiya.

Though they mixed as well as oil and water, Bete had the longest relationship with Filvis out of anyone in *Loki Familia* after Lefiya. Knowing her true motives now, the werewolf had nothing more than an intent to kill. He had moved to battle preparations to bury the enemy before his eyes.

"W-wait, please! There's still—!"

"Cut the crap."

"...?!"

"That's a traitor. An enemy. That's all it is," Bete said, mercilessly brushing away Lefiya's entreaty.

Bete had watched their discussion without interrupting, only now bringing his own harsh words to bear. They were filled with an anger of a different sort from what he usually expressed. His hostility was intense, and the adventurers who had been standing by watching instinctively readied their weapons.

"Hey, elf. Hey, traitor, how are you feeling?"

"…"

"Me? I'm feeling awful after listening to your sob story."

"…"

"Why bitch about it now?"

The fact that Bete would bother to berate Filvis before fighting was proof that he was feeling some sort of doubt and anger, because he usually attacked without any questions. He would normally never talk about himself or lend an ear to the nonsense of a weakling. He would just have scorned Filvis's weakness and cursed the world's irrationality. The tattoo etched into his cheek warped as he shouted at her at the top of his lungs.

"I don't give a shit about your stupid pity party!"

"…"

"Just keep festering for the little left of your life!"

Bete started sprinting, not hiding the annoyance in his howl, winding up to land a full-strength punch on the transformed fairy monster. However, he made a slight miscalculation—

"—You were always like that, werewolf."

The girl in front of him was currently more powerful than he was.

"?!"

She *easily caught his attack* as he bore into her with his whole body, an attack from a Level-6 adventurer. Bete's eyes were shocked as she caught his fist with a single hand. A tremor of unrest shook the room. With floor-length hair the color of night, Filvis spoke quietly as Bete's fist creaked.

"You were always looking down on me…but you never abandoned me."

"Gh…?!"

"You always tried to break down my walls with that foul mouth, trying to encourage me. You are *kind*."

Bete was surprised again at the physical strength he could feel through his fist. Even as she was talking indifferently, her force kept increasing dramatically. He pushed and pulled, but he could not budge her. His amber eyes became bloodshot as it felt like she was trying to crush his fist.

And then a crack rang out, the sound of the bones in Bete's fist fracturing.

"I had always looked down on you for that and mocked you in my heart."

She unleashed her power. Clutching his fist, she swung her slender arm, tossing him down with arm strength alone. There was no trace of any refined technique. Yet Bete could not do anything to resist her as he was slammed into the floor.

"—?!"

On impact, cracks webbed out on the stone floor, and stone chips bounced into the air as a crater formed where Bete had hit the ground. The shock against his spine left him paralyzed and speechless for a second—

Letting her long black hair flutter like a wild yaksha's, she unleashed a simple kick, tearing into Bete's stomach.

"*Gaaah?!*"

The rough kick landed directly. Coughing up blood, Bete was blown away to the back of the chamber like a piece of trash caught in a tornado.

"Mr. Be—?!" Lefiya's scream was cut off because the shadow started moving with an unbelievable speed, rampaging through the rest of the adventurers.

"*Gaaaaaaaaaaaaaaaaaaaaaah?!*"

It raised its hands and mowed them down with its arms. That was all it took to finish them off. Armor was shattered. Arms and legs broken. Adventurers cried out as they were swept aside like dust. It was over in the blink of an eye. The shadow passed right by Lefiya, and it felt like a whirlwind tearing at her earlobes. As she felt the wind blow by, Lefiya immediately turned around, but by the time she did that, she was the only one left standing.

"What?!" Lefiya shuddered.

"While *Einsel* is active, my Status is *halved*," Filvis said simply after wiping out all the upper-tier adventurers with her bare hands.

That was the requirement for activating the cloning magic. Because it was not just an illusion but actually created an entire second self, there was a strict restriction to accompany this incredibly powerful ability: The user was granted only half her Status.

Lefiya immediately understood what that meant and froze in place. That meant that Filvis, who had worked with Lefiya's group, and Ein, who had fought with Finn's crew, had had only half their original strength. Her battle strength was no less than Aiz's when she was cloaked in wind. That was the true strength of the girl who had become a creature—

"Ironically, it seems I was made for this...Right now, I'm even stronger than Levis."

"___"

Lefiya's thoughts were cut off by that declaration. The implication of those words filled her with despair.

It was not just Lefiya, either. The adventurers collapsed on the ground. Even Bete was frozen, halfway through struggling to stand up. The strength to handle a Level 6. The movements that had blown away an entire squad of upper-tier adventurers. All of it lent credence to what Filvis was saying.

"Why did you come, Lefiya? Why did you have to come here...?" Filvis moaned as she looked down. A sorrowful murmur crossed her lips.

"...?!"

The green eyes befitting a servant of the corrupted spirit were concealed behind her hair. Her bitter words sounded like a curse.

"I did everything I could...I even hurt you...I even killed myself to keep you away from here."

Immediately after that, the girl-turned-monster raised her head and screamed as tears fell from one eye.

"I didn't want to have to kill you!"

As her emotions boiled over, Filvis turned into a blur. She closed in on Lefiya in an instant. Her fist encased in a metal glove clawed into Lefiya's stomach, causing blood to burble past her lips.

"Gah—?!"

Lefiya had immediately launched herself backward, but despite dampening the impact, Lefiya's vision was still rocked. The shock felt like an explosion going off inside her body. In an instant, she crashed into the wall.

"There is no letting anyone go anymore! I can't let anyone leave alive! For the sake of Lord Dionysus's wish, I will kill everyone! Everyone!"

Lefiya rose to her knees as she hacked up blood. As she gazed before her, she saw the creature that was stronger than everyone flailing its hair wildly, tears pouring down its face as it wept.

"All of it! Everything! *All shall perish! Aaaaaaaaaah!*"

It was the cry accompanying the birth of the strongest monster, the howl marking the beginning of a feast of violence.

They had been forced into an overwhelmingly disadvantageous battle.

In the chambers spread around the tenth floor, everyone was engaged in combat.

While the main bodies of the demi-spirits were continuing their chant apace, the three faces on the pillars' lower halves were activating the spirit altar's magic and rapidly launching wave after wave of spells at the adventurers.

It was a literal storm of attacks. The chain of flashes containing the power of each element poured down on everyone indiscriminately. Dealing with high-powered magic from all angles was a first even for the top-tier adventurers, and it created a hell that could not be just described as "the unknown." It was far more threatening than the Dragon's Urn below the Dungeon's fifty-second floor.

In the blink of an eye, the comrades who were running were blown away. In the very next moment, a party up front was completely dashed from view. In the middle of hell, the adventurers howled. Even knowing they would be lost in the thunderous boom from magic, they screamed with their entire body and spirit, leaving behind their friends who had fallen to break through the enemy's barrage and take down the altar's defense mechanism. Encased in stout armor, their bodies pooled with blood and tears.

They pushed on—even as the advance was blown apart. Mages chanted even as their staff and arm were blasted away. The adventurers were paying a horrific toll, shaving away at their lives as they continued to attack.

"Eat this! *Aaaaah!*"

The fourth squad.

Tiona's Urga landed. Her whole body was covered in burns, and smoke was coiling off her skin, but she managed to land a heavy blow to the left-most face on the spirit altar, slicing through its thick lips. Once there, she unleased a reckless rain of attacks with Urga. It looked almost like a dance, or perhaps like a spinning top.

Using both her Skills, Berserker and Intense Heat, to create a combo attack with maximum output, Tiona immediately carved away at the giant face, creating dozens of huge gashes.

"*Graaaar?!*"

The spirit altar's left face coughed up a stream of blood as it cried out its death throes. In an instant, it suddenly swelled, popped, and then scattered. Tiona had broken the magic stone of the Treent at its core.

"*Raaaaaaaaah!*" Tione quickly followed up. Her body was just as wounded as her little sister's; she jabbed with her twin Zolas, obliterating the right face with her fists of steel charged with fury.

"————*Gh!*"

"*Aaargh?!*"

"Damn it! After all we did to break it…!"

The two Amazons were pushed back from the spirit altar by the central face that screamed as it swung its enormous tentacle. Its defense mechanism was half-destroyed. But to make up for that, the remaining face redirected its resources to dealing with intruders in passages to the chamber, focusing its attention on exterminating the troublesome ants. It howled with rage as it unleashed a rain of magic.

"Healing droplets, tears of light, eternal sanctuary—!"

Even in a formation that didn't afford them any protection, the healers did not stop their casts. On a battlefield that would inevitably end with annihilation, the only reason the adventurers could still keep fighting was because of the efforts of the healers of *Dian Cecht Familia*—because they continued to chant for recovery until their throats were rubbed raw, because of their well-timed use of items. The adventurers managed to maintain their battle lines, and all the parties were managing to cling to life. If it were not for them, Tiona and Tione's squad would have long ago bitten the dust.

"Aaaah?!"

"Amid?!"

Amid's pure-white magic circle flickered. The enemy's magic had landed right at the feet of the girl who was practically maintaining the entire squad's constitution by herself. Dea Saint had the frightening ability to sustain a battlefront by herself, but even she could not continue healing at this scale if she was being attacked herself. The tanks protecting the healers had reached their limit, which would mark the beginning of the end. As the adventurers holding up big shields steadily lost their strength, Amid started getting exposed to the enemy's barrage, along with the healers in the back lines.

"Gareth, the healers are down! This is bad!"

"Damn it! Gimme a shield!"

The same scene was playing out elsewhere. In Gareth and Tsubaki's third squad, the healers had taken the brunt of a blast, forcing Gareth to fall back from the front lines to handle the defenses.

"Lady Riveria?!"

"Don't leave my defenses!"

In the second squad, Riveria activated her defensive barrier and endured the full artillery assault. However, she could not counterattack while she was turtled up, defending against the monstrous magic attacks from every direction. Riveria's jade eyes focused on the spirit altar as she analyzed the situation. She understood that trying to challenge the spirit altar with its enormous reserves to a test of endurance would end only in defeat.

It was not a coincidence that the healers were being targeted on each battlefield.

The colossal magic circle and the six pillars of the spirit altar connected by that circle had a singular mind. Upon discovering the heart of the adventurers' resistance, the defense system prioritized aiming at it. The three faces learned the subtleties of the battlefield quickly, inorganically, smiling, raging, weeping—as they turned their nigh-unlimited magic power into spells to launch at the adventurers' back lines.

"It's no good, Lido! The trolls can't hold on any longer!" the red-cap goblin warned.

"Damn it…! We're all monsters here, right?! We should be fighting with claws and fangs, not magic!" Lido said as he wildly swiped the blood from his face with an arm that had lost most of its scales.

The only squad that had not been affected by the spirit altar's focus on the back lines was the Xenos's sixth squad. However, because they did not have any healers to begin with, they had less ability to recover than the adventurers, leaving them already in worse shape than any other squad.

They were running out of the elixirs made by Fels to heal up Wiene the vouivre and all the other monsters with lower combat abilities.

"Where the hell did Fels take Gros anyway?!"

The lizardman cried out, telling the gargoyle to hurry up and get back as the enemy's rain of magic continued without pause.

The spirit altar was more militant than imaginable. To the first-tier adventurers of *Loki Familia* and Tsubaki, they estimated the six pillars' abilities to be lower than those of the demi-spirit in the unexplored territory of the fifty-ninth floor, but they also noticed the labyrinth itself that made up the altar provided an effectively inexhaustible supply of magic. Like the passages covered in green flesh, the pillars had a regenerative ability to recover if they were wounded. Even though most of the magic power was being used for the spell to destroy the city, the spirits' vitality was extraordinary, and to top it off, they even had a petal armor protecting their bodies. The spirit's actual body was protected from a knockout blow.

The only effective place to aim was the three Treents whose magic stones were embedded in their faces, but now that their collective consciousness recognized the adventurers were aiming for that, they were on guard against those targeted attacks. Between battle-fields, they had managed to take out two of them, but they could not finish the final face.

The assault coming from all directions was menacing to say the least. With the aid of the spirit cloths, the adventurers could barely hold their ground, but it took all they had to maintain this position. With the healers starting to fall, the moment of annihilation crept closer.

"Captain! This is the fifth squad! We can't attack the target!"

"…!"

"Even if all five other spirits are taken down, if there is still one left…!"

They were short on forces. There was a decisive lack of firepower. Because they had been split into five squads, each group of adventurers was lacking in power to break through the monster's defenses, and Bete's fifth squad had been split in half. As she came through the oculus to Finn, Anakity sounded uneasy.

"The tanks have been wiped out!"

"Captain, we can't defend against the magic! If Amid gets taken out, we…!"

"Do any squads have anyone to spare?! Can anyone back us up?!"

A variety of different voices echoed through the oculi as their forces encountered problems on every front. The reports coming in almost sounded like cries for help as they merged with the shouts of adventurers from behind Finn.

As the overall commander, Finn was trying to maintain control of six different boards at once. While listening to the unending stream of reports, he gave accurate commands to battlefields that he could not see, all while still maintaining control of his own fight with the first squad. He was effectively playing chess blindfolded on five different boards even as he wielded his spear and crossed blades with the enemy before his eyes.

It was a deific level of multitasking. He must have been the only one in all of Orario who could pull off that kind of stunt. However, it also put an extremely heavy burden on Finn.

"Gh…!"

The spray of the lightning blast singed his cheek as he slipped past it. He continued firing off orders without a break, even as his lungs screamed for oxygen. His breathing was ragged, and he could not get it under control.

His body begged him to activate Hell Finegas as it started to lose its luster, but Finn immediately dismissed that option. If he turned into a berserker now, the squads on every battlefield would lose their commander. That would mean defeat for their alliance of forces. In something as insane and menacing as an entire labyrinth, the adventurers were all relying on Finn for support.

A bead of sweat trickled down Braver's cheek as he kept revising the situation for each squad in his head and firing off order after order.

"…Overlap your attacks! If it's focusing fire on the back lines, then the barrage hitting the front lines has to let up some! I'm calling all squads! I don't care how you do it, but crush that defense system!"

He was laying out a command to attack together.

Throwing his spear, he pierced one of the faces on the lower pillar, but the return fire of magic was immediate. The soldiers were putting their faith in him, but their morale wavered like candlelight in the wind.

While the adventurers were struggling on a battlefield out of sight, there was a change aboveground.

"What is that?! What's happening?!"

On her way back from her part-time job, Hestia noticed something—a red ray of light rising from the ground. It was dim, but as time passed, the amassing rays shone from crevices in the stone pavement, from below buildings, and from the sewers. Polluted by an odious red fog, the dark-blue night sky was nowhere to be seen.

"And…do I hear a song?"

Accompanying the fog, a singing voice seemed to reach her ears. It was distant, but the tone seemed like a calming lullaby to put everything to sleep. Or maybe it was more like a solemn requiem to purify all. There was a destructive intention hidden behind its melody.

The song resounding belowground had finally started to be transmitted aboveground, too.

"No way. Is this…a chant?"

Right when Hestia murmured to herself, there was a commotion nearby. The wave spread through the crowded streets, taverns, and other shops, caused by the mysterious light that was visible for all to see.

Adventurers and deities realized behind the scenes that "that time" had come. However, the adventurers were blown away by the scale of what was happening, and the deities recognized just how bad it was as it dawned on them that this was no joke.

Six singing voices merged in the red rays of light, a dissonant sound accompanying the warning bells. There were tremors rocking the ground. The singing was starting to melt into the earth beneath them. They finally noticed the footsteps of destruction that were hidden in the shadow of the tranquility that had cloaked the city, and panic began to spread.

"What is this? Why do I have a feeling that this is really… reaaally bad?"

Hestia started to sweat, expressing what all the deities were feeling at that moment.

"Ouranos, we're at our limit! We can't hide it from the residents anymore!"

The city's core, Guild Headquarters, was intense with bustling bodies as Royman's ragged voice echoed in the underground altar.

The head of the Guild, who had worked together with every familia and secretly taken the lead in supporting the second assault on Knossos, looked ghostly pale. To avoid unnecessary panic, he had not told the lower-level members of the Guild what was going on, but that selective information was threatening to lead to the worst possible result. Royman's overweight body was drenched in sweat as he barged in, but Ouranos remained silent, staying in his seat.

"..."

There was one last oculus sitting within reach of his hand, but it had not yet buzzed with victory cries. It had not made any noise at all—

"It's too late…Dionysus's plan was perfect," Demeter cried.

Watching from her second home in the mountains, she saw Orario transforming into a different realm. From a distance, it was clear to behold. There were crimson waves emanating from the ground around Orario. They even enveloped the city walls. From a distance, the innumerable red rays of light rising into the sky looked like a prison surrounding the city.

It was as though the city itself was being transformed into a magic circle.

The monstrous spirit's ring taking shape underground was emerging on the surface. The final countdown was closing in on them.

Defeat in this battle would mean the destruction of the Labyrinth City as prelude to the complete annihilation of the mortal realm. And as Orario approached its fate, Demeter was overcome with grief. She crumpled into tears.

"Because of my weaknesses…because of my betrayal…the city… the whole mortal realm is going to be destroyed," she sobbed out, as if confessing her sins.

The night air carried a warm breeze from the direction of the illuminated city, causing the balcony to sway slightly.

With no more reason to hide themselves, the members of *Hermes Familia* were standing there, gazing at the city, unable to move as the crimson scenery filled their vision.

As Demeter and the adventurers watched, it looked like Dionysus's plan of destruction was about to reach its completion.

"No," Hermes said. *"Not yet."*

A violent crash jostled Knossos. It was the aftershock of the extreme artillery blitz the spirit pillars were still firing at the adventurers.

That tremor was incomparable in power to the aftershocks of the ritual that were being felt aboveground. The green flesh continued to undulate, and the visible magic circle running along the floor of the passages was glistening.

Amid all that, a single shadow appeared noiselessly.

"—I'm a little ashamed to be able to move around in secret while Braver and Lido and the rest of them are fighting for their lives…"

Fels appeared like a ghost, dropping the reversible veil, which granted invisibility to its user, much like another item maker's handiwork. Following the instructions that Finn had provided before the operation, Fels had been moving around Knossos alone. To accomplish those orders, the mage had made liberal use of magic items, avoiding not just sight but each and every manner of detection. Because of that, Fels had not been noticed by the green flesh or exposed to the bombardment of magic, despite moving all around through the depths of the labyrinth.

"But thanks to that, I found it."

Fels was in a stretch of a passage that seemed absolutely ordinary. However, looking closely, the lines of the magic circle on the floor were entangled, merging with a side path, gathering by the keystone.

"There are several points on the tenth floor where the magic circulates. This is the last one."

All told, there were eight locations. Using Daedalus's Notebook, the blueprint of Knossos, and the information about the composition of the spirits' ritual gathered from the gods, the mage had quickly found the targets.

They were the hearts that circulated magic through the altar, so to speak.

"With the six demi-spirits at its core, this won't stop the ritual to destroy the city, but—"

Small gold and silver orbs scattered along the lines of the magic circle. The mage in the black robe matter-of-factly proceeded with the preparations, and finally, a black glove clenched around a magic stone.

"—I can at least disturb the altar covering Knossos."

And then the mage set off an explosion, smashing a jewel. A crest shone on the black glove, igniting a ray like a lightning bolt and blasting into the magic filling Knossos.

In the next instant, all eight points were consumed in a giant explosion, knocking out the hearts.

"?!"

The demi-spirits' real bodies all reacted, looking up as one as they realized the change that had occurred inside the altar. The synchronized explosions that Fels had set off in the hearts had temporarily blocked off the pipes circulating the magic. The supply of magic power to all the altar had been severely disrupted.

"Braver, I've finished up on my end."

"—! *Really?!*"

"The chambers housing the main bodies of the demi-spirits won't run out of magic, but the same can't be said for everywhere else."

The spirit altar was attempting to repair the hearts as quickly as possible. But all the circulatory features had been destroyed at the same time. Even if it tried, it would not be able to distribute the magic power well enough, and it would slow down its process.

And because most of the magic power was relegated to recovery, the storm of magic blasts hitting each squad would be forced to weaken.

However, that was just a convenient side effect.

"With this, the obstacles that might hinder our follow-up have been removed, just like we planned."

Fels spoke into the oculus.

"Sorry to keep you waiting, Ouranos. The time has come."

"Huh?"

"I said 'not yet,' Demeter. It's far too soon to give up." Hermes tipped the brim of his hat up with his finger. "The wedge has been shoved in. Now is when Ouranos will give his order."

His eyes narrowed, and a smile appeared on his face.

"They're going to move now. *All our forces.*"

"It's here, huh?"

The exchange with the mage was short. Ouranos opened his eyes.

"Send in all the forces."

As he stopped wailing, Royman hurriedly knelt in acknowledgment and dashed out of the Chamber of Prayers, conveying his master's divine will through the city.

"Go, Ottar."

The queen's order was quiet.

"—Milady!"

And the warrior's response was short, as if he had been awaiting that command from her. There was no doubt in his eyes. Behind him, the chariot's silver spear shimmered. The four prums' weapons chattered like a beast's fangs. The black-and-white fairies' weapons gave off a bewitching gleam.

They were all filled with militance—the fighting spirit of the goddess's followers who devoted themselves to the pursuit of being the strongest.

"F…*Freya Familia*…" someone murmured.

As panic enveloped the city, the strongest army gathered in

Central Park at the base of Babel, imposing and inspiring. The scene caused the residents who had been thrust into confusion by the mysterious red light to forget their fear and agitation for a moment.

Standing before the strongest warriors was the embodiment of the world's beauty, with her silver hair swept up by the wind: Vanadis, the Goddess of Life and Death, Battle and Victory. It was almost like a page had been taken out of myth and brought to life. The scene was burned into the eyes of the onlookers.

"Th-they're here!"

"*Freya Familia* really came!"

The reserve force from *Ganesha Familia* cheered the appearance of the goddess's army of more than eighty troops, counting those who were not first-tier adventurers. The reserve force had been desperately hoping for the appearance of the reinforcements, causing a stir: a quarter in awe and three-quarters joy.

"With the stage set with precision…there's no way we wouldn't come," Freya said.

The goddess's eyes narrowed in amusement as she watched her followers descend the stairs from the tower while basking in the roars of *Ganesha Familia*'s reserves.

"To think Braver himself would come to me," she marveled as she reflected on their meeting that had occurred after the end of the strategy meeting with the others, including Shakti and Fels.

"Goddess Freya, I'd like you to hear my request."

The prum had gone directly from the meeting room on the thirtieth floor of Babel to its highest floor, apologizing for the sudden visit before he had gotten straight to the point.

Freya could not help but be intrigued and a little surprised when he had causally explained that Loki was very busy, which was why she couldn't make it here and why he had come directly himself. Finn was not so foolish as to fail to recognize what it meant for the leader of a hostile faction to enter Freya's castle without any protection.

"I'm sure that Hermes's letter has reached you, so you should understand the situation."

It was true that there was a letter in Freya's hands. It was one of several that Hermes had left with Asfi to be delivered to several groups of reinforcements. Basically, it was "an invitation to the banquet where the fate of the mortal realm will be decided."

But Freya had no intention of heeding Hermes's request. She had no interest in being dragged around by another god's divine will. She would use her forces at her own leisure and intended to take down Knossos in her own time. She would wipe out the vermin infesting her garden, but she would do it herself.

"You are going to tell me that you can win on your own, I'm sure. Even still, I would ask you to please fight together with us."

"!"

"That way, we can be absolutely certain that we defeat this enemy. And most importantly, we can win this battle where there will be no wealth or glory to be won," Finn said grandly. "There are those of us who have sworn to protect the innocent people in this city and those of us who have sworn to protect this place where they belong. But whatever the motivations, we must win this together with everyone."

For the sake of lost comrades. For revenge for those who had died. Finn left those other reasons unspoken as he boldly stood before Freya.

"That became clear the moment the enemy chose the name 'city destroyer.'"

From Freya's side, Ottar's rusty eyes watched on as Finn faced the goddess.

"Like the heroes of the past who brought peace to the mortal realm, we are going to weave together another *Oratoria*."

Freya was silent as the room fell quiet, but there was a smile on her lips.

"Braver. You've changed."

The old Finn would never have spoken of something as idealistic as the *Oratoria* created by the true heroes. Even though Finn was one of Loki's children, Freya still understood his true nature. But Finn just shrugged and grinned back.

"It is hard to become the real hero the gods wish for," he responded fearlessly.

*   *   *

"This is not for Loki but out of respect for your honor, Braver. I shall heed your request. That child came before me all alone and demonstrated both the resolve to achieve victory and the temperament befitting a hero...To fail to acknowledge that would render me more naked than an emperor with new clothes."

In addition to love, heroism and bravery were some of Freya's most valued things. And because Finn had so embodied both, Freya had given him her word—for the sake of a united victory.

"Ganesha? Loki's vanguard has already cleared the path to the demi-spirits. So my children can just hit them to their hearts' content... Correct?"

"I am Ganesha, the one who rises to the situation when the city is in danger! *Because we are Ganeshaaaa!*"

"Ganesha?" Freya's eyes narrowed coolly.

"Yes, that's correct!" The god behind the elephant mask dropped his needlessly excited boasts and snapped to attention.

She smiled at the cat person beside her.

"That's all there is to do, so I'm asking you as well, Allen."

"..."

"Or are you still going to throw a tantrum?"

"...I will not. If you say that prum has demonstrated the capacity of a hero, then I will demonstrate an even greater allegiance to you."

As Freya's smile widened, Vana Freya, Allen Fromel, readily obeyed. His silver spear rang as he charged into the Dungeon ahead of everyone else.

Ottar watched as he slipped from view with an unbelievable speed, an almost visible aura of the desire to fight around him, and then the boaz called out with a booming voice.

"The goddess loathes rotten flowers! Do you know what that means?"

"*Raaah!*"

"The goddess did not extol us but Braver! Do you understand what that means?!"

"*—Raaaaah!*"

The taciturn warrior spurred on the warriors whose utmost desire was their goddess's favor. The Goddess of Beauty's followers roared again, the flames of militancy fanned even higher by the respect she had paid to Braver. As the goddess lovingly looked on, the Warlord raged.

"We are going to exterminate the weeds wreaking havoc on our goddess's garden! Let's go!"

"*RAAAAAAAAAAAAAAAAAAAAAAAAH!*"

A thunderous shout roared out. Vowing an unshakable, absolute victory, the strongest army moved out.

"Heh-heh-heh…Heh-heh-heh-heh! What a wonderful night!"

As the adventurers' terrific shouts rang out under the sky, a young girl—a goddess—licked her lips in anticipation.

"A supreme night filled with the battle cries of powerful warriors!"

Eyes peered out from the holes in a mask and through wavy red hair. Kali trembled in excitement as she looked to the sky and clapped. In her hand was the same letter that Freya had received. Granted the ability to enter the city freely—Asfi had arranged for the city gates to be opened—the goddess turned back to her followers and shouted.

"This will be the greatest feast! To make up for a fight against Freya! Let's run wild!"

"Yes, Kali."

"Wait for me, Finn—the strong male who defeated me!"

The twin Amazons with sandy hair had responded. The younger Bache was calm, while the older sister Argana was overcome with excitement—of a different sort. The two of them were gone as quickly as the wind, and the rest of the warriors of Telskyura followed.

"*Ra wehga! Ra wehga! Ra wehga!*"

We are the true warriors.

Paying no heed to the red rays of light dancing through the city, they raised a battle cry and rushed down the streets like wild beasts, causing the residents to dive to the sides of the road in an effort to avoid them.

The intensity caused *Ganesha Familia* to panic a little as they directed the Amazonian reinforcements into the transformed Knossos—

*   *   *

"You think we'll lose to Kali?! Let's go!"

"*RAAAAAAH!*"

Not wanting to lose to their fellow Amazons from Telskyura, Antianeira Aisha Belka and the Berbera of the former *Ishtar Familia* roared on Daedalus Street.

After getting wrapped up in the incident caused by Valletta Grede and the Evils, they had been saved by *Loki Familia*. The hot-blooded Amazons had come to repay their debts and reclaim their honor.

"Let's go quickly, Aisha! To rescue Bete Loga!"

"To save the city, you mean. Sheesh, didn't that werewolf tell you to stay back?"

"Like I would listen to him in a situation like this!"

As Lena got particularly wound up, she spun her scimitar over her head. Aisha was exasperated, but the girl just smiled.

"What kind of woman can't protect her man?!"

"Everyone's getting all worked up..." Lulune the chienthrope grumbled to herself as she covered one of her ears to dampen the thundering shouts pouring out of the oculus in her other hand.

"Well, shall we go quietly?"

Inside, the Dungeon was filled with the same red rays of light, rocked by the same tremors as aboveground.

While the other adventurers were turning pale and scrambling to escape to the upper floors, she turned to her companion.

"I'm counting on you this time, Miss Helper."

"Yes, I'll make up for the trouble I caused before."

The masked adventurer nodded quietly as she readied the gear that *Hermes Familia* had provided.

The forces gathered, churning, becoming an amalgamated mass.

Thanks to Ouranos's order, *Hermes Familia*'s influence, and Braver's oath, every last influential force met up in Knossos—to save the adventurers who were already fighting and to defeat the evil that would destroy the city.

The trail that *Loki Familia* had blazed would come to fruition on this night and become the blade to save the city.

"Wh-what was that? Those voices sounded different from a panic..."

Hestia froze in the middle of the street and looked left and right when she heard the battle cries. The Goddess of the Hearth could not grasp the subtleties of the battlefield, so she was confused at first, but she finally realized she was hearing the roars of adventurers: the battle hymn of the gallant people who charged to take down the danger threatening them all.

Standing among the residents who had been kept in the dark, Hestia could feel the breaths of the people who embarked to fight in secret.

"...Sheesh, and I already said I'd had enough of dangerous things..."

After a little bit, Hestia pursed her lips.

"Is it really going to go according to Hermes's plan?"

"That's right. The world wants heroes."

In a place removed from the Labyrinth City, Hermes stared off into the darkness and murmured in his way.

"Hermes...?"

"There weren't enough pieces on the board, so I had to play the ace up my sleeve. Even with all our forces gathered."

He was not facing Demeter, who looked bewildered, as he continued to speak, as though he was talking to himself.

"To drive away darkness, you need a bright light. A resounding bell to save the chosen ones. The final hero who will someday shoulder the promised era."

The breeze caught his words and carried them toward the city where the battle was unfolding. His words could have been a realized prophecy. It was indefinite, vague self-righteousness. The words of an oracle, tinged with longing, conveying something that he alone could see.

"The truth is, I wanted to keep this in reserve, but...I don't see any other way around it. In a battle that will never be sung in the epics, please save the world—this one time."

And then Hermes smiled, like a child reading an unequalled tale.

"For the sake of the world—I am playing the joker."

"Is this okay?" asked the final reinforcements quietly.

"Yes, go ahead." Asfi nodded in response to the young boy.

They were in the dark Labyrinth District. As the voices of the other reinforcements surged, the final hero who Hermes sought was looking down at the hole leading into the distant abyss.

"Sheesh. Getting into risky business right after we got back from the expedition...I mean, what can we even do down there?!"

"It's a mission, so there's no choice but to go, Li'l E."

"Yes. Besides, if we can be of any assistance, we should help."

"I heard Miss Aisha's voice...Let's go."

Four more voices spoke up. In appearance and scale, this group was clearly inferior to the other reinforcements, and yet to Asfi, they looked more reliable than anyone. They had grown. The familia led by the boy her patron god called the "final hero."

"Orario is in danger. Miss Aiz and *Loki Familia* are already fighting. And I want to help them."

His determination was met with smiles from three of them, and the remaining prum girl nodded begrudgingly.

He had white hair—the color of virgin snow. It rustled in the wind. His rubellite red eyes were filled with determination. His arm wasn't fully healed, but he could manage to move it.

The joker. The incomplete hero. Bell Cranell.

He joined the fray with *Hestia Familia*.

"Let's go."

CHAPTER 7

Final War II

Гэта казка іншага сям'і.

Апошняя вайна

Starting with the strongest, the reinforcements were dispatched into Knossos. Inspired battle cries echoed in the skies over Orario.

However, just as they moved belowground, something suddenly appeared, as if taking their place, as if waiting for them.

"A-aaaaaack?!"

Aboveground.

As the spirit's great ritual began to take shape and the red light rose, peals of cries started to fill the air. A swarm of man-eating flowers tore through the cobblestones and emerged from the sewers.

Their hideous jaws were dripping mucus, and their flower petals opened as tentacles undulated.

"Is that some new kind of monster?! Wait, isn't that what came out at Monsterphilia?!"

Absorbing some of the surging magic from the demi-spirits to destruct, the man-eating plants started rampaging. It was the work of Enyo, a trick to amuse himself as a prelude to the feast of frenzy to come.

"What the hell is this weird red light?!"

"The tremors aren't dying down…!"

"What's going on?!"

The appearance of monsters everywhere in the city was the final straw that caused the residents to lose control. All who had been cowering in fear of this clearly abnormal situation finally fell into frenzied panic.

The scene fit for a mad feast spread to every inch of the city. Residents and merchants who had no real power screamed in fright, scrambling desperately for their lives. As the tears of children resounded, adventurers rushed out to deal with the monsters.

"Aaaaaaah?!"

"Th-they're really strong!"

But the man-eating flowers had a potential that surpassed the great majority of adventurers. Blunt-force attacks did not work, and they reacted to magic, turning to crush any mages who attempted to cast a spell. Even upper-tier adventurers were cornered into defensive positions in the face of unknowns that did not appear anywhere in the Dungeon.

The strongest adventurers who formed the core of the city had all gone to support the battle in Knossos, meaning they were no longer aboveground. The city would have to pacify the current situation with only the forces still on the surface.

The bulk of the response came from *Ganesha Familia*'s reserves. They quickly came to the aid of the citizens, but the rampaging monsters were menacing. With bad reports cropping up from everywhere without any ready solutions, the panic started to accelerate.

"Oi! Come here, you monsters!"

All of a sudden, dozens of fishermen appeared.

"Don't push yourself too hard, Rod!"

"I'll be fine, Njǫrðr! I've seen enough of them to last a lifetime, but I know how they work because of that!"

It was *Njǫrðr Familia*.

Kali Familia had been staying in Meren, and when they had moved out, the fishermen had rushed to Orario in its hour of crisis. Their captain, Rod, smiled at his patron god's warning.

"This is the leftover magic-stone dust from Borg's father! We'll use it all up here!"

Rod and his men were hauling big bags over their shoulders. The bags were filled with crushed magic-stone powder that could be used to lure the violas. It was an item that Njǫrðr and Borg had created to protect the coasts near Meren and served as proof of their sins. The fishermen vigorously powdered their surroundings, causing the swarm of man-eating flowers to stop attacking the fleeing people and redirect their attention toward them.

"Wh-why do *I* have to do this?!"

"Oh, piss off, Rubart! Just do your job and lure them to the upper-tier adventurers!"

Rubart had changed jobs from head of the Guild branch to fisherman. He whimpered as Rod took the initiative and started leading the monsters.

"This is bad, Bors!"

"Damn it! I come up for the first time in forever, and *this* is what I have to deal with? I saw enough of these ugly pieces of shit in Rivira!"

In the city's northwest quadrant, Bors Elder happened to be aboveground for once, cursing up a storm. It reminded him too much of a certain nightmare: when he had gotten mixed up in the incident with a crystal orb fetus that had nearly destroyed Rivira. This whole situation was rearing its ugly head again. As his henchmen turned pale, Bors stared at the violas and then charged into battle, annoyed.

"Shit! Fighting with cheap weapons isn't gonna work! The blade will give out first!"

Unfortunately, the violas boasted tough skin that not only resisted bludgeoning but even caused nicks in swords and axes that tried to slice through it. Considering their own safety, they were getting ready to run away.

"Use this."

"Are y-you...Old Man Goibniu?!"

A short old god stopped the ruffians. It was Goibniu, God of the Forge.

"I'm opening my familia's stockpile. Take our weapons and fight."

Judging it the right thing to do, the smiths of *Goibniu Familia* were calling out to the adventurers, bringing weapons to those who were on the front lines.

The offer had reached the ears of Bors's group as they were being pushed back by the monsters. Stunned by the proposal, they turned around and leaped at the treasure.

"T-top-tier gear made by *Goibniu Familia*...!"

"This is stuff that we'd never hoped to get our hands on!"

"Hot damn! I'm so happy! I'm so glad to be alive!"

As a weapon maniac, Bors was moved to tears, and the rest of his henchmen went from terror to excitement. They cried out in joy as they started to push back the swarm of monsters, their new weapons capable of slicing through the enemies' tentacles and hardened skin.

"I had anticipated the worst case, but…it really did turn out as Loki said."

Elsewhere, in the city's northeast Industrial District.

Witnessing the excitement of adventurers, Hephaistos, Goibniu's fellow Goddess of the Forge, watched on, her uncovered left eye narrowing sharply.

"Tsubaki and the other high smiths are with Loki's kids. I know it's a heavy load, but I'm counting on you."

""Yes, ma'am!"" the lower-level smiths shouted in response.

"Focus on fighting with the magic swords! Leave the front lines to the adventurers!"

The smiths roared at their patron goddess's instructions. Turning the passion that they put into their forge into a burning battle spirit, they unleashed a barrage of attacks using *Hephaistos Familia*'s prided magic swords. Hephaistos assumed command, and they showered the monsters with a storm of flames and lightning in an area that had been evacuated of civilians.

Swinging around the high smiths' works, the craftsmen rose to the challenge in the city's moment of need.

"Work together with the mages, fools! Those plants are reacting to magic! Draw them away from the residents and annihilate them!"

Even the members of the Guild were doing what they could. And at the center of it all, his earnest voice ragged from all the yelling, was the head of the Guild, Royman.

"What?! Weren't you the one always talking about how the use of magic in the city was prohibited due to its potential dangers…?"

"There's no time to argue semantics! Look around you! Take a good look at this situation! Tulle! See to it that every familia works together! Frot is useless!"

"Y-yes, sir!"

"What did I do?!" Misha Frot yelled in tears as her fellow receptionist—a half-elf—headed out.

Royman continued to fire off instructions.

He was the only one in the Guild at the moment who had a firm grasp of the situation, and he looked extremely pale. He could not stop sweating as all his worries snowballed out of control. If he could, he would have liked to gulp down his stomach medicine like a cold beer and tell himself it was all a dream as he hid under the covers. But he continued to stay there because he understood that there was no one other than him who could give the right instructions in the current situation.

"Frot, go to the Benevolent Mistress! Even you can handle asking them to help out!"

"What?! A bar?! Guild Chief, did you forget that in the confusion—?"

"*Just go already!*"

"Y-yes, sir?!" she yelped back.

He had no more concerns about appearances. He was dredging up *all the top-tier adventurers who were in his memory*—trying to secure their locations and abilities—and making a mental list of anyone who could be useful in their forces.

"Have *Takemikazuchi* and *Miach* and *Dellingr Familias* move to the east of the city!"

Whether they were lower-tier or a mid-level faction, he set all of them to work. He even mobilized the powerful familias that had been given the mission to clear out the green flesh, sending them out again to pacify the monsters.

"Grrr, Finn! You bastard! Saying you'd leave what happens to me after you left…! You *knew* it would end up like this!"

Royman was the head of the Guild. Selfish and devoted, the man would use anything in his power. The Guild's Pig.

"If you can't save everything in the city, there'll be hell to pay!"

However, his feelings for Orario were genuine and stronger than anyone's. If they were not, Ouranos would never have given him the most powerful position with all the responsibility it entailed. In terms of a familia, he would be the captain.

Royman channeled his chronic stomach pain into an explosive shout.

"Protect the city, adventurers! Protect my—protect *our* Orario!"

As the sweaty Pig sent orders, even his fellow elves who held him in contempt chose to obey him.

"A battle involving all of Orario...It's been a while," Freya commented.

"Yes, ever since the conflict with the Evils," Ganesha responded.

Upon sending out their followers, the two deities watched as people flowed into Central Park. Most of the deities in the city were entertaining themselves in their own ways, not wanting to be late to this party. They all realized the fate of the mortal realm rested on the conditions surrounding this battle.

"This has really turned into something crazy...Did all my actions to try to help my sea play a part in causing this?" Njǫrðr murmured, his voice tinged with regret as he looked on.

"We'll take care of things up here! So make sure you win this, Loki!"

"―――――――――!"

It was a rush of combat boots. The adventurers advanced, roaring through the Dungeon and from the entrance at the Labyrinth District, pouring into Knossos. There was nothing to get in their way.

They raced through the ninth floor and the tenth floor that the vanguard of *Loki Familia* had cleared out, charging straight to the chambers where the demi-spirits waited.

It had all been for this: Finn's obstinate insistence on damaging the spirit altar—the labyrinth's defense mechanism—and getting Fels to cut off the supply line of magic with their tricks. All of it.

"The following forces must reach the demi-spirits without taking damage."

Before the start of the second assault, this was the plan that Finn had designed at the strategy meeting. With a single battle to determine the fate of Orario, it would have been nonsensical not to send in all the city's major forces. Now that they had directly felt the menace of Enyo, it was essential that they forget any personal holdbacks and work together as a team, including *Freya Familia*.

"I expect resistance from Knossos, now that it's been transformed into an altar. It will exceed anything we can imagine. We will secure the route to the target and use the strength of the following forces to finish it."

Loki Familia and *Ganesha Familia*, *Hephaistos Familia* and *Dian Cecht Familia*, their forces were actually just the vanguard.

Their job would be to charge into enemy territory, gather information, open the way, and make sure the following forces could reach the target unharmed. Finn had immediately concluded that cooperation with *Freya Familia* would be impossible, so he had designed a two-stage attack instead. He had tried his best to convince Freya about the necessity of a united front, but he had also discarded any possibility of true cooperation between their forces. He was not some simple idealist; he was a shrewd and shameless hypocrite.

"*Advance!*"

Fels had stealthily covered most of the passages on the tenth floor. The mage in the black robe was currently using an oculus to share the optimal routes to the forces aboveground, allowing the reinforcements from the Labyrinth District and the Dungeon to reach the six chambers as quickly as possible regardless of the entrance they used.

The counter magic that had jeopardized the lives of *Loki Familia* and the rest of the vanguard squads had ground down to a halt. In the chambers, the defense mechanism had been crushed. With Fels's help, the source pipe of magic was still being restored, which was why the spirit altar was forced to allow the new intruders to pass by untouched.

Their efforts to open the way had a definite return on investment. The labyrinth was not searching for enemies or launching counterattacks. The follow-up squads were able to race through the passages without any difficulty. And amid the reinforcements, the first ones to land on the stage of the decisive battle was the other familia said to be the city's strongest.

There was an explosion of magic and the flash of a blade severing through a tentacle. It was a brave charge by the reinforcements whose arrival rescued *Loki Familia* from their pinch.

"*Freya Familia!*"

As the spirit altar continued to sing its terrific song, the appearance of the new forces was met with equal parts joy and shock from *Loki Familia.*

The reinforcements were a party composed mostly of fairies. And among the new arrivals, a white elf and a dark elf stepped forward, the ones who had just unleashed the simultaneous attack using magic and weapons.

"It's been a while, noble lady."

"You're..."

Riveria's second squad.

The two elves did not kneel before Riveria, who was using her barrier in a one-sided defensive war, but they paid their respects nonetheless.

"While we normally feud in such an unsightly way, at a time like this, let's fight together."

"Hildsleif Hedin Selrand..."

"I have sworn my loyalty to Lady Freya, but just for now, allow me to become your right hand."

White skin and long golden hair. A white elf adventurer like Riveria. He adjusted his glasses, speaking dispassionately. At first glance, he might be thought as dainty, but that would be a mistake. He was holding a twin-bladed rhomphaia taller than his height. It was a first-tier piece of equipment that increased magic power and a weapon that could cut through any enemy.

"We're before royalty. Say something, Hegni."

"............"

With dark skin and silver hair that almost looked lavender, he was wearing black clothes and a black mantle, wielding a sinister black longsword.

He was a dark elf, a rare sight in the current era where white elves were thriving. Despite his partner's nudge, he remained silent. His sharp eyes of a warrior flared, his irises twitching at a speed that only Hedin could understand. The white elf sighed in annoyance.

"You ceremonious prick..." he muttered.

"Dáinsleif Hegni Ragnar...The black and white knights."

The two were first-tier elf adventurers, one piece of *Freya Familia*'s strongest force. Riveria's eyes narrowed at the appearance of the pair who were known as the most *brutal* magic swordsmen.

"...Buy me some time. I'll finish things up with my magic."

""Understood.""

There was no need for unnecessary words. She left the front lines to the brave warriors who were the pride of their race, and the two knights responded in unison to the high elf's edict as they dashed off.

One was Concurrent Casting while the other slashed into the hideous pillar with a gust of wind.

A thunderclap went off, and a cosmic slash carved a path like a black shooting star.

Slipping through the altar's full bombardment, their magic canceled each other out, and the dark elf's slash burned through the tentacle.

For the second squad that hadn't been able to land a finishing blow without Aiz, this violent attack did the trick—and then some. The battle was almost one-sided as the two magic swordsmen caused the enemy to cry out in agony. They were just too strong.

Paying no heed to the shocked looks from *Loki Familia* and Ilta, the rest of the fairies from *Freya Familia* followed the high elf's instructions and started to fight.

Flowers of magic bloomed. They fired off barrages that did not pale in comparison to the spirit altar's counterattack. Ignoring the chain of explosions that illuminated their faces, the black and white knights proceeded to trample over the demi-spirit without waiting for Riveria's magic.

"I never would have imagined fighting shoulder to shoulder with our bitter enemies."

"We're quadruplets, which means all annoyances are quartered. Forgive and forget."

"And to see a filthy dwarf when we were done running? It's not just unforgiveable: It's unforgettable."

"At least it isn't that shameless hero who acts a symbol for all prums."

The same voice represented the opinions of four different people. The small warriors appeared before the third squad.

"If it isn't the only prums who are more impudent than Finn! Of course you'd be the ones to come here!" Gareth groaned at the four prum brothers who had led the reinforcements for his squad.

Sword, hammer, spear, and ax. Those four weapons were clearly oversize for their height, repelling the magic circle's light. Their childish bodies were covered in a sand-colored armor, and their faces were covered by matching full-face helms. The four of them almost looked like armored toy soldiers, but there was no one who dared look down on them.

Bringar. The Four Knights of the Golden Flame. They were prums like Finn and little monsters who had climbed all the way to the rank of first-tier adventurers. As heroic figures, the Gullivar brothers were rightly feared.

"As usual, there's no telling you apart. Maybe I should try seeing which of you feels the best to cuddle? And then I could compare to Finn to see who feels the best of all!"

"Don't touch me, half. Stay away."

"Oh, don't make me laugh. Who'd want to get hugged by you? You've been singed by the forge! I would never want to be sandwiched between your giant chest!"

"Hey! Don't come for Lady Freya like that! Beg her for forgiveness."

"Quit it! I don't want to spend even more time cleaning myself."

"Ha-ha-ha! Ha-ha-ha! Hey, Gareth! Can I slice up these little assholes?!" Tsubaki asked.

"Quit screwing around! This isn't the time or place for that crap!"

Even Tsubaki got offended, laughing out loud as the four prums insulted and expressed their utter distaste for her. Gareth shouted, reminding them it was still a battlefield as the spirit altar launched a barrage, seemingly in agreement with him.

The prums quickly evaded it along with Gareth and Tsubaki, and their four pairs of eyes stared down the enemy, chattering among one another.

"That, huh?"

"That's it."

"Pretty disgusting."

"So what do we do?"

""""Eliminate it, obviously.""""

"Then let's go."

Their little dialogue sounded almost like someone talking to themselves, expressing an uninterrupted stream of consciousness. Following the declaration of the eldest brother, Alfrik Gullivar, Dvalinn, Berling, and Grer moved forward. Realizing the purpose of the spirit flags, they quickly stole all the flags that Tsubaki and *Loki Familia* were holding and charged. In the blink of an eye, flames, lightning, blizzards, and flashes of light were raining down on them, but they were all nullified by the matching spirit flags.

Alfrik knocked away the flames, Dvalinn knocked down the lightning, Berling mowed down the blizzards, and Grer shifted the path of the rays of light. And repeat. An unending series of teamwork. Those four small frames nullified the tremendous storm of magic blasts by working as one. Their charge did not lose any speed, splitting the battlefield in half while basically laughing at *Loki Familia*, who'd faced major trouble trying to fend them off.

"————————————————————?!"

Three weapons were thrown at their respective targets. The sword, spear, and ax pierced the spirit altar's giant face, causing it to let out an earsplitting scream as a full swing of the hammer slammed into the bridge of its nose.

That was the end. That attack shattered the nose and smashed the entire face, along with the magic stone, effectively silencing the spirit altar. That was the result of the greatest teamwork in all Orario.

"You're kidding…They already managed to shut it up…" said Sharon, a second-tier adventurer from *Loki Familia*.

"It pains me to say it, but…they're really strong," Tsubaki admitted.

"There's no use trying to measure their strength. When you put all four of them together, their teamwork is multiplicative—not additive," Gareth responded, readjusting his helmet.

Even though Gareth's squad had already taken out two of the faces on the spirit altar, the prums were the real deal. It was not an exaggeration to say they could beat any first-tier adventurer if the four of them fought together.

"All that's left is the main body! Show your backbones!" Gareth roared.

In response, the adventurers in the vanguard strained their voices and moved to attack the demi-spirit's main body with *Freya Familia*'s reinforcements.

"Shall I lend a hand, Tiona?"

The spirit's attack was pushing the fourth squad to the brink of destruction. And amid that, a group of powerful Amazons saved the adventurers.

"Bache?!"

When the Amazon appeared, Tiona doubted her eyes. The strong-looking figure standing before her resembled someone in her memories. Bache Kalif had been her teacher and mentor, training her when she was still young and weak.

"What is this?! Weak! You've gotten weak!"

"Argana...!"

Tione had the same reaction.

Telskyura's strongest warrior clamped on to the enemy's tentacle with both hands like the fangs of a snake, tearing it off. Tione held her wounded arm and looked in shock at Argana Kalif, with whom she'd had a death battle in Meren.

"You...It can't be...Did you all come to help us...?"

They were reinforcements who even Finn had not anticipated. *Kali Familia* had joined the fray at Hermes's request. They roared as if praising the hot-blooded battle that Tione's squad was locked in.

A helping hand had come to the rescue from her hated homeland, channeling the warriors' reliable battle cries. Right now, Tione could not figure out the feeling welling up in her chest, at a loss for words.

"—What about Finn?! Tione! Where is Finn?!"

"—What?!"

She was taken aback by Argana, whose cheeks were flushed and whose face had become markedly more feminine.

"The strong man who defeated me! I was asking the location of my husband—the one who conquered me!"

And on hearing her say it again, the temperature of the air around Tione dropped to absolute zero. Amazons fell in love with powerful males. Argana had lost to Finn once, and she was no exception to that. She forgot all about being a brutal warrior, totally in heat.

"The captain isn't yours! *He's mine!*"

"You've got it all wrong, Tione! Finn is my male!"

Tione roared with rage, forgetting the situation. Argana was obviously passionate, which could be felt even through her stilted Koine.

As the two girls butted heads, the spirit altar fired off another blast, without any care for their coarse argument. The two of them leaped away from the blast like feral beasts. To the spirit's misfortune, their dangerous glares redirected toward it.

"How about this? Whoever defeats that thing can be Finn's woman! The victor can have Finn to herself!"

"Bring it on! I'll be the one to claim the captain's fidelity!"

Argana's face transformed into that of the strongest warrior, and Tione swelled with determination, totally forgetting about her wounds. They looked exactly like teacher and student as they stood shoulder to shoulder before charging at the demi-spirit. As if in sync, the rest of the warriors of Telskyura unleashed a full-out attack.

Even the spirit was overwhelmed by the otherworldly intensity. In another location, a certain prum hero felt a mysterious chill.

"Since when did the holy ground of Amazons turn into the cradle of perverts...?" grumbled Olba, an exhausted Level-3 animal person from *Loki Familia*.

"With their squabble, the enemy has shifted its focus away from the healers...! Now we can regroup!" Amid said as Olba provided a shoulder for her to lean on, her robes scorched. She carried out her recovery magic to heal herself.

"...Whoa, they're putting the pressure on the spirit!"

"Argana has changed…to a scary degree…"

As their older sisters composed a serenade of blows that overpowered the enemy, their little sisters had a distant look.

However, that was just a brief moment. Bache faced Tiona as if collecting herself.

"I lost to you once. I'll sacrifice my life…the one I should have lost that day…for you." There were traces of a smile hidden behind the veil covering her face. "I've come to help, Tiona."

At those words, Tiona broke into a sunny grin.

"Thank you, Bache!"

"…To think you'd be the one to come here," Finn said as his eyes narrowed.

"Put a sock in it, shrimp. I just came to the place that was left. That's all."

A single cat person appeared at the first squad. The swift adventurer coolly berated Finn. He had not brought any other familia members. Well, he had just been so fast that he had left them behind.

He wore black battle clothes with shoulder armor on just his left shoulder. There was a flowing mantle attached to that shoulder. In his hands was a long silver spear. The first-tier adventurer with the second name of Vana Freya, *Freya Familia*'s second-in-command.

Allen Fromel tossed down the map of Knossos that *Ganesha Familia* had provided and glanced at Finn.

"More importantly, what's with this predicament?"

"What? The enemy's attacks were more powerful than anticipated. Our squad has taken casualties."

"You piss me off. To think she would praise you when you look so damn unsightly."

He spat venom. It was a bit too callous to be called jealousy, disappointed in the state of Finn's squad that was beaten-up and battered. But it was also a window, a glimpse into his respect for his goddess.

While he did not deign to hide his annoyance, he muttered to Finn as they passed each other.

"I'll finish that ugly piece of shit. You've got a mountain of other shit to deal with, so get to it, asshole."

"…Yeah, I think I will."

Allen did not give Finn a second look as he glared forward. There were countless magic circles forming in the air. Even now, the demi-spirit still continued its chant. The spirit body on the upper part of the pillar looked pleased as it lorded over Allen and the rest of the adventurers.

"Just singing that grating shit." The ears at the top of Allen's head twitched. And then the light of the magic circles' barrage went off.

"—Just die."

A tremendous boom rang out. It was the sound of him kicking off the ground. The green flesh covering the floor blew away like gravel. He dashed at high speed, taking a wide angle toward the pillar. Only Finn and Shakti were able to keep track of him as he closed in on the spirit's face.

"*Glegh—*" burbled the flesh as it was pierced, instead of the chant.

The movements were instantaneous. None of the adventurers would have objected if this was described as teleportation.

Allen dashed—leaping, maneuvering through the air, leaving the oncoming magic behind, slipping through the gap between magic circles, and *jabbing his spear into the spirit's mouth.*

"Quit regaling us with that awful singing voice, you ugly thing."

"*Ah…Gah…?*"

"Don't contaminate Milady's garden."

Slamming the bottom of his boots against the spirit's face, he spun the silver spear that was piercing its mouth. A mix of confusion, shock, and uncertainty went through the spirit altar. Its stagnant golden eyes cried tears of blood.

"He broke the incantation?!"

He had closed the distance between them in just an instant. It was an amazing acceleration that sent shudders down the spine of Shakti and the other adventurers. That was Allen Fromel, Level 6, the first-tier adventurer. Not surprisingly, Allen and Bete got along like cats and dogs, and he had another title, Vana Freya—the city's fastest. There was no comparison. He had the fastest legs of any adventurer.

Ignoring the spirit altar altogether, Allen had cut off the chant faster than any squad or any adventurer. He spat on the unsightly spirit from his position atop it.

"—Aaaaaaaaaaaaaaaaaaaaaaaaaaaaaaaah?!"

A tentacle whipped out from the female body, but Allen quickly dodged it. However, he did not retreat. He used the wall and pillar and even the enemy's tentacles to intricately ricochet himself, performing a sonic-speed hit-and-run. The spirit let out a screech that raised their hairs as it was dissected, shredded to pieces in the blink of an eye.

"Leave the spirit's main body to him! We'll take out the pillar!"

Finn ordered, getting the rest of the adventurers to attack. He did not want to lose to the cat person. The battle had reached a tipping point.

"It's…Warlord…"

The undisputedly strongest person in the city arrived at the chamber housing the spirit. As a fellow animal person, Anakity felt awe more than relief or joy. The boaz warrior wielding his giant black sword had *come alone.*

"Out of the way, Alsha. Wounded animals serve no use."

Anakity had no time to be honored that the city's strongest fighter knew her second name as she cleared the path for him.

Since they had lost half their squad to Ein's trap, Anakity and the rest of the fifth squad had not been able to deal much damage to the spirit altar. The pillar's lower part still had all three of its faces intact. On top of that, there should have been counter magic in the passage leading to the chamber. And yet, the boaz warrior had made it there untouched.

His giant body—made of pure muscle—passed in front of her eyes like a massive boulder as he stood across from the spirit.

"…Mm?"

For the first time, the spirit reacted to something. It still continued to sing its song, but even through all the collective efforts of the fifth squad, it had only smiled its sadistic smirk.

Its body stirred in a way that even it could not comprehend, recognizing that man could not be trifled with, even though he was far away. To an onlooker, it seemed like a giant being overwhelmed by a child.

A crimson magic circle formed in a flash. Feeling the fluctuating emotions of the main body, the spirit altar prepared an extra-powerful blast. It unleashed a ball of flames charged by a colossal amount of magic power.

Ottar gripped his black sword in both hands and split that ball in half.

"_____"

Anakity, and the other adventurers, and even the spirit froze. The blast exploded behind the warrior as if it had finally remembered its original purpose, forming a tremendous sea of fire. The city's strongest adventurer advanced with a wall of sparks at his back, and the demi-spirit showed a hint of fear.

"Begone with you at once. This is the garden where the goddess resides. Any who dare disturb it will not be forgiven."

The assault began. Neither tentacles nor magic could stop the man who sauntered closer. After he spoke, he accelerated, rapidly approaching the base of the pillar with a speed unbefitting his hulking body, swinging his black sword vigorously.

That was all it took for the spirit pillar to tilt.

"_____*Ghhhh?!*"

Though it did not manage to sever it at its base, he had *cut halfway* into the giant pillar.

As the spirit cried out, it prioritized its regeneration, but it was not able to recover its leaning posture.

With the enemy's head at a lower position, the dauntlessly valiant warrior did not speak a word as he mercilessly destroyed it.

"...Captain, Warlord has started fighting by himself...He's already overpowering it," Anakity whispered with a trembling voice into her oculus.

"*Of course he is. He's Ottar.*"

There was a playfully annoying tone to the voice that responded immediately. The prum hero's joking voice rang out from inside the crystal. Despite being enemies, he trusted Ottar completely.

"*Ghhh...*We're going, too! We're *Loki Familia*! We're no cowards!"

"*Raaaaaaaaaaah!*"

Even covered in wounds from head to foot, Anakity raised her sword with a powerful battle cry. The rest of the familia there rose to their feet and followed her. Ottar gazed at the proud cat person, but he did not question her, allowing her to join the fight.

The smile had been completely wiped off the demi-spirit's face.

As the reinforcements arrived at each front, they were able to regroup. The tides were turning in Knossos.

"Fels! Are there any reinforcements for us?!" Lido shouted into the crystal in his hand.

As *Freya Familia* and the other reinforcements reached the squads to save them, there had not been any backup for the Xenos. They had somehow managed to take out two of the faces of the spirit altar, but it was still casting magic in the chamber as it pleased. Even the hardy scales and fur of the Xenos were getting battered. It was just a matter of time before they gave out.

"*You don't need anything from us.*"

"What?!" Lido went wide-eyed when he heard this cold response from Fels.

"What do you mean by that, Fels?!"

"*I mean what I said. You don't need anything from us.*"

There was a hint of anger in the voice of the lizardman warrior, but Fels's tone was still unchanged.

There were not many adventurers who would come to help the Xenos, knowing who they were. Even if reinforcements had come, they would not protect the Xenos, leading to both groups getting attacked by the spirit. But Fels's voice came across as far too aloof.

Lido started to suspect it might be because they had run out of reinforcements.

Lido was about to unleash all the human swears he had at his disposal.

Thud! Thud!

Something brushed up against Lido's eardrums.

"What?"

"...Are those...?"

"...Footsteps...?"

Something very heavy was sending tremors through the ground as it approached. As Lido and the rest of the Xenos looked around to locate it, suspicion appeared on the demi-spirit's face.

"—Seems I made it in time."

"Gros?! Where were you?!"

Gros the gargoyle appeared, flapping his stone wings. His beastly face looked annoyed.

"You know, I got stuck running errands for Fels. I was the welcoming party."

"Welcoming party...?"

Before Lido could ask for whom, the answer appeared with a loud thump.

A giant body stepped into the chamber—one made up entirely of chiseled muscle. It could have been a huge hunk of steel. It was wearing an adventurer's full-plate armor. Due to its muscular build, it looked like it was only light armor. In its hands was an enormous Labrys that was stained bright red from the blood of slaughtered prey.

Masculine horns and jet-black fur. A human body and a bull's head. His chest swelled as he unleashed a roaring battle cry.

"Graaaaaaaaaaaaaaaaaaaaaaaaaaaaaaaaaaaaaah!"

The howl caused even his comrades to shrink back as it pealed around the chamber. Ignoring Wiene and the others as they covered their ears, he looked at the demi-spirit, wondering what the hell it was.

"See? I told you, you don't need any reinforcements from us."

As Lido was overcome with surprise, a voice rang out from the oculus in his hand. The mage's shameless voice reached his ears.

"Because the strongest Irregular *made it in time."*

The howl ceased to end. The labyrinth did not stop quaking. With the rest of the Xenos, Lido was frozen in place as that monster's name crossed his lips.

"A-Asterios..."

Just one month prior, the strongest Xenos had cast untold masses of adventurers into the depths of fear—as the black minotaur. He had appeared to reinforce Lido's group.

"After going to rescue that brat in the deep levels, Aruru and Helga tracked down Asterios's location on secret orders from Fels."

"Kkkr!"

"Woof! Woof!"

The al-miraj next to Gros raised her short, soft arm, and the hell-hound barked with pride. Among the group of Xenos who had gone to the thirty-seventh floor for a certain mission, they had continued down even deeper to search for Asterios. Relying on information from a guardian who had come to the Xenos's hidden village to rest once, they had finally found him, and Gros had gone to meet him and persuade him to join the battle.

"There's no sense in letting his strength go to waste. Or, rather, if I had, who knows what Braver would do to me instead," Fels explained from inside the crystal with a wispy sigh.

Lido and the rest had still not broken free from their stiffness when Asterios stopped howling and slowly looked forward, fixing his gaze on the spirit pillar standing at the back of the chamber.

And then his mouth cracked into what seemed to be a smile. He hung his Labrys on his back and planted his fists on the ground, lowering his center of gravity and his head. Before Lido had time to wonder if he was really going to do that, Asterios started running.

"OOOOOOOOOH!"

It was a black charge that did not wait for any signal to begin.

As the Xenos and even the spirit looked on in shock, he sprinted straight at the spirit altar.

"Hey, wait, Asterios!"

But Lido's warning fell on deaf ears as his giant body accelerated like a cannonball. The demi-spirit's eyes widened, unable to believe what was happening. The counter magic flared, and a barrage of spells rained down from all around.

Shots hounded him from every angle: a blast of flame, ice, lightning, earth, light, and dark magics. They tore through the minotaur's fur, burning muscles, freezing flesh, drawing blood from his stout body. But he *did not stop.*

"?!"

His speed did not drop in the slightest, and the volley could not budge him from his trajectory as he kept charging forward. The demi-spirit's main body stopped chanting its ritual, feeling a chill at the sight of the minotaur bulldozing across the ground like a meteor, and it switched to its own high-speed cast.

A magic circle appeared and unleashed a thunder ray. This flash of lightning could erase everything into the distance, but Asterios managed to break through it.

"_____"

The immeasurable monster shredded the flood of lightning as he charged through, freezing time for the demi-spirit that should have been just as immeasurable.

His unbreakable horns were readied. The unmatched strongest charge slammed into the spirit pillar.

"OOOOOOOOOOOOOOOOOOOOOOOOOOOOOOOOOOOOOOOH!"

There was an explosion that sounded like the world splitting in two. The Xenos were all taken aback. A shock wave rocked the entire chamber and the last remaining face on the spirit altar literally exploded into dust. The spirit pillar whose base had been completely pulverized shook violently as it tilted forward.

"*Aaaaaaaaaaaaaaaaaaaaaaaaaaaaaaaaaaaaaaaaaah?!*"

The pillar crashed to the ground, accompanied by the spirit's pained cry. As the second earthquake caused by that shock knocked Wiene and several others into the air, Asterios's fellow Xenos's faces looked pale.

"He broke it…with a damn tackle…"

It had been a charge without any thought for the damage he had taken himself. A brute-force rush forward without any need for tactics or strategy. The embodiment of power that even Finn had feared had used all his strength and shattered the pillar.

As if copying his teacher from a previous life, Asterios resolutely tore down the spirit pillar.

"*Hraaaaah.*"

"*Aaaaaack?!*"

The green flesh along the floor was shredded, causing smoke to rise in the center of the chamber. As the monster approached, the spirit trembled like a butterfly whose wings had been plucked. The bloody black body had taken serious damage, but his intense hostility had not disappeared from his eyes.

Asterios had been begged to return from his solo training journey in the deep levels, equipping his Labrys again. Determined to make up for the lost training, he began rampaging like a natural disaster in search of a grand battle that would make his heart beat faster.

"…Hey, Fels! Bellucchi and his familia are coming here, too, right?"

"…*Yes, according to the report I received,*" replied the raspy voice from the crystal.

After a moment's silence, the lizardman whispered.

"…We should probably not tell him that Bellucchi is here…" Lido concluded as he watched the minotaur rampage from afar, accompanied by a series of unbelievably loud booms.

Battle cries began to overlap. Thousands of sword slashes and magic blasts transformed into violent tremors. Even at a great distance, the adventurers' roars in the battlefield were audible.

"Aren't we really out of place here...?!" said Lilliluka Erde, the prum girl, putting her true feelings into words.

She was moving through the passage of Knossos with the rest of *Hestia Familia*. Even though they hadn't reached the battlefield yet, she was already getting cold feet.

On a certain expedition, they had just experienced the highs of a new adventure. But the signs of a deadly battle were so thick that this exhilaration was immediately dashed. She recognized this was a battlefield beyond human understanding, a battlefield for the chosen ones with the qualifications to be heroes.

"Quit blabbing and give us our orders, Commander!"

"Please grant us guidance, Commander."

"What should we do, Commander?"

"Uh, ummm, do your best, Commander Lilly?"

"Oh, 'Commander this' and 'Commander that'! You only call me that when it's convenient for you! And, Bell! Don't force yourself to say something! You're bad at it!" She blew up in a fit of rage at her comrades, who were pulling her foot.

Asfi could not help giving some advice.

"First of all, let's link up with one of the squads. There's no point in moving around aimlessly."

It was a reasonable suggestion, but...for some reason, Lilly could not really picture it happening. All the strongest factions from *Loki Familia* on down had gathered in Knossos. She was still dubious even now, wondering what they could accomplish in there. Of course, she was super interested in a battle with the fate of the city on the line. But even for her, it was hard to imagine what more could be done. In fact, it would be hard for most any normal person to figure out what the best steps were in that situation.

"Lilliluka Erde!"

"—Fels!"

At that moment, the mage in the black robe ran to them from the other end of the passage.

"When I first heard it, I thought I was imagining things...but *Hestia Familia* has really come."

"If Orario's going to be blown away without a good fight, we don't have much of a choice! It doesn't matter if it's a good idea for us to come or not! More importantly, what's the situation?! What's happening?!" Lilly snapped back.

Slightly taken aback by her menacing glare, Fels responded quickly.

"Thanks to the wave of reinforcements, we finally have the upper hand. But a single mistake and the situation could go south in an instant."

"What...? But this is all Finn. Isn't he the one in command of this operation?"

Lilly was shaken by Fels's tense mood and the implied warning that their victory was not a foregone conclusion.

Lilliluka Erde had been viewing things optimistically. She had assumed that because the hero of the prums was in command, his forces would be in an advantageous position from start to finish.

"Braver is currently in control of all the battlefields with the demi-spirits—the targets. Six battlefields, six fronts. While he fights on his own front. Even he doesn't have any room to breathe in this situation."

"*Six fronts?!*"

He was dealing with six different battlefields. That caused Lilly's face to twitch. Directing troops across five battlefields spread around the labyrinth *while* physically fighting on his own battlefield? Was there no limit to the absurdities he could pull off?

Lilly had recently taken the position of commander herself. Obviously, she knew this feat was crazy talk. She almost doubted her own ears, barely believing this stunt was even possible, trembling with fear just imagining it. But at the same time, she finally understood that this situation was precarious: The alliance must have had its back against the wall if Finn had been forced into taking this absurd position.

"*Fels! The enemy's attack has intensified at the second and third squads! Can you move now?!*"

One of Fels's crystals lit up with an intense message. Lilly jolted. It was Finn.

"*I don't want to move the reserves! Now that the labyrinth's counter magic has been silenced, I want Raul's forces to focus on saving the hostages and clearing up the remaining concerns there! It can be from the wave of reinforcements! I don't care who—!"*

As Finn's powerful voice rang out from the crystal, they could hear a *hair-raising* battle thundering in the background—an otherworldly explosion and what sounded like the screams of adventurers. On top of that, the booming voice of what could only feasibly be an impossibly large monster. The sounds in the background caused *Hestia Familia* and even Asfi to gasp.

Lilly started turning pale and tried to back away by herself, but—

"Mr. Finn! Is there anything we can do?!"

A single boy courageously stepped up.

"That voice...Is that you, Bell Cranell? Why are you—? No, am I right to assume this is Hermes's doing?"

Lilly's face twitched. She'd had no time to stop him. His rubellite eyes were burning.

That was right. Bell Cranell was that kind of boy. He was not the sort of person to stay quiet when the city was in danger. He was not the type of adventurer who would run away.

If anyone, even a complete unknown stranger, was asking for help, he would step in to the fray to save them. It did not matter who. The boy had always yearned to be a hero, and he had become one of the people running headlong down the path to becoming one.

Even if he had not realized it himself yet, after he had made it through the Xenos incident, Bell had become the newest adventurer at the bottom of that list of chosen people Lilly had imagined earlier.

This is bad! This is really bad!

Finn had definitely seen through Bell's nature. With Bell at his disposal, the boy would surely be worked to the bone. Lilly's crush was going to be thrown into the danger zone with all the other first-tier adventurers! That would be bad! She didn't want that! But there would be no stopping Bell! Damn it!

Her thoughts ran wild like a tsunami. Her chestnut pupils

narrowed and darted chaotically as she glanced around. In her head, the doomsday meteor had basically slammed into a swarm of Lillys running in terror while a fiery inferno of flames raged.

Before Finn could say anything, the strategic girl was cornered into a decision and immediately opened her mouth.

"—Give me *two fronts*!"

Lilly chose an unbelievable move. While Bell, Fels, Asfi, the rest of *Hestia Familia*, and even Finn were shocked, she requested a transfer of command.

"I'll take command of them *in your stead*! Let me shoulder some of your burden!"

It was absurd. Entirely impossible. Even as she was saying it, Lilly could not help those thoughts welling up in her mind. Even if it was to protect Bell, a supporter commanding a battlefield filled with first-tier adventurers? It was hysterical. She was laughing at herself. To think she could somehow take on some of the burden for Braver of all people. How misguided could she be? If the adventurers had been there, there would have been no end to the shouts telling her to know her place. Those thoughts were also crossing her mind. She understood the absurdity of her request better than anyone. What she had said was a delusion.

But…!

Could she really deny there wasn't a small part of her that was frustrated when she had heard he was handling six different battlefields? Did the sparks flaring in her heart not exist? Did she really have no reason to say it other than to cover for Bell?

Her worry for Bell and a small sense of pride, combined with the impending doom for the city, transformed into duty to help the heroes and exploded. It was very unlike her.

She was still new to it, but Lilly had stood in the same commander's position as Finn, and she did not want him to take her Bell—or for Bell to go off without her.

"You're…Is that Lilliluka Erde?"

"I've learned from you, and I've been training as a commander! Let me take one or two squads! I can imitate you if that's all!"

There was no going back now. She could not take back what had been said anymore, so Lilly cast aside the regret, moved her face closer to the oculus as if to bite deep into Braver on the other end, and let the big talk flow. As a storm of uncontrollable emotions overtook her, she pushed forward impulsively, adding even more false bravado to what could already be called "irresponsible boasting."

"But just two fronts, okay?! And the simpler ones! I definitely can't do more than that!"

"Do you want to help or don't you, Li'l E?!"

Lilliluka Erde had to be desperate if it had gotten bad enough that Welf was talking sense into her. In truth, she was asking for too much responsibility. As basically secondary commanders, Fels and Asfi were about to put a stop to her recklessness.

"All right, I'll trust you."

A voice came back through the oculus with a prompt decision. Before Lilly even had time to voice her surprise, Finn was handing down his decision.

"I'll give you some squads! Take command of two fronts in my stead!" boldly proclaimed the voice, startling Asfi and the rest. Even Lilly was frozen as Fels's flustered voice flared.

"Wait, Braver! Do you understand the situation right now?! Lilliluka Erde's quick wit is certainly valuable, but in this situation…!"

"Tell me, Fels, could you say what she said?! Or you, Perseus?! Could you actually tell me to give you command in this situation?!"

Fels and Asfi were hard-pressed to respond. Finn continued, exhilaration audible in his voice.

"My fellow prum has demonstrated her bravery! There's no reason not to welcome her support!"

For a second, they could almost see a smile on Braver's lips in the light shining within the oculus. Was it a smile of delight or exaltation?

"I'll leave you command of the second and third squads! Riveria and Gareth will be able to smooth over a few rough spots for you!

Don't be scared to command them as you see fit! And don't you dare mistake cowardice for discretion!"

Of course, Finn would not go along with Lilly's suggestion in the heat of the moment without any plan at all. He knew her abilities well from what she had shown during the skirmish on Daedalus Street. From observing her movements on the board when they had been enemies, he had judged that she was sufficient to be trusted.

Finn Deimne trusted Lilliluka Erde.

"I wish you a luck greater than anyone's! Brave prum, take my breath away!"

A chill ran up Lilly's spine. For some reason, she had goose bumps. She felt the trust of the hero who boldly inspired all the armies, and her heart started racing.

——*There's no backing out now!*

——*I can't get away!*

——*Now I'll have to actually direct adventurers far stronger than I am!*

A pandemonium of cries rang out in her head. Her back started to bend as her head tried to tell her it was impossible, but amid the crushing pressure, a different feeling took root in her heart. A desire to meet Finn's expectations. He was not the one she loved, but as a member of the prum race, she wanted to live up to his trust in her.

"—Please tell me the makeup of the second and third squads!"

"Eh, ah, okay!"

"Tell me everything we know about the enemy, too! Starting with its means of attack! As precise as possible!"

Immediately after, Lilly had transformed, ordering them in a strong tone that caused Asfi to follow her lead reflexively. The image of her even caused Fels to break out of his frozen state, drop what he was doing, and help her. In addition to his map that covered all of Knossos, he provided oculi connected to both squads.

The rest of *Hestia Familia* glanced at one another and smiled. They knew that once she had made up her mind, Lilliluka Erde was strong.

"Your scars are mine. My scars are mine."

As Lilly was hammering all the information about the sprawling battlefield into her head, she chanted. Closing her eyes and singing her spell, her voice and body transformed.

"What...? Finn Deimne?!"

Asfi was amazed to see the prum hero appear before her eyes. Using transformation magic, Lilly had copied everything about Finn. Opening her eyes, she responded to the confused gazes.

"If those fighting realized that command had shifted from Finn to me, it would just cause confusion. No one there knows who I am—obviously, they wouldn't listen to me."

"!"

"So I'll transform into Finn and take over command with none the wiser."

Fels and Asfi were taken aback by her explanation.

The number of people with oculi was limited, but it was possible for people nearby to hear the voice coming from the crystal. All the more when she would have to shout over the explosions and yelling crisscrossing around the battlefield on the other end. Because of that, she had become Finn.

At the same time, Fels and Asfi realized that the reason Finn had been able to yield command to her was because he knew of her transformation magic.

Lilliluka Erde was the only one who could take Finn Deimne's place.

"Haruhime, cast Level Boost. Use Concatenated Casting, please."

"Y-yes!"

"Bell, prepare for hit-and-run assaults. Welf and Mikoto, ready equipment for facing a super-large-class monster. Once Haruhime's magic is finished, *I'll be using the three of you out there—separately.*"

"Got it, Lilly!"

"All right!"

"Leave it to me!"

A switch flipped in Lilly when she completed her transformation. There was a tremor of tension in their movements as Haruhime and the others obeyed the instructions delivered with a different voice and gaze.

"Wait, Lilliluka Erde! You aren't going to move them as a familia but individually? Bell Cranell aside—he's Level Four, after all—Ignis and Eternal Shadow are…!"

"Other than Bell, everyone in *Hestia Familia* is extremely unbalanced. In localized…No, perhaps it would be better to say that they will absolutely hit specific openings that will be very effective.

"Of course, I'll see to it that they get sufficient back-line support, too," she added as she responded to Asfi's concerns. Her voice was the same as Finn's, but the tone was totally different, flustering Asfi. At the same time, her resolute stance was reminiscent of the real Braver.

Taking the oculi that had been provided to her, she daringly transformed one corner of the passage into a temporary command post as she looked down at the map spread out on the floor.

"Counting the skirmishes on Daedalus Street, this is the second time that we're using oculi to command forces, huh…?" she murmured as she held the crystal magic item in her right hand. She had experienced it once before during that mission. *Bring it,* Lilly thought as she licked her lips.

"I'll show you I can do it…!"

The time had come for her to repay the debt she owed the hero of the prums—the one from when she'd been had during that incident with the Xenos.

"I'm sending reinforcements for the second and third squads now! Continue the front line's attack while gathering forces in the mid lines!"

Two people felt something out of place when they heard Finn's voice calling from the oculus.

Finn?

His direction has changed.

Riveria and Gareth. The two had known Finn longest. They immediately realized that this was a fake. But it was not just that—they realized that whoever was behind it was a commander without much experience who had a skilled ability to envision the battlefield, even if it was no match for the real Finn's skill.

"What's that, Finn? Changing course now? Got more wily tricks up your sleeve, huh?"

The third squad.

Gareth grinned into the crystal as he endured the enemy's barrage, playing up the act.

"*...Yeah, Gareth. I'm sure you're used to it by now! Since it's a wily trick by none other than Finn Deimne!*"

The person at the other end was clever. They had recognized the implicit question in his response and conveyed that everything was happening according to Finn's plan—all while keeping the rest of the squad from noticing to avoid any confusion. In that case, Gareth would not say anything, either. He decided to work with the fake Finn, since that was what the real Finn wanted.

"Listen, Finn! Right now, *Freya Familia* is attacking something fierce, but we're missing a decisive finisher! And those guys are just moving around willy-nilly, so there isn't any real coordination!"

For the fake Finn's sake, Gareth summed up the battle conditions. They had shifted toward a siege of the actual target. With the spirit altar silenced, the demi-spirit had temporarily paused its chant, halting the ritual while it finally joined the battle in its own right.

"*Flash, rays of light. Tear through the darkness. Your envoy beseeches thee, Lux. Incarnate of light. Queen of luminosity—*"

It could fire only a single spell at once, but its blasts were utterly menacing. The magic that the demi-spirit's main body used was incomparable in power to the spirit altar. After successfully recycling part of the defense mechanism's ability, there was no end to the magic circles fixed in the air next to it, firing off rays of light, a torrent of destruction that reshaped the field of battle with each blow.

Because of that, the battlefield was in an appalling state, even after receiving backup from *Freya Familia*. Because they made no effort to coordinate, it might be better to call their addition "harmful." Either way, they were attacking all out. And because of that, Gareth had been forced to the back lines to work as a defensive tank. They had achieved a position of superiority, but that had distorted their fighting style.

"I'd like to join the front, too, but I can't move until we can do something about the enemy's blasts!"

The demi-spirit had an impregnable defense in addition to its extraordinary firepower. It was making use of its strong petal armor that had caused *Loki Familia* heartache during the fight on the fifty-ninth floor. It was intercepting all attacks from weapons, magic, and everything in between and beyond. Even the Bringar were left frustrated.

They just could not manage to break through the enemy's defense.

"*—Perfect timing. Gareth, you and Cyclops should prepare to move up to the front lines.*"

"What?"

"*Reinforcements are coming your way. Use them as a shield!*"

The voice in the crystal had the ring of a commander who was able to see the board's movement clearly, precisely perceiving what was happening. Before Gareth had time to ask what the voice was talking about, the aforementioned reinforcement appeared.

"*—Descend from the heavens, seize the earth—!*"

A Far-East human girl dashed into the chamber while Concurrent Casting, cowering at the rays of light.

"*Shinbu Tousei!*"

"*Stop the mages' fire! Let Eternal Shadow go first!*" yelled the crystal, reaching the other members of the squad and the single reinforcement. With a Level Boost spell, Mikoto Yamato was now Level 3, unleashing her magic as ordered.

"*Futsu no Mitama!*"

At the same time, the enemy's cannon exploded.

"*Light Burst.*"

The adventurers' faces were illuminated by the onrushing blast of light. However, a gravity barrier appeared in the spirit's magic's path, intercepting it.

"?!"

The barrier's sudden appearance surprised the adventurers and the demi-spirit. It was not clear whether the blast had actually hit the barrier, but the spirit's wave of light crashed into the ground and exploded before reaching the adventurers.

The gravitational force is so powerful, it can even bend light. With Mikoto's Status, nullifying the spirit's magic was impossible, but she could just use the unique property of gravity to change the spell's path, causing it to explode harmlessly into the ground. Right now, there was a gravitational field between the demi-spirit and the adventurers, a giant shield.

With the spirit altar gone, the enemy could no longer unleash attacks from all angles inside the chamber. The mouth of the enemy's cannon was fixed in place. Because of that, it was near impossible for it to override the barrier that Mikoto had erected and actually target the adventurers. If the barrage could come from only the front, her *Futsu no Mitama* could stop all its spells in their tracks.

"I'm still inadequate, but...this is the battlefield's watershed. I shall become a shield to protect everyone from the enemy's light!"

Mikoto was sweating as she maintained the powerful gravitational field, boasting in front of adventurers stronger than she was. Gareth grinned as she displayed a spirit to fill the role of a tank, not even losing to a gallant dwarf.

"Eternal Shadow! Can you hold out ten—no, five minutes?!"

"I'll definitely do it!"

"Nice response! Let's go, Tsubaki!"

"Aye!"

Freed from their defensive position by Mikoto, Gareth and the others collectively threw down their shields and equipped their big weapons. Their target was the enemy's main body, where *Freya Familia* was even now attacking at close range.

"*Back lines, shift behind the gravitational barrier! Frontline fighters, leave all the protection to Eternal Shadow and move up!*"

Understanding the commander's goal, the adventurers obeyed with perfect coordination. The vanguard raced off, and each party scattered. And the commander's voice did not stop there.

"*The enemy will lose its temper eventually and switch to a long-cast wide-range destruction spell. Aim for that!*"

"I don't need you to tell me that!" Gareth roared back at Lilly, whose read of the situation resembled Finn's. It was almost annoying. Gareth led the forces across the battlefield.

"The dirty dwarf is coming."

"But it's good timing."

"Let's use it."

"He can open a hole in the enemy's defense."

As Gareth's group pushed up from behind, the Bringar's hive mind activated.

They would use the dwarf's destructive power to blow open the petal armor. The prum quadruplets saw Gareth and his forces as a battering ram to break through the enemy's defenses.

With Mikoto's gravitational barrier, Lilly's command had taken control of the entire battlefield. The third squad took the support from *Hestia Familia* and used it to obliterate the enemy's armor.

"It's way bigger than I was expecting…!"

A single reinforcement appeared at the second squad. Welf Crozzo hid his shudder behind a smile as he laid eyes on a monster bigger than any he had ever seen before. The demi-spirit was more imposing than he had expected.

"*Riveria, protect him! Don't let him get hurt!*"

"…Understood, Finn. But if he's our backup…"

Riveria acknowledged the instructions from the fake Finn, but she did not hide her doubt.

"Ignis from *Hestia Familia*? What's the meaning of this?"

Freya Familia, including Hedin, and even *Loki Familia* all shared their doubts. They knew the firepower of Crozzo's Magic Swords, but the speed with which they hit their usage limits meant that they would be of almost no use in a prolonged battle with a superlarge monster.

"Tsubaki is fighting, and all those guys from way back are in combat, too…So I've gotta do my best, or I won't be able to face Lady Hephaistos!"

With his great sword and magic swords on his back, Welf did not run or hide as their dubious looks zeroed in on him. Thinking of the Goddess of the Forge with crimson eyes and hair, he ran forward empty-handed.

"*Riveria, protect Ignis!*"

"…*Ilta! Take care of him!*"

Riveria called out, conveying "Finn's" instructions. The Amazon and others from *Ganesha Familia* took up formation around him as he moved. Welf made no effort to dodge or defend against the rain of attacks from the enemy's tentacles as the stout first-tier adventurers used their weapons to deflect them and change their course. Welf looked like he might be knocked back by the force of the jarring clashes in front of him, but he just squinted and pushed forward. It was a do-or-die approach to get into range to fire. Welf perfectly understood his role without Lilly telling him. His ability would be most effective against an enormous monster chanting magic.

"*Pierce, spear of lightning. Your envoy beseeches thee, Tonitrus. Incarnate of thunder! Queen of lightning——*"

And the moment swiftly came. The demi-spirit was casting at a high speed. Combined with the short-spell cast, the adventurers would not be able to immediately defend against it. *Loki Familia* and *Freya Familia* prepared for the enemy's blast in frustration, but Welf continued moving forward by himself.

"*Blasphemous burn.*"

The blacksmith had been waiting for that once-in-a-lifetime opportunity, and his super-short cast was faster than the spirit's high-speed casting.

"*Will-o-Wisp!*"

Starting at Welf's hand, a heat haze seemed to shimmer in the air. The moment it touched the enemy's magic circle, an enormous explosion went off.

"*Graaaaaaaaaaaaaaaah?!*"

"What?!"

He had caused an explosion while the monster was trying to fire its magic and stopped the blast from going off. An Ignis Fatuus. And it did not stop with just that. All the magic circles around the demi-spirit went off in a chain of explosions.

Above the adventurers' heads, a deafening series of fiery explosions bloomed in the air.

"Th-the demi-spirit..."

The demi-spirit's main body looked like a disaster zone from the explosion from Ignis Fatuus that had gone off right in front of its face. Half of its face had been blown away, and its eyes the size of a human's head were hanging out of their sockets. The giant pillar had been hit by the shock wave at point-blank range, and the damage it had taken was commensurate.

"The bigger the spark, the bigger the fireworks!"

Welf brushed away a cold sweat at the blast that had been bigger than expected, a fearless grin pasted across his face.

Anti-magic fire. His ability could force an Ignis Fatuus to occur. It wouldn't be a stretch to call it a magic killer. That was Welf's rare Skill, which could turn the tables on enemies' magic and force them to self-destruct.

"One of the Crozzos...Utterly incompatible with us elves," Hedin murmured, gazing in wonder as he adjusted his glasses once the shock wave passed.

It could ignite magic and cause it to self-destruct. That was difficult to swallow for a mage. And it was more effective on magic users like elves.

Half the fairies in the chamber paled as they imagined having to face off against Welf. The other half had mixed feelings, because as a race, they had a deep connection with the Crozzos. But they all recognized Welf's utility in battle.

"Riveria, if you're interested, feel free to use him as you please. I'm willing to bet he'll be able to completely seal the enemy."

"...Yes, I'll have him do just that!"

Riveria praised the trump card from *Hestia Familia* in her mind.

As far as the battle against the spirits was concerned, there was nothing more menacing than Welf. Given that the scale and force of the anti-magic fire was proportional to the enemy's magic, the demi-spirit was like a powder keg that could go off at any time, especially with its abundance of magic. Its destructive ability had rebounded back at itself.

As a part of Crozzo, Welf had descended from spirits himself. With the help of the Level Boost magic, he was currently maintaining a pseudo–Level 3, more than capable of becoming an effective force.

"I got more to come!"

As the demi-spirit cried out in anguish, Welf drew his magic sword. He swung the crimson longsword without any reservations.

"Kazukiiiiii!"

An enormous crimson lotus started to bloom. The current of the flames was like a giant waterfall, flowing in reverse as it delivered a follow-up attack to the suffering demi-spirit.

It was an unbreakable magic sword that blew away the adventurers' concerns. Equipped with something as absurd as an everlasting magic sword, Welf continued to unleash roaring red flames.

Their eyes reflecting the fire, the elves mustered themselves, not wanting to lose. Riveria's voice rang out, the black-and-white fairies cut in sharply, and the rest of the fairies immediately joined the fray. The alternating blasts of the magic sword and magic impediment hit the spirit hard.

"Run! Ruuuuuuuuun!"

In a place far from the six chambers, the reserve forces of the second squad were sprinting, rushing through the labyrinth. Raul's shout guided the mixed force of *Loki Familia* and *Ganesha Familia* members.

"With the enemy confused, this is our only chance! Hurry!"

The location was the eleventh floor, one floor below the primary battlefields. With all its energy concentrated on the floor above them, the vegetation filling the labyrinth seemed to have rotted away, turned into a treacherous path.

Shaking off their disgust, Raul's squad advanced toward one of their targets. They followed the directions of Rakuta, who had a blueprint of Knossos. Plus, they could rely on the ears and noses of the animal people accompanying them. When they removed the green flesh covering the corner, they discovered a hidden door and pried open the thick stone entrance.

"!"

On the other side of the door were several men and women lying on the floor as if they had exhausted all their energy. Raul lifted one of them and checked for a pulse. The body was completely dry, almost like a desiccated mummy, but there was just the faintest sound of a heartbeat.

Raul took out his oculus and shouted, "They're alive, Captain! The hostages are safe!"

"Gaaaaaaaah!"

Holding out her staff, Elfie Collette continued to stream out fire magic. Her reserve force was currently on the ninth floor.

Trusting Elfie's assurance of all she'd seen, the group of adventurers and mages had burned the green flesh obstructing their path and headed to the designated location.

"We're here! This is the place!"

Upon scorching the flesh, they had stumbled upon a familiar passage. The gap in the wall had been completely sealed. Splitting up, they examined everything in the surroundings before discovering a hidden door—just like Raul's squad.

"Are you okay?!"

There was no source of light at all in the hidden room where they were cowering in tattered clothes. Elfie rushed to one of the girls, who was little more than skin and bones.

"Ugh...?"

Her bloodshot eyes that she barely managed to open were a testament to the negligence. Her voice was hoarse, whispering with her cracked lips, like a zombie in the rumors that the gods found so funny. Staying in the darkness for this long must have messed with her psyche, because her fingernails were bloody, ground down from clawing at the wall. Heavy chains were clamped around her arms and legs. She had been the mysterious eye that Elfie had seen through the crack in the wall during the first assault.

"Is Lady...D-Demete...?"

As Elfie watched, her opened eyes filled with tears. Her wispy voice was desperately trying to confirm the safety of their patron goddess.

They were part of *Demeter Familia*. They were the goddess's followers who had been caught by Enyo, left suffering in confinement. There was no trace left of their beauty in their current condition, emaciated.

"*Gh*...I'm sorry! I'm so sorry!"

Elfie blamed herself for not noticing the voice begging for help, turning her back on them during the first assault. She tightly hugged Persephone, who had been trapped in the darkness all this time.

Early on, they had decided on the plan to rescue the hostages. As soon as Loki had figured out Dionysus's true identity and Demeter's situation, Finn had baked it into the scheme for the second assault himself. They wanted to save the members of *Demeter Familia* to cut off the opportunity for any devilish hostage tactics by Enyo. To avoid the repetition of a tragedy—like what had happened with *Dionysus Familia*.

"Rei, please!" shouted Alicia.

"Leave it to me. Cover your ears!"

Following the elf's instructions, Rei the siren tried to echolocate them. After indulging Loki, she had linked up with the reserve forces as planned. Her echolocation was perfect for searching out hidden rooms. As long as there was the tiniest of air vents, it would seek the location of the hostages. With the help of a Xenos, the Fairy Force members who had rampaged through Knossos were racing around saving people.

"Hurry up and carry *Demeter Familia* out of here! Perform first aid as necessary! Save the full treatments for once they're out!"

And the final member of *Loki Familia*'s second-string forces, Cruz the chienthrope. They were on the tenth floor. The captured members of *Demeter Familia* had even been kept on the same floor as where the demi-spirits were concealed.

Because Fels had destroyed the supply lines providing magic to the altar, the green flesh had slowed its regeneration. Before it could finish recovering, they were carrying hostages out from their prison, hauling them away.

The mastermind must have intended on using them as spares—in the case that magic ran out. There were many people held captive on the tenth floor—those who had been cruelly killed to demonstrate a point to Demeter.

Cruz had a hard time maintaining his cool at the sight of Enyo's ruthlessness.

"Cruz!"

"!"

Because of that, he was slow to notice his surroundings. Narfi's warning alerted him to the gang of monsters approaching from down the hall. Because it could no longer activate its counter magic, the labyrinth had summoned a swarm of violas and vargs: All had gnarled green flesh eating away at their bodies, creating a muddy green cloak. It was as if the altar had *spat out* the things that it had swallowed. The rampaging shouts were more intense than before, and it was clear that their bodies had been enhanced.

This is bad!

The bulk of the squad had their hands full, carrying hostages who could not move themselves, and the fiendish monsters closing in had both quality and quantity to their advantage. Intercepting was hopeless, and even successfully running away was unlikely.

"OOOOOOOOOOOOOOOOOOOOOOOOOH!"

"Gh?!"

As the monsters approached, screeching, howling, Cruz and Narfi readied their weapons to act as a physical wall to protect the rest of the squad.

"_____"

A sudden flash entered Cruz's field of vision. A white shadow appeared without warning from one of the labyrinth's side paths, slicing off the head of the leading viola. Leaving the frozen adventurers and monsters in the dust, it spun, and a black arc followed the white flash, bisecting three approaching vargs.

The absurdly fast shadow did not stop there. The flash was too fast for their eyes as it entered the swarm of monsters from the front and laid waste to them. Even when the violas finally started to counterattack, it slipped close to them and gouged them with a jet-black knife.

And then there was a *Firebolt*. Using a quick attack, the enemy's body exploded from the inside.

"?!"

The flaming lightning flowing into the viola's long body turned it into a red lotus, and the explosion knocked the monsters behind it backward. As the explosion and an accompanying flash of light went off in front of them, Cruz and the others immediately covered their eyes.

In a moment, the dust settled. Inside the flying sparks, they saw his back as a young boy stood there.

"...R—" Upon seeing the white hair swaying in the light of the flames, Narfi choked out, "Rabbit Foot..."

"...Bell Cranell...?" Cruz said, which reached the back of the boy clad in light armor. The boy with white hair glanced around at the reserve squad carrying injured people and then charged into the main force of monsters letting out enraged howls.

"Wha—?! Wait! Don't—?!"

The reckless charge drew blows from all the violas' tentacles. Narfi immediately tried to stop him. *But it was useless.*

Even though he seemed to have nowhere to escape, Bell managed to dodge all the tentacles. Cutting through the bare minimum of tentacles, he slipped through a gap scarcely large enough for a single person. Lowering his body to the ground like an animal, he approached with a counter.

From the moment he engaged with the swarm, it was a lopsided rampage.

His jet-black knife and shining white long knife were not very reliable when dealing with a large-class monster as an opponent, yet they created a storm of lacerations that sliced everything in half.

Because the range of his knife did not go far, it could not cut all the way through a viola's body with one attack, but he simply added two or three more gashes to finish his prey. A moment later, he was sending another monster's unsightly jaw flying along with the rest of its head. There was no time wasted on the smaller vargs. They were dashed from this world in the blink of an eye. Many tried to spit out acid from midrange, but he quickly undid the scarf around his neck and lashed out with it like a whip, mowing them all down at once.

"…Miss Aiz…?"

For some reason, Bell's combat style reminded Narfi of the Sword Princess. As *Loki Familia* and *Ganesha Familia* stood in place, he was locked in solo combat, demonstrating his speed.

"Hah!" Bell himself was using all he had to protect the reserve forces as he scattered the swarm of monsters without any fear.

That had been Lilly's order.

The battles against the demi-spirits required extreme impact and firepower, which meant she would not be able to fully make use of Bell's strong points. If he used his Skill, he would certainly be able to contribute, but Lilly did not want to discount the rabbit's advantage…At least, that was what she'd said to them. The truth was, she wanted to protect Bell. His left arm was still severely injured. If Bell was sent to a battlefield with a boss during his recovery, he would definitely do something that could not be undone. In fact, if Amid knew that he was taking part in the battle at all, she would explode in rage. After all, she was in charge of his full recovery.

For those reasons, he was raiding—as a one-man light cavalry reinforcing the reserve squads, who were running around freeing hostages.

And just as she planned, Bell was flourishing on his own. The vibrantly colored monsters were no match for his growth. Though the enemies' potential power exceeded Level 4, he was cutting through them like a seasoned adventurer who had descended to the deep levels by himself.

He was incredible—almost too strong. In fact, Cruz and the rest of *Loki Familia*'s second string had just heard about the new level, and they could not help but feel like he was already racing ahead at the forefront of all Level 4s.

"...I think I might finally understand how Lefiya feels," Cruz said.

As he watched the boy before him, he remembered her irritability whenever she heard reports about him.

The battle was already over.

"Are you all right?" Bell asked after rushing over to them, brushing off his scarf like nothing had happened.

"Ah, y-yes! Thank you very much..." Narfi responded.

"...Um, sorry, but do you think I could borrow a bigger sword?"

"Huh?" She was flustered as she looked at the boy's back.

"With all that I have equipped, it's a little hard to fight those monsters."

At times, the rescue squad had carried out the role of the emergency reserve forces, which was why they had supporters carrying gear and items. While Bell spoke with Cruz and Narfi, his eyes drifted behind them to a girl, who had larger weapons attached to her backpack.

"I'll hold off all the monsters," he declared, which sounded like neither bravado nor a lie.

It was just a simple statement, which triggered a feeling of déjà vu for *Loki Familia*. He was reminiscent of Aiz and the other first-tier adventurers. They immediately nodded and answered his request.

"Carmillia! Give Rabbit Foot a longsword!"

"O-okay!"

"..."

As Narfi and the rest readied themselves, Bell observed the squad. Or, rather, he looked at the state of the hostages. They were all weakened. It was clear that they had not been given much to eat or drink for a long time. And several had their tendons cut in all four limbs to prevent them from moving freely.

Bell balled his hand into a fist. A wave of disgust and fear crashed over him, but those emotions were immediately followed by a blazing anger.

A desire to protect the city and to help his idol: He had joined the assault on Knossos with vague motivations, but now his feelings had taken on a more concrete form.

His left arm was already starting to ache, warning him that he was reaching his limit. He had started to bleed inside the support covering his arm. However, even at the cost of blood, he had to keep fighting.

He was determined not to allow evil to win.

And as if manifesting those feelings, his clenched fist started to chime.

"Rabbit Foot! Here's a longsword. Will this work?"

"...Thank you. Go on ahead."

Taking the sword from Cruz, Bell's eyes were already focused on a new swarm of monsters coming from a side path. Cruz's brow furrowed as he looked back at Bell.

"I'll leave this to you," he said apologetically, and then he left.

Attaching the sword belt and sheathed longsword to his back, Bell held out his right hand, which had a white light gathering around it. Targeting the swarm of monsters approaching with hideous roars, he responded with his own roar of *"Firebolt!"*

"We've taken out sixty percent of the enemy's tentacles! I count thirty-seven left!"

"The demi-spirit is still continuing its cast!"

There was no end to the voices from the battlefield pouring out of the crystals. Estimating the scenes described through the oculi, Lilly continued to give orders in Finn's voice.

"Bring up the parties from the middle lines! Two parties! No! Three of them! Use them to cycle the front lines back for a bit so that they can recover with the healers!"

"Now'd be a good time for that, Finn! Of course you'd notice that! But three won't be enough! I'm bringing up four!"

"Leave the front lines to *Freya Familia*! *Loki Familia*, start casting! And *Ganesha Familia*'s middle-line party needs to protect them! Riveria, use your judgment for when to fire the spells!"

"Understood. But that will be hard to do without some disruption. I'll lead a party as a feint and leave the signal to you, Finn!"

Commanding large forces was something that Lilliluka Erde had never done before. For her first time, she found herself on a stage of this caliber, suddenly ordering two different fronts. Put bluntly, she was in over her head. Her eyes were bloodshot, and she looked like she was about to start smoking out of her ears at any moment. But with support from Gareth and Riveria, she was somehow managing to hold on.

Fels and Asfi were watching from the side with indescribable looks on their faces as they eyed her ghastly expression—one that the real Braver would never have shown.

"You're amazing, Lilly..." whispered Haruhime, the renart girl, as she watched everything play out.

She had been left behind because she could not be sent out. It was too dangerous on a battlefield with extreme volleys of magic all around. Even the shock waves from impacts would be enough to kill a Level 1. Haruhime was biting her lip at her own powerlessness, just like she had during the battle in Meren before.

"H-hey! Where is Bete Loooga?!" shouted a girl through Asfi's oculus.

"?! Is this channel...? Aisha?!"

"I can't find Bete Loga anywhere! He isn't in any of the squads fighting the spirits! My man is waiting for me—"

"Don't go sending off stupid transmissions, you dumbass!"

"YOW?!"

There was a loud smack, followed by an annoyed woman's voice.

"Asfi, we're moving down the passage now! It's taking some time because of the monsters that are coming out, but we can go wherever we're needed!"

The transmission had come from the squad of Berbera that Aisha was leading. In the background were battle cries and a frenzied skirmish as they asked for instructions. Fels whispered to Lilly.

"Lilliluka Erde, where should they—?"

"I don't have any capacity to think about that! Please do something about it yourself!"

"Ah, very well…"

With this new intensity, she had lost all traces of Finn's mannerisms, and it overwhelmed Fels.

"…Then we can have Antianeira's squad reinforce the fourth squad with the other Amazons—" After thinking about it for a moment, Fels looked down at the map, starting to direct the surplus forces.

"Wait a minute." A voice cut in from a different oculus. It was Finn.

"Can you send any forces we can spare to the members of the fifth squad who were cut off? To Bete's group?"

"To Vanargand? What do you mean, Braver?"

"According to Aki's report, Bete's fifth squad was caught in a trap by the masked creature. Our best guess is that she might be the biggest threat in the current situation."

"…!"

"And my thumb is aching. Please send some reinforcements to Bete."

Silence settled in their makeshift command post. No one doubted Braver's foreboding.

"…Antianeira."

"Yeah, I heard. I've got a score to settle with that stupid werewolf. Figure out where the trap was triggered and tell us where we need to go."

"Hooray! We get to go to Bete Loga!"

One girl was obviously in high spirits. They could hear them preparing to move from the other side of the crystal. As the Amazons raised their voices and changed course, Aisha had one last thing to say.

"Is Haruhime there?"

The voice called out past Fels and the other leaders, aimed at a renart girl. Haruhime's eyes opened wide.

"Are you coming?" Aisha asked.

Direct and to the point. A confirmation without any kind of explanation. Just a simple question that demonstrated her intentions. The weak girl froze in place, and then her lips slowly moved.

"I—"

The blood flowing from wounds made it seem like an armor of blood. A pained groan escaped the gaps between gnashed teeth that creaked under the pressure. The armor on both his arms was already broken, and he had lost count of the insane attacks that had slammed into his stomach. His blood had turned a darkened red, proving serious internal injuries. There was still blood flowing out of his injured head, matting his gray fur.

But even still, the wolf raised a ferocious battle cry.

"Goddamn monster!"

Bete sprinted. The howl erupted from the pits of his stomach. Flecks of red scattered from his body as he ran, and he bared his fangs at the monster in front of him.

"Well done. To be able to stand back up before me..." she spat.

Her dark, muddied green eyes were unmoved. Standing there with composure, Filvis handled Bete's fierce attack, easily deflecting it.

The isolated remnants of the fifth squad had been devastated. All around the chamber, adventurers' *broken bodies* trembled as they sank into pools of blood. Bete was the only one left putting up any kind of real fight. In fact, the squad had not already been wiped out entirely because Bete had continued fighting Filvis by himself. It was an uneven affair with no hope of winning, but he still kept throwing himself into the fray, bearing the full brunt of her attacks.

"Mr. Bete…!"

Lefiya was one of the handful who could force their quivering bodies to stand back up. She brushed aside the oncoming pain from her own wounds, readying herself to chant, looking to support the werewolf who continued to weather the storm of violence by himself.

"Just quit already, werewolf. Don't struggle before me anymore."

"Gh…?!"

"The figure of your noble self protecting your comrades is just an annoyance to me now!"

The monster's fist clenched with hatred, slipping past Bete's series of attacks and slamming into his shoulder. The shock of the blow rang through Bete's lungs, causing him to cough up blood, but she did not stop there. A succession of punches landed on his battered limbs, and unpleasant sounds garbled inside his body.

Bete was nothing more than a musical instrument for Filvis at this point. She composed a muddled melody of a breaking body to accompany the act of shaving away at his life. Flesh was torn, bones were broken, and he struggled to breathe.

With *Einsel* canceled, Filvis's strength was abnormal. For six years, she had continued working behind the scenes at her patron god's orders—day in and day out, fighting through two different battle-fields with her clone and main body. Because of that, her familiarity with battle and these locations was effectively doubled. That experience was in no way inferior to a first-tier adventurer's experience.

Bete had a slight advantage in technique and tactics, but that was all. It was not enough to overcome her edge in potential.

Her eyes narrowed sharply. Filvis stole Bete's Dual Roland swords in the blink of an eye and thrust them into both of his thighs. His legs, the source of his mobility, were stolen away from him, but Bete was left standing for only a moment before she unleashed a critical hit.

"*Gaaaaah?!*" he groaned.

A sharper and stronger kick than one from Vanargand himself blasted into the side of his head. Cracks ran through his skull, gushing with blood from his temples, as his brain ricocheted around in its bone cage. It was a decisive blow that severed Bete's will to fight and his consciousness. His body flew into the distance with the force of a river breaking through its dam.

"*Loose your arrows, fairy archers. Pierce, arrow of accuracy!——Arcs Ray!*"

Instead of a shriek, Lefiya shouted her chant.

She unleashed her completed magic with an incomparable amount of Mind poured into it. The spell made full use of her Fairy Cannon Skill. It was the most powerful instantaneous attack that she had in her arsenal. It contained all the firepower she had built up to Level 4. The giant ray of light flew through the chamber. Its tracking ability ensured that it would not miss.

But Filvis reacted to that ray of light.

"What?!"

To Lefiya's shock, the creature's brow furrowed just the slightest as she knocked it to the side with a swing of her arm. It was thrown off its path; the ray landed in the corner of the chamber. It was a feat that Levis had achieved in the past, something capable by only creatures. Despite the fact that *Arcs Ray* was significantly more powerful now, it was still sealed.

"Tch—!"

Having finished with Bete, Filvis turned her attack on Lefiya.

She made a simple move, as if waving a fan, but her arm swung down so fast that it turned into a blur. Her fist slammed into the floor, unleashing a shock wave. That one attack easily broke through all the way to the adamantite floor, causing a disgusting wave as the green flesh clinging to the floor rolled back.

"?!"

The wave of green approached Lefiya, rushing forward like a tidal wave. She immediately tried to evade it but did not make it in time as the wave slammed into the right side of her body, bending her back and sending her flying. Fractures ran through her arm and her magic staff, Forest Teardrop, was shattered to pieces.

She's too strong!

Lefiya's heart beat wildly as she lost her armor, and half her body was racked by intense pain. Filvis left no opening in her attack or her defense.

"*—Raaaaaaaah!*"

At that moment, with both Bete and Lefiya knocked away, the adventurers on the ground leaped to their feet as one, taking advantage of the single moment's opening that Filvis gave them. They had feigned their inability to move, but they were the members of *Ganesha Familia* who had been part of the fifth squad. Some of their stomachs were gouged, some were missing limbs, some had lost eyes. They were all bleeding out. There was no helping them anymore. Realizing that, they had prepared a suicide charge.

Death before surrender.

Leaving the rest to the mages who wove their spells with tears in their eyes, they would hold down Filvis for a moment so that the oncoming volley could take her out, bringing her down with them.

Eyes wide, Lefiya cried out in grief but had no time to stop them as they rushed toward her.

And Filvis reacted.

"Purge, cleansing lightning."

She had chanted emotionlessly.

"_____"

Lefiya froze in place. The entire chamber was filled with a brutal magic for an instant. A magic circle appeared, dyed a sinister black instead of pure white. That menacing circle evoked dread in all the mages as Filvis held out her arm and cast the spell.

*   *   *

"Dio Thyrsos."

The creature unleashed a destructive lightning bolt. The atrocious thunder wave rendered the adventurers' determined suicide charge meaningless as they *disappeared* in a flash of light.

"―――――――――?!"

The charging adventurers and even the mages behind them all vanished. The torrent of lightning swallowed up everything that lay in its path. It slammed into the chamber wall, demolishing it and breaking through with a boom that could rupture eardrums. The roar of the thunder cannon was momentarily deafening, and by the time Lefiya's ears started to work again...there was nothing left.

The black crackles of remnant lightning and the tiniest bits of charred ash in the air announced the fate of those adventurers.

"...No. Way..."

It was an attack and defense with no openings, a spell that was off the charts. Even though it was an ultrashort-cast spell, its output was a match for the magic of the demi-spirit on the fifty-ninth floor. Or maybe even higher.

The strongest of all monsters.

With the full power of the united Filvis and Ein, those who had witnessed it from start to finish began to cry out in fear and despair.

"Aaaah...*Aaaah*...?!"

They were dead. Without a doubt, they had been killed. The adventurers from *Ganesha Familia* had been killed by Filvis—their lives stolen without a moment's hesitation.

This reality left Lefiya trembling. Nausea pushed at the back of her throat. There was no more denying the reality before her eyes. In every sense of the word, Filvis had flaunted sin, her extraordinary karma, by taking so many lives there.

With his body obliterated, Bete lay unconscious, and the rest of the members of *Loki Familia* on the ground turned pale.

Grief shattered Lefiya's heart.

"I knew this would happen..." Filvis said.

Lefiya was unable to stand. She saw Filvis look up to the ceiling. There was no expression on the face of the monster in the form of a girl. It was as if she were a doll. It was breathtakingly beautiful, chaotic, sad.

"I knew this was how it would end. I knew it would be like this… And yet you still came here, Lefiya…I made you make that kind of expression."

"?!"

"Starting now…I'm going to have to kill everyone, including you."

Her neck shifted, tilting her head. Her green eyes reflected Lefiya's face. Filvis finally revealed the monster that she had always been keeping inside, starting to talk to herself.

"Why did you have to come, Lefiya?…Why? Why?! Didn't I tell you…to get away from Orario? If you had just said yes…Or if you had just stayed a broken doll until it was all over…"

Her long hair, black as night, trembled, and her dead eyes focused on the wounded elf. Her voice was filled with a mix of emotions—grief, rage, hatred, despair. She was gripping her fists so tightly that chunks of broken flesh were falling to the floor.

"I didn't want to kill you…You were the only one I didn't want to kill…But if you have to die, then at least it will be by my hand…Ah! But wait."

It was as if she had had a divine revelation. Letting go of her wrath and anguish, she suddenly smiled faintly.

"Should I embed a magic stone in you and turn you into the same as me?"

"Wh—?"

"Maybe…you can be corrupted, too."

Euphoria appeared on Filvis's face as she paid no heed to Lefiya, who was speechless.

"Ah, that would be good! You always said those self-important things! You always acted like an innocent child, Lefiya! Oh, Lefiya! You are so beautiful! I was always irritated by you! Your brilliance made me miserable! I can just cast you down into an inescapable despair—where you can suffer like I do!"

Lefiya gasped. The smile on Filvis's face was like none Lefiya had seen before. This was the first that she had heard joy in Filvis's voice. Filvis's laughter was tinged with dark delight. Exposing her true feelings, she became intoxicated with the sweet destruction of dragging Lefiya down her same path.

However, she stopped moving. As if resisting that dark desire, she gripped her head with both hands and listlessly shook it from side to side.

"...No, I can't. I can't do that. Lefiya must not be sullied...Lefiya cannot be corrupted...She must not become the same as me."

"...Miss...Filvis..."

"Then I guess there's nothing else but to kill her...Bury her... Ha-ha-ha, I guess there's no other choice than killing Lefiya..."

Drip. Drop.

Rain dampened the floor—they were drops of water that fell from Filvis's eyes, splashing on the stone flooring where the green flesh had been torn away. Filvis was laughing while crying. It was as if her uncontrollable emotions were shattering her personality as she spoke an incoherent soliloquy.

Acknowledgment and denial. Joy and grief. Acclamation and reproach. A fairy's pride and a monster's hatred. It was as if the white Filvis and the black Ein were shouting back and forth at each other.

Lefiya finally understood something—the reason why Filvis always used her magic and maintained the clone.

——"*Rage, despair, hatred...You hoisted all of that to me. Quit acting like some tragic heroine.*"

——"*You pushed all the dirty work onto me.*"

Her heart was already at its limit. If she had not pushed her darkness onto the clone, all her negative emotions, she would not have been able to maintain a soul of any kind. Filvis Challia had been broken long ago. The fact of being a monster was a poison that tormented and ate away at the fairy and was even now killing her. Antinomy, self-contradiction.

Unable to die, she could do nothing but cling to Dionysus's sweet talk, becoming a pitiful puppet—a lonely fairy forever tormented by her spiritual disintegration. Ever since that nightmare six years before, Filvis had been wandering, lost in a maze with no exit. Searching for a light that did not exist, she became darkness.

Lefiya's teeth grated. Her limp hands slowly turned into fists.

"…Why are you crying, Lefiya?"

Her precious friend asked her why there were tears flowing down her cheeks. She marveled at the tears pouring from those blue eyes like a clueless child.

"Are you scared? Don't worry. I'll end it quickly so you don't feel any pain."

Her voice was cold and inhuman, simultaneously conveying mercy and cruelty. Despite the fact that it bore no resemblance to the girl's voice that had once encouraged her so, it caused even more tears to pour down Lefiya's cheeks.

Lefiya Viridis had been clinging to an illusion. Knowing that Filvis was still alive, she had clung to the convenient belief that there could be a do-over somewhere deep in her heart. That even though Filvis had sinned, they could spend their lives atoning for it together.

But Filvis was crying now. She was suffering more than anyone. In her damning despair, she desperately sought affirmation by worshipping her patron god. She just kept suffering, and her pure heart imposed destruction onto herself. Filvis could not stop anymore—she could not be stopped. Even if she lost Dionysus, she would continue to follow his divine will, martyring herself to destroy Orario. Otherwise, all her sins would be meaningless. That would be the same as denying herself. And even if the corrupted spirit was defeated, she would be destroyed, too, since she was one of its servants.

The promise of destruction was all that waited at the end of Filvis's path. The only path to achieving even a fake salvation would be in accomplishing her patron god's divine will.

This is the first time…

Lefiya clenched her fists so hard, they started to tremble.

This is the first time I've ever hated a god like this…

Her rage seeped out of her fingers, and her heart beat so hard that she was afraid it might explode.

Now is the time for my choice. I have to answer her—not as some kind of holy saint or even as a hero. But as just one fellow elf. As her friend.

Or else the city will be destroyed at this rate...

Strength flowed back into her clenched fist. She looked at the girl who had shouldered many sins, suffering under their weight even now.

At this rate, Miss Filvis will keep suffering...

Her battered body swelled with purpose, even though it was covered by wounds and screaming in pain. Finding Filvis's old gaze in those green eyes, she made up her mind.

That's why I...!

She rose to her feet. Filvis's eyes widened.

"—I will defeat you!"

Lefiya Viridis would surely end up regretting those words and choice. But she didn't want to forget this remorse as they reached this crossroad. She stood before it and did not look away.

Lefiya would cry. She would shout. She would bear eternal dismay herself. And she would bear that to save Filvis—before any more sins could corrupt her further. To prevent her from becoming plagued by that paradoxical smile and tears. *To return the virtue that she granted me.* Lefiya chose the option that would grant Filvis both salvation and destruction.

"I will defeat you and stop you! I won't allow your honor to be sullied any more than it already has been!"

She drew two weapons from her waist to replace her destroyed magic staff, Forest Teardrop—a sword and a wand. The spell blade Tear Pain and the wand Protector's White Torch. Lefiya would save her with the weapons that Filvis had cast aside.

"...You'll defeat me with those weapons? You can't, Lefiya. That's impossible."

"*Ngh...!*"

"Right now, you don't have anyone with you, not even that were-wolf. As you are, you cannot defeat me…"

Filvis slowly turned, giving off an air of sadness tinged with murder.

Filvis's read of the situation was correct, but Lefiya would not go back on her resolution. She readied herself to attack her friend who was pivoting to face her.

"Bete Logaaa!"

Someone could not read the vibe.

"To save her man from his pinch, Lena is making her gallant appearance! Bete Loga, your wifey is here!—Wait! *Noooo?!* Is Bete Loga dead?!"

The uproar of a single Amazon stole Lefiya's and Filvis's attention. The sweet child somewhere between a young girl and a woman trembled when she found Bete's battered body, and her excitement transformed into a panicked fear.

She was the Amazon girl Lena.

"Shut up, dumbass. Indoor voices."

"YOW?!"

And she had brought reinforcements with her.

Aisha had hit Lena in the head to shut her up, and the Berbera of ex–*Ishtar Familia* poured into the chamber.

"Why did I have to come, too…?"

Even Asfi had been brought along against her will. As the members of *Loki Familia* looked on in shock, the reinforcements did not stop there.

"I brought someone else, too, Asfi!" shouted Lulune the chienthrope, appearing from a different passage, waving her arm. Following behind her was a single elf wearing a hooded long cape.

"Leon!"

"I'm sorry for being late, Andromeda. I'm still recovering, but… I've come to pay back my debt."

Lefiya recognized the adventurer who was equipped with several different blades borrowed from *Hermes Familia*.

"And as recompense for my dishonorable dereliction of duty, I will aid you in this fight."

She was the masked adventurer who had saved Bell and Lefiya on the eighteenth floor.

"It's good that you could make it in time!"

"I'll do the best I can. I was filled in on the way, but are there any reinforcements other than me?"

"Yes, Bell Cranell's familia has come as well!"

"_____"

"Wait, what?! Did she just trip on air?!"

"Leon?!"

It was almost a slapstick routine. Lulune had shouted, starting to doubt whether the masked elf was really the rumored body-guard with skills, and Asfi followed up with her own concerned interjection.

Time stopped as even Lefiya started to sweat, but the masked adventurer rubbed her nose with one arm and stood up like nothing had happened.

"Could you not say his name in front of me? It knocks me off my stride."

"Did something happen between you...?"

"I don't know. There's just a weird palpitation."

Lefiya was taken aback for several reasons as she watched the elf ignore Asfi's suspicious gaze.

"Miss Asfi, Miss Lulune...You guys..."

Lefiya could not hide her surprise. She had fought together with Asfi and Lulune, but there were even some of the odd acquaintances who had been by her side in her journey in life.

Aisha and the Amazons had tense looks on their faces.

"We followed the directions and a certain loudmouth raised hell as she tagged along...But what *is* that?"

"Could that be...a fellow elf?"

Aisha and the masked adventurer could not help but shudder as they observed the enemy. Even Asfi was taken aback by Filvis, even though Finn had filled her in earlier. They had all experienced many battles. They could readily recognize the potential hidden in her overpowering presence. Lulune gulped audibly as she looked at Filvis, whose figure could not really be described as that of a person or a monster.

"Antianeira and Perseus...and Gale Wind? Whatever. It doesn't matter. Level Fours are virtually meaningless." Filvis ominously sighed as she glanced at the reinforcements with a look of annoyance.

Aisha and the others were Level 4s like Lefiya. Even in the Labyrinth City, they were powerful people who were recognized as a cut above the rest. But faced with the current Filvis and seeing that she had defeated Bete, a Level 6, their strength was entirely outclassed. The creature's words were not hyperbole but a disinterested statement of fact.

"...It's true. You're scary as shit. I hate to admit it, but you probably could kill us easily," Aisha said, agreeing with Filvis's claim without taking her eyes off the creature. A bead of sweat trickled down her cheek, but she still grinned boldly. "If we were Level Four, that is."

The next instant, the sorceress hidden in the shadows of the Berbera unleashed her magic.

"*Uchide no Kozuchi—Dance!*"

Golden sparks zipped through the air. Haruhime the renart used the sorcery that only she could use. Aisha, the masked adventurer, and Asfi were bestowed with light.

"This light...!"

"You've experienced it before, right, Gale Wind?"

"So this is Level Boost...An unfair form of sorcery that brought ecstasy and destruction even upon the goddess Ishtar."

Gold particles gathered around them.

A Level Boost. *Loki Familia* had encountered that hack-worthy power several times before, during the fights in Meren and on Daedalus Street. As its name implied, it was a sorcery that increased the target's level by one. Haruhime Sanjouno was the user. The renart who had converted from *Ishtar Familia* to *Hestia Familia* grew a tail of light. Her breathing became ragged from the sorcery's combustion of her stamina, but she desperately tried to regain control of it.

"My strength is…!"

And the blessing of the Level Boost was bestowed on Lefiya. Feeling her strength expand as the light touched her, Lefiya shuddered at the power of that broken ability. It was a pseudo-level-up, bestowed on four people at the same time.

"—Four Level Fives…"

Even Filvis, the embodiment of an Irregular, could not help but be shocked.

"Lena, slap Vanargand awake! We're going to need his strength, too!" Aisha said.

"O-okay!" Lena nodded.

"Lulune, you and the rest of the Berbera protect Haruhime Sanjouno, no matter what it takes. You don't need to bother trying to take part in the attack. When her magic gives out, we lose!" Asfi said.

"G-got it!" Lulune responded, springing into motion.

"And, Lefiya Viridis…Please support us. We can't hold that thing back by ourselves," Asfi requested as Lulune and the others formed an extensive defensive formation.

Their factions and allegiances were across the spectrum. They had never even tried to work together before. They were a dream team in every sense of the phrase.

Should I borrow their strength to challenge Filvis, even though we have no history of working together? Lefiya did not know if that was the right thing to do. With the sense of omnipotence that came from the sudden boost to pseudo–Level 5, she could not judge whether she was excited or agitated. Lefiya was at a loss for how to respond to Asfi's request.

"…Thousand Elf. I don't know the situation between the two of you," said the elf adventurer who had not addressed her before. Her sky-colored eyes peeked out from behind her mask. "But stopping a fellow elf in this condition should be your duty, regardless of what is required in order to achieve that."

"!"

After hearing that from a fellow elf, Lefiya made her decision. Filling her chest with her purpose, Lefiya responded as a mage.

"Please protect me!"

It was a loud voice that filled the battlefield. Wielding the one weapon allowed to her as a mage and clutching her friend's sword in her other hand, she called out to them.

"I am a magic user! Protect me, and I'll save us all!"

Those were words that Asfi and Lulune had heard once before, during the battle on the twenty-fourth floor—the proclamation she had made when she transformed her resolution into a vow.

"Because I must stop her!"

Her gaze sharpened on her greatest enemy, the girl who had once been her friend. Asfi watched Lefiya and Filvis exchange stares and silently adjusted her glasses.

"…We'll move following Thousand's directions. You don't mind, right? Leon? Aisha?"

"She's Lady Riveria's successor. And more importantly, she has demonstrated an adequately strong motivation. I have no objections."

"In the first place, she's the only one who'll be in the back lines. We won't have any time to spare with giving orders."

Neither the masked adventurer nor Aisha had any complaints. In fact, they did not even glance at Asfi. Their eyes were glued to the unprecedented monster before them. They readied their weapons and shifted to a battle stance.

"…Fine, I'll crush you all at once."

Opening her eyes wide, Filvis showed them her intent to kill as she squared off against the adventurers who were cloaked in a blessing of light.

A HEROES' CHORUS

Гэта казка іншага сям і.

Герой Цын

In Knossos, there were eight main battlefields, ignoring localized conflicts with monsters.

The six halls where each squad was fighting a demi-spirit.

The chamber where Lefiya and her reinforcements were facing Filvis.

And one other.

"*Raaaaaah!*"

"!"

That was the cavern where Levis and Aiz's death match was unfolding.

Crashing against each other were the creature with corrupted flesh armor covering her body and the swordsman veiled in a jet-black storm. The chamber that had become their battlefield had been torn, smashed to pieces. On one side, there was human strength. On the other, shock waves encased in a black current of air caused by the silver sword. Strands of blood-colored hair whipped around, and a few long golden locks zipped through the air, severed by a slash.

There was a boom, sparks flying where their swords crossed. They both used the opposing force to leap back. The fierce storm of wind allowed Aiz to steady herself and land easily on the floor. The winds could hardly be called "breezes" anymore. Meanwhile, Levis left tracks carved into the floor as she stopped her momentum using only her brute force.

With an opening between them, they glared at each other without letting down their guards.

"Damn adventurers…You had this much strength hidden in reserve?" Levis muttered in annoyance.

For a while now, stone fragments from the ceiling had been crumbling down to the floor from the aftershocks from the battle occurring on the floor above. Those were not the tremors from a rampage by the spirits. The thundering, repeated shouts from adventurers indicated that much. The labyrinth trembled with their brave roars, and those tremors even reached Aiz and Levis on the twelfth floor.

"In every era, Orario is still Orario, huh?" Levis said as she suddenly looked up. She was looking toward the shaft they had fallen down. The hole that Aiz had excavated using her wind was slowly being repaired as the green flesh gradually tried to cover it. Levis stared into the hole, measuring the depth they had fallen before turning back to Aiz.

"But…this is the end," she murmured.

Aiz's brow furrowed in confusion at those words. That profound statement aroused suspicion in her mind.

"You are lucky, Aria…that we fell all the way to here," she muttered emotionlessly as steam caused by her regeneration rose from her body.

"They've rallied, huh…?" Loki murmured.

The adventurers' roars were audible. Their brave cries from her oculus spoke to the increasing morale. The crystal itself was trembling from their shouts.

There were no foregone conclusions on the battlefield, of course, but it was safe to say that with this situation, the adventurers had managed to fight to get them the advantage in this battle. Loki sensed that Finn's plan was succeeding and they had taken the upper hand.

"Sounds like the board's been flipped on you, Dionysus." Looking up, Loki shot daggers at him with her eyes.

They had thrown in all of Orario's forces for this decisive battle: all the notable upper-level factions and even some borrowed help from Meren. Even if there were six demi-spirits, as long as they could mobilize their forces, they would be able to break through.

That was what it meant to be an adventurer. That was Orario. It was the promised land that gave birth to heroes. With the fate of the world on the line, it was the mortal realm's final stronghold that had defeated destruction an untold number of times.

"........." Dionysus looked down.

His crazed laughter from a moment before had fallen silent, and he accepted Loki's words and gaze silently. The torches' light caused his shadow to flicker on the floor.

"Dionysus, your plan—"

—*ends here*, Loki was about to say.

"Hee-hee…Hee-hee-hee…"

The impulse that the god had been desperately trying to hold back crossed his lips.

"Hee-hee-hee-hee-hee-hee…! Ha-ha-ha-ha-ha-ha-ha-ha-ha-ha-ha-ha-ha-ha-ha-ha-ha-ha!"

Dionysus laughed—chortling and guffawing at her.

At that moment, Finn shifted to a lengthier analysis.

——*What comes next?*

Thanks to the reinforcements from *Freya Familia* and the proposal from Lilly, he had gained a little bit of leeway. Instead of using every last one of his resources to command the forces, he finally had a little time to think.

Of course, he still had things to do, but compared to his former responsibilities, it was like night and day. He could leave the command of the first squad to Shakti and the front lines to Allen.

With the reinforcements from Ottar and the likes, we've basically turned things around. The creatures are still a problem, but at this rate, we should be able to suppress the six demi-spirits.

Legions of adventurers had gathered in Knossos by this point. It could even be called overkill. On the boards where the enemy resistance was particularly intense, he could throw in some of the surplus forces from *Hestia Familia* and other groups. The reserve forces were rescuing the hostages. Antianeira and the other reinforcements had been sent to Bete's group. The course of the battle was clearly trending in their direction.

Finn was doing everything in his power to eliminate any sources of uncertainty. He was nipping every last bud of a potential counterattack by the enemy before it could sprout.

But this is going too well.

Premonition flashed through Finn's mind. A hunch that it would not end like this. That Enyo would not let it end in this way.

As the adventurers' morale rose and they started to see a light at the end of the tunnel, Finn alone was not basking in premature elation. The victory was tilting toward them, but he would not allow himself to mistake that for an omen of a win.

I had this same feeling during the first assault. We pushed Knossos right to the brink, but that was precisely when the board was flipped on us.

That was when a blade from outside the board had cut it in two. While Finn was sitting in a chair moving pieces around the board, Enyo had suddenly appeared out of nowhere and thrust a sword through the board, taking the match that Finn had been close to winning and rendering it meaningless.

This bore a striking resemblance to how things were going now.

I won't make the same mistake twice. From what we experienced last time, I can be sure that Enyo is not even fighting on the same field as us.

The activation of the spirits' spell and their attempt to prevent it.

The former meant their loss; the latter secured their victory. Was their battle really that simple? The doubts swirling in Finn's head could be summed up in that single question. As he listened to the voices of each squad fighting the good fight on all battlefields, he considered the situations and possibilities, given his understanding of Enyo from the previous battle.

Enyo doesn't care about a tactical victory or even a strategic one. That's not how gods play. They don't care about losing the battle or the war; they only care about the results. As long as he gets the desired goal, he doesn't give a damn about how he achieves it. He doesn't have any sense of standards or chivalry or aesthetics. He doesn't have even the slightest respect for his enemies. Enyo definitely has that sword in hand, waiting for the right time to slice the board in half—

Was that Finn's pessimism? It was not. His thumb was aching. Finn's intuition was alerting him to danger, a warning in the form of an ache like never before. It was shouting at him not to misread the flow of battle this time, screaming that he had to defeat the deity.

Enyo is intelligent and crafty. A merciless, inhuman god. That's for certain. But at the same time, there is a part of him that seeks amusements like Loki!

Searching for the culprit. Challenging the other gods. Misdirecting Demeter. Carrying out his plan was absolute, but it was clear that he wanted to enjoy the struggles of those investigating the incident and the thrill of the chase.

On top of that, he loves the cries of defeated enemies! He wants to enjoy the orgia *as our hope withers away and we fall into the pits of despair!*

He created a profile of Enyo in his mind. With a taunting grin floating in the darkness in front of him, Finn's thoughts accelerated.

Everything Enyo has done has a meaning! Is some kind of hint!

He reflected on every incident leading up to that battle.

The female form that appeared at the safe point on the fiftieth floor: That was almost certainly the work of the corrupted spirit.

The man-eating flowers at Monsterphilia: That was part of the enemy's plan that had misfired when it coincided with Freya's game.

The conflict with the creatures on the eighteenth floor surrounding the crystal orb fetus: That was a complete irregular, thinking back on the details of it.

The twenty-fourth-floor pantry: That was the first hint at the enemy's goal.

The battle in the unexplored territory on the fifty-ninth floor—

——*The fifty-ninth floor...*

At that time, those words set off sparks in Finn's mind.

That was the first time that we confirmed the existence of a demi-spirit, but why was it there? Was it a threat? Was it part of the plan? Was it a reward from a god for those who cleared the challenge?

But that chain of questions led to a paradox.

We wouldn't have even known about the existence of demi-spirits.

If we hadn't seen that giant thing with our own eyes, we would have been too slow in responding, and this ritual would have been completed. Orario would have been destroyed for sure.

Which led to a suspicion.

In fact, my theory only shifted to thinking that the spirits would carry out the destruction because we experienced the menace of that demi-spirit—

And made him come to a *certain conclusion.*

——*In other words, he was* manipulating *my thought process.*

The world around him split open. A flash of light bolted through his mind, dyeing everything white. Finn's head jerked up.

The simultaneous attack on the six demi-spirits in six locations that they had been forced into. The situation where they would be inevitably forced to concentrate all of Orario's strongest forces. All the noteworthy forces protecting Orario were currently gathered in Knossos.

"—It can't be!"

The enemy's true aim *wasn't the destruction of the city* but—

"Hurry! Free all the hostages while the captain's group is still fighting!" Raul called out to the party of adventurers he was leading.

Footsteps thundered as they rushed through the passages coated in green flesh. Their current location was still the eleventh floor of Knossos.

They were searching for hostages. They had discovered several clusters of *Demeter Familia* members. Other groups had split off from Raul's squad as well, both people to help carry the hostages and guards to protect them. Because of that, his team was down to just ten people.

We'll have to head out to the Dungeon ourselves when we find another group of hostages…! he thought.

"What?"

That was when he heard an ominous sound.

"R-Raul…"

"This is…"

"…"

Judging from the other familia members' reactions, he immediately realized it was not just his imagination. Raul fell silent for a moment, gazing down at the map in his hand. It was the copy of the blueprints of Knossos that he had referenced while running around before, eyes bloodshot as he looked for spaces that might have hidden rooms. This time, he was looking for something else, but—

He turned around. The mapper Rakuta also had a copy and seemed to recognize Raul's fear. She shook her head, flustered, indicating there weren't any giant spaces hidden in the surrounding area.

Even with that confirmation from her, a cold sweat trickled down his back. Raul did not have transcendental intuition like Finn. But when stretched to their limits, even an ordinary person like Raul could experience a vague apprehension that was difficult to put into words.

"…Let's go."

He could not verbalize it, but for some reason, it miraculously appeared in his mind. Raul pointed in the direction of the sound he was hearing. They had no choice but to go there. The others in the group did not even remember to respond as they followed his lead.

A mysterious bass echoed. It sounded almost like the labyrinth itself was making the noise. And it was getting louder—growing stronger.

As they approached the source of the sound, rounding corners in the narrow passages, the sound's resonance gradually increased. They started to hear a hair-raising pitch. It could have been created by a being who had crawled its way up from the depths of hell. Despite that, it was now clearly audible without having to strain their ears. The members of the party were still silent. Their lips started to quiver as they desperately tried to keep calm.

Standing at the head of the party, Raul gradually turned paler as he advanced.

"_____"

And then he saw it.

"Velgas!"

Bache's poison fist hit the spirit's tentacle. The enchantment concentrated into one point. In the blink of an eye, the mortal poison rotted the green flesh, turning it a blackish purple. The demi-spirit screamed as it detached the tentacle.

Without a moment's delay, Tione and Argana thread through the gap that this created and cut into the spirit's body. The twin Kukri knives sliced its arm, and bare hands coiled around the body like a snake to snap it. And then Tiona slammed Urga home.

"Just a little more!" Tiona said, licking her lips.

"It's really hard to get to the magic stone!" Tione responded.

"But it's at death's door! Ha-ha-ha-ha, I'm going to kill it!" Argana boasted boldly.

The spirit had desperately flailed its tentacles, pushing them back, but they could feel the damage they were doing. And as Argana had said, the demi-spirit had already been deeply wounded. The number of tentacles had dropped dramatically. Bache's group was intercepting and severing many of them. Others had been rotted off, falling prey to her mortal poison. And its invincible regeneration had slowed dramatically as it finally reached the limits of its magic. The demi-spirit writhed in agony as it regenerated its arm. Its chant had been paused long ago.

The situation has completely turned around...Is that the power of Telskyura...? No, of the Amazons, including Tiona? Amid wondered.

Even in the healer's eyes, the flow of the battle had become clear. In addition to over fifty Amazons holding the line, there was support from the back lines by mages from *Loki Familia* and *Ganesha Familia*. And more than anything, the assault and disruptions caused by four Level 6s. With Finn's commands to top it all off, even a demi-spirit would be on the verge of collapse.

At this rate...

Amid started to be sure of their victory...

"What?"

Tiona, Tione, and the rest murmured at the scene that unfolded before their eyes.

"Hey, Gareth…What is that?" Tsubaki asked, dumbfounded.

"Like I know!" Gareth roared back.

The third squad.

In another location altogether, the adventurers were seeing the same thing as the fourth squad.

"Is that like the recovery from before?"

"No, something is different about it."

"Its body is swelling."

"Something…weird is happening."

Carrying the spirit flags that they had forcibly taken from *Hephaistos Familia*, the prum brothers' eyes narrowed as the Gullivars glared at it from behind their helmets.

"Gh…!"

The spirit's figure was clearly transforming with a burble. It was becoming more hideous, more repulsive.

Mikoto Yamato was gripped by terror, unable to speak.

"Come on…I'm seriously gonna run out of Mind here."

In the second squad, Welf's eyes narrowed as the strain started to get to him. He had done more than his share, repeated uses of his anti-magic fire, and indiscriminately fired his magic sword.

The demi-spirit was giving off steam—more than it had spouted when it was regenerating itself all the times before. The steam was superheated, causing the temperature of the entire chamber to increase, as if the demi-spirit was turning into a volcano.

"Watch for the magic's element and prepare the resistance to it…Try to calculate the timing to nullify it. That isn't just flesh anymore…It's a shell steeped in magic."

"…"

Hedin muttered to himself as he observed the change while firing off a super-short cast spell with lightning speed. Hegni held his black sword silently as he looked up at it.

Ganesha Familia's force, led by Ilta, watched in shock at the change.

"Damn monster! Masquerading as a spirit…We managed to drive it this far into the corner, and it has *another* trick up its sleeve? Don't screw with us!" Riveria accidentally voiced her thoughts.

She had expressed what the adventurers were feeling as they paled at the transformation occurring before their eyes.

"A-Aki…!"

"…!!"

In the fifth squad, Aki gritted her teeth unconsciously.

As it gave off steam, the demi-spirit's transforming body turned black. As its darkened skin cracked, a red light shone out from inside it. The crimson lines spreading over its body looked like they were infecting the spirit itself. It swelled, turning black. It was consumed by pure power.

"This is…"

Even Ottar could not help gazing in wonder.

The blackened, contaminated spirit raised a repulsive cry as it was born right in front of the adventurers' eyes.

"Aaaah…? *Aaaaaah…?!*"

Raul struggled to keep his head on his shoulders as he saw the being in front of him.

A big chamber on the eleventh floor.

Technically, it was not actually a chamber. It was a series of spaces forcibly created by breaking through walls, joining together dozens of rooms and passages.

A giant body was enshrined there. It was so big that it could not be contained except in a giant new chamber that did not exist on the map.

"A…a dragon?!" Rakuta cried out.

Its body was modeled on a dragon species. It had three pairs of wings; crooked claws that looked like they had been carved from a rugged mountain ridge; an enormous torso that was covered in scales, of course; and the head of a devilish dragon.

It was linked to the labyrinth that had become an altar, just like the demi-spirits.

It was giving off an ominous red light. The surrounding green flesh seemed to pulse, as if resonating with the heartbeat of the extraordinary dragon.

Its entire body was pitch-black. It was covered in sinister red lines that looked like blood vessels. Beneath its giant dragon head, a demi-spirit was embedded in its chest. The spirit's upper body with arms spread looked like it had been crucified. It had been assimilated as a magic stone. Its face was not visible. Everything above its mouth had been eaten away by the dragon's body, making it faceless.

The spirit was no longer the parasite. It looked as if it had been entirely consumed.

The monster's imposing appearance was so horrific that Raul was convinced the black dragon slumbering at the ends of the earth could not possibly be more repulsive than it.

"No way…No. Way. *No way?!* Captain! The six rings shouldn't be our real goal!"

Its appearance was more than imposing. Those who saw it were immediately convinced that it was Enyo's actual trump card.

Even they could clearly tell that it was absorbing an enormous power from the *magic circle expanding on the ceiling* above it.

Raul shouted, the blood draining from his face, as he completely lost his cool.

"The enemy's real goal is this—an explosion!"

The woman embedded in the dragon's chest sighed. Her body writhed in an enchanted ecstasy as all the power gathered throughout the labyrinth concentrated into it. The dragon's pulse beating around them was quickening, as if warning that critical mass was near.

The spirit did not even bother trying to attack Raul's party appearing before it. No, it was not even paying them any heed, as if they were just ants crawling around beneath it. It did not care about their presence as it awaited the brutal destruction to come.

"At this rate...?!"

The adventurers would all be wiped out.

"A seventh one?!" Loki shouted in rage.

"Exactly right! That is what I actually prepared to enact my *orgia!*" Dionysus boomed, reveling in the act of announcing his secret. Brushing away his hair with one hand, he arched his back to look up to the heavens. The shadow extending from him on the floor reached to the walls, dancing like a devil.

"Come, Loki! Did you really think I would just make an enemy of Orario without any thought at all?"

"What...?!"

"I'm sure I know more about all of you than anyone else in the world. Yes! That is precisely why I would call myself the city destroyer. I fully acknowledge the strength of those adventurers—who have the capacity to be heroes! I understand them to an annoying degree! A detestable one! But that's why I would have a trump card ready, obviously!"

As Loki stood there on guard, Dionysus's body twisted as he laughed, looking down on her perceived superiority.

"I left hints, Loki!" His scorn was almost palpable, and a smirk spread across his face. "Your follower saw it, right? My collection? The mural of the spirits' spell of six rings?"

"!"

"Because of that, you invaded Knossos! Realizing my plan, you poured all your forces into the labyrinth! *Exactly as I intended!*" Dionysus raised his hands as if singing.

"You thought, and you thought, and you thought! The target was the six bodies that made up the circle! You fixated on that! But wasn't there something more wicked than the spirits on that mural?!"

"…?!"

"A symbol of darkness that would destroy the mortal world! An abominable evil dragon!"

Nidhogg. The dragon that had thrust the mortal realm into the depths of despair in the Ancient Times. That was the true hint that Dionysus had provided them.

"What kind of logic would lead me to use the spirit ritual that sealed *away* the destruction? Isn't that obviously wrong? My plan will be carried out by the dragon, a symbol of the destruction of the mortal world!"

The dragon at the center of the mural was the seventh demi-spirit. It was the trump card that was the crux of Dionysus's plan.

——*And I wonder if Enyo wants to eventually become that dragon.*

The words of a certain God of Death crossed Loki's mind.

"Was it because of Ishtar?! When you first entered Knossos, the heavenly bull left a strong impression on you! You thought there were seven demi-spirits hidden away in Knossos, including that bull!"

It was just as Dionysus said.

Aiz had seen the giant flasks deep in Knossos. There were seven installations for nurturing the crystal orb fetuses. After defeating the heavenly bull, *Loki Familia* had calculated back that there were six demi-spirits.

As if it was all the height of amusement, Dionysus's face twisted into a sad smile.

"Of course not! What fool would give Freya one of the carefully nurtured cornerstones of this plan?! I gave her the crystal orb fetus that was one of the rejects! A defective one!"

The gears were spinning in Loki's head. She finally reached the same conclusion as Finn, getting there even faster than he did.

The spell of six rings was a lure. It was the reason he had used an exaggerated bait to lure them into Knossos—

"Planning to destroy the city was to throw us off your trail? Your real goal was…!"

"Exactly right—the adventurers!" Dionysus admitted. "Even if I blew Orario away, Babel and all, as long as the adventurers were still alive, they would eventually construct another lid! *Zeus* and *Hera Familias* were decimated fifteen years ago, and yet those with hero potential were quick to resolve the Dark Ages! Even if the city was destroyed, they would undoubtedly display their tenacity like little pests!"

"…!"

"But what if all the adventurers driving the current age were to disappear? There would be an unstoppable reversion! No one would be able to strike back against the monsters pushing out of the Dungeon, and I would be assured a long *orgia*!"

That was Dionysus's true aim. The destruction of the chosen adventurers. The loss of those with the potential to be heroes would bring a wave of chaos to the mortal realm, snuffing out the seeds of revival and restoration. The reconstruction of the final fortress on the mortal realm would be a long time coming. In fact, it might not ever come again.

All that to see the dream of an eternal *orgia*.

"In the worst case, I wouldn't even really mind if Ouranos managed to get away. The annihilation of those who would bear the next age on their shoulders is the true key to the destruction of the mortal realm! Oddly enough, Zeus and Hera's defeat at the hands of the black dragon proved that for me!"

By no means had Dionysus underestimated the adventurers, the beings worthy of hero-dom. In fact, he had judged them to be the ultimate obstacle to the success of his scenario, refining his plans with them in mind.

He had caused *Loki Familia* to fight the demi-spirit on the fifty-ninth floor during their expedition. He had used them, the city's strongest faction, as witnesses to testify to its menace. He had led them on to think that the demi-spirits he had brought into Knossos had to be exterminated, inviting the adventurers in.

It was all for the sake of this day: to summon every last crumb of Orario's principal forces into Knossos.

"If I had not let on to anything and just activated the spell of six rings, the key familias would have been able to escape during its interminable cast time. At best, a bunch of innocent children—unworthy to be considered fighters—would have been the only ones wiped out."

"*Ngh...!* You piece of scum!"

"Heh-heh-heh...I wouldn't have complained if I had managed to shave off a few of your children and destroy your familia during the other two attacks on Knossos...but my Filvis did some unacceptable things. But it's fine. I forgive her. Because this way, I get to see your pained expression, Loki."

Dionysus started walking, glancing at Loki as he approached one of the murals.

"The seventh demi-spirit is named Nidhogg, of course. The being that that crystal orb fetus was attached to is an infant dragon. A nameless dragon that Levis and the others captured and brought up from the deep floors. It has the same origin as the ancient monster of lore."

The final spirit had been granted the name of the dragon that had destroyed cities and killed heroes. Dionysus's eyes narrowed as he lovingly caressed the image of the great spirits and evil dragon.

"It's a calamitous bomb that absorbed the magic of the six spirits. It will blow up everything above it. Into smithereens...It isn't as powerful as the six-rings spell, but it will be more than enough to eradicate the adventurers and deal a fatal blow to Orario!"

The seventh spirit was on the eleventh floor.

Nidhogg would unleash its enormous energy upward, taking out all the forces above it. At the very least, every one of the adventurers currently fighting the demi-spirits would be obliterated.

The area below Nidhogg, below the eleventh floor, was the safe zone. Dionysus intended to live on comfortably and watch over the wild and frenzied feast of madness that would consume the mortal realm.

"Loki, it's been fifteen years!" Dionysus announced loudly. "This has been in the making for fifteen years—since Zeus and Hera's downfall!"

Six years ago, the foundation of the plan had taken shape, as Loki had deduced before, but Dionysus's intrigue had been going on for more than twice that length of time as he worked out the details of his plan.

"At that point, the forces had the potential to become an obstacle to my plan—you, Freya, Ganesha, and Hephaistos. Those four large factions. Astrea had the potential to become a menace as well, but after her and Rudra's followers went and killed each other, she became a nonproblem."

"…!!"

"In terms of battle strength, the remaining points of concern were Ishtar's and Ouranos's personal forces, which had to be hidden somewhere! Aside from those six groups, no one could get in my way!"

At the point when he had contacted the corrupted spirit six years ago, Dionysus had judged that no other forces could threaten his plan. Because of that, he had concentrated on dealing with those six forces in some form or another.

Loki Familia, Freya Familia, Ganesha Familia, Hephaistos Familia, and Ouranos's personal forces, the Xenos.

It was unexpected that *Kali Familia* had joined the fray, but he had considered the possibility of *Ishtar Familia* turning against him before the Evils had won her over. The hole left by the absence of Ishtar was filled by Kali. That was all.

And to deal with those six forces, he had prepared the spirits' six rings to keep the true goal, Nidhogg, hidden by his bluff.

"With the activation of Nidhogg, the other six bodies should be transforming now. Their job isn't to activate the ritual anymore. They are transforming to exterminate all the adventurers!"

Loki Familia had been underground from the start, but now *Freya Familia*'s members were all fighting against the six demi-spirits with the other reinforcements.

The nameless dragon had gotten some strength from Nidhogg, which then flowed to the spirits, enhancing them as if it were a Monster Rex. It had been designed that way. The ritual had been modified so that that would be the result.

Even if it was Finn's crew, they would not be able to crush the enhanced spirits quickly. And if they abandoned the field to go take out Nidhogg, the spirits would just continue the six-rings spell and turn the city to ash. There was no escaping the fated destruction.

"There is nothing left that can stop Nidhogg! Ask for reinforcements from aboveground? That's hopeless! There's no one left who can save you! Because you were the only threat to begin with!"

Dionysus's voice took an operatic twist as Loki clenched her fists.

But she understood what he was saying. Dionysus was sure that even if they had seen through the fact that there was a seventh demi-spirit, it would still have been impossible for them to stop his plan.

If they stopped the ritual, the bombs would go off, and if they defused the bomb, the ritual would complete and the spell would go off. The magnificent two-stage scheme had been perfectly calculated to exhaust all of Orario's forces.

"It's my victory, Loki! Ha-ha-ha-ha-ha-ha-ha!"

Enyo was drunk on victory as his laughter resounded through the labyrinth.

"Captain! The enemy's on the eleventh floor! There's a seventh spirit!" Raul called out urgently from the oculus.

Finn had come to that conclusion even before he received Raul's report.

We were forced into this hellhole to deal with the six rings of the spirits. We were dragged *onto this battlefield.*

He had correctly interpreted Enyo's insidious will, realizing that the battle on the fifty-ninth floor had been foreshadowing this. Obviously, Enyo would have gladly finished off *Loki Familia* then and there, but letting the familia defeat the demi-spirit was necessary to lead to the next best result.

Gathering all the adventurers who have the potential to become a threat…That's his real goal!

Around the same time that Loki was probing Dionysus's divine will, Finn realized himself that Enyo's real aim was the adventurers themselves. That realization was accompanied by a horrible shudder.

"Tch, quit thrashing!"

"Is its strength increasing?!"

Looking up, Finn saw a different battle unfolding. Allen and *Freya Familia* and Shakti and *Ganesha Familia* were continuing to attack, but the blackened demi-spirit was rampaging without any concern for what was happening around it.

Even when it took damage, it continued to swing its tentacles all around. It did not recoil, regardless of the blasts of magic targeted toward it. Its blackened skin resembled dragon scales, blocking any incoming attacks. And just when it seemed to have transformed into a bundle of destruction threatening all the adventurers near it, without any heed to Allen's attacks, it suddenly started a staticky chant and fired off a spell. The power behind the spell had dropped noticeably, but the chaos caused by its total lack of control turned it into a destructive storm.

The bit of power that had flowed into the demi-spirit from the seventh spirit had stimulated it, allowing it to complete its final transformation.

"All squads! Does anyone have any forces to spare?!"

"No! We've got our hands full dealing with the transformed spirit!"

"Even if we gather all the reserve forces, the quality and quantity is…"

He called into the oculus, clinging to a last shred of hope, but cold reality was the only response.

A crack formed in Finn's metaphorical mask as his face twisted at the responses from Fels and Lilly. There was no force that could meet his call.

It was the same for Aiz, who was engaged in single combat.

"""————————————Gh!"""

The two of them roared as they clashed and crashed into each other. Aiz was cloaked in a black wind and Levis met her attacks with her monstrous strength. The armor of flesh covering the right half of Levis's body undulated, pushing aside Aiz's full-bodied attack from the front, seemingly provoking an increase in the creature's power.

Shock and fury. Fighting spirit and murderous intent. The two women's emotions blended for a split second.

Aiz's momentum was not slowed by the deflection, accelerating even faster, using the current of air to unleash a spinning slash. It was an attack carried out without any preparation and without anything held back for the next attack. It surpassed Levis's response speed, but she absorbed the blow with her right arm that had reflexively readied itself, clad in a gauntlet of crimson flesh.

Her arm was half-severed by the slash, but the momentum of the blade was completely halted. The flesh armor expanded like an amoeba consuming its prey, trying to swallow the sword and Aiz's body, but a blast of wind exploded out from Desperate as soon as she chanted "*Nizelle,*" and she was able to escape.

It seemed like a space had opened up between them, but in the very next moment, she dashed forward so fast that her body seemed to blur and swung her sword, crossing blades with Levis.

"Your armor…!"

"Don't give me any crap about fairness. As far as I'm concerned, the same goes for your wind!"

Levis's flesh armor could withstand a slash powered by the strongest Skill. At this point in time, it was arguably the strongest armor in existence in the mortal realm. It was an armor of red flesh forged in the spirit's magic. And in addition to its defensive power, it provided its host with an unexpected superhuman strength—the finest armor for both offense and defense.

Cloaked by wind, Aiz clashed with Levis.

Each attack added to the next, creating a brutal shock wave powerful enough to leave a second-tier adventurer unable to continue. When their blades crossed, the air around them vibrated, and the green flesh clinging to the floors and walls near them peeled off as if crying out in anguish. Their attacks easily cracked the adamantite that was laid bare.

In truth, Airiel was faster and stronger with the synergy from the effect of Avenger. But even when Aiz managed to get behind Levis with her insane speed, the giant eye in the right shoulder of the creature's armor quivered, reacting to her movements and allowing Levis to counterattack from her blind spot almost automatically.

Aiz looked irritated as Levis blocked the blow with her red sword without even turning around.

"Wind!"

She increased the output of her wind again. Using the greater force and acceleration, her series of slashes finally surpassed the creature's ability to defend.

"Guh?!"

The sword encased in a black wind cut off several pieces of the flesh armor.

"—Come to me!"

But the *labyrinth responded* to Levis's call. From the walls, ceiling, and floor, the green flesh oozed out, clinging to the right side of her body and turning crimson—transforming into a new corrupted armor. Her broken sword grew anew from the floor. The moment she drew it, she cut in toward Aiz, accompanied by a gust of wind of her own.

"...*Gh!*"

Aiz's face twisted. The enemy had an *infinite supply* of equipment. Having received the divine protection of the altar—and the demi-spirits that had become the labyrinth—there would be no outlasting Levis. Aiz would run out of strength before the creature who had abandoned her humanity.

It was one girl versus an entire labyrinth. As demonstrated by the history of Orario, the only thing that waited was victory for the labyrinth. How could a single adventurer win against a dungeon, the world itself?

"—*Haaaaaaah!*"

Cast aside your doubt. Raise a battle cry. Subsume yourself in your fighting spirit.

Throw away all room for thought. Just stand and fight.

Without even the time to breathe, the sword of wind and corrupted blade performed a rondo accompanied by thunderous clashes. The preposterous series of blows sent tremors through the entire chamber.

It had become a battle between two inhuman creatures.

On the one side, a spirit of deadly wind engaged in a wild hunt, paired with a black wind that surpassed human understanding. On the other was an unsightly undead ruler clad in an armor of flesh, similar to those spoken of in legends. Raging wind and undulating flesh clashed ruthlessly, trying to destroy each other, summoning one battle cry after the other.

——*I can't win.*

Aiz understood that from their intense mortal combat.

At this rate, I can't overcome her. At this rate, I can't finish her.

The enemy was a genuinely indestructible monster. Her strongest enemy. And desiring the most fitting battle for their final confrontation, Levis consumed even more flesh, becoming even stronger.

My powers!!

It's not enough. It won't be enough! It's really not enough!!! I need more! More!

The desire to win called forth her will to fight, which ascended to a murderous intent. The outline of the monster reflected in her eyes started to morph into the silhouette of a dragon. Her instincts howled and her spirit raged as she tried to draw out even more power.

Linked with Avenger, Airiel grew more and more violent. One by one, she removed her restraints. The black flame burning her back flared with ecstasy. Her will was gradually consumed by the hellfire she had resisted. The intense battle had robbed Aiz of everything she had held back, and her body and soul began their descent into darkness.

"Gh!"

She faced her blackened urges and accelerated. Her body cried out. Her flesh and bones creaked. Her nerves were on the verge of burning out. But she ignored all of that and moved to kill the monster before her eyes. There were more black sparks emanating from her golden eyes. The original Aiz was being revived, the one who had been called the Doll Princess and War Princess. Her bloodlust was as potent now as it had been in the past, threatening to claim Levis's life.

"…Ha-ha!"

As Aiz slashed, cloaked in the whipping wind, Levis unconsciously started to laugh as she tore through her own limits. The hidden cost of that forbidden armor was that it was puncturing her internal organs. Her flesh exploded, and blood vessels popped as an unsightly amount of blood burst out from her skin. The magic stone at her core was heating up as if on the verge of burning out. However, she still attempted to meet Aiz's challenge and kill her, as if she considered this damage trivial.

"""————————————————————————*Gh!!*"""

Their roars overlapped. They were determined to kill no matter what it entailed.

Crack. Aiz's Desperate split.

Even her Durandal sword, which was *supposed to be unbreakable,* could not endure the power of her black wind. But Aiz did not notice the damage to her weapon as she continued rushing down the path to self-destruction. Her trusted blade's warning fell on deaf ears. The pleading cries of her other half were not enough to stop her.

Her demise was quietly approaching her.

"Gh…!"

The sounds of countless battles poured out from the oculi. Everyone had their hands full with their current battles, roaring in desperation.

Finn thought he could hear Enyo's laughter. On every board, they were lacking the decisive firepower to break through, running out of options. Even if Finn used his head or played his cards, the current situation was just one step ahead of his reach.

It had been fifteen years in the planning. That span of time was an overwhelming difference in prebattle preparedness, the difference between victory and defeat.

He felt uneasy. A warning of defeat and destruction sent shivers down his spine.

"—Shakti, take command!"

"Finn?!"

"Cynthia, come here!"

"Y-yes, sir!"

Finn immediately dashed away from that battlefield. Leaving the first squad and the demi-spirit to Allen and Shakti, he took as little forces as possible and headed for Raul on the eleventh floor.

——*This is hopeless. What am I doing? I won't make it in time.*

The voice in his head told him the cruel answer. It was too far from the first squad's battlefield to the stairs to the next floor. He would not be able to reach Nidhogg before the timer finished counting down. The warning ache in his thumb might as well have been meaningless pain at that point. Every fiber of Finn Deimne was screaming the word *defeat*.

"—Shut up already!"

However, Finn's feet did not stop. He had no intention of ever stopping. Honorable resignation could eat shit. There was no way he would just applaud Enyo and acknowledge defeat graciously. Even if it looked shameful, he would never resign. Faced with an unavoidable checkmate, Finn refused to give up and continued to look for moves.

He would never give up. He would never stop struggling. He would try every path on the way until the end to create even a single glimmer of hope out of their hopeless situation.

Because he was an adventurer—he would greedily, desperately cling to life with no concern for appearances.

We can't hope for more reinforcements from aboveground! And there's no point hoping for the appearance of a convenient third party out of thin air! Praying to the gods? Yeah, right! We're here to beat one of them!

As he sprinted down the passage, he redirected every ounce of energy into his thoughts. He examined every possibility, as many choices as there were stars in the sky; scrutinized them; studied them from every possible angle; and groped for the one move on the board that would resolve everything.

In his head, time compressed, and Finn plumbed the limits of what could be achieved in a single moment of time.

Don't stop thinking! Move! Move! Move!

Split up the forces. Gather a few troops from all six squads and send them to the eleventh floor.

—No good. It would take too long. The bomb would go off before we could gather enough strength.

Send in Fels and all the other forces in reserve. If they could just delay the activation of the bomb...

——They can't. Nidhogg's strength is unprecedented. A superficial force will just be wiped out.

——And if Fels and Lilliluka have to join the fray along with me, the command center will be broken.

An infinite loop of trial and error, a flash of static, alerts blaring over each other. All his nerves were moving as one. His brain started to overheat. His thoughts still did not slow, even as his head started to burn red as shrill alarm bells continued to ring.

Currently, everything was going according to Enyo's plan. In that case, they just had to do something that Enyo had not accounted for. Use everything. Put everything in. Bet with everything. Overcome the divine will of a deusdea and stop the ache throbbing in his thumb.

Isn't there anything?! Do I—do we have anything left?!

In the depths of his thoughts, he was sitting by himself at an enormous round table in the darkness.

There was a single giant board composed of eight different boards. Pieces were scattered all around, trying to take down the six black queens and the rest of the enemy pawns. There was no one across from Finn. Just an empty seat.

Laughing ominously, Enyo had approached from somewhere outside the board and lobbed a bomb in the form of a ninth board, looking to turn all of Finn's pieces to ash.

It was a deadlock that was impossible to break. There was no move that could reach the ninth board from his position.

Motionlessly staring down at the board, Finn changed tack. If Enyo had already accounted for all the pieces on the board, he had no choice but to fight back with a piece that Enyo had not foreseen: something that was currently on the board, outside the realm of Enyo's considerations. A piece that fell outside the god's field of view.

Enyo's plan had been envisioned fifteen years ago. The preparations had begun six years ago. All that time had been spent calculating. Finn needed to hit the god with an unknown that would render all that time meaningless. Something beyond his predictions. Something of the mortal realm that could surprise even a deity—

"_____"

In that instant, Finn's vision lit up.

Amid those boards and those pieces. Amid infinite choice. Amid all that, he reached his hand out to a single piece that was hidden, buried, yet shining with a faint light like a glittering star.

Finn grabbed that single piece that the god had not seen—that the god could not see—a piece that was visible only to Finn. The moment he touched that piece, his body jolted and his slowed internal clock sprang back to normal.

"—Rei!"

In the next moment, Finn looked up and took out an oculus. It had taken him less than a second in real time to reach his decision, shouting into the crystal.

"Lend me your strength!"

Fifteen minutes.

That was how long the miracle would last. The time limit for the effects of Level Boost. In other words, they had to finish the battle that was about to begin within those fifteen minutes.

"It's been a while since I fought with this kind of lineup. Since that tumble with the black minotaur," Aisha said as she licked her lips.

"So we're going to have to slug it out with another Level Seven–class monster, huh...?" Asfi sighed.

"Yes. It's fate," the masked adventurer responded, unruffled as she drew her weapon.

They were all looking at the true monster in the form of an elf. The creature Filvis watched them cover Lefiya, her green eyes reflecting her despair at the world.

With her mind made up, Lefiya was no longer troubled. She readied the sword and wand, which had been Filvis's weapons.

The air rippled with tension. The final calm before the battle began. It was so tense that Lulune and the others subconsciously paused their movements to aid the adventurers collapsed on the ground. For just a second, there was no sound, as if they had detached from the world.

"—*I beseech the name of Wishe!*"

Lefiya was the first to move.

"*Talaria!*"

She was followed by Asfi.

The rear guard chanted, which announced the opening of battle. At the same time, she activated the magic item Talaria on both feet. She just barely lifted off the floor, hovering, and then all of a sudden, she flew like a gust of wind without any warning.

"!"

To Filvis, who was standing across from her, it seemed as though Asfi had shifted to the side instead of advancing. It was a sidestep that could be accomplished only by flight. With that, she quickly disappeared from Filvis's line of sight.

The effects of Talaria were influenced by the user's Status. For Asfi, her flight was much faster than normal, since she was a pseudo–Level 5 with the Level Boost.

That sudden unexpected movement caused Filvis to lose sight of Perseus. As that happened, Aisha and the masked adventurer advanced, pressuring the creature.

"All right, let's get this started!"

"Here I come."

While Filvis was forced to deal with the two vanguards approaching from the front, Asfi skimmed over the floor, gliding around the room and scooping up the adventurers' weapons that had fallen to the ground. Then she shot up into the sky like a bird flapping its wings. Making use of her ability to move in all dimensions, she came over Filvis's head and threw down the weapons in her hands.

"Hah!"

Having stolen the high ground after escaping Filvis's gaze, Asfi's surprise attack annoyed the creature, interrupting her when she had been just about to hit back at the other two attackers, but she stopped and dodged the attack.

Sabers and longswords stuck into the floor where Filvis had been standing just a moment before, but Asfi did not stick around to watch, going back to pick up more weapons, fly up, and throw them again. Not just once or twice but multiple times, repeatedly. She retrieved weapons, flew up, and fired them off.

It would be generous to say that her aim was true. Filvis did not even have to defend herself, easily dodging all of them. She pushed back the persistent efforts of Aisha and the masked adventurer with ease, swinging a single arm as she looked on dubiously.

"What are you trying to do?...Wait...Is this...?"

That was when Filvis realized something. In less than ten strafing passes, Filvis had been surrounded by a circle of weapons around ten meders wide. Swords, spears, glaives, halberds, all sorts of weapons were thrust into the ground, forming a circle around her.

"...Are you trying to make a cage to close me in?"

It wasn't even a fence! She snorted in annoyance as she stared at Asfi floating above her head.

"...I suppose you could call it the foundation for your defeat."

Asfi looked stretched thin, tossed about by the newfound power that she was not used to yet from the Level Boost, as the strongest monster looked up at her. She grinned as sweat streamed down her cheeks.

Immediately after, the masked adventurer kicked the ground.

"Wsssh!"

Her dash evoked images of a gale. A high-speed slash caught the enemy off guard. As the attack came in diagonally from behind her, Filvis swung a single arm, judging the entire charade to be utterly pointless.

"Gh?!"

The swinging blade shattered tragically. A destruction of weaponry. A complete nullification that would knock down an average adventurer. She lost the excellent blade that she had received from *Hermes Familia*.

It spoke clearly to their hopeless difference in strength. However, the masked adventurer was not shaken, nor did she lament the loss. As the shards of metal were still flying through the air, she slipped past Filvis and moved behind her, *drawing one of the swords sticking out of the floor.*

In the blink of an eye, she had swung around to unleash another slash at Filvis.

"What?!"

Equipping a new weapon, the masked adventurer speedily and decisively moved on to the next attack, surprising Filvis for the first time in the whole battle. The creature reflexively intercepted the sword, breaking the blade again, but the masked adventurer did not hesitate to discard the hilt and draw a glaive from the circle of weapons that was not even a fence for Filvis. As the masked adventurer's whirlwind charge picked up speed, Filvis was finally too slow to respond. The purple robe she was wearing was cut.

"I did not make a cage—or a fence. If you must call it something, then I suppose *armory* will suffice," Asfi said, adjusting her glasses.

From them, she could see Filvis was being exposed to a surging series of attacks by the masked adventurer. The thing that Asfi had prioritized at the opening of hostilities was readying the battlefield.

To best make use of Antianeira Aisha Belka and her peerless strength in hand-to-hand combat and the masked adventurer, a skilled vanguard by the name of Gale Wind, she had set the stage.

After losing her beloved wooden sword, the masked adventurer kept drawing more weapons from the armory, running riot to her heart's content. Filvis was experiencing the same precise divine attack that the Sword Princess had faced just one month ago on Daedalus Street.

"*Gaaaah?!*"

As she added more power to her sprint, she kicked up speed and the impact of her attack. Upon seeing the effects of Gale Wind, Filvis lost a shred of her composure. It was imperative that they not miss any slight hint of agitation—to snare her feet. That was the key to toppling her and slaying Goliath.

"Hey, where are you looking?!"

"Tch?!"

As the masked adventurer retreated after landing a blow, Aisha attacked from another angle altogether. The Amazon unleashed her assault with the optimal timing, forcing Filvis to defend with her bare arms. The large pudao slammed into her readied metal gloves, sending sparks flying. The force of the blow caused Filvis's knee to buckle slightly.

While the masked adventurer was the embodiment of a raging whirlwind, Aisha Belka was skillful all around. Without spending any time reasoning in her head, she instinctively worked together with the two of them to utilize the results to their utmost limits. Using her warrior's intuition, she observed the high-speed combat of her Gale Wind, weaving in her own attacks without getting in the way. On top of that, she had filled the gap right when the creature was preparing for a counterattack. Because of Aisha, Filvis could not prepare a response, forced to absorb the onslaught one-sidedly. As the creature gazed in wonder, the gale passed through again, scratching her cheek.

"Ghhh! Don't look down on me!"

Filvis punched in fury. It was a move that betrayed common sense, causing the two attackers to shudder. Even though she hadn't taken a proper stance, her attack was strong enough to kill with a single hit, speaking to her insane potential.

And it was aimed at Aisha.

"Gather, breath of the earth—my name is Alf!"

But Lefiya rejected that oncoming slaughter with magic.

"Veil Breath!"

Right before the attack landed, Aisha, Lyu, Asfi, and Lefiya were covered in a film of jade light. As Aisha looked in wonder, she adopted a defensive stance, almost as if guided by the armor of light. Filvis's fist rammed into her crossed arms, and she was sent rolling across the floor—but a second later, she stood up.

"What...?!"

"...Sheesh, I swear I saw my life flash before my eyes."

Aisha grinned mischievously as her arms hung limply, the bones fractured. Filvis's amazed gaze shifted from the woman standing up to Lefiya at the edge of her periphery, her wand out.

Veil Breath. Riveria's forte. Defensive magic. Its effect increased resistance to physical and magical attacks. When Riveria used it, it was enough to protect an adventurer from even a valgang dragon's big fireballs. With a long cast, Lefiya had prioritized buffing, which was indispensable when dealing with a powerful enemy.

It was the correct decision as the rear guard.

"Thanks, Thousand!" Aisha yelled as her fractured bones healed as a side effect of *Veil Breath*, launching herself back to the battle-field. Watching everything, Lefiya shifted to her next round without pause.

"Unleashed pillar of light, limbs of the holy tree. You are the master archer."

She was composing another spell. Casting it at an impossible speed, it rang out without any hesitation.

"Loose your arrows, fairy archers. Pierce, arrow of accuracy!" She completed the short cast quickly: *"—I beseech the name of Wishe!"*

Lefiya *immediately began chanting a new spell* as soon as her spell had moved to standby.

"That's..."

Among the adventurers who had distanced themselves to avoid getting wrapped up in the battle, Haruhime was the only one who noticed the oddity and doubted her eyes.

The magic circle from Lefiya's first spell shrank, becoming a small ring that wrapped around her left wrist. And while that was happening, she continued the second chant, and a large magic circle expanded at her feet. There were two magic circles active at once.

That impossible scene caused the renart sorcerer to gaze in wonder.

"Gah?!"

"Leon!"

On the front lines, Filvis launched an intense attack that peeled off one of the allies. The creature hit the masked adventurer's weapon and arm, moving to follow up the attack.

"Cannon!" Lefiya paused the second cast she was chanting. *"Arcs Ray!"*

The magic circle on her left arm activated and expanded in the palm of her outstretched hand, unleashing a blast with an astonishing output—a large homing ray of light. It was a stupidly powerful spell that would cause significant damage if it hit directly, regardless of their difference in level. With that, Filvis was forced to give up on chasing down Lyu.

While that was happening, Lefiya picked up the cast that she had cut off partway.

"My name is Alf——Luna Aldis!"

Her completed Summon Burst activated Riveria's healing magic.

"?!"

All were blown away by this: Filvis, who endured the light ray, and Lyu, who was healed, and even Aisha and Asfi.

"Wait, did she just fire two different spells at once?!" Lulune shouted.

"No, that isn't it! She held back the magic and activated it with a time lag...!" Haruhime responded.

She was the only one who understood the fairy's trick, upon witnessing it from start to finish while Lulune and the others were moving around, retrieving fallen adventurers.

All knew of the general idea of holding magic on standby. They understood it was possible not to immediately fire spells once the chant was complete, maintaining the magic circle to fire it at the optimal time. It could be called one of a mage's key techniques.

But while it could be used to activate a spell after ascertaining the flow of battle, the downside was that they could not start a new spell when mages held a spell on standby. Starting a new cast canceled the spell on standby. The followers in the present day were not equipped with the circuits to use two different types of magic at once. If they tried to force two spells concurrently, it would simply cause an Ignis Fatuus. Even Riveria, the strongest mage, could not do it.

However, Lefiya's new Skill had flipped those rules on its head. Double Cannon. Its effect allowed the expansion of two different types of magic circles. It was a rare Skill, allowing the first magic to be maintained on standby while she shifted to chanting a different spell. The first spell on standby could be activated whenever she wanted using the spell key.

In other words, Lefiya could construct a new spell while staying capable of firing off a broadside at a moment's notice. It was effectively manipulating two different spells at once: a dual control that was impossible for any other modern mages. Dual-wielding magic.

At the same time, this whole thing was ironic. After she'd sobbed tears of grief, finally resolving herself to face a cruel reality, she had developed Double Cannon, as if she was still longing to continue her duet with Filvis.

To defeat Filvis, Lefiya was using the rare Skill she had attained when she leveled up.

"Gh...!"

As a mage on the back lines, she knew Double Cannon wielded a tremendous effect, but it was not all good. Using the Skill drained her Mind, combining two different types of magic, which made it all the worse.

It feels like my head is splitting in half...!

And on top of that, there was the difficult task of choosing the right casts. At this moment in time, Lefiya was serving as the rear guard on the battlefield, where it was host to a super-high-speed fight that did not allow even a single second's wasted time. There was no time for her to abandon a cast and choose a new spell. Once she started chanting, she had no choice but to finish the cast. Lefiya had to guess the next ten moves to choose the right spell to have in her arsenal once she finished casting it.

Should I choose an attack to deal with Miss Filvis next? Defense? Recovery? Or a Status buff for everyone?

As she mentally sifted through her myriad of options, asking herself for the correct answer, the voice in her head reached a fever pitch.

For a regular back-line mage, who was normally expected only to unleash her strongest cannon blast, the combined weight of all the considerations was too much. Lefiya's head felt like it was being crushed. And Lefiya Viridis, the mage with the name Thousand Elf, had too many options to begin with. But those were liable to cause chaos, which could easily short-circuit her thoughts if she let them.

"Grrr. *Cannon! Wynn Fimbulvetr!*"

But Lefiya kept choosing the correct answer. When Aisha and Lyu moved to attack, she fired a supporting shot. She correctly timed when the buffs ran out, reapplying them as necessary. And when Filvis went on a raging counterattack, she defended against it by creating a wall of ice that froze everything in sight.

From the back lines, they could overlook the entire battlefield. That was a crucial ability for a mage—to read the flow of battle. The spirit of the Great Tree helped cover for these gaps in ability when these two conditions were not fully up to the task.

The method of powerful mental tuning that Riveria had taught her had become a kind of skill. In this extreme situation where a single mistake was not allowed, she faced the pressure placed on her head and cast it aside.

Lefiya's mental state had ascended into a higher dimension after reaching Level 4 coming to terms with this new reality and still choosing to fight.

Her spirit was like a great sacred tree with roots digging deep into the earth. She controlled her heart, overcame her confusion, and continued to read the subtleties of the battle.

And Lefiya's chosen spells as the rear guard influenced the vanguard. If she chose a cannon blast, then they could attack resolutely. If she chose a defensive spell, it was a warning of a follow-up attack from the enemy. If she chose recovery, the other two would maintain the front line.

Mutual understanding between front and back lines gave birth to coordination that was even smoother.

Perseus, Antianeira, and Gale Wind—adventurers of great renown—were being guided by Lefiya.

—*The rear guard is too strong!*

As Leon engaged in a fierce battle with the powerful creature, she was astonished by the cover fire she was receiving. If there were multiple mages providing support, then it would make sense to her. But could anyone believe that a single person was supporting with attack, defense, and recovery spells all by themselves?

"Thousand Elf…To think you have grown to this height!"

The immature mage was nowhere to be found—the one who had been with Bell Cranell when she had saved them. The masked adventurer felt no shame as she complimented her fellow elf with the alias of Thousand Elf.

"Protect you? Quit joking. This fight has felt unequal so far!" Aisha said, exalted, as she crossed blades with the creature.

Lefiya never stopped readying the next round even as she held on to a spare spell to fire off whenever she needed it. The elf was currently standing still, devoting herself to the back lines, but if she was ever able to Concurrent Cast and move around at the same time, there would be no touching her. Aisha could see that future potential, and it was a scarily reliable one.

"I suspect Thousand feels the same about coordinating with us."

Swooping into a dive to unleash an attack before circling back around in the air, Asfi, coolheaded, observed the battle with a bird's-eye view, unlike the other two. She could see that Lefiya's Double Cannon would have been meaningless if she was facing

Filvis by herself. This was the first time that she would have been able to use her Skill to its fullest: when she was working together with the three of them—with a party of skilled front- and midline fighters. Lefiya must have been feeling the same sort of awe toward them that Aisha and Lyu felt about her.

As all four of their thoughts converged, they glanced at one another. And then they accelerated, charging at Filvis.

"Gah?!"

They did not let her recover, continuing to press her before she regained her composure. That was their only chance of winning. All four of them were certain of that as they continued their waves of attacks, gradually cornering Filvis.

Gale Wind raced, Antianeira danced, Perseus supported, and Thousand Elf sang. Even the inhuman creature was on the back foot when faced with their strongest quartet.

"Come, reckless conqueror!"

"Distant forest sky! Infinite stars inlaid upon the eternal night sky!"

"!"

All of a sudden, two voices began Concurrent Casting. Skilled at chanting, the Amazon warrior and masked adventurer were gathering an immense amount of magic.

It was a tactic, a trick they had thought up together. Which would Filvis prioritize stopping? Or would she take the risk and try to crush them both at once? They were forcing Filvis to make a choice, to react.

"—Tch!"

The one she chose was Aisha. Because she had to split her focus off chanting, her speed of evasion would have to take a serious hit. With that conclusion, Filvis turned to deal with the woman closest to her.

"Well done."

"____"

But Aisha halted her casting without a problem. Her movements regained their brilliance, and, luring Filvis into a certain position, she avoided the creature's impatient attack to retreat.

"Wsssh!"

Just as Aisha slipped away, Asfi lobbed the Burst Oil that landed where she had been standing just moments before. Even a creature would be caught by surprise. She was unable to avoid the item, but the toss had not been aimed at her. Its target was a spot where weapons were sticking out of the ground—the armory that Asfi had prepared. And the weapons sticking out of the ground next to Filvis were not just simple ones—

—Is that a magic sword?!

The magic sword with a golden copper sheen reacted when the Burst Oil exploded, setting off a secondary blast.

"Gah?!"

A giant explosion went off. Perseus was experienced in reading into the battle to turn things in her favor, and she had hidden her actual move by pretending to set up the armory.

Filvis stopped moving, wrapped in a swirling explosion. Judging that this would be their first and last opportunity, Lefiya activated the magic she had just finished casting.

"Fusillade Fallarica!"

Flame arrows arced through the air. It was an unending barrage targeted at Filvis.

"Luminous Wind!"

And the masked adventurer had continued her Concurrent Casting, too, firing off an artillery blast of her own. Giant balls of stardust were cloaked in a green wind. She launched another spell with a wide range like Lefiya's *Fusillade Fallarica*.

"———————————?!"

It was a simultaneous blast from the two Level-5 elves—an unparalleled high-power assault. The twin attacks unleashed a chain of light and flames, forcing Haruhime, Lulune, and the bystanders to brace themselves against the shock wave that it set off. The monster in an elf's body disappeared, consumed by the bright light of the explosion.

"...Miss Filvis..."

As the ferocious sea of flames gave off a veil of smoke, Lefiya pressed her hand to her chest, where she was confronted by a confused mix of emotions. Her whisper was swallowed up by the crackle of the flames. The other three glanced at Lefiya before staring into the heart of the explosion, not letting their guards down.

It was a combined barrage by two Level-5 elves, inherent magic users. It was an attack powerful enough to take down even a floor boss. That was the greatest firepower that the four of them could bring to bear.

Even a creature would not be able to brush that off.

"_____"

——Just as they became convinced that was the case, a single arm thrust out from behind the smoke. Time froze for the four of them as a giant black magic circle unfolded, like the maw of darkness hinging open. Green eyes gleamed behind the smoke as Filvis mercilessly fired her cannon.

"Dio Thyrsos."

She unleashed a pitch-black bolt of lightning—an attack magic with a spell so short, they didn't even have time to realize she was casting something. The sound of its blast outdid the combined assault by Lefiya and Gale Wind.

While everyone was desperately trying to get out of the path of the lightning, unable to say anything, Filvis's arm tore through the smoke, swinging to the side. The single-target magic should have moved forward only in a straight line, but it was fired in a sweeping arc.

"?!"

The bolt turned into a lightning whip that incinerated the entire battlefield. By changing the area of effect from a straight line to a fan, the four of them were placed in the destruction zone.

It was an absurd use of magic. Because they were caught off guard, the adventurers had no choice but to deal with it head-on. The black gleam of lightning shone on their faces as they took emergency action to evade the oncoming attack.

"Aaaaaaaaaaaaaaaaaaaah?!"

All of the green flesh in that part of the chamber was burned to ash. The swords and spears stuck out of the ground, and their armory disappeared in the flash of light, too. The crackling tendrils of lightning charred their equipment, their battle clothes, and their skin. The electric shock in the air even reached Lulune, Haruhime, and the other adventurers, causing them to cry out in pain.

The thunderous boom temporarily deafened everyone in the room. Their field of vision was dyed white. All told, as the electric current dispersed, half of the giant chamber had been charred.

"A…Asfi?!"

"Aisha?!"

As the reverberations finally died down, Lulune and Samira the Amazon cried out at the scene.

The four of them were still alive. But they were clearly just barely hanging on. They had all been burned seriously, and smoke was rising from their bodies. Asfi was collapsed with Lefiya, as if she had tried to cover her. Everything below her knee on her right leg, including the Talaria, had been charred black.

Aisha and Leon were charred and collapsed on the ground. The glow from *Veil Breath* had disappeared, consumed by the black thunder. In truth, that was what had saved them at the last moment. If not for that, they would have been disintegrated without a trace.

"…Had I not been corrupted, that would have been your victory."

As the smoke cleared from the source of the lightning, Filvis appeared, battered but without any major injuries. She had lost her right ear, that long ear that was emblematic of elves, and her face was burned badly enough that red flesh was visible. Her left arm that she had used to protect herself from the fire arrows was still burning. But that was all. As her body gave off steam, her ear and skin were regenerating. The flames burning on her arm were extinguished by the touch of that healing steam.

Filvis paid no heed to the onlookers consumed with despair, focusing on the four who had damaged her.

"*Ah…?!*"

"Damn monster!"

She targeted the masked adventurer and Aisha, who were struggling to stand up. Even discounting their wounds, the two of them had no hope of winning without everyone's teamwork. Filvis's furious assault left them spitting blood and collapsing to all fours in the blink of an eye.

"No! Ah...*Unleashed pillar of light!*"

As Asfi struggled to control the spasms and broke out in a cold sweat, Lefiya gritted her teeth and pushed herself to her feet. She muttered a spell to herself, trying to support Aisha and Lyu, who were being cornered.

"Lefiya...I'll get to you last."

Filvis had sensed the magic and swung her leg, kicking the floor where the green flesh had been burned away, unleashing a blast of rock fragments to disrupt the spell. Rocks the size of a child's head pummeled Lefiya: her right elbow and thigh, her left armpit and shoulder. When the rock fragments slammed into Lefiya, she coughed up blood and slumped over to her back. Filvis's green eyes narrowed, looking almost sad as she cast aside her lingering attachment, but the moment she turned back to Lyu and Aisha, her face, that of a merciless monster, continued its rampage.

"Agh...Gah...Ha...?!"

As Lefiya breathed in a mix of blood and air and started to cough, Gale Wind fell.

The fist of an ex-elf mercilessly slammed into her, knocking her to the ground. And then Aisha. The last one left standing, she kept fighting to the end, plastered in blood and sweat, but it was all meaningless before the creature who looked on with Ein's cruel expression. No extensions were allowed as the sound of the impact of her metal gloves cruelly sliced away at what remained of her life.

It had not yet been ten minutes since the fight began. The battle had been decided before their fifteen-minute time limit was reached.

"Don't you dare, you piece of shit!"

Samira howled, and the Berbera who had been kept out of the fight on strict orders charged as one. Even if it was utterly reckless, the Amazons chose a savage valor. Aisha cried out for them to stop, but it was too late.

Filvis mercilessly swung her arm, knocking back all the women charging at her. Some had their arms snapped by that attack, cracks resounding from their spines, and others continued charging despite being filled with intense pain. The creature watched their determination to rescue Aisha with sober eyes and then crushed it with cold fists.

It was an image of hell as blood splattered and they cried out in pain. No one was left able to move.

Lulune, Haruhime, and the surviving adventurers had no choice but to watch as the Amazons were brutally murdered and Lefiya, Lyu, Aisha, and Asfi were left groaning in anguish on the ground. It took all they had to stand up to their fear and not flee in terror. Teeth chattering and tears flowing at the scene of destruction, the image of that powerful monster was burned into their eyes.

At this rate…!

Coughing over and over, her consciousness dim, Lefiya was filled with unease. If she did not stand up, if she did not persist, if she didn't do anything, then the winds of victory would not blow over them. Shaking away the image of defeat, the vision of utter destruction, Lefiya scolded her limbs for not heeding her commands.

"…?"

While everyone else's heart was wrenched into two and all were losing their will to fight, Lefiya saw someone hurrying at the edge of her blurred vision, dashing across the chamber.

"Bete Logaaa!" shouted a little girl.

Ever since the battle had begun, that was all she'd managed to say.

"Hey, stand up! Please get up, Bete Loga!" Lena kept calling out to the unresponsive werewolf.

He was lying on his back, his hair covering his eyes, his wounds refusing to heal. She tried potions and elixirs, but nothing was working. It was as if Filvis's pitch-black thunder had been accompanied by a curse. Every single means of healing she tried was rejected.

"If you don't, everyone will die! Aisha and the other Berbera, too!"

The scene of her comrades being trampled was unfolding before her eyes. As her comrades collapsed, her tears became unstoppable.

Her shuddering, too. She could not contain the fear that was causing her slender limbs to tremble. Lena was being consumed by fear, just like Lulune and the rest of them.

"Wake up! Get up! Are you really going to just keep sleeping?! That's so lame! That's not like you at all!"

But she kept shouting. Kneeling beside him, grasping his right hand, she kept shouting. Her voice had grown hoarse, and her throat was starting to bleed from all the yelling. Coughing and hacking, she kept pleading with him. She almost looked as if she was praying.

"...This version of you isn't strong at all! Y-you're gonna break the illusion!"

However, despite all that, the wounded werewolf did not move. Lena's eyes filled with tears as she peered at his unopened eyes and gazed upon his unresponsive hand that would not squeeze back. She looked determined.

"You're always acting tough! Talking crap about how weaklings should just stay in their lane! You can't lose—obviously! That would be so stupid! Like, really uncool! I misjudged you! You're just a loser with your tail between your legs!"

She forced herself to stop crying and insulted him with all her might. She mustered all the scorn and disdain she could in order to set him off. She was obviously forcing herself, as her teary voice and unseemly dripping nose attested. Trying to control her voice that threatened to collapse into a fit of sobs, Lena desperately feigned a scornful sneer.

"You were the one always telling me not to come, Bete Loga! Right? Then stand up! Win! Show me that arrogant-strongman act and beat the shit out of the enemy!"

Lena Tully was weak. She was a burden, which was why Bete had tried to keep her away. She could not save her beloved man. Fighting together with him had been impossible from the start, and even just supporting him from the sides was hard enough to make her despair.

Lena Tully could not protect Bete Loga.

"If you can't do that, then you're just talk! Just like all the other stupid men!"

But Lena Tully could make Bete Loga mad.

"With everyone else, Aisha always said you were a pain in the ass and a real nasty wolf! That you only cared about lycans. I was always standing up for you, but I dunno if I can do that anymore!"

Lena was an expert at pissing off Bete. When she'd leap on him like a puppy, he'd send her flying with a solid jab to the stomach, and when she'd cling to him like a cat in heat, he'd kick her aside, and when she'd get all excited like an innocent girl, he would be there to bring her back to earth with his fists. Her boisterous voice seemed to spur his rage. Her shouts made Bete's wounds ache. Her very existence was so aggravating to him that Bete would actually call her by name.

"...Hey, didn't I fall for a strong guy? Someone coarse and mean who still wanted to save us? Even though he would say the worst things imaginable, he would never, ever abandon us!"

Tears like jewels splashed onto Bete's face.

She had long since been reduced to tears during her attempt to mimic the usual mockery of her beloved wolf. Her face melted into overwhelming emotions.

"He would totally look down on us and fight even if he was alone, but even then, he'd shrug it off, trying to play it cool like a little kid!"

The drops became as dense as rain, soaking into the tattoo engraved in his right cheek, penetrating his hidden scars.

"You would push us away and try to bear all the pain yourself!"

Twitch. One of the fingers of the hand that Lena was clutching trembled.

"I don't want to see you like this! But I can't protect you, either! I can't even support you because I worry that you might end up in an even worse situation if I'm there!"

The wolf's left hand clenched into a fist, as if filled with irritation. His fangs ground together at her continual tears.

"I'm so weak. I can't do anything other than believe in your strength!"

At that, the wolf's lips trembled.

"…—P…"

That weakling's tears bothered Bete.

"…—T up…"

That pip-squeak's cries made Bete's scar ache.

"…Shut up…"

That wimp's tinny howl ignited the flame of Bete's rage.

"I'm begging you, Bete Loga!" Lena screamed as she grasped his hand in both of hers. "Don't lie to me!"

"Aaaaaaaaaaaaaaaaaaarrrrgh, shut up!"

The wolf's eyes snapped open.

"Ah…"

"Shut your damn trap! You're really starting to piss me off! Who wants to hear your stupid sobbing?!"

Lena's eyes opened wide as Bete crushed Lena's hand. He had recovered. Peeling himself off the ground, he ripped away the chains of pain that had bound his whole body.

"I was never planning to let it end like this, and I don't need a weakling saying shit to get me to move!"

The manly image of a strong wolf rising brought tears to the weakling's eyes.

"Get back, Lena!"

She struggled to smile as emotion swelled in her chest and then nodded in acknowledgment.

"Uchide no Kozuchi!"

"!"

Another wuss provided a blessing of golden light.

"Haruhime?!" Lena shouted.

The renart girl had appeared before Bete. She had been the blurry figure that Lefiya had seen from afar, cutting across the battlefield while avoiding getting wrapped up in the battle. The renart girl granted Bete the final golden foxtail she had left.

She had been waiting for him to stand back up to pour in all her magic.

This was the third time she had stood across from Bete. The first time, she had been a coward who could not even fight. During the second meeting, she had appeared before Bete as a weakling who had nonetheless resolved to fight. And now, this was the third time they took each other in. Haruhime was still a wimp, but she faced Bete with an even stronger gaze than before. Her breathing was ragged from the repeated stress and impending Mind Down, and she was struggling desperately not to collapse as she stared into Bete's eyes and believed.

"*Grrrr!*"

Faith was the most scathing revenge. The weakling he had tormented and insulted did not resent him, continuing to believe that he would stand back up. She had believed in Bete's revival even more than he had. She had had a stronger determination than he had.

The wolf was consumed by his rage. His amber eyes became so bloodshot that it looked like a red web was covering them. His anger exploded. He was infuriated with himself for letting howling weaklings set the stage for him.

What followed went without saying. The animal had long passed his boiling point. He unleashed all his hidden animal instincts, turned the hot blood flowing from his wounds into strength, and raised a powerful howl, swearing to those two girls who had believed in him that he would hunt the creature down.

"Gh...Gah...?!"

"This is the end."

Filvis stood alone, grasping a single woman's neck as all the Amazons lay collapsed on the floor around her like gravestones. It was Aisha. The last left standing, she was smeared in blood, and her beautiful figure was battered. Filvis's slender fingers squeezed tighter, biting into Aisha's neck as she struggled to breathe, sounding like a broken music box.

Despite all that, the warrior's eyes had not lost that determined look, continuing to stare back at the creature looking down on her.

"...*Purge, cleansing lightning.*"

Filvis's eyes narrowed as she chose to finish her in the cruelest way possible. There was a crackle as she started giving off light. The left hand clamped around Aisha's neck became electrified. When the magic was cast, everything above Aisha's neck would be incinerated, instantly transforming the beautiful vixen into a tragic corpse.

Turning a deaf ear to the soundless and heartbreaking pleas to stop from Lefiya and the others, Filvis was going to make sure that Aisha's heart would never beat again.

"——*Gh?!*"

At that moment, a howl resounded in the chamber, causing everyone's hairs to stand on end. It was not the cry of a wounded animal. It was the howl of a giant wolf who would devour everything that lay before his eyes. Filvis could feel the bloodlust—a homicidal fury that was intense enough to make the creature's body sense danger for the first time.

She immediately spun around just in time to see a wolf, fur matted with blood, already right in front of her, brandishing his fangs.

"*Gaaaaaaaaaaaah!*"

Bete's flying kick used all his strength. Filvis immediately raised an arm to defend, but it was so powerful that it tore through her skin, shattering her bones. She dropped to her knee, letting go of Aisha. Taken by shock, Filvis shook off her confusion and thrust her left arm at the wolf about to sink his teeth into her.

"*Dio Thyrsos!*"

That was what she had finished chanting. She decided to activate it at short range. The result was a destructive blast of thunder that even scorched the air, but Bete knocked her electrified arm up with his own.

"——"

Blown back, the lightning cannon went off with her arm pointed up, blasting through the ceiling, piercing into the upper floor. As the bolt flickered above them, a tremor shook the entire chamber. While the lightning was running wild, the wolf paid it no heed, howling from the very depths of his soul as his clenched fist slammed into Filvis's stomach.

"*Gaaah?!*"

An instantaneous body blow slammed into her. The light-red roots spread across Filvis's upper body *predicted the blow*, swelling, hardening to protect her magic stone. His fist tore into her defenseless side rib, crushing the creature's internal organs, causing her to cough up blood.

"*Aaaaaaaaaaaaaaaaaaaaaaaargh!*"

And there was no end in sight. He kept attacking, refusing to let go once he had sunk his fangs into his prey. Peppered with painful blows, the creature did not even have time to stagger back as a raging stream of attacks, punches, knee-ups, elbow jabs, and kicks slammed into her body. The bloody blows landed one after the other, each dealing serious damage. The unending barrage cut off the monster's consciousness for a few seconds.

This whole thing should have been impossible. It left Filvis mentally scrambling in confusion until she finally saw it—the beautiful golden light cloaking the rampaging wolf. *Level Seven*. Level Boost. Having temporarily reached the pinnacle with the help of that most powerful of sorceries, Bete's strength was finally enough to kill the creature. Using that extreme boost to his advantage, he had locked Filvis in a jail cell—with prison bars of violence—scorching her body like a raging fire.

"A werewolf...?! Impossible!"

He should not have been able to stand back up. There was no way he should have been able to return to the battlefield—not after how thoroughly Filvis had destroyed his body before. The mortal wounds she had left on his body should have made it impossible to fight again. And yet—

Filvis looked uneasy, bewildered, as the wolf covered in wounds howled.

"I mean, even a bunch of damn wimps managed to raise a cry of their own. What excuse would I have if I couldn't beat the shit out of you?!!"

After raising a battle cry befitting one of the strongest warriors, the wolf's fangs ripped into Filvis again. For the first time that day, Filvis felt a chill run down her spine as the revived wolf started to destroy her, the force of his series of attacks shaving away at her magic reserves.

The fear of impending death. The absolute and vivid feeling of her life getting chipped away. The creature who should have been a tyrant standing alone was forced to recognize the enemy before her eyes: The wolf she had always scorned in her heart was the most dangerous being she had faced.

"—*Don't get in my waaay!*"

Her eyes flared as she pushed back his fierce charge. Her metal gloves flashed, causing Bete to cough up blood, landing with a heavy *thud* on his body encased in golden particles of light.

"I can't die! Not now! Not after coming this far!"

"Gh…?!"

"Die! Just die already, werewolf!" she barked, derangement seeping into her voice as she unleashed a storm of counterattacks. Her true feelings and her inner violence were being drawn out now that her life was finally being threatened for the first time. She turned her hatred and resentment into power and attacked back, pushing into his body in return.

Specks of what little blood he had left splattered out, his upper body trembling. Right when it seemed he was on the verge of retreating, Bete's eyes turned even redder and he kicked the ground and pushed in.

"Just shut up!"

It was a headbutt that contained every ounce of his strength. That brutal blow had been unleashed with perfect timing, smashing right into Filvis's forehead, halting her counteroffensive.

"You're the one who's gonna die!"

His tightly clenched fist thrust out, landing hard. They traded haphazard blows, leaving both of them drenched in blood. It was a head-on match. Without even considering defense, they howled, using all four limbs to slaughter the enemy in front of their eyes.

Explosions blasted on both sides: A palm thrust and upper kick clashed. It was a never-ending struggle where as soon as one seemed to get an upper hand, the other countered it.

Even with Bete's hacks, Filvis still had the greater potential. The intrinsic strength of a monster would not allow a mere adventurer to have the advantage. Clenched fingers smashed. Bones started to crack. Skin peeled back as the struggle for supremacy continued to unfold.

But even so, Bete's howl did not reach its end.

"Ghhh?!"

"*Aaaaaaaaaaaaaaaaaaaaaaaaah!*"

For the first time, Filvis was overwhelmed as the wolf swallowed his pride and mustered every last bit of his strength. Lena supported Haruhime and Lulune and the rest, all standing there in amazement as he demonstrated the persistence and will to overcome granted to the strong.

"Mr....Bete...!"

And that resounding howl reached Lefiya, too. The girl who had just been suffering on the ground gathered her strength and moved her lips.

"*Proud warriors...marksmen of the forest...!*" she sang with a quivering voice. To support Bete. To bring victory. To stop Filvis.

Stand! If you don't get up...! If you don't stand on your feet now, when will you?!

She mentally whipped her body that would not heed her cries. She shook off the pain and everything else, moving to collect on the oath she had sworn to defeat Filvis.

And at that moment...there was no warning or any advance notice. But something rang out, as if synchronizing with the song composed by the battle of adventurers whose hearts had not given in.

"_____"

A certain sound reached Lefiya's ears.

"This is the end, Loki! Nidhogg is about to activate!"

The song of destruction became clear as it passed through the floors, closing in. It was a prelude to the destruction of the mortal realm, to the reproduction of the *orgia* that had consumed the world in the Ancient Times. The ritual to activate the bomb was not even minutes from completion as Dionysus celebrated.

"Ha-ha-ha-ha-ha-ha-ha-ha! I'm the victor! I took the name of Enyo and brought destruction to this aggravating land!"

Dionysus's guffaws echoed, filling the chamber. Loki's teeth ground together. He was celebrating with a wild drunkenness, as if her suffering were the ultimate appetizer to go with his drink.

"Ha-ha-ha-ha-ha-ha————...?"

His laughter suddenly stopped. When she heard it, Loki instinctively looked up.

"...What's that?" she whispered.

Something was trembling, resounding, and certainly *ringing*.

Dionysus was frozen, and Loki's eyes widened. They could both sense it—the same sound that Lefiya had heard.

Gong. Gooong.

Its pure timbre was clearer than anything. That magnificent tone was more heroic than anything. That bell's unceasing ringing thundered through the labyrinth.

"This is—?"

"...From the great bell tower?"

A master smith and great dwarf warrior stopped moving, listening carefully.

"Where is it coming from...?"

A high elf mage's elven ears twitched as she spun a spell.

"This sound..."

"It's so pretty..."

Amazon twins forgot all about fighting as they listened in delight to it.

"It can't be—"

The strongest Warlord's eyes opened in shock.

It reached every corner of the transformed Knossos. It was a soul-stirring melody that reached the adventurers in the large chambers, in the passages, in every place where battles were unfolding. There was no holiness to be found anywhere. And yet that bell resembled a blessing from the heavens, resounding through the ground, repelling the song that would destroy the city, and transforming into a sacred rhythm to purify evil.

To the adventurers' ears, it was a battle cry. A shout of encouragement to jolt their spirits. Everyone stopped moving. Everyone listened to that sound. Even the evil spirits were frozen by it, creating a moment's pause in Knossos.

Gong. Gooong.

Like an illusion composed by that bell's solemn tone, they all recollected a scene from a few minutes in the past.

"Y-you're..."

A single feather fluttered to the ground in front of Raul. It was a golden feather that sparkled as if it had been interwoven with a single thread of hope. High above the adventurers' heads, a single siren was flapping her brilliant wings and releasing the being she had carried there in her talons. His shoulders free, he landed on the ground after a brief descent. He was equipped with a battered longsword. A black scarf and snow-white hair fluttered. His eyes were tinged with red rubellite. Someone among the frozen adventurers murmured that he looked almost like a hero.

"Gh..."

The boy shuddered. Faced with the true dragon monster that appeared only in fairy tales, he showed a glimpse of fear. However, he closed his eyes, and when they opened again, they were more courageous than anyone's. His gaze housed an understanding of why he had been brought there, of what he needed to do.

Bell Cranell had made up his mind.

"Please protect me," he said as he took the longsword in both hands and held it before him.

And leaving that to Raul and the rest who were standing there, he activated his trump card—the one shot granted him by his goddess.

His Skill was triggered by the thing he admired most—*Loki Familia*, those grand adventurers.

Braver Finn Deimne.

Nine Hell Riveria Ljos Alf.

Elgarm Gareth Landrock.

Amazon the Slasher Tiona Hyrute.

Jormungand Tione Hyrute.

Vanargand Bete Loga.

Thousand Elf Lefiya Viridis.

And Sword Princess Aiz Wallenstein.

Those gallant adventurers had shouldered their pride and duty, continuing to fight the darkness hidden away in the city, unbeknownst to everyone. Borrowing the strength of that unattainable peak for which he desperately longed, the power of the next generation of heroes, he overlapped his purpose with theirs and loaded all of it into that one attack.

"…!"

Raul could see it—the torrent of power rushing into his readied blade, the moment that hero's blow would cut through that pitch-black manifestation of despair.

"—Protect hiiiiiiiiiiiiiim! Protect Rabbit Foot!"

He was carried along by instinct and impulse. With no concerns for appearances, he fired off a decisive order to everyone there, swearing to protect that boy until the end. And as Raul drew his sword and dashed forward, the rest of the members of *Loki Familia* raised a battle cry and followed him.

With the help of the siren who had changed course in midair and switched to a diversionary attack on Nidhogg, they became a lure, a shield, composing chants and risking their lives to create a defensive line.

Beads of white light gathered together. A bell's chime transformed into the gong of a grand bell. And that sublime sound resounded across all the battlefields.

Gong. Gooong.

"—Go, Bell Cranell!" Finn murmured as he ran through the passage, clutching the oculus in his hand.

He had given orders for the siren Rei to carry Bell to Nidhogg on the eleventh floor.

With her ability to freely fly through the air, she could move through Knossos faster than anyone, and with her echolocation, she could locate both Bell and Nidhogg. She alone could carry out all the way to completion the one move that Finn had discovered. She could find the light that Finn had discovered and carry it. Guide it.

"Enyo, I'm betting it all on that white light."

It was an ambush from where Enyo was least expecting it—a blind spot that the god had missed on the board, that he had no way of noticing.

Because the boy had been nothing more than a pawn.

He embodied the potential of the mortal realm, an unknown factor with which to smash the god. Something that could betray the predictions of a god. A being who had not been around fifteen years ago or even six years ago.

It had nothing to do with strategy or predictions. It was just faith—a belief in the adventurer he had seen that day with Aiz, the adventurer who had defeated the minotaur, overcome the impossible, and gained the qualification of a hero.

It was just a bet, a gamble on that incomplete hero who had rushed headlong faster than anyone, overcoming all kinds of hardships, fueled by his desires.

"But that's why it'll *cut all the way through*. To defeat a god, there's no choice but to gamble on the unknown!"

That was the trump card that Hermes had snuck into Finn's hands. That was the piece from outside the board that should not have been there on that day. This time, Finn was the one slamming a sword down onto the board from outside as Enyo stood frozen.

Reflected in the oculus, Nidhogg noticed Bell Cranell and raised a dreadful roar, but its movements were dull. With the ritual progressing this far, it had become little more than a bomb waiting to go off. This was their only chance. He slammed a pawn—a piece that had been promoted to a hero—down onto the ninth board that Enyo had brandished.

"This is it, Enyo!"

Your evil and our light. Which will win?

Finn shouted a declaration of war at Enyo, who had finally been forced to sit in the empty seat on the other end of the board—at Dionysus, whose face had grown pale.

Gong. Gooong.

As if synchronizing with Braver's will, the grand bell rang louder. There was no stopping the sound. It was a signal to everyone, a single blow marshaling all the heroes' feelings. It was a roar of hope that railed against absurdity. Everyone who could still fight was reinvigorated, drawing swords, raising shields, wielding staffs.

"It's Bell! It's Bell! Everyone!"

"Wiene...?"

"Bell is fighting!"

The dragon girl shouted his name. Her crammed thoughts turned into tears and a smile.

"Sir Bell!" Mikoto cheered as she looked up.

"Come on—what are you all doing?! At this rate, my buddy's gonna take all the good stuff!" Welf broke into a grand smile.

"Focus on the enemy in front of you! There's nothing left to fear! He will defeat the seventh!" Lilly proclaimed in Braver's voice.

"—Follow the bell of victory!"

And finally, Finn's voice overlapped with another version of himself as he ordered an all-out attack.

"AAAAAAAAAAAAAAAAAAAAAAAAAAAAAAAAAAAAAAA AAAAAAAAAAAAAAAAAAAAAAAAAAAAAAAAAAAAAAA AAAAAAAAAAAAAAAAAAAAAAAAAAAAAAAAAAAAAAA AAAAAAAAAAAAAAAAAAAAAAAAAAAAAAAAAAAAAAH!"

The counterattack began as every adventurer in the labyrinth raised a battle cry. The adventurers embarked on the final clash, guided by the sound of the great belfry. The sound of that bell stirred the hearts of the adventurers and even the monsters. It was the bell ringing in the heroes' dawn, stirring those who had fallen to stand back up. People who should not have been able to get up again were standing one after the other, wiping away their blood, taking their weapons in hand, and facing off against the spirits trying to destroy the city.

Everyone reacted, following that grand signal to begin.

"—*Gh!*"

And the boy's cry reached Lefiya.

This ringing bell is...!

Lefiya knew it. She had heard the grand bell ringing out when she had fought together with him before. When they had fought together on the eighteenth floor.

"Master Bell!"

Even if she had not heard the renart girl's rejoicing cheer, she would have known. That boy was fighting, too. Ringing the bell that signaled a new dawn, he was preparing to defeat the enemy before him!

"—Me too!"

As her fingernails clawed into the ground, Lefiya dragged herself to her feet. The pain tormenting her whole body disappeared. Or, rather, the blaze of emotions swirling in her heart burned it all away.

I can't lose. I won't lose. Absolutely not. Not to that tiny hero in the making. If he can ring a bell to clear away the darkness, then I will sing the song to bring victory.

"This ain't the time to be sleeping...!"

"Yes...!"

"...Let's go!"

Aisha, Asfi, and the masked adventurer all mustered the last of their strength at the sound of the bell.

"—*Gaaaaaah!*"

And Bete, too. Confronted by that magnificent howl from a weakling who had become strong, the bell's gong stirred a mix of irritation and gratification in him as he rampaged.

"Why are you standing?! Why are you getting up?! What is this sound?!"

Filvis alone shuddered, agitated by the sound, getting pushed back as Lefiya and the rest rose to face the final battle.

Gong. Gooong.

The sound became clear, causing Dionysus to stand still.

"What...?"

A rasping whisper crossed his lips. The torches' flames flickered at the sound of the great bell. The flickering flames caused the mural of the evil dragon and the spirits to fade in and out of darkness.

"What *is* that...?"

The game board had changed. The adventurers had moved from disadvantage to equal footing. No, beyond that. From the oculus in Loki's hands, the adventurers' shouts rang out as they attempted to cut through the cruelty. It was as if they had been revived.

Time had stopped for Dionysus, and slowly, his body began to tremble in fear. He was assaulted by a premonition that was difficult to bear. It was the harbinger of failure, of his plan falling apart.

Loki said nothing. Her half-opened eyes just stared at the face of the god whose laughter had died. It was just a belief—faith in the ending of the *Oratoria* written by her followers.

"—What *is* that damn bell?!"

Dionysus lost his composure and raged at the sound that had caused even a god to shudder.

"Push them baaaaaaaaaaaaaaaaaaack!"

As if stirred up by the grand bell that continued to ring, every battlefield raged. The adventurers raised their swords, their backs lit by magic being cast behind them as they pushed the blackened demi-spirit to the edge.

"—Ha-ha! Ha-ha-ha-ha-ha-ha-ha-ha-ha-ha-ha!"

"Hegni! Hey, Hegni!…Damn it, snapped, huh?"

The dark elf exploded into laughter as he kept axing the spirit's enormous trunk with black flashes like a storm on a dark night. The white elf shook his head at his partner's excitement and unleashed a white flash of his own with a massive lightning strike.

"*Incinerate, sword of Surtr—My name is Alf!*"

"Fall back, everyone!"

As the two elven knights pushed back the spirit, a sweet singing voice rang out. Ilta's order thundered, and when Welf and the adventurers had pulled back from its giant area of effect, Riveria activated her extermination spell.

"*Rea Laevateinn!*"

"*AAAAAAAAAAAAAAAAAAAAAAAAAAAAAAAAAAAAAAAA AAGH?!*"

The city's strongest mage scorched the spirit in a towering pillar of hellfire.

"Bell Cranell?"

"It's Bell Cranell."

"Really?"

"He was just a Level One. That's insane."

""""Exactly.""""

"I don't want to tell Lady Freya because she'll just get more obsessed."

""""Exactly!""""

"Quit bitching and move your asses, you damn prums!"

As the Bringar sprinted by with a frightening speed, dismembering a black tentacle as they passed, Tsubaki's own sword flashed. She shouted at them, as if their little conversation was getting on her nerves. The Gullivar brothers leaped into the air, throwing their four weapons. Combined with Tsubaki's quick-draw ability, this attack ripped through the last of the abused and battered petal armor, finally breaking through.

"Hey, Finn! Riveria! That youngster is really interesting! But we aren't gonna lose to him, right?!"

The spirit was dumbfounded, having lost all its defenses. The old dwarf warrior charged, more excited than anyone by the soul-stirring song of the new generation. A fanatical grin covered his face as he took a giant leap and brandished his battle-ax.

"Rest in pieces!"

Charged with every bit of strength, the swing caused a flashy explosion of flesh.

"It's Argonaut! That's gotta be Argonaut!"

"'Argo-knot'? That story you made me listen to?"

"That's the one, Bache! There's this amazing guy who's, like, a hero from those epics brought to life!"

"Argo-knot...Argonaut."

As Tiona got excited and forgot the situation, Bache pondered the name.

"I see...You're telling me there's a man like that here?"

The warrior who had only ever known battle smiled behind her veil. And in the next moment, her eyes flared as she sprinted. Tiona joined her with a smile, accelerating alongside her.

"Tione, give me some blood!"

"Just take it already! This isn't the time for that!"

Tione shouted as she used her Restrict Iorum to obstruct the spirit's movements. Argana did as she said and licked her blood, activating her Kalima and increasing her stats. Tione and Argana tugged on either end of a magic whip of light, holding the suffering spirit down, threatening to rip it to pieces as it struggled to break free. While they were doing that, Tiona and Bache dove in.

"Here we goooooooooooooooo!"

"Velgas!"

There was nothing that would not have been killed by the full swing of Urga and Bache's mortal poison punch.

"AAAAAAAAAAAAAAAAAAAAAAAAAAAAAAAAAAAAAAAA ARGH!"

"Wait, quit it! Stop it, Asterios!"

"Don't let him join the boy!"

"We have to finish this thing first!"

The minotaur went into a wild rampage on hearing the white battle cry of his ultimate rival, causing mayhem for his enemy and allies. The Xenos desperately pleaded with him, and the single minotaur finally, inevitably turned and faced the spirit with blood-shot eyes.

"—He's getting stronger. I will, too. For the sake of our conclusion."

The jet-black minotaur spoke in brusque human words for the first time that battle and then smiled. That brutal grin masked an irrepress-ible hunger, and that glimpse of reasoning was consumed by his battle instincts. His battered body filled with an even greater power, and he aimed another charge at the demi-spirit, whose eyes turned pale.

"OOOOOOOOOOOOOOOOOOOOOOOOOOOOOOOOOOOOOO OOOOOOH!"

The second attempt at his strongest charge smashed everything in its path.

"That bell is pissing me off..."

While everyone was exalting at the magnificent sound, he alone was not. More annoyed than anyone else, Allen swung his silver spear.

He refused to acknowledge anyone who was not stronger than him. He would not allow anyone to be faster than him. His desire to fight was so strong that he welcomed anyone who might be able to catch up with him. Allen was the embodiment of the primitive emotions of man.

He took off, annoyed at himself for being annoyed by that boy. It was his single fastest sprint of the day—a near-infinite acceleration that no one could follow. The chariot became the personification of force as he left afterimages in his tracks, dashing all around, trying to knock down the spirit.

"Clear the way! He'll trample you!"

Without being able to give support or even backup, Shakti could only shout a warning, which the rest of the adventurers heeded as one, retreating. The mantle attached to his shoulder fluttered, about to tear off, as he revealed why he had been given the name Vana Freya. The giant spirit pillar was covered in dozens of ruts of light.

"GAAAAAAAAAAAAAAAAAAAAAAAAAAAAAAAAAAAAAAA AAAAAAAAAAAH?!"

Its body was shredded so badly that its regeneration could not keep up. The spirit groaned as it lost its eyes, nose, ears, mouth, and throat, unable to utter a proper sound anymore.

As it gave off an earsplitting cry of death, Allen had just one thing to say.

"Die."

He did not hesitate to send the spirit's head flying and mercilessly crushed its entire chest—and the magic stone along with it.

"Lady Freya…Your insight was correct," Ottar acknowledged. "A new hero has been born."

His eyes narrowed sharply as the sound of the great bell filled the labyrinth.

He quietly walked forward, approaching the spirit that had *already* been turned into a fleshy corpse. Carrying his enormous black sword on his shoulder, the boaz advanced with the air of a king. Anakity and the others gasped and cleared the way, yielding the final blow to him.

Raising his black sword to the heavens, he slammed it down like a guillotine on the spirit that was at death's door.

"This was a good battlefield, giving birth to a full-fledged hero."

His praise felt somehow out of place as he finished everything with his absolute power.

And thus…

After four minutes on the seventh battlefield, the final proclamation was handed down. One that did not reach the six other battlefields.

The only ones allowed to see it were a plain, mediocre young man who was nonetheless roaring indomitably. Those comrades who followed him. A single siren flying in the air. And finally, the sinister dragon spirit that was trying to bring about the destruction of everything.

As the song of destruction approached its critical mass, he was faster. The particles of white light gathered closer. The sword of light was held aloft—a single blow with his whole soul. Everything was riding on it.

A full charge. As the grand bell rang out, he unleashed that pure-white aurora.

"*AAAAAAAAAAAAAAAAAAAAAAAAAAAAAAAAAAAAAAA AAAAAAAAAAAAAAAAAH!*"

It was a heroic battle cry that no one would ever know. A world dyed white. A labyrinth engulfed in tremors. The Hero's Attack to be recorded in the passage of the *Oratoria* roared.

It was the melody of a deadly combat. The sounds of a sword fight born of crossed blades. The sounds of destruction and regeneration composed by wind and flesh. And the sounds of screams and shouts rose from both their throats.

With will and purpose, combativeness and murder roaring together, blending together, rejecting each other.

It was undoubtedly the harmony of a decisive battle.

""——————————————————————*Gh!*""

Aiz's and Levis's swords clashed.

Instead of sparks, the shock wave and wind caused their hair to blow back. They were in the eye of the storm for just a second as they glared at each other and reversed their blades.

They had gone beyond their limits. There was nothing left holding them back. Their bodies were filled with a wild power. It was as if they could accomplish anything, and with that, they dashed beyond the realms of possibility. They were long since past the point where they had time to think. They simply moved as soon as the idea crossed their minds.

Airiel blew back the corrupted sword, and a swelling flesh armor repelled the blade cloaked in a violent wind. Levis retreated from Aiz's attack, sacrificing an arm that was sent flying in order to push back, but before the regeneration could make any progress and the flesh fully inched over her skin, she took a powerful blow to the body.

There was no longer any shock or valor. Pain and hesitation had been cast aside. She was filled with a determination to fight and kill her opponent. Everything was for the sake of becoming a sword with which to slaughter her enemy.

"—*Gh!*"

She sank to her knee. Her arm was on the verge of splitting apart. Even though the pain had long since disappeared, her field of vision narrowed. It was as if she was losing some of her eyesight every time their blades crossed. It had reached the point where she could see only the enemy standing before her, could see only that grotesque black outline—that repulsive monster.

"Come, Aria! Come again! Give me more! Hit me with that wind, with all that you offer!"

The black shadow was enthusiastically shouting something, laughing incessantly.

"After rotting away! Encountering you and this battle have been pure entertainment!" Levis, the illusion of a sinister dragon behind her, caused the flame of Aiz's rabid obsession to blaze still higher.

Wild slashes and a ferocious storm of wind. Whenever she swung her sword, it broke the enemy further and the air roared around them, causing everything to tremble. Her own body was being torn apart.

But that just caused the black flame within to rage more.

"—*Aaaaaaaaaaaaaaaaaaaaaaaaaaaaaaaaaaaaaaaaaaaaaaaaaaah!*"

To kill the enemy in front of her, she let out a battle cry from the pit of her stomach. Even her will to fight took on the form of a blazing black inferno. She could no longer tell where her arm holding the sword ended and the wind began.

Maybe this was how Father felt that day. And Mother, too...Maybe she had these same thoughts.

As she tried to justify herself, she continued to transform into a demonic war princess.

——*You're wrong.*

She heard someone's voice.

——*You've got it wrong.*

It took her a moment to realize it was the voice of her younger self.

—*Father and Mother*—

She could not hear the rest of what she was saying. Static was disrupting the voice. Her eyes were consumed by darkness as she deemed it trivial. Her fragment of consciousness now cut loose, she wandered in the deep sea of roiling flames.

She had not wanted to become a hero. And she had not wanted to save the world, either. There was just something that she'd wanted to get back, and she'd had to become strong to do it, even if she lost sight of her goal in gaining that strength. She'd had to sacrifice everything of herself to attain that strength. In order to defeat the being before her eyes, she'd had to turn even her hatred into fuel for the fire.

Every time I fought, I optimized myself.

Every time I killed, I shaved off a little more excess flesh.

I lost my expressions. My emotions became more limited. Thanks to my friends, I didn't become a killing puppet, but this version of me and the me in my heart are entirely different people. This version is a fake, an imaginary "what if" that the real me could never reach.

"Aaaaaaaaaaaaaaaaaaaaaaaaaaaaaaaaaaaaaaaaaaaaaaaah!"

"Ooooooooooooooooooooooooooooooooooooooooooooh!"

What reflected in the creature's eyes was an Aiz who was no more and no less repulsive than Levis herself. She entrusted herself to the pitch-black storm, wielded the murderous blade that had butchered tens of thousands of monsters, and took on the form of death itself. As if she herself were an incomplete spirit, just like the woman who was effectively a tendril of the corrupted spirit. That was the fate that the current Aiz Wallenstein had reached.

There is no going back. I can't turn back anymore. I can't remember anymore. But didn't you already realize that long ago?

She did not understand why the Aiz in her heart had a sad look on her face. Consumed by resignation and loneliness, Aiz wandered in that sea of flames, seemingly not realizing anything as she devoted her everything to the battlefield.

It's hot—

The blackened sword of wind and the wicked crimson blade clashed. Her long golden hair was so dirtied by blood that it had lost its golden sheen as it blew in the air. As each second ticked by, she slashed faster, more sharply, more instantaneously, more overwhelmingly.

It's scorching—

No matter how often Levis was painted in blood, she just laughed and kept rising to the challenge. The black wind trembled under a powerful blow. There was a sizzling sound as if the wind was weakened, and then in the next instant, it swirled and regained its strength.

It's hot—

That sound was the sound of her life burning away. The sound of the black flames consuming her life.

But that's fine—
There is no going back. I can't turn back anymore. I can't remember
those memories.
I'll defeat this monster and go beyond this—
She entrusted all of herself to the black flames that had taken up
residence in her. She embraced the hellfire that would turn her body
and soul into ash, heading for what lay beyond the darkness—
Her cry was swallowed up by the black wind that joined her in her
descent to hell.

At that moment, she heard the sound of a giant bell.

"_____"

In a world closed off from everything but the enemy before her, it
still reached Aiz's ears. The Aiz in her heart opened her eyes wide
and snapped her face up.
It was the sound of a blessing. The morning bell signaling the
dawn. It was a song of recovery. A light appeared beyond the hori-
zon in a world that had been swallowed by an ocean of darkness. It
illuminated Aiz's heart, like the declaration that the sun would rise
again—that there was no such thing as a never-ending night.
——*Bell!*
She knew it was his battle cry—from the culmination of all her
feelings up until that day.
The ringing tickled Aiz's ears, resounded through her whole body,
and reached her heart—chipping away at the force of the rampaging
black fire. The dark flames that were burning her back—that she had
lost all ability to control—were purified by that white light.
"This is…?!"
Levis looked irritated as the bell continued to thunder magnifi-
cently.
Aiz's arms moved as if being led. They traded blows. An evenly
matched tremor. Even though the black blaze withered, her wind

continued to blow strong. As her Skill fell silent, Airiel increased its output, as if wrapping her in its embrace.

Each chime of the bell that reached their battlefield shook their bodies. Its sound overlapped with the swords' melody.

Remember that sunrise at the top of the wall.

Remember the image of that pure boy's advance.

Remember the smile that crossed my lips reflected in his eyes.

That had been a remnant of Aiz's face left over from days past.

——There is no going back. I can't turn back anymore. I can't remember those memories.

——But is that really true?

The younger Aiz was smiling with teary eyes as she responded to the grown Aiz's thoughts. And then, as she rubbed the tears from her smiling cheeks, the young Aiz unraveled and became the wind.

"HAAAAAAAAAAAAAH!"

A resolute voice thundered out. A single decisive blow drew near.

Levis sensed danger as the bell continued to grow stronger and swung her sword, signaling the conclusion of the battle was nigh. The floor shattered as she stepped in, and she sliced even the air as the weapon advanced, slamming into the black storm.

The next instant, the wind encasing Aiz's sword and the current covering her entire body *burst*.

"What?!"

After a moment's struggle, the black storm *dispersed*. The force field disappeared. Levis's deadly blow was pushed from its path by the wind, its power and momentum losing their direction as the deadly blow slipped past Aiz's side. As the corrupted sword grazed by Aiz, her right arm, gauntlet, and shoulder armor were blown away. Slipping past Levis, Aiz felt her eyes go wide, as if her mind were elsewhere.

Her field of vision had been eaten away by the black blaze, until it suddenly widened again. White feathers seemed to scatter before her, and her monochrome world filled with color. The young Aiz had disappeared, becoming a gentle breeze blowing a tuft of her beautiful golden hair.

An instantaneous transition.

"Ghhhh!"

She stopped right in her tracks, dramatically *pulling the brakes*.

The speed that the wind had brought her was canceled out by the gust blowing in the other direction as she moved past Levis.

Ignoring the cries from her body that she was abusing to its limit, Aiz turned around. Meanwhile, Levis immediately recovered her stance, her eyes focused on the battle drawn out in her head as she took aim and charged—intercepting the attack with her inhuman strength. Even though she was caught off guard, her sword still unfairly moved faster than Aiz's.

Faced with that impending blow, Aiz called out the wind's name, repeating the words whispered in her heart.

"Tempest!"

She was clad again in the spirit's wind—the clear gust that had been purified of all traces of darkness wrapped the girl in an untarnished white. Her sword became like the wind, transforming into a white flash as she drew a golden arc. The bell rang out over them, and the white wind whipped wildly. Levis's eyes filled with shock, but in the next instant, they widened, brimming with murder.

Her corrupted sword groaned as it crossed blades with the roaring sword of wind.

"AAAAAAAAAAAAAAAAAAAAAAAAAAAAAAAAAAAAAA AAAAAAAAAAAAAAH!"

At the same time as Bell unleashed his Hero's Attack, the decisive blow was made in their fight. As the grand bell shook the entire battlefield, time stopped for Aiz and Levis, who passed each other again, their swords unmoving from where their completed slashes had stopped.

In the next moment, one shoulder burst open, sending a set of armor flying as blood spilled forth—it belonged to Aiz. Her body shook violently and sank, but she chewed her lip and stepped forward forcefully, just managing to stay standing.

Levis's eyes narrowed coolly. The feedback from the slash assured her that she had surpassed her enemy's blow—

"—What?!"

Her chest was ripped open. There was a track of a single slash running diagonally across her chest. The white flash had cut through the armor of flesh and reached her magic stone, splitting that vibrant, gleaming mass in two.

"Impossible?!"

As she looked down at her chest, her right hand instinctively reached up to cover the wound, but it turned to ash. That was the fate of all monsters whose cores had been destroyed. The corrupted sword slipping from her hand and clattering to the floor caused the creature's eyes to fly open in shock.

After landing the superspeed slash, Aiz turned around, still clad in the white wind, and resumed her stance.

As the ends of Levis's arms and legs crumbled, the creature's shock was met by Aiz's piercing gaze. Seeing those golden eyes certain of victory, Levis's eyes trembled and became bloodshot.

"Ariaaaaaaaaaaaaaaaaaaaaaaaaaaaaaaaaaa!"

She swung around, her left hand outstretched, as if reaching for something—but the arm crumbled to ash before Aiz's eyes.

The creature's entire body collapsed, turning into a formless pile of soot. Her shouts, her rage, and her body were all erased.

With a sandy rush, there was just a big mound of ash and a few fragments of richly colored magic stone. Nothing else remained. There was no swell of victory or regret that this was all over. There was only the faint ringing of the bell and strained breathing.

As those two sounds echoed ephemerally around the solemn battlefield, the white wind blew between them. It tousled her golden hair, guiding Aiz's gaze upward. Her eyes narrowed as she listened to the reverberations of the bell that were still audible.

After all the tremors had passed, the adventurers whose bodies had been dyed white slowly opened their eyes.

"...He...did it..."

It filled Raul's vision. The spirit had been entirely obliterated. The last remnants of Nidhogg were disappearing together with fading white light. And the boy was standing there frozen like a statue in the stance of drawing that ultimate blow of light.

Finally, the sword crumbling away, his arms dropped as he collapsed to the ground, his body and spirit having reached their limits.

There was a long silence that Raul finally broke with a shout at the top of his lungs.

"—You did iiiiiiiiiiiiiit! That was fantastic! You were amazing!"

He and the others cheered as they surrounded the boy. There was no concern for trivial things like being from different familias. Raul ignored Bell's exhaustion and hugged him, wrapping his arm around the boy's shoulder like an old friend. And it was the same for everyone else. They ruffled the boy's white hair as he struggled to smile, sharing the rough sort of praise that was standard for adventurers. In her excitement, Rakuta the hume bunny hugged the siren who had slowly descended to the floor, shocking her.

As everyone mobbed the boy, Raul looked to the ceiling.

"He did it, Captain!" he roared.

"Well done, Raul!" Upon hearing the cheers coming through the oculus, Finn smiled in praise. "And you too, Bell Cranell!"

He clenched his fist as tightly as he could, squeezing out every last bit of joy and excitement. In the wide passage he had stopped in, he forgot his usual leader's facade for a brief moment and let the plain smile of just another adventurer cross his lips.

Finn had found the move to finally stop Enyo's plan.

"Captain!"

A second later, Alicia's group, which Rei had left on Finn's order, rounded the corner. Quickly regaining his composure, Finn had more orders ready.

"We've confirmed the defeat of all seven spirits! Riveria, Gareth, gather everyone who can still fight and have them head for the remaining enemies. Reinforce our allies who are still fighting!" he shouted into the oculus.

"Understood."

"I'd like to ask you to let us rest, but I guess there's no other choice!"

"We're going to head for Loki!" Finn said, turning to Alicia's group.

"'Yes, sir!'"

As their response came in unison, he turned and started running, taking the lead.

The battle was not over yet. The finale was still to come.

"...Im...possible..." Dionysus barely managed to murmur.

The battle cries from the crystal, the sound of that bell, and the tremors shaking the labyrinth had all passed.

The appointed time approached, but his plan for great destruction would not happen, and it took all Dionysus had not to fall to the ground as that fact staggered him.

The song of self-destruction that Nidhogg was chanting had been stopped. That meant that his plan—that Enyo's plan—had failed.

"...You lost, Dionysus," Loki said. She stood there, facing the god who was completely stupefied. "Your plan was perfect. But Finn's crew still stopped it."

"...Gh?!"

"While you were laughing to yourself outside the game board, those children kept struggling. And because of that, they were able to draw victory from the jaws of defeat. The cause of your defeat was fitting for your *deific* pride and the arrogance of omniscience."

The adventurers' struggles. The familia myth that had even conquered a god's divine will. Loki's lips curled up. From the very depths of her heart, she was exhilarated by what she had witnessed.

"That...and an unknown factor that they had hidden up their sleeves."

Dionysus's plan had been founded on a calculation of the strength of various factions from fifteen years ago. And it had been broken by just a single adventurer—a single ray of white light. That boy had appeared in Orario only *six months ago*. In just that short period of time, he had raced down the path of the hero. Dionysus would never have guessed that he would keep running with a wholehearted aspiration in his heart and grow into an existence that could threaten Enyo. That was not something anyone, even a god, could have predicted. That was the potential of children.

"You lost to the mortal realm's potential for growth."

Dionysus's face twitched as she explained the cause of his defeat. The difficult and determined struggle of heroes and the existence of a heretical one had crushed his perfect plan.

"...*Damn iiit!*" Dionysus suddenly roared.

His pride crushed, he seemingly lost it, exposing a disgraceful side of himself. His eyes flared and his hair was a mess as his sweet mask was warped by anger and hatred.

Dionysus flew into a rage. He seemed to be running his hand through his hair when all of a sudden, he drew a gleaming dagger. It was a blade with grape designs on the hilt—the one he had used to send Penia back to the heavens.

"*Die, Lokiii!*"

His mad actions were spurred by the undying lust and obsession with which he had pursued his *orgia*. If he could send Loki back, her familia members would be robbed of their Statuses. Then he could send in monsters to deal with them. But more importantly, if he could just survive, there was still hope—a wish that he could draw up a new plan for a feast of frenzy.

A sinister grin appeared on his face as he readied his dagger and charged Loki, but she just quietly watched him. Right as he got in range, she tossed the ash she had secretly been holding in her hand.

"Ugh?!"

It was ash she had picked up from the monsters' corpses she had come across along the way there. He hesitated as his eyes filled with soot, and Loki was able to avoid him with ease. As he passed, she held out her leg, sending him tumbling to the ground in an unsightly heap.

"*GAH…?! That's dirty, Lokiiiii!*"

Dionysus raged, his eyes shut in pain from the ash, and stood up with a childish shout, swinging his dagger randomly. His desperate thrusts were a far cry from the attacks of Finn and the other adventurers, and Loki was able to weave around them without any trouble as she silently moved behind him. And from there, she kicked upward as hard as she could, right into Dionysus's crotch.

"*—GAAAH?!*"

Though he might be a god, it was still a critical hit, and her kick drew a deep groan that was even more vulgar than the last as he crumpled to the ground again. His stubbornness was all that kept him from losing his grip on the dagger. Loki did not laugh even though he was ridiculously, wretchedly unsightly. She just continued to unleash a series of kicks.

"*Gh?! GAH?!* S-stop! Quit it!"

"Can you even hear yourself, dumbass?"

"*Ahh! AH?! AAAAAAARGH?!*"

"How oblivious can you be?"

There was no mercy, no pardon—just cruel, unending punts.

Covered in shadows cast by the torches, Loki's face had a cold-blooded intensity to it. The smile she always had for her followers was nowhere to be found. She was revealing the true nature of a deity—just like Dionysus had.

"I'm *Loki*. The moment you bothered to call me dirty, you were already beyond saving!"

She was the greatest trickster in the heavens—the one who brought demise to all creation. She hammered a reminder of why deities feared her into the god trembling on the ground beneath her.

"Just how many of my children did you steal with that smooth smile of yours? Just how many of my followers did you murder? How stupid can you be?!"

"Q-quit it! Sto-*PPPPTFF*?!"

"There's no way I wasn't gonna settle the debt with the piece of shit who did all that!"

Loki's barrage did not let up, even as Dionysus's fine features became more and more disfigured. Her wide-eyed expression was more sinister than Dionysus's had been. She had unleashed her true nature, revealing the goddess who had once schemed to kill deities back in the heavens, as she continued to torture him to avenge her followers.

She transformed into an embodiment of sadism, accompanied by the dull *thump* of flesh being kicked, the dry snap of bones breaking, and the gargles of a voice being smothered. There was no trace of a loving goddess. She was a full-fledged goddess of destruction.

"*GAH—DAMN IIIIT!*"

As she kept kicking him, Dionysus mustered the last of his strength and swung his blade, rolling away as Loki easily evaded the blow, desperately trying to put some distance between them. Blood trickled down his tortured face as he breathed heavily, and he was covered in wounds. There was no trace left of the princely, noble appearance from before.

Loki had held back just enough to keep him from being returned to the heavens. Because of that, he could still move, which meant she could keep torturing him. Even in his humiliated state, he still did not try to use his Arcanum to kill Loki, which must have been the last bit of pride he had as a god who had descended to the mortal realm. Or perhaps it was because it was out of his utter devotion to the cause of starting another *orgia*.

With his plan, his body, and his composure pulverized, his breathing muffled, Dionysus screamed as if deranged.

"Damn it! Damn it, damn it, damn it! You garbage creatures, kill her!"

"…They aren't here."

"Thanatos?! What are you doing?! Call the Evils' Remnants or some monsters! I don't care what you use, but come here already!"

"They aren't here, either. Weren't you the one who cast them aside?"

He was cornered. Dionysus was backed into a small space, and he did not bother with any kind of explanation or apology. This was the proper fate for a god who had manipulated everything from the shadows. For a god who had discarded everything and everyone after they had served their purpose.

His face was plastered in blood. He swung his blade over and over, his eyes losing all traces of sanity as he shouted.

"Filvis! Where are you, Filvisssss?!"

It was the final battlefield. She was down to her last dregs of strength. She had nothing left to put on the line except her own spirit. Dragging a battle roar out from the pit of her stomach, she turned the pools of spilled blood into strength and devoted everything to her purpose, weaponizing her limbs to defeat the enemy reflected in her eyes.

"*AAAAAAAAAAAAAAAAAAAAAAAAAAAAAAAAAAAAAAAA AAAAAAH!*"

Unleashing a furious shout, Bete and Filvis continued to clash in an unending struggle—punches, kicks, sprays of blood. All could hear the destruction as shock waves and tremors merged into a maelstrom. They paid no heed to victory or defeat, life or death, glory or destruction. Their shadows danced as they stood on the decisive stage, edging toward the brink.

A single blow from the hungry wolf cloaked in light smashed Filvis's bones, and a blow from the monster's unprecedented strength crushed Bete's flesh.

He was covered in wounds, yet he never stopped howling: The hunt was not over yet. He broke through his limits and continued to bare his fangs at the enemy before him, using everything in his power to kill her.

Why—?

As the intense clashes and the storm of blows consumed all her senses, Filvis murmured that thought in the depths of her heart. She was sure that her attack had landed, certain that it should have been a mortal wound. However, his determination, his murderous intent was unbroken. His howl had only intensified.

For some reason, her murderous fist that could obliterate a dozen people in a single punch could not kill that single beast. She could only keep asking herself why as she beheld that contradictory scene.

Why—? Why won't he fall?!

As a creature, Filvis was superior from start to finish. But Bete would not fall. He would not break. He would not be destroyed. And not just that, his counterattacks were starting to do lasting damage to Filvis. Every time his sharp kicks landed, they were powerful blows that caused her insides to thump around her body. Her green eyes became bloodshot, stained a red that was reminiscent of her former self.

Neither Filvis nor Bete could have predicted that they would take each other as far as they had gone, that the incompatible pair would still be there smashing their bodies into each other, chipping each other away.

"Heed this foolish one's voice, and once more grant the starfire's divine protection. Grant the light of compassion to the one who forsook you!"

"Oh brave warrior! Oh strong hero! Oh covetous, cruel champion! "

"Haaaaaah!"

Three shadows rose again to fight with Bete, offering up their determination to defeat Filvis—chanting, dancing, becoming the wind, threading the needle between his attacks to prevent Filvis from landing a deadly blow.

The beautiful adventurers flew into Filvis's line of sight, looking to turn the tide with their divine coordination.

Why won't they give up?!

The masked adventurer and Aisha were Concurrent Casting as they knocked away Filvis's attack, and Asfi resolutely slashed in with only one Talaria to control herself. Filvis could not understand how they kept fighting with their worn-down bodies.

How can they stand against despair? How can they struggle against the irrational? How can they stand against me, when I have become degraded to this most hideous monster?

They were adventurers—those who pushed past adversity, who rejected difficulty, who did not know what it meant to give up.

Filvis had no more use for that indomitable spirit after becoming a creature, so she had forgotten what it meant to be an adventurer.

"Unleashed pillar of light, limbs of the holy tree. You are the master archer!"

And the girl who had been singing louder than anyone. The eyes of her fellow elf had continued to pierce Filvis the entire time. That gaze was sharper than anyone else's, more direct than anyone else's. The proud fairy archer had rejected Filvis's mercy, still crying in her heart for the girl who had no more right to grieve.

Why, Lefiya?!

Why won't you let me kill you? Why won't you understand?

Why won't you understand that trying to defeat me is pointless?

I must walk down the path of destruction. That's all I have left. This was my fate ever since my corrupted heart fled from reality and clung to a salvation that was impure.

If that were not the case, if she really could have stopped, then the mountain of corpses that Filvis had constructed would have been for nothing. All the people she had killed, all that she had stolen, all the countless lives she had ended to make things easier for herself, the sacrifices she had continued to make, it would all become meaningless. That was why Filvis could not stop. There was nothing left that could stop her.

"Miss Filvis!"

Don't look at me. Don't look at me with those eyes. Don't call my name!

In the depths of her heart, Filvis screamed and shook her head, her hair flying wildly as another Filvis scoffed, her face cloaked in Ein's scornful mask. The girl who hid her rage and her tears in a cloak of darkness raised a battle cry that matched the adventurers' and completed her transformation into an atrocious monster. In order to push further down the path of destruction, she would brush aside her fellow elf's arrows, the adventurers' swords, and the wolf's fangs.

"_____"

That was when Filvis sensed it. The scream of the abominable being connected to her. The reality that Nidhogg had been destroyed by the Hero's Attack. The sound of her patron god's plan crumbling.

Because she was a tendril of the spirit herself, a part of that larger being, there was a resonance, allowing her to notice it first. That realization gave birth to a blank moment in her consciousness. A split second later, the quakes caused by that ultimate attack shook the hall. While the noncombatants struggled to endure the tremors, the wolf, his eyes flashing, did not miss that opening.

"*RAAAAAAH!*"

"*GAH?!*"

Bete's kick landed squarely on Filvis's body. Bete leaped back himself as the powerful blow sent the creature flying. He glared at Filvis from across the gap that had been opened and broke his one commandment.

"*Chained Fenris, king of wolves!*"

He began to chant a spell.

It was not just Filvis. Even his allies were taken aback. But he ignored all of that and decisively cast his magic.

"*The first wound: Gelgja, the fetter. The second wound: Gjöll, the cry. The third wound: Þviti, the hammer. The ravenous slaver your only hope, may it form a river, mixing in the tide of blood, to wash away your tears!*"

Bete was filled with a murderous intent, exchanging glances with Lefiya, whose shoulders trembled in surprise.

He did not have a decisive blow. He could not devour the enemy. At this rate, he would lose. Lena and the others would die. That alone could not be allowed to happen, which was why he unleashed the restrictions he had placed on himself.

Filvis Challia had cut everything away, choosing isolation,

continuing to follow the path of destruction. So Bete would have to cast aside everything as well. His trivial pride. Hs scorn for himself. It was all meaningless in the face of death.

"Never forget those irreparable wounds. This rage and hatred, your infirmity and incandescence!"

There was no hesitation as he invoked that curse and fanned the dirty flames. The source of Bete's strength started to spike in preparation for liberation.

"—Gh!"

However, there was no way that the creature would allow that to happen. A werewolf with no training in Concurrent Casting—one who wasn't even a mage—made a perfect target. Standing up, Filvis indignantly thrust out her arm.

"Denounce the world! Acknowledge fate! Dry the tears!"

"Purge, cleansing lightning!"

Their two spells overlapped, but the super-short spell left Bete's magic in its dust. As his face twisted, Filvis put her finger on the trigger of her cannon. Dionysus's plan had failed, but it was not over yet. She would not allow it to end. The magic circle became the size of her body as she prepared to unleash a black ray of lightning.

"Wsh!"

"What?!"

In that instant, Asfi flew in close and unleashed an item that froze Filvis. Her outstretched right arm and the right half of her body and even the magic circle itself were encased in a prison of ice.

Freeze Oil. A new prototype developed by Perseus. Inspired by Fels, she had managed to complete just one bottle before the final battle. Her trump card. It was a freezing explosive that prevented all movement and even froze magic.

"May the pain become your fangs, the lament your roar—and your lost companions your strength!"

The creature was shocked by Perseus's attack, but the wolf continued to prepare his rampage, taking advantage of the time Asfi had bought for him. Faced with Asfi's critical hit, Filvis forcefully activated her magic anyway, without any thought to what might happen.

"*Dio Thyrsos!*"

The thunder ray went wild because of the wall of ice blocking the barrel of the cannon. The result was a tremendous explosion similar to what happened when something blocking a barrel caused a catastrophic backfire. The ice shattered into fragments that exploded out, electrified by the magic. Filvis's body was scorched by the backfire, but her artillery still shot through the air with a thunderous blast.

"*Gah?!*"

"*Asfi?!*"

Asfi was knocked away by one of the scattering thunder whips as she looked on in amazement at the creature's brute force. She fell to the ground, unconscious, as Lulune's cry was drowned out by the thundering blast shooting forward.

"*Bete Loga?!*"

Lena's cries scattered into the air as the lightning charged straight at Bete, who was still casting his spell.

Just as the deadly blow was about to consume the werewolf and everything else, three shadows appeared in the shot's path.

"*Hell Kaios!*"

"*Luminous Wind!*"

Filvis's eyes widened as she saw the Amazon and elf. Aisha and the masked adventurer had continued their Concurrent Casting, letting loose their magic at the giant ray of lightning.

"*Arcs Ray!*"

And Lefiya, too, wielding Filvis's wand. A combined blast from three Level 5s slammed into the black lightning.

"""————————*Gh?!*"""

But resistance was futile. Even as they continued to unleash their magic, their bodies were slowly getting pushed back. The force of the lightning had been significantly lessened by Asfi's Freeze Oil, but even still, it had an outrageous amount of power behind it.

Their eyes stretched open as they realized, despite all their combined efforts, they were still being fended off by the black lightning.

Shock waves ran along the floor, chipping away at the ground as they endured. There were only a few orbs of light and stardust left in reserve after so many had already been fired. And the fairy's ray of light that tried to stop the lightning was withering, as if groaning under the strain.

The unending burst of sparks threated to consume them whole and incinerate them.

"Free yourself of the chains that bind you, and unleash your mad howl! O lineage of enmity, pray use this vessel and devour the moon, drinking greedily from its overflowing cup!"

"!!"

However, upon hearing Bete's chant resounding behind them, the adventurers gritted their teeth. They demonstrated an intent to defend him to the last. They entrusted everything to the roar of the wolf waiting behind them as they poured all the sublimating golden particles they had been granted, all their remaining *Mind*, and everything else into resisting the lightning.

Amid all that, Lefiya, who was purely a back-line mage, risked the entire meaning of her existence as she screamed.

"AAAAAAAAAAAAAAAAAARGH!"

She mustered all the magic in herself and all her emotions. The giant ray of light regained its luster.

And in the next moment, the magics canceled each other out.

"What?!"

As the thunder dispersed, Filvis's magic and the spells of Lefiya, Aisha, and the masked adventurer dispersed.

Filvis's demonic lightning that should have been unstoppable had been shaved down by Asfi, stopped by Aisha and the masked adventurer, and finally scattered by Lefiya. The shock wave knocked the three of them back as the fragments of light and lightning disappeared.

In the split second of calm and quiet, Bete spoke. *"Bare your fangs— and devour all."*

The final line of the chant. Reaching the end of his cast, he called out the name of the spell.

"Hati."

Filvis saw it all. With that quiet declaration, a blinding light was born. Flames erupted from the werewolf's entire body. And the moment when that inferno trembled, howled, and swelled in the blink of an eye, it flared up into what looked like a giant flaming wolf.

The gray wolf was cloaked in flames, his eyes brimming with murderous rage. His body slowly fell forward and then *disappeared*.

"_____"

An explosive sprint. A flaming charge that made any distance between them meaningless. That wolf's dash was faster than anyone. Turning the flames and shock wave into propellant, he ran on four flaming legs, like the embodiment of a hungry wolf, closing in on Filvis in the blink of an eye.

The entirety of that world-destroying flame enchantment gathered in his right arm. As the creature immediately crossed her arms, the wolf's fang slammed the blaze into her body.

"RAAAAAAAAAAAAAAAAAAAAAAAAAAAAAAAAAAAAH!"

The chamber became crimson. The flames of demise consumed Filvis and enclosed her in an inferno. The rampaging inferno crackled as her skin and flesh were burned, and even her cries evaporated. But she endured.

Despite the living hell of raging flames, it was bearable. The creature was certain that with only firepower, she would not be devoured. Her inhuman life force would be able to overcome it.

She gathered strength into her arm. Once the inferno weakened, the moment the enemy's fang scattered, she would tear off the wolf's jaw.

"Cannon!" Someone shouting a spell key pierced Filvis's ears.

Even consumed by that torrent of raging flames, her eyes still froze over as she saw the image of an elf, scolding her trembling legs as she struggled to stand and turning her wand on the creature.

——*No way!*

Bete howled right as Filvis filled with dread.

"Get her!"

Lefiya had not missed the signal from Bete and unleashed her barrage with perfect timing.

"Fusillade Fallarica!"

Flaming arrows poured down on Filvis, causing *Hati*'s inferno to explode. It was a suicide attack. No, it was covering fire and a boost to *Hati*'s power. Thanks to the magic and damage drains, Bete's fangs became infinitely more powerful. The werewolf gritted his teeth and endured the burns, and Filvis was consumed by rage as dozens of flaming projectiles hit her. She was speechless as the flames lapped at her.

I can't endure this! This is absurd! I'll burn! I can't stand this! If I don't protect my magic stone—?!

The roots across her upper body cast aside all other considerations as they tried to protect the creature's chest. In the next moment, the flames glowed from the inside, swelled, and then lost their form.

"_____?!"

There was a violent boom. All the flames that had been poured into her swelled and bloomed into a staggering explosion.

Bete was blown away, since he was at the center of it all, but even Lena and the noncombatants watching from afar were knocked off their feet. The masked adventurer, Aisha, and Asfi were all blown away.

A volatile earthquake rattled the chamber. A wave of hot air burned their lungs, filling the hall, carrying a wave of sparks. A sea of flames pooled across the ground.

Flying through the air, Bete landed on the floor lifelessly. The Level Boost was released, and the werewolf finally reached the limits of his strength—but the monster was still there in the sea of flames, both feet planted on the ground.

——*An immortal.*

——*A monster.*

Aisha's and Asfi's faces twisted in despair as the creature refused to fall even after Bete's final attack. Collapsed on the ground, able only to lift their heads, they saw Filvis's body consumed by flames. Her metal gloves were broken, she had lost several fingers, and her throat had been scorched. Every celch of her body had been badly scorched. The roots on her chest that had barely managed to protect her magic stone had all been burned away.

"………*Gh…Aah…?!*"

Her burned skin was regenerating, like a phoenix rising from the flames, but it was slow. Very slow. She had taken so much damage that even that superregeneration that surpassed human understanding could not immediately heal her. The little magic left in her reserves was all being redirected into recovery. She could not move at all.

It was clearly a fatal blow. She was cornered. If they could just deal one more blow…But no one could move. No one could stand up. The adventurers had reached the limits of their power, and they had no way to land the finishing blow.

——Except for her.

"I beseech the name of Wishe."

"———" Filvis heard it.

"Ancestors of the forest, proud brethren. Answer my call and descend upon the plains."

She could hear that melody, that fairy's song.

"Connecting bonds, the pledge of paradise. Turn the wheel and dance."

Filvis saw it.

"Come, ring of fairies."

The fairy's wings spread as she exhorted her staggering legs and stood even though she should not have still been able to get up after all she had been through.

"Please——Give me strength."

Filvis could see the image of Lefiya preparing a blow that she could not yield to anyone, charging at her.

"*Elf Ring!*"

A dazzling yellow magic circle appeared when she sang the spell's name. It was her last bit of Mind, her final spell, the last of her willpower. Calling on the vow that she had carved into her heart, she encouraged her body, crossed the sea of flames, and charged at Filvis.

"—*Lefiyaaaa!*" Filvis screamed as her eyes flared. She raised her arm even as the very fibers of her muscles audibly tore, holding it out toward the girl.

——*I'll make it.*

In a haze as her body was racked by pain and destruction, Filvis analyzed the situation.

——*She's casting a Summon Burst.*

——*She could chant anything in the world, and I'll still finish faster!*

Lefiya was injured, too. She had lost more than 90 percent of her power, and the creature was sure that she would finish her cast faster.

—*I can't die. I will fulfill Lord Dionysus's wish!*

In her heart, Ein shouted, declaring her duty—ordering her to destroy her former friend for the sake of her beloved master.

—*This is all that's left for me and my corrupted soul!*

The white Filvis left in the corner of her heart wailed in lamentation, crying that this was not the end that she had wanted.

——*Why? Why did you appear before me, Lefiya?!*

She sobbed like a toddler. Her memories flashed in her mind, passing through her heart like a glittering wind, sending cracks through her chest.

——*If I had just never met you!*

For Filvis, their meeting had been a promise of loss to come.

She could do nothing but give up on everything, cursing her corrupted body and heart as she accepted her miserable fate.

——*Then I... Then we could have continued to be cruel Ein!*

For Filvis, Lefiya Viridis was too brilliant. She was so radiant that her broken heart would be stirred up by her.

It's scary. It hurts. It's so painful.

The spirit's voice echoed in the back of her mind—the despair and urges that would never disappear. The suffering that she could forget only in those few moments when she was comforted by her god's hands, when he had wiped away her tears and affirmed her.

That's why…!

"Purge, cleansing lightning!" Filvis shouted with a primal moan, marking their separation.

She summoned the black lightning that would erase Lefiya and all Filvis's remaining conflicts. That sinful thunder strike symbolized her current self, a single blow of her original sin, the reason she could no longer save people or protect people, why she could only kill.

"Dio Thyrsos!"

Filvis would return everything to ashes to reach a conclusion with her own lingering attachment.

"Shield me, cleansing chalice!"

However, as the chant echoed, the pure-white gleam filled her eyes, causing time to stop for Filvis.

"_____"

It had been a short spell. The magic circle turned from a bright yellow to a holy white light. It was Filvis's magic—a barrier spell that protected the user from any obstacle.

"Dio Grail!"

The white gleam that unfolded was like a mirror, reflecting Filvis's heart.

Aaaah—

The pure-white shield resisted the corrupted black lightning.

My magic—

The noble light symbolized her past self.

My light—

Her virtuous soul might have been able to save someone, to protect someone.

"I'm entrusting you with this spell, Lefiya, so...come back alive," she had said in return, which had circled back to protect Lefiya.

The memory of that day disrupted Filvis's hold of her magic. Her ephemeral lightning could not begin to reach its original power. The thunder exploded and hit the shining barrier. A flash of light went off, followed by an intense whirlwind. Created by the fairies' resonance, the gust blew away the surrounding sea of flames. The clash lasted for just a moment, letting out a shrill sound like crystal shattering. The black lightning dispersed, and the white shield burst open. The shock wave slammed Filvis backward.

And there, her eyes opened wide, Filvis saw it: the sprint that had not stopped despite the force of the wind. Filvis's old sword drawn, Lefiya charging, tears falling from her face as she cried out. A voice that would not become words.

It was beautiful. Almost like a fairy's flight. It was a noble, sublime, proud figure, the embodiment of the ideals of their race.

Filvis had adored the girl's light. It was one that she had wanted to protect.

——*Nooo!*

Filvis cried.

—*Thank you.*

Filvis smiled.

As she was torn apart by her two hearts, the beautifully hideous girl accepted that blade.

"Aaaaaaaaaaaaaaaaaaaaaaaaaaaaaaaaaaaaaaaaaaaaaaaaaaaaaaaaa aaaaaaaaaah!"

Lefiya screamed. The sword thrust into Filvis's chest. Cracks ran through the stone, signaling the end of that life that she had never been able to take hold of with her own hand. As Filvis fell backward, carried by the momentum of the blow, Lefiya also collapsed, unable to stop herself.

As Asfi and the rest looked on in wonder, the battle finally reached an end.

"*...Ahhhhh...Arghhhhhhh...?!*"

The first to make a noise was Filvis. As the cracks spread through the magic stone in her chest, her fingertips turned to ash and drifted to the ground.

When she realized she had only minutes left to live, she writhed in agony.

"_____?!"

Standing up, she extracted the sword from her chest, and she cried out, her face filled with panic. And as she shouted, losing her mind, something incomprehensible was chanted at high speed. Then her heart was split in two, and Filvis collapsed to the ground as a second Filvis remained standing.

"Lord Dionysus! Lord Dionysuuuuuuuuuus?!"

Without glancing at Bete or the others who were barely still breathing, she even abandoned the second Filvis. Driven mad, giving off a magic light as she went, Filvis rushed from the battlefield.

"Loki!"

Footsteps rang out in the pillared chamber on the twelfth floor that housed Loki and Dionysus. Finn's group rushed in. When they exited the hidden passage, they saw Dionysus, who was still shouting wildly.

"Where are you, Filvis?! *Save me, Filvis!*"

Finn's group gathered around Loki to protect her as Dionysus continued to screech the name of his last remaining follower. And then, as if the god's voice had reached her, Filvis appeared from a passage at the other end of the room.

"Lord Dionysus!"

The familia members immediately readied themselves, but Finn and Loki both stopped them. Her body was giving off rays of light. It was like an hourglass breaking the laws of nature and flowing in reverse. Her long black hair was disappearing from its ends. It was clear that she was on borrowed time. Her eyes could see nothing but Dionysus.

"Lord Dionysus! Lord Dionysus! I…I…!"

She stumbled weakly and called her patron god's name like a child as she clung to his chest. As he stood there, unmoving, the last thing to cross Dionysus's face was a look of resignation. He would not be able to use the strength of his follower to escape. It was a checkmate.

And then his face twisted dramatically.

"Tch…Useless."

His ugly scorn shocked Filvis.

"Just how much must you disappoint me before you're satisfied, Filvis?"

"Lord…Dionysus…?"

"How many times did you ignore my orders? How many times did you fail to finish off Loki's children because you were trying to save Lefiya Viridis?"

"Ah…Argh…!"

"That's what got you cornered, right? If you can't be of any use now, then what good are you?"

"Ah…*Aaaaah…?!*"

Every scornful word caused another crack in Filvis's face. The god's disappointed voice and contemptuous gaze lashed at her, scoring deep gouges into her heart.

"A foolish, half-witted follower. What an utter disappointment."

Tears fell from Filvis's eyes. Her face was filled with despair as she was cast aside by the one pillar of support she'd had.

"*Gh…!*"

Upon seeing that, Alicia knit her eyebrows together. She had not had much interaction with Filvis Challia. But to see someone toy with the heart of her fellow elf and cast it away on the whim of a prideful god ignited the same kind of pure rage that Lefiya had felt. Even if he was a god, Alicia was about to leap in and peel him away from Filvis.

"But—"

She was stopped where she was standing by Dionysus's confession.

"But you are still lovely."

"_____"

Dionysus's smile was simultaneously unsightly yet somehow entrancing. Filvis, Alicia, the other familia members, and even Finn were frozen. In silence, Loki alone watched, unsurprised as the god's right hand cupped the fallen elf's cheek, as if trying to cradle something broken.

"You're truly foolish, Filvis. You were my Maenad. I made you cry. I broke you down with my commands...That was more pleasing than anything else...Ah, how I adored you."

"*Ah. Ahhhh...!*"

"That's right, the voice of your *orgia drove me madder* than anything else. In the end, it is my own failure in granting you too much freedom that led to this. Sheesh, how aggravating..."

Rage. Annoyance. Frustration. And love. He was beautiful despite being stained by blood. His repulsive face bore a smile that was both utterly hideous and beautiful.

His words and gaze contained no fiction. Even the mortals in the room who could not see through the lies of deities could understand that much. As Filvis was overcome with emotion, her eyes flowed with tears of a different kind.

"—Be proud, Filvis. My heart is yours."

It was a soft voice and a dark smile. He almost seemed to be enjoying himself, as if still searching for the limits of the girl's joy and sorrow. As if chuckling at himself for becoming captivated by that broken girl.

It was unsightly, and yet this was an expression of love by a twisted god.

"You are mine. Yes, I would never let anyone else have you...Even when you return to the heavens, you must stay by my side."

"Yes, Lord Dionysus...!" Filvis responded in delight. She trembled in joy that someone was willing to accept her corrupted filth. Embraced by a pitiful happiness, she closed her eyes as Dionysus hugged her tightly to himself.

He wrapped the beautifully tormented girl in his arms as she seemed to fall asleep, only an arm and shoulder, chest and head remaining. And then, as if his previous disgraceful behavior was a lie, he stroked her beautiful hair while she disappeared into rays of light, and his eyes seemed disconnected from earthly concerns.

"...It's my loss, Loki."

In a complete reversal, he raised his head, a twisted smile on his face. Knowing that he did not have any chance of winning, or even any way to escape, he resigned.

"You were strong. You foiled my plan, turning me into a foolish jester! It's galling! Be proud, great heroes and deities!"

He freely praised Loki and Braver who had defeated him, the smile of a loser on his face.

In the next moment, his lips curled gruesomely.

"But you've noticed it, right, Loki? The Dungeon is *at its limit!*"

"..."

"You've thwarted my ambitions, but there is no stopping fate! Even without waiting for the promised time, this mortal world will be transformed into a realm of the dead and the *orgia* of my dreams will come!"

There was no changing that.

Dionysus's words sounded almost prophetic, accompanied by his mad laughter. Then, with the hand that was not wrapped around Filvis's body, he raised his dagger.

And then stabbed it down forcefully into his own chest.

"What?!"

As Alicia and the others looked on in amazement, he coughed up blood. In the blink of an eye, his body was enveloped by beads of light.

"I'll be watching! From the heavens above! Watching the *orgia* that you perform!"

His Arcanum activated. The supernatural power activated to prevent a god who had sustained a fatal wound from dying. He hugged Filvis, whose eyes were closed, her body on the verge of disappearing completely. In the next instant, a tremendous flash of light rose into the sky.

"Ha-ha-ha-ha-ha-ha...Ha-ha-ha-ha-ha-ha-ha-ha-ha-ha-ha-ha-ha-ha-ha-ha-ha-ha-ha-ha-ha-*ha-ha-ha-ha-ha*!"

The blinding pillar pierced through the labyrinth and shot into the sky. The god's return, signaling the end of everything. He had ascended to heaven, bringing Filvis, who had entirely scattered into rays of light, with him. As the god's laughter slipped into the distant sky and the ground rumbled intensely, dancing beads of light fell on those left behind.

"…What is this terrible aftertaste? Even though we won…" Alicia murmured as everyone else remained silent.

Alicia was clenching her fists.

Loki responded, as if seeing into her heart, "You can't let it get to you, Alicia. That's just one aspect of a god's love. Don't try to judge it by children's standards."

"…Was Filvis Challia saved?"

"Of course not. She was ensnared by an awful god, who completely and utterly manipulated and toyed with her."

"…"

"But…if you are asking whether she herself thought she had been saved, then I couldn't say."

Loki looked up as she responded to Alicia. Through the hole Dionysus had made, there was a glimpse of a sparkling sky. A starry night sky. The crimson light covering the ground had disappeared, and it was faint, but the sounds of cheers from the city were audible. A victory song bestowed on the nameless heroes by the people who would never know what had happened.

"It's over…" Finn announced.

"Yeah, it's over…There's still a big problem left…but this part has come to an end," Loki responded. Her eyes narrowed slightly as she gazed at the sky.

Along with Alicia, the other familia members closed their eyes, some held hands, others raised their weapons, and the rest prayed.

Looking to the heavens, a goddess whispered, "Leene, you guys… we won."

EPILOGUE

RAINING LIGHT

Гэта казка іншага сям'і.

Дождж святла

She heard a ringing that reached up toward the heavens.

She felt like she heard a song of tears sung by someone's loving voice. A sense of actually claiming victory, the joy of protecting their home, a feeling of accomplishment. The sadness over the comrades lost and the mourning of the victims. All those emotions and thoughts could not be expressed or repaid with a simple word such as *victory*.

"..."

In the labyrinth where it all ended, Aiz was walking by herself. She did not have any more strength left to swing her sword. Her wounded body was shrieking in pain. If she relaxed for even a moment, her knees would give out. Her body pleaded with her to rest. There were no more enemies. All the demi-spirits had been taken down and the green flesh in the labyrinth had turned a yellowish-brown color, rotting away. The passage that Aiz was walking down was the original stone of Knossos. There was no trace of monsters, either. The vibrantly colored monsters that were like feelers for the spirit had stopped functioning.

But Aiz kept walking. Just a little bit more, as if she was searching for something. She kept moving through a labyrinth that had fallen silent.

"A-Aiz!"

At the end of a winding path, members from *Loki Familia* appeared. Raul called out to her and ran over.

"Y-you came all the way here? Th-those are some serious injuries! Are you okay?! But if you're here, that means you won…That's great!"

Raul's squad had set up a temporary base in the passage there. A little while before, the order for all squads to retreat had come over the oculus. They were to gather up anyone who could not move and wait for rescue teams to come. Aiz did not have an oculus, but she had been told the order by a Xenos who had kindly stood on the ground, wearing a robe to appear more human. It was the siren who had been flying around, searching for adventurers who had been separated from squads.

This base had been the closest to her, and it also had the person Aiz had wanted to find.

"F-for now, let's get you healed…! Ah, but we've already used up all the items, which means it would probably be faster to just get you out of here…But I guess walking by yourself or getting carried outside would also be rough…I-I'll go get a healer and a cart!"

It could have been simple exaltation from winning the war, but Raul was a bundle of energy. He kept switching between concern for her wounds and joy at finding out she was safe. As he confirmed the state of her wounds and got ready to head out, Aiz smiled.

"Okay…I'll be waiting for you."

Raul's cheeks flushed, and he stared at her for a second. When she tilted her head a bit, confused by his reaction, he hurriedly stammered, "I-I'll be right back!" and dashed off.

There were several adventurers there besides just Raul's squad. They were all wounded and exhausted. There were some celebrating victory, but there were others whose mouths were shut. They must have lost comrades. But there were others, too, who must have been remembering what Finn had said before they set out that night, smiling at their comrades in arms who had been added to the funeral procession in the heavens. And there were those who took out a hip flask stashed away and downed half the alcohol before pouring out the rest on the weapons left behind by those who had been lost.

She dragged her body along, watching the scene after the decisive battle with all its cocktail of emotions. Rakuta and the others were happy to see her safe as they passed each other. And then finally… she found him.

"Bell…"

The boy was sleeping. He was sitting on the ground, his upper body leaning against the wall. He seemed utterly exhausted. There was no indication that he would wake up any time soon.

Aiz smiled and sat down next to him.

"...You...saved me."

They were words that he would never hear, but she still looked at him as she whispered in his ear.

No one noticed them there. The group was mostly of *Loki Familia* adventurers, who were already pushing themselves, walking around the encampment, checking on the condition of those who were wounded. Watching all that in the background, she continued to whisper.

"I won...thanks to you."

Aiz had defeated Levis with his ringing bell. If it were not for that, Aiz would have been consumed by the black flames without ever making it back.

It was always like that. Like when she had found him collapsed in the Dungeon and gotten close to him. Her heart had become clear, like her spirit was being cleansed. The black flames had disappeared. It was as if she had reclaimed just a little bit of something—of her more innocent self. Not realizing that her expression was still softening, Aiz's lips spread into a wider smile.

"I could hear...your voice."

Finally, the boy's head slid to the side, falling against Aiz's shoulder. But that weight felt comfortable. Letting go of her last bit of strength, Aiz leaned closer to him.

"Thank you, Bell."

She did not know whether she had gained anything. In exchange for victory, some people must have lost things that were important to them.

But right now, in that one moment, she allowed herself to lean against Bell and sleep peacefully.

There was a melody ringing in the distance. The tremor of light connecting the heavens and the earth was gradually fading. And Lefiya was crying without noticing any of that. She had fallen to her knees, supporting a single girl's body.

"Miss Filvis...! I...I...!"

Her tears fell on the girl's body as she wept. And then the girl's tear-stained skin turned to ash and crumbled. She was the girl whose life Lefiya had brought to an end—the fairy freed from her fate of destruction.

The magic stone that Lefiya's sword had pierced cracked further, the fissures spreading. That she still had any time left was a miracle in and of itself.

The life of the girl who had become a monster was drawing to a close.

"Don't cry, Lefiya...It's fine this way...It's better this way..."

Filvis smiled faintly as Lefiya kept sobbing. There was no energy in her whisper. Every word caused a new crack in the magic stone, and her body continued to turn to ash. Both her legs had already crumbled to dust. Her left arm was in the process of turning to soot and fluttering away.

The sight of it caused Lefiya's chest to constrict.

"I didn't know...! I never understood...! I never knew which was the real you or what you really wanted...I never understood anything...!"

There was the Filvis who had cried out and rushed to Dionysus's side—and the Filvis who had stayed there in Lefiya's embrace. Which was the real her? What had been her true salvation? Lefiya bawled as the grief sank in again, the powerful image of her unyielding resolve long gone.

"The one who clung to Lord Dionysus is me...and the one saved by you is also me..."

"...!"

"They're both the real me..."

Filvis was worn out to the point where she could not control herself, splitting into two using magic. She was unstable and broken. That was why she had said both instances of her were real. It was no lie that Lefiya had freed her from suffering.

"My heart was in shambles...I didn't know what I should do...or what I could do..."

"Miss...Filvis..."

"...I'm not strong. And I'm not beautiful, Lefiya...I was always unclean...and corrupted..."

Her eyes lost their focus, and she whispered as if falling into delirium.

Hearing Filvis's confession, Lefiya bit her lip as she fought back her tears. There were so many things she wanted to say, so many thoughts that she could not convey. She wanted to turn back time. But she knew that she could not let that confession be Filvis's last words.

"You weren't strong...You were a weak elf who couldn't live without relying on someone else—like me!" Lefiya spoke her own truth. And those honest feelings reached the girl who was consumed by regret.

"But that weak and proud side of you—!"

Fragments of memories of all that had happened leading up to that day flickered in her mind. There were so many happy memories, the numerous times that she had been helped. Their arguments, too. All the times that Filvis had doted on her like a kind older sister. Images of Filvis's anger, her suffering, her embarrassment, and her smile punched Lefiya's heart.

Her voice was on the verge of giving out as she desperately gathered herself.

"That was far...far more beautiful than anyone else!"

Filvis's eyes that had grown distant opened wide. Slowly, she looked at Lefiya, who was crying a river of tears. Tears fell from her red eyes, as if to stop Lefiya crying.

"—Ahhhh."

Her lips cracked slightly. She smiled as tears fell down her cheeks. And that was the most beautiful thing Lefiya had ever seen.

"..........."

"Mn...?"

Mustering the last of her strength, Filvis drew her lips close to Lefiya's ear and whispered, as if singing a lullaby to a bawling child.

"If you are ever…in trouble…Just remember. I promise…to…"

She was turning into ash. The shapes of her arms and legs disappeared, stealing away what little was left of her time.

Lefiya was at a loss for words. She could not make a sound. She shook her head like a child throwing a tantrum, refusing to part with her friend despite knowing that it would have to end.

"Thank you, Lefiya…I'm glad I met you."

Filvis smiled one more time. Lefiya's tears streamed down.

"I'll always be with you."

——*Let's go see the crown of light together.*

Those words were not spoken, disappearing in the crumbling ash, but Lefiya still heard them.

Filvis Challia disappeared. She vanished into soot and cinders, smiling for Lefiya until the very end. What remained of her rose in a pillar of dust, setting off on a journey as it left Lefiya's arms.

Her body was trembling as she desperately tried to hold back her emotions. That was when Lefiya realized something.

There, underground, there was a light rising upward. It was as if all the magic in the chamber were dancing. The beautiful white light was diffused as the light and ash danced together. The rays of light quivered, gathered together, and formed a ring, as if to prove that a single fairy had been there.

"_____"

It was like the crown of light. It was exactly like the scene in Lefiya's home forest that they had promised to see together. The rays of light scattered and rained down on Lefiya. At a loss for words, Lefiya watched, sure that she saw Filvis smiling at her from inside that light.

She could see a crown of light—a ring of diffracted light suspended in the air, woven together to create a white stairway ascending to the heavens.

She had promised to see this together with Filvis—which meant this had to be an illusion. Her battered consciousness should have already slipped away, but it showed her this fragile, transient, final hallucination reflected in her eyes. That was but a sliver of a beautiful dream.

Even if it was a trick of the eye, she had conviction that it was lovelier than anything she had ever seen.

It was the Elf Ring in Lefiya's home forest.

As she looked up, the radiant light burned into her eyes. And as her eyes were scorched by its radiance, all that was left was to give in to the impulse welling up inside her.

She cried, weeping aloud. Praying that her tears would dry up. Praying there would be an end to her sadness. Her tears mixed with the white gleam pouring down to become a rain of light. It was unfairly beautiful, held a cruel purity, a rain more precious than anything in the world. Those tears became a song that echoed out and back again.

Watching on, the renart wept quietly. Supported by an Amazonian girl, the lone werewolf turned his back and left the chamber, as if shunning those tears. As if turning a deaf ear to that weeping voice. As if just for now, he was letting the girl be by herself. The renart and others trailed after him.

Left alone, the fairy continued to cry—continued to sing. And she would carry on that song always and forever, a melody of tears that would emerge whenever she thought of that lost girl. And as the white light shone down on the ash, what was left of that girl's slender shoulders disappeared, praying that she would be able to always look over the girl who remained behind.

Filvis · Challia

BELONGS TO:	*Dionysus Familia*

RACE:	Creature (Elf)	**JOB:**	adventurer
DUNGEON RANGE:	sixtieth floor	**WEAPONS:**	sword, wand
CURRENT WORTH:	2,018,000 valis		

Status   Lv.0

STRENGTH:	000	**ENDURANCE:**	000
DEXTERITY:	000	**AGILITY:**	000
MAGIC:	000		

MAGIC:

Dio Thyrsos	• Lightning element. • Single-target magic.
Dio Grail	• Barrier spell. • Obstructs physical and magical attacks.
Einsel	• Cloning magic.

SKILLS:

Fairy Senior	• Amplifies magic. • Increases effect in relation to grief.
Monstrum Union	• Hybrid. • Neo-Irregular. • Status buff. • Anima erosion.

Dark Light

- Active trigger. • Modifies the wavelength of magic and emanated.
- Adds an enchantment to magic that rejects recovery.

EQUIPMENT:

Tear Pain

- A second-tier shortsword. Intended to be equipped by a magic swordsman, it has a Mind-heightening effect.
- A custom item that Filvis ordered from Lenoa after the Twenty-Seventh Floor Nightmare.
- The base was a fairy's blade that had been made in Filvis's home, Asthenia Woods. On a whim, the witch had added in the magic effect.
- Because it would break to pieces if wielded by the unified form of Filvis and Ein, whose presumed potential pushed the upper limit of Level 7, she had not retrieved it, marking a break with her past.

Protector's White Torch

- A wand-size magic staff that's easy to swing around.
- Constructed from the root of a sacred tree from an elven village outside her homeland. It was made when she developed Dio Grail, given to her by the rest of her familia. It was a source of pure pride before she was corrupted.

Corruption-Concealing Heavenly Garment

- Vestments made entirely under Dionysus's watchful eye.
- Paying no heed to defensive capabilities, it focused on allowing as little skin to show below her face as possible. In order to prevent any deities seeing through the existence of creatures, it was thoroughly crafted using an abundance of drop items, magic concealers, etc.
- Because the creature was an unknown Irregular of the mortal realm, no deities were able to see through her true identity. Even her fellow creatures would not have recognized her if they did not know her already.

© Kiyotaka Haimura

Afterword

The twelfth book of *Sword Oratoria* occurs after the fourteenth volume of the main series, before the fifteenth volume.

The first edition of the fifteenth volume of the main series was released on June 15th, 2019, a full month before this book was released. It would have been nice if they had been released at the same time, or even for this book to be released first. I guess I'm trying to say I'm sorry for this late release!

It was totally the author's fault for not keeping the deadlines. And I apologize to all who were involved for causing extra problems.

In the twelfth volume, the fight that has continued since the first volume has finally reached its conclusion. And yet, I don't really have much to say here. I thought that I would have so much to share about the final battle, but nothing comes to mind at all. This must be what it feels like to have poured in everything that I could offer until there was nothing left.

First of all, I can say with confidence that among all the books in the main series and side story, this book was indisputably the hardest to write. It was so bad that while I was writing it, I kept saying "This sucks" to myself, like, 177 times. And I'm sure the editor who watched me suffering laughed out loud 177 times. It was like a picture of hell.

I think that pain had as much to do with the fact that I was wringing out every bit of my strength together with the characters and expressing it on the page as it did with the fact that it was so hard to finish this story. Or at least my intention was to tell a story on a larger scale than anything else that I've written so far. That I still had so many characters I still wanted to write was surprising—and a little scary.

I'd like to believe there won't be a battle to surpass this one (he says, while pretending not to see the plot for the final book of the main series).

* * *

If I just stopped here, it would feel a little empty, so I'd like to try to touch on one of the characters. Which means that there will be spoilers after this. Consider yourself warned.

This book marks an ending for a girl who could be called a heroine for the first time in any of these stories. At first, I avoided trying to express how she was feeling on the inside. That was because I didn't want to write it. I didn't want to see what was going on in her heart that was filled with contradictions. I suspected that the more I delved into it, the more I would get sucked into those depths and I wouldn't be able to escape. It was just that exhausting.

However, at the very last moment, I selfishly insisted on rewriting the very final battle. Normally, I write battles from the perspective of an ally, but for the first time, I put it together with the focus centered on the opposing side. It was definitely hard, and I fumbled around a lot, struggling to find her inner voice, but in the end, I managed to hear it. And as expected, I regretted it.

But even with that remorse, I finally understood that she felt deeply for her fellow elf, and just how much their initial meeting had saved her. Her actions were undeniably evil, but if I was asked whether she was an enemy or ally, even as the author, I would have difficulty answering. But I believe that her friendships and desires were real. Well, real enough that she would selfishly disobey (someone who was, in my personal opinion) a god whose facade was beautiful but whose true feelings were filled with meaningless things.

I picked up the book again and reread the scene where those two met, and I realized I hadn't devoted many pages to it. I was trying not to foreshadow anything, but when I imagined her smile after they held hands, I started to tear up a little bit. So yeah. That's essentially that.

Good job. Good night. Until we meet again. I'd like to continue watching over the girl who was left behind, to take responsibility for my promises.

With that, I'd like to move to my thanks.

To my editor Takahashi and chief editor Kitamura, I'm extremely sorry for causing trouble with the schedule again. And likewise for Kiyotaka Haimura. It was thanks to your illustrations of Aiz, Lefiya, and the rest that I was able to get to this volume, which was a critical turning point in the series. Thank you very much. And my deepest gratitude to all the people involved who have continued to support someone like me.

And most importantly, thank you to the readers. I appreciate you for reading this far. Because of your support, we were able to continue publishing the twelfth volume of a side story, which is always a difficult sell. If I've been able to give you anything in return with my story, then I'm truly happy.

Sword Oratoria has reached the end of a chapter with this twelfth book. But even with that, I have plans to write more. But with the time line for the main series, I would like to give the strongest protagonists a break. I hope you can wait a little longer for their return.

With this, the third part of the side story is finished. Starting with the next book, it will be a new chapter, the fairy's awakening arc.

Thank you very much for sticking with me until the end.

With that, I'll take my leave.

Fujino Omori